Faery Moon

A Tess Noncoiré
Adventure

P. R. FROST

DAW BOOKS, INC.

DONALD A. WOLLHEIM, FOUNDER
375 Hudson Street, New York, NY 10014
ELIZABETH R. WOLLHEIM
SHEILA E. GILBERT
PUBLISHERS
www.dawbooks.com

First Paperback Printing, June 2010
1   2   3   4   5   6   7   8   9

DEDICATION:
For all the mothers out there who dedicate themselves to raising their children to have manners and coping skills so they can go out there and achieve what they need to do to live life to the fullest.

In Memoriam
Miriam Elizabeth Bentley Radford

2/14/1915–8/28/2004

Acknowledgments

Many thanks to Gwen Knighton for permission to use the lyrics of her song "Fairytale" from her CD "Box of Fairies." Please visit her at www.gwenknighton.com for a full list of lyrics, more music, and a glimpse into her life as a harpist. Interesting how our lives have connected through this piece of music. Almost every song on the CD would have fit for Tess, Gollum, and Donovan and their journey. I had a hard time choosing. In the end, "My Fairytale" seemed the right choice.

I'm always amazed at how many memories I can trigger with just a snippet of a song. I hope you've enjoyed my trips backward in time with the featured songs in *Faery Moon*.

The history and full lyrics of "Mairzy Doats" can be found at en.wikipedia.org/wiki/Mairzy_Doats. I'm glad I looked up this interesting and favorite memory from my childhood.

And for "Three Little Fishes" and other camp songs, please visit www.backyardgardener.com/loowit/song/song193.html. Another favorite from Girl Scouts.

Many thanks to Deborah Dixon, her sister Pam, and niece Tonya for their gracious hospitality and help in researching the Las Vegas landscape and history. Without them, I might never have gotten it right. Any errors are mine, not theirs.

I highly recommend a side trip to the Valley of Fire Nevada State Park next time you happen to visit Las Vegas. The landscape is an awesome contrast to the city. The park employees patiently answered my questions and directed me to great research texts. And check out Cirque du Soleil's production of "Mystere" at the Treasure Island to find my inspiration for "Fairy Moon." I found "Las Vegas Trivia" by John Gollehon invaluable as a resource about the city and its culture.

My long-suffering and special friends who read early drafts of my feeble attempts at this book deserve a favored place in heaven. Without Lea Day, Deborah Dixon, and Jessica Groeller, I'd never have whipped those stumbling paragraphs into a real book. I cannot forget my editor Sheila Gilbert for her untiring excavation of my manuscript to separate the true gems from the dross and help me make them shine bright and true.

Last but not least, I need to thank my mom for ... well for being My Mom.

Prologue

WHILE MY DAHLING Tess flies from here to there on a big mechanical machine that makes so much noise it hurts my tender little ears and smells too ripe, I'm wandering around the chat room looking for something to do.

The vast whiteness that stretches on and on, broken only by an occasional door to another dimension is strangely quiet today. I can't even find the demons that are supposed to be on guard duty. They keep beings inside their home dimension, only allowing passage to a privileged or wily few.

I'm one of the few. Imps may go anywhere. Convincing the guard demons of that is another issue altogether.

I stumble across a round stone door I haven't noticed before. It smells odd. My pug nose wiggles overtime trying to discover what lurks behind before I open it.

Stone, copper, dust, and sage.

I've smelled that before.

Instantly wary, I tug on the handle until it squeals in protest on rusty hinges.

I freeze—waiting, assessing.

No one comes to pummel me into submission or back where I came from.

So, like a good little imp, I poke my nose inside the scant inches between the round stone door and the arched stone jamb.

"Gargoyles!" I chortle. "Gargoyles in their natural form." Translucent spirits flit about. The smallest have hardly any features at all, just amorphous wispy forms. The larger ones begin to show signs of eyes, nose, and mouth. Nothing individual about any of them.

They all play tag with inanimate cutouts of demons, practicing pushing over bad guys with only the power of their aura. Some are better than others.

They are all good enough to keep me out. I can only watch from the doorway.

An old guy, his wrinkled and threadbare robes made of smoke sagging around his potbellied form, follows the youngsters about with a clipboard. He peers over half glasses at the antics of one particularly talented child. The twisted grimace on his face appears carved out of stone. He's lived long enough to develop features and a personality. A grim one from the way he frowns.

The kid he concentrates on can't be more than two or three centuries old. He won't stand still long enough to get a bead on his developing features. I get hints of bat wings.

"Report," the old guy barks, quill pen poised over his notes.

"Six Damiri lurking behind that pillar," the kid nods toward a Gothic column I hadn't seen before he pointed it out. Maybe it didn't exist before he mentioned it.

"Check. What else."

"Two Cthulhus in the moat, reluctant to come out. And a pair of Windago hunting innocents who enter the forest trying to find sanctuary."

"Very good. We have an emergency vacancy," the old guy intones. "You are young yet, but you are the best student we've had in three centuries. Go now. Replace the ancient one who fell asleep. His corner is a vitally strategic post. We need younger energy to fill the gap."

The kid salutes, bouncing up and down in his enthusiasm. Then his misty body trails off and escapes through the door I left partly open for my own escape.

The venerable gargoyle tutor makes a check mark on his clipboard and moves on to supervise another pupil.

The distinctive smell of stone, copper, dust, and sage shifts. Now I get granite, moss, and clay tiles.

So that's how they do it! The spirit form of the gargoyle inhabits the stone or metal body which gives them definition. Their magic exists only in their apotropaic ability to repel demons away from the edifice they protect.

Hmmm. I wonder if the kid's smell is unique to him, or merely his type. I know that scent. I do not trust the man who cannot mask it behind a musky aftershave.

This is info my babe may need.

Time to check on her. She should have changed planes and started on the final leg of her journey.

Chapter 1

Gambling became legal in Nevada in 1931, the same year the divorce laws were relaxed.

"TESS, MY DARLING." Donovan Estevez cupped my face in his long-fingered hand. His thumbs rubbed circles against my cheekbones. The rasp of his calluses on my skin awakened nerve endings and sent flaring signals of welcome to my fevered brain. Then he traced my scar from temple to chin, trailing kisses along the ridge.

"I find this scar very sexy." He feathered more kisses behind his fingers' trail. "I can't see it, but I know it's there. Clouded with mystery and promises."

I waited, willing him to move closer, linger, and savor. Magnetic tingles drew our mouths closer. He held back.

"Are you certain?" he whispered. His warm breath drifted across me like the softest of spring breezes.

A new face appeared in my vision. Gollum peered at me from behind Donovan's shoulder, a stern frown of disapproval and . . . aching pain marring his lean face. He pushed his glasses up to hide his eyes.

I tried to banish the image of my friend and mentor; my Gollum. I could never think of him as Guilford Van der Hoyden-Smythe, PhD.

"Yes," I said to Donovan, doing my best to ignore my misgivings.

Our bodies pressed against each other in an explosion of sensation, bonding us together. Our mouths blended and molded, opened. Our tongues entwined in an eternal dance, mimicking a more intimate joining.

Clothing disappeared without seeming to have ever been worn.

I stood on tiptoe, stretching to feel as much of him as I could. His hands ran the length of my back and lifted me higher by my bottom.

I nestled my face into his shoulder and inhaled his unique scent of copper, sage, and hot dust, enhanced by a dry cologne. A sigh rose, constricting my chest with anticipation. I belonged here. We fit. We were meant to be together.

"No, you don't," Gollum said, the erudite scholar, not a lover or a friend. "You belong with me."

A sharp pain in my neck wrenched me awake, out of my pretty dream. My head jerked forward and back against the airplane seat. The jet engine grated on my ears and my nerves. My balance skewed to the left.

I automatically keyed my laptop to save, and to back up to a flash drive.

One night. I'd had one wonderful, erotic, special night with Donovan.

Then I had three comfortable nights sleeping on Gollum's sofa, the only intimacies between us on the level of dear friends.

One friggin' night with Donovan. *Not enough,* part of me screamed.

Never again, my common sense replied. Not until he honestly told me of his past and his current agenda.

"Tess Noncoiré, you snore in a most unladylike manner," Mom said with a delicate sniff. Then she turned her lost and fragile gaze back to contemplating the agricultural patterns of the Midwest thirty-five thousand feet below us.

"Where are we?" I asked on a yawn. I scrubbed my face with my hands, trying desperately to banish the dream, the wanting, the need for a man I could not trust.

"We're somewhere south of Chicago," Mom replied. She played with her pearl necklace, more out of habit than nervousness.

Well, duh. I looked at my watch. An hour and a half after we'd lifted off from O'Hare. About another hour to Las Vegas.

A frisson of alarm suddenly clawed at my spine from tailbone to nape. I twitched in the too-narrow airplane seat, two seats side by side on our side of the aisle, three across the aisle. The tingles spread down my arms, making my fingers itch to hold a weapon.

The underlying smells of plastic and cleaning fluids combined with stale air, stale coffee, and stale bodies suddenly intensified. My nose is keen. My otherworldly imp's nose is better. Something was off here.

What?

Beside me, my mother glared at me, mentally ordering me to sit still, just like she used to do in church.

Nervously, I closed my laptop, secured it in the case, and shoved it beneath the seat in front of me. Then I unfastened my seat belt. Once free of my lifeline and slave driver of a novel, though little more existed than an outline and first chapter, I slid into the aisle, stretching and arching my back.

I used the innocuous movement to scan the other Las Vegas-bound passengers. Mostly couples in casual shirts and slacks headed out on vacation. They bubbled with excitement. A constant susurration of sound rose from their discussion of show tickets, excursions, and spa treatments. Discussion of the show "Fairy Moon" flew about more than any other. I hoped to get tickets for me and Mom to the hottest show in Vegas.

When excursions came up in the conversations, more than one mentioned the geological wonder of the Valley of Fire, only an hour north of Vegas. I'd have to think about that one if time allowed, with a full conference schedule and babysitting Mom.

Scattered throughout the nearly full coach seating, I

spotted a few intense men and women flying solo. Their garb varied from business suits to jeans and Tees. They had the haunted look of addicts. Gamblers.

Then there were the business people. Suit jackets off, ties loosened, working furiously on their laptops.

No one person stood out in the crowd as different. No one person kept their gaze locked on me.

If I had a stalker, he wasn't going to be easy to spot. But then that's what stalkers do. They stay in the shadows and watch. Waiting for the opportunity to lunge. Like a crocodile.

Ambush predators.

I prefer fighting demons. At least with monsters from other dimensions, I know who I'm fighting and why.

"Mom, I'm walking back to the restroom." I spoke slowly and distinctly, making certain I had her attention before I touched her shoulder.

She nodded and drifted back into the tangled world of her nightmares. Last month she eloped with a demon: Darren Estevez. He was also the foster father of my former lover Donovan Estevez.

Fortunately, an escapee from a pan-universal prison had murdered him thirty-six hours later and Mom only had to endure one night of his inhuman attentions.

She coped. She went about each day's routine without protest. Darren had drained a vital quality from her. I'd never forgive him for that.

I had a few issues with him over the way he'd manipulated Donovan as well.

I hoped this five-day junket to Vegas would help Mom separate her mind from those horrible days of existing in demon thrall. I could stretch it to a week if I had to. Maybe some natural wonders out in the Valley of Fire would do the trick if all the glitz and neon of Las Vegas didn't.

A writers' conference was paying me and covering most of my expenses. For four days I had workshops to present. Up-and-coming writers wanted to pick my brain on breaking out of midlist into best sellers. New writers wanted my secret formula (there isn't one) for getting published. But that should only involve a few hours each of four days. The rest of the time I could show my mom the wonders of the oasis of light and noise and frivolity (not to be confused with *le frivolité* or tatted lace, a pile of which sat tangled and ignored in her lap).

Something, anything, to bring back the twinkle of mischief to her eyes. Normally, she delighted in playing the martyr—especially after Dad moved in with the love of his life, Bill Ikito. Mom had a right to feel used and abused since Darren and should revel in her martyrdom. Now, she lapsed into too-long sessions of silence and depression. No complaints. No trying to make me feel guilty for her problems.

What was worse, she no longer tried to play my sister Cecilia and me against each other. Cecilia with her architect husband, her three children, her PTA meetings and garden clubs, no longer exemplified Mom's definition of a proper woman. I, the black sheep of the family, who fought demons and dressed up in costumes at Science Fiction/Fantasy conventions, was now her crutch and anchor in life.

No fair. I shouldn't have to take maternal responsibility for my mom. I was the baby of the family, the one all the others should take care of.

I took my time strolling along the aisle, nodding casually to anyone who looked up. Making myself as skinny as possible and plastering up against a seat back so the flight attendants could move about collecting drink and snack debris—no such thing as meals aboard anymore. Good thing I'd fed Mom in Chicago, not that she ate much.

Nothing out of the ordinary caught my attention. No suddenly averted glances or angry glares. Not even Scrap, my interdimensional imp, showed on my radar.

And now that I was moving about, the sense of danger and foreboding had vanished.

Just my imagination working overtime.

Yeah. Right.

While I was up and about, I might as well use the facilities.

"We'll be preparing to land soon, ma'am," an attendant in her prim gray jumper and white blouse, informed me. "The captain will ask you to resume your seat within minutes."

Sure enough, the floor had begun a gradual downward tilt.

"I won't be long," I reassured her.

The miniscule cubicle—barely enough room for me to turn around in—gave me just enough privacy to ask for other-dimensional help. Blue room smells dominated here, almost pleasant after the staleness of coach.

"Scrap?" I whispered into the ether. "You anywhere close, buddy?"

What? he answered querulously.

"Well, excuse me for interrupting your sojourn in the freeze-dried garbage dump of the universe." Scrap said he'd visit his mum while I flew south. He didn't like airplanes much.

A few mumbled grumbles passed through my mind. *What's up, babe?* he finally asked in an overly bright tone, like he was hiding something.

"Have I acquired a stalker?"

Not that I can tell from here. I'll let you know when you hit Vegas.

"And if that is too late?" This time I sent the mumbled grumbles his way. Mine were more specific and less polite.

No stalker worth his salt will cause an incident on a plane. No way to escape.

"And if it's a demon? Some demons can open the door and fly to safety." A Damiri demon, like Darren Estevez, took a bat form naturally.

I was pretty sure that Donovan Estevez, his foster son, could do the same, though I'd been told by semireliable sources he was now fully human. I didn't want to risk pushing him too hard, too far, too fast to force him into his natural form.

If you'd picked up a demon stalker I'd know, dahling. Trust me, the only danger you are in is from the fashion police. Faded jeans and stained golf shirts are for gardening, not flying to Las Vegas. And couldn't you do some-

*thing else with your hair than cut it as short as a boy's?
You look like a poodle.*

Visions of short, fat, cranky dogs that yapped continuously flashed across my mind. I might have lost weight
as part of the ritual that gave me Scrap—ten days of
one-hundred-three-plus fever will do that to a body. But
in my heart, I was always short, fat, and cranky.

"I thought you liked boys?" I needed to change the
subject.

Boys, dahling, not girls looking like boys. I could almost smell the smoke from his favored black cherry
cheroot.

I snorted as I washed my hands and checked my
image in the wavery metal mirror. The mass of dirty-
blonde kinky curls had brightened a bit over the last
year thanks to a magical comb Scrap had given me. But
the curls hadn't relaxed and I was tired of the tangles,
so now I sported a bob that would have been cute if it
didn't tend to stick out like an uneven afro.

Still feeling like a pair of eyes tracked my every move,
I meandered back toward my seat, just in front of the
wing.

A slender young man of no particular note in dress or
form twitched as I passed. He looked pasty. His equally
young companion, wearing an unremarkable suit, dozed
in the center seat. At least I presumed they were together. Mr. Twitchy had both hands on the other man's
arm.

An acrid scent whispered across my senses. Fear.

"Sit down, lady," Mr. Twitchy hissed at me.

"What?" I hadn't touched him, hadn't done anything
to attract his attention other than walk past him.

"I said sit down! We're going to crash. I know it. I just
know it." The smell of fear on stale sweat nearly overwhelmed me.

Chapter 2

*The building of Boulder Dam (now Hoover Dam)
in 1931 and the creation of Lake Mead behind it
changed the economy of Las Vegas from an agricultural railroad town to a tourist destination.*

*M*Y HEART LEAPED to my throat. My balance tilted again. I had to grab the back of my
seat to remain upright.

"Tsk," an older woman behind me clucked. "Flying
is safer than walking across a street." Her hours-too-old
perfume told a different story. Mr. Twitchy's fear began
to infect her.

You might want to listen to the guy, Scrap said.

I didn't like his tone. Anxious. No sarcasm. No
drawled "dahling," or affectionate "babe."

"Everybody sit down!" Mr. Twitchy moaned. "Please
sit down before we crash."

I plopped back in my seat and fastened my seat belt.
Then I made sure the laptop was secure under my feet
and the flash drive clipped to a lanyard about my neck and
safely tucked into my shirt pocket. I'd e-mailed the work in
progress to myself from O'Hare. If both the computer and
the flash drive trashed, I'd only lose about an hour's work.

I'm obsessive about backups. Or hadn't you noticed?

Of course, if the plane crashed hard enough to trash both the laptop and the flash drive, I'd be dead and wouldn't have to worry. The novel and its sequel became the problem of my agent, my editor, and my literary executor, all good friends of mine.

The plane bounced and plunged. I felt like I'd left my stomach a hundred feet above me.

Mom clutched my arm so tightly I knew she'd leave bruises. I don't bruise easily.

Yelps and gasps all around us. Mr. Twitchy moaned, "I knew it. I knew it. We're all going to die."

The canned air permeated with staleness became claustrophobic. More than one person tugged at a collar or neckline, seeking more air.

A steward emerged from behind the curtain separating us mere coach passengers from first class. He blanched as the plane banked right and then sharply left. He grabbed the curtain with both hands, nearly ripping it from its cable support.

Sweat poured off Mr. Twitchy's brow. He rocked forward and back, enduring his own private agony.

That's when I got scared. The guy had to be a sensitive. He knew things, bad things before they happened.

"Ladies and gentlemen," a reassuring male voice came over the intercom. "We are experiencing a bit of turbulence. The captain has turned on the seat belt sign. Please return to your seats immediately. We ask that you put away all carry-on items and secure your trays. Return your seats to an upright position."

All of the flight attendants disappeared to their own seats.

"In other words, prepare for a crash," I muttered. This was much more than the slight sideways jiggles we'd had off and on all the way south from Chicago.

The incandescent blue of Saint Elmo's fire shot around the wing tip.

"A bit of turbulence? I'd say that was an understatement." Mom sounded like her old self. Then the flash of fire in her eyes faded and she resumed staring out the window.

I followed her gaze. Weird, red rock formations flowed and twisted out of a gray-brown background below us. Splotches of black drizzled over the top. Like looking at the bottom of a seabed without the sea. The shadows promised mysteries. I'd hate to get lost in that trackless and waterless wilderness.

"The Valley of Fire," the man sitting behind me whispered. "It's awesome."

The plane lurched again. We lost more altitude. The gasps and cries of alarm grew louder. A small child wailed in distress.

We passed the Valley of Fire and approached volcanic formations. This landscape was born of fire and tumult; just as trackless and without water.

"Las Vegas has put us into a holding pattern. We're experiencing some severe crosswinds at this altitude. So please, ladies and gentlemen, sit back and relax. We'll keep you updated."

"Scrap, I could use some help here."

"Who are you talking to?" Mom whispered back at me.

"Myself."

"Fine time to start talking to yourself."

What's ya need, babe?

"A little information."

On my way, but I've got to fight my way through some pretty ugly energy in the chat room first.

Scrap always had to fight his way into or out of the chat room—that's the big white place with no sense of size or shape that exists between dimensions, giving access to all other dimensions. Some called it limbo.

I called it purgatory.

"Are these crosswinds normal?" I whispered, hoping Mom wouldn't hear me and get any bright ideas about ghosts or demons. Another encounter might tip her over the edge of sanity.

The plane banked again, smoothly. The jumping about ceased.

Everyone breathed a sigh of relief.

"Las Vegas informs us that we will be circling for

about another fifteen minutes. We've climbed above the severe crosswinds," the copilot said, almost cheerily.

"They're coming back," Mr. Twitchy shouted. "We can't escape them. Not now, not ever! They're coming to get me. You all are just collateral damage."

Excited murmurs all around us.

I peered around Mom out the window. Plain old desert undulated beneath us like the bottom of a seabed. But the weird red-rock formations northeast of the city were coming into view again.

The plane took a nose dive. Bounced. Tilted. Climbed. Rocked. Dove. The wing tips moved a fraction of a second after each jolt.

Worse than a roller coaster.

Screams. Wailing cries. A miasma of unpleasant scents. Mom looked like she'd lose her lunch.

Mine wasn't sitting too well either.

Mr. Twitchy jumped up and ran toward the front. "We've got to get out of here. We're all going to die!"

I stuck out my leg.

He fell face first. Lay there pounding the deck.

More people got up. Some paced the aisle in agitation.

A steward tried desperately to push them back into their seats. The more he tried, the more people tried getting into the aisle.

Screams deafened me.

"Tess, you have to do something." Mom turned wild eyes on me. Her grip tightened on my arm.

"What can I do about crosswinds?" I returned.

"Are they truly crosswinds born of this Earth?" Her eyes took on an unearthly red glow. Demon thrall. Some-*thing* other than my mother spoke with her voice.

I shuddered and leaned as far away from her as I could.

Are they otherworldly, Scrap? If so, there might be a rogue portal that bypassed the chat room hidden in the red-and-black shadows. I really hoped Scrap would catch my telepathic message. He didn't always. Our bond is not perfect. I couldn't risk Mom or anyone else hearing me talk to an imp that was transparent in this dimension except when he transformed into my choice of weapon.

I don't know! he wailed. *They're winds, but the source? I can't find the source.*

Where are they strongest?

Silence.

Another steward appeared from the rear and tried desperately to get people to sit down.

Mr. Twitchy pulled himself up, eyes wild. I saw the same panic reflected in the faces and cries of all those around us.

I unfastened my seat belt and pried Mom's hand off my arm. Then I rose and hauled Mr. Twitchy to his feet from the deck. "Sit down and shut up. You are only making things worse."

"They're coming for me. Evil spirits use the winds to find their victims. We're all going to die!"

I edge my way toward the Earth portal in the chat room. New guardian demons have sprung up since I looked into the gargoyle nursery. Can't let these guys know where I'm really headed. A weird-looking demon I've never seen before tracks my every movement. He's all full of red scales and flits like a faery. He smacks me with the force of a fully loaded semi going seventy in a fifty-five speed zone. A little morphing and removal of the hard edges, this could be a faery on steroids dressed in unnatural neon colors of clashing orange and pink over the red scales and black hair, lips, and nails.

He smells of rancid tobacco and burning sewage.

This is not good.

From infancy, imps are schooled in many types of demons and their weak points. We have to know so that we can help our Warrior companions fight these guys.

If new demons are cropping up, then there's trouble brewing. The balance of the universe is going cattywhumpus.

What else is new?

The not-faery demon raises his hand for another blow. I duck underneath and scoot toward the wooden door with heavy iron crossbars. Iron doesn't bother me, but it should hold back a faery—even a not-faery—for long enough for me to open the door and duck back into reality.

Curses and taboos. The door sticks.

No, it's not stuck; the not-faery is holding it shut with his big hand resting on the iron. I smell flesh burning from the contact. My opponent doesn't care. A real faery would have flitted home whimpering and affronted by now.

I gulp.

My road back to Tess is rarely easy.

I still my inadequate wings for half a heartbeat. An endless time in the chat room where time is just another dimension. No way to know if the gargoyles I saw are in training now or a thousand years ago.

Then, with a mighty swoop, I push myself straight up and butt my knobby head right into the family jewels.

Mr. Stoic-pain-means-nothing jumps and howls and screams like a banshee deprived of robbing a soul and backs off.

I grab the door and am outta here.

Gray-brown desert with splashes of khaki plants is a welcome relief from the bare whiteness of the chat room that goes on and on and on without definition. Khaki is so not my color, but it's an improvement over white.

I look around, trying to orient myself. Shivers run up and down my spine so hard they almost shake loose the beautiful warts on my bum. I worked hard to earn those warts in battle; I won't lose them now to the creepy crawlies. No sirree.

I'm in the wrong place. I should have popped out on Tess' shoulder. She's near. But not close enough.

A plane cruises by thousands of feet above me. That's where Tess is. And she needs me. I sense the plane is in trouble. If it doesn't get out of the holding pattern that loops it through this space soon, the pilot will lose control and crash. The magnetic forces of this place are screwing up his instruments. The winds spiral up and assault the plane from every direction. The pilot can't steer clear or outrun them.

He's as lost as I am.

More shivers and portents of doom.

I'm surrounded by weird rock formations. Lots and lots of red, both broken and flowing. Something draws me here. Something that feels like death and liberation at the same time.

A mural of writhing petroglyphs dances across a rock face above me. I can't read the exact symbols of horned figures and broken lines, but I sense a human running, endlessly running in circles away from evil, only to confront it again at the next turn.

This area is a maze of dead ends, and caves, and winding canyons that lead right back to the starting point. Or off into another dimension.

My senses reel. I can barely tell up from down, north from south, good from evil.

Dust, drier than a mummy, clogs my nose.

I try to pop out of the here and now, through the chat room to go back to Tess. The magnet of this place keeps pulling me in.

This is too creepy even for me.

Not a gargoyle in sight to repel me.

Chapter 3

The oldest rocks in the Valley of Fire are only six hundred million years old, compared to four billion years for the oldest rocks on Earth.

"NO ONE'S GOING TO die. Not on my watch." I shoved and twisted Mr. Twitchy into the nearest seat. Then I clamped his seat belt closed.

He immediately reached for it as if it cut off his breathing.

"Stay there," I said in my teacher voice, the one no teen dared brook.

His emotions continued to infect the rest of the passengers. No one, it seemed, except Mom, was willing to remain seated.

The plane tilted again. And again.

Screams.

I longed for a strong dose of Mom's lavender sachets to counter the hideous air.

A good belt of single malt scotch wouldn't hurt either. I preferred Lagavulin, but I'd settle for Sheep Dip.

A man ran forward from the extreme rear, clawing his way past the rest. Three stewards couldn't hang on to him. His eyes wouldn't focus. "I've got to get to the captain. I've got to make him land. Right now."

A steward tried to follow him. Too many people blocked his way.

I couldn't let him get past me.

He outweighed me by a good one hundred pounds and stood nearly a foot taller than me. He looked like a fullback with the ball under his arm and the goalposts within easy reach. I didn't have a weapon. I didn't have enough mass to stop him. Especially since the plane nosed down again, giving him momentum and challenging my balance.

Some god or goddess must have been looking over my shoulder that day. Not that I believe in such things. A little kid, wailing like a banshee, trying to get away from her mom's too-tight hug, raced forward, between and beneath the maze of legs. She got ahead of Mr. Fullback.

I grabbed her up and held her so she could see my face.

"Mairzy doates and dozy doates and liddle lamzy divey," I sang in my brightest voice.

As if I'd conjured it, I caught a whiff of freshly laundered sheets, dried in a warm spring wind, and folded away with sprigs of lavender. Home, comfort. Safety.

The little girl blinked at me in amazement.

"A kiddley divey too, wooden shoe?" she whispered in the high lisping toddler monotone.

Then we giggled together. I raised my voice and continued the nonsense song.

"Mares eat oats
And does eat oats
And little lambs eat ivy
A kid'll eat ivy too
Wouldn't you."

Mr. Fullback stopped short, grabbing the seats on either side of him. He blinked in confusion. Like he didn't know where he was or how he got there.

The little girl and I sang the ditty again from the top. Cautiously, I eased back into my seat. Mom belted me in. Then she raised the arm between us and helped me shift the child to the more secure place. She joined us on the third round of song. Her strong contralto balanced my soprano nicely.

Mr. Twitchy picked up on the chorus, in his quivery tenor, fighting panic with every word.

Slowly, quiet and order prevailed. Soon the entire coach section was singing. And seated.

I tired of the nonsense words and started up an old campfire song.

"Down in the meadow
In an iddy biddy pool
Swam three little fishes
And a momma fishy, too!"

Mom picked up on it—she'd taught it to me after all. She gave me my first voice lessons in church choir, too.

The crowd around us took a few moments to catch on. Eventually, they sang the chorus with us.

"Boop Boop Diddim Daddum Waddum Choo!"

"Thanks," the hapless steward said quietly, touching my shoulder. "I'll take Jessie here back to her mama. And I owe you a drink when we get to Vegas."

"Make it Lagavulin, single malt."

He grinned at me and held up one thumb in agreement. Then he gathered up the little girl, both happily singing, and deposited her with a relieved mother.

"You did good," Mom said.

"We're entering final approach for landing, ladies and gentlemen. Thank you for your patience."

Ten minutes later we landed in Las Vegas. I could feel the sun beating on the outside of the airplane the moment we stopped at the gate. The whoosh of fresher air entering from the airport relieved much of the olfactory stress. I sat back, eyes closed, and soaked up the heat, letting it banish the anxiety of the last half hour. It felt like a week.

I let the other passengers scramble for their bags in the overhead and scurry for the exit. No sense in fighting them to get out first. I'd learned long ago that on airplanes and in airports the hurrier I go the behinder I get.

Mom seemed content to wait.

When I opened my eyes, Mr. Twitchy was still strapped in the seat across from me. The captain stalked back to lecture him firmly about the panic he'd caused. "We've added your name to *the* list," he warned. "Next incident and you're banned from flying again in this country, maybe arrested for causing an incident."

His angry presence blocked my easy exit.

When the aisle was clear, I looked over at the abashed Mr. Twitchy. He looked like he wanted to cry. "I can't help it," he said to no one in particular. "I'm clairvoyant."

"Not a great one. We ran into trouble, but we didn't crash, and no one got hurt—except for some bumps and bruises. And that wouldn't have happened if people hadn't reacted to your panic and started running about. If they'd stayed seated, nothing would have happened. You're also a projecting empath," I said. "You need to work with a competent psychic on controlling that talent."

"You're one, too," he said defensively.

I started to protest. The events of the flight replayed in my mind like a videotape on fast forward. "Maybe I am. I used it to calm people for a positive outcome. If I hadn't, Mr. Fullback, or even you, might have opened one of the exit doors, causing depressurization and sucking a lot of people out the door to their deaths. Think about that next time you have a vision."

I stood up and yanked my computer bag out from under the seat.

"You don't know that," Mr. Twitchy retorted.

"I know that if I hadn't stopped you, you might

have made your 'vision' come true. A self-fulfilling prophecy."

"Listen to her, young man. She knows what she's talking about," Mom said. She handed me her overnight bag from beneath the seat, and marched down the long aisle to the exit, as full of majesty and determination as I'd ever seen her.

I whistled a jaunty tune and followed her, very happy to have my mom back.

"Took you long enough," I admonish Tess as she steps into the terminal from the long walkway off the plane. I flit around and around, then land on her shoulder. I have to hold on for dear life. Her life as well as mine. I do my best to disguise my tremors of fear as indignation. "You could have warned me you were going to be late getting off the plane."

Actually, I was the late one. I'd tugged and twisted and yanked myself away from those awful magnetic rocks with a great deal of difficulty. If Tess had gotten off the plane a moment earlier, I'd have some serious explaining to do.

And I will explain. Just as soon as I figure out what went on. Or if she treks out there on one of her mad excursions. Tess does love to explore when she visits new places.

You'd think she'd lose her fascination with rocks now that she's ditched the ghost of her geologist husband; and the demon construct made to look like the late and barely lamented Dillwyn Bailey Cooper. We'll see if the delights of Las Vegas keep her on the straight and narrow. I don't think we can fight whatever lurks out there in the desert. I don't think we need to.

Yet.

"You couldn't amuse yourself rigging the slot machines?" Tess rejoins, sotto voce. Her gaze goes to the bank of computerized one-armed bandits not ten feet away. A number of people exit the plane and make a beeline for the bright lights and clanging bells, eager to begin losing money.

"Come on, babe. Let's go shopping. I need a new feather

boa, and you need a little glitz in your evening gown! We have an awards banquet to go to Saturday night!"

"Later. I've got show tickets to buy," Tess mutters angrily. Like she'd really rather go shopping with me but knows she has to come up with those tickets because it's the only thing Mom has asked for since Darren died.

Chapter 4

Most workers in Las Vegas make little more than minimum wage, even in the biggest and most impressive casinos. They rely upon tips to survive. Everyone in Vegas expects a tip, from the bellhop, to the dealer, to the massage therapist, to the bus driver.

"I'M HAVING A massage in half an hour," Mom announced as we checked in at The Crown Jewels Hotel and Convention Center. The noise from the casino ten paces away and down three steps from the narrow lobby nearly obscured her words. The writers' conference had opted for a small hotel/casino off the strip. Much more affordable for a gathering of under one thousand people.

Not able to compete with modern glitz and glitter, The Crown Jewels had gone for the genteel poverty look of an English manor. Dark wood wainscoting and hardwood floors, accented with deep red velvet drapes and upholstery, dim lighting from Tiffany style shades on floor lamps, and an abundance of potted palms and rubber trees gave welcome relief from the bright desert sun outside.

That and the air-conditioning. The red Oriental style

carpets, and the upholstery had just the right touch of threadbare shabbiness. I thought it succeeded quite well in providing a comfortable and welcome ambience.

However, the sour reek of tobacco smoke drifting in from the casino and embedded in the upholstery spoiled the atmosphere.

I can smoke in here! Scrap chortled. *Everyone else does.*

Just what I needed. "You will not smoke around any of the conference people," I replied under my breath. "Offend one of them with your cigars, and I'll feed you to Gollum's cat." Scrap had a running feud with the long-haired white monster that owned my lodger back home.

I accepted our key cards and room assignment from the hotel desk clerk.

"You do realize, Mom, that you will have to remove *all* of your clothing for the massage." I tried to keep the surprise out of my voice.

"Not in public, Tess. They give you a bath sheet and keep it very discreet and professional. I'm not totally ignorant of the world." She hmfed and trotted off toward the elevator, leaving me to collect our bags. Again.

"I'm going to try again to get show tickets for tonight. If I do, we'll need to be at the theater by six," I called after her.

She waved an acknowledgment.

I flagged down a bellhop. Gone were the days when I could flit off to a weekend science fiction/fantasy convention with only a change of underwear and my toiletries crammed into a small backpack. I also found room in there for half a dozen books to be signed by the authors attending the same con. Now I traveled with professional clothes, banquet/party clothes, rugged clothes and hiking boots for excursions, a whole suitcase of my own books in case the convention dealers didn't have enough copies, and my trusty laptop with backup CD burner and flash drive. I also brought a cache of other people's books to read and to have signed.

While I sorted and organized my gear plus Mom's, Mr. Twitchy entered the hotel lobby and sidled up to the registration desk as if he didn't want to be seen. I saw no trace of his luggage or a bellhop in tow.

"Welcome back, Mr. Sancroix," said the perky desk clerk. She handed him a key card. He didn't fork over a credit card or sign a registration form like the rest of us had to. Even though the writers' conference paid for my room, I still had to leave a credit card number on file against incidental charges.

With barely a nod of acknowledgment, Mr. Sancroix marched toward a broad flight of stairs leading to the mezzanine.

I smell imp, Scrap wiggled his pug nose and slapped my back with his barbed tail in excitement. I could almost feel it.

"How can you smell anything over the stale cigarette smoke?"

Scrap alit from my shoulder and flitted around the lobby on stubby wings working his pug nose overtime. He honed in on Mr. Twitchy Sancroix.

"He a regular?" I asked the bellhop, jerking my head toward Mr. Twitchey's retreating back.

I betcha he's related to that last Sancroix guy we met. I just know it. I smell an imp. Scrap bounced from rubber tree to lamp to drapery pull.

I hoped he wouldn't break anything. Sometimes bits and pieces of him materialized in this dimension just enough to wreak havoc.

The bellhop pursed his lips and rubbed his thumb against his fingertips.

I sighed and slipped him a ten.

He looked at it with a frown, then back to me hopefully.

I stared him down.

This time he sighed. "Junior pops in and out a couple times a month for ten days at a time, practically lives here. His uncle has been here for the past three weeks solid, visiting."

"That would explain the lack of luggage, if he keeps

clothes here. The uncle wouldn't have a first name of Breven would he?"

Betcha he does! Scrap chortled. *Just betcha. How much you wanna bet? This is Vegas, after all. They bet on everything here. How much, babe? How much you wanna bet?*

We'd met a Breven Sancroix briefly a few weeks ago. My Sisterhood had sent him to help me with a little demon problem. Only by the time he showed up, I'd solved the problem, or rather beaten it back to the otherworld. Breven and his dominant male imp Fortitude (Scrap called him Guts because the grumpy senior imp didn't return his affections) were the only Warriors of the Celestial Blade I'd met outside of a Citadel. We solitaries, or rogues, aren't too common.

For two of us to show up at the same off-Strip hotel in Las Vegas at the same time seemed too much of a coincidence. I don't believe in coincidence.

The bellhop stared at his empty hand.

"I'll find out myself." I smiled at him and trotted off to the elevator. "Scrap, what's appropriate to wear for the hottest show in Vegas?"

That little midnight-blue number with layered chiffon and just a touch of beads and sequins.

"I don't remember buying a dress like that."

Because you haven't bought it yet. I spotted it in the underground mall on the discount rack. Let's hurry before someone else snatches it!

"Sorry, ma'am, those tickets for 'Fairy Moon' have been sold out for months. I can get you two single seats, separated by half the theater in August."

I glared at the young man working in the box office for the show Mom had asked to see.

"Who in their right mind comes to Las Vegas in August? The heat . . ." No windows or clocks in any of the casinos to hint at the harsh sunlight outside. My eyes already hurt from the glare. Mid-April was bad enough in the desert. No way was I coming back in August.

"Ever heard of air-conditioning?" The attendant signaled the next person in line to move forward. The middle-aged blowsy bottle blonde wearing a bright orange tank top and green shorts three sizes too small shoved me out of the way.

"Psst, missy," a weak little voice whispered in my ear.

Back off, dude, Scrap hissed back.

I whirled, hands up, expecting Scrap to stretch and morph into my Celestial Blade.

He remained firmly attached to my left shoulder, leaning over and baring his multiple rows of teeth at the sharp face of a skinny man about my own height. Unusual to find a fully grown man as vertically challenged as myself.

"I got tickets." The little man looked around nervously, twitching his nose a lot like a weasel.

Don't trust him, babe, he smells funny. Scrap spat out his cigar only half smoked.

"I don't trust him. But if he's got tickets to 'Fairy Moon,' I'll listen." Two steps away from the ticket counter and I was close enough to smell something rancid on the man's breath, barely masked by an overly sweet and oily hair tonic.

No kidding he smelled funny.

He backed up with small mincing steps, subtly leading me toward an exit, a fire door nearly hidden behind a huge potted palm. We had privacy. I had him in the corner. He couldn't grab my money and run.

"Name?" I demanded of the scalper.

"Names aren't necessary between friends. And right now I'm your best friend with tickets. Two seats together. Not the best, but not the worst either." He smiled, revealing small, pointy teeth.

"Okay, Mr. Weasel." He smelled of very ripe musk.

He winced but didn't lose the smile.

"Scalping tickets isn't exactly legal. How much are we talking?"

"Five hundred apiece."

Ouch.

"Even my mom's heart's desire isn't worth that much. One hundred apiece or I call hotel security." Or I'd bash in his pointed nose myself.

"My boss will bite hard if I sell for less than four-fifty."

"Bite hard? What is he, a vampire?" I almost laughed. I can't believe in vampires. I may write fantasy fiction, but that is one topic I won't touch. No one comes back from the dead. I'd learned that the hard way with the ghost of my husband.

"Yes. She is a vampire. A very old and powerful vampire."

He really believed that. His eyes glittered in terror. His almost offensive aftershave intensified.

Best I play up to his fears.

Scrap trembled and flicked his barbed tail. *I don't think this guy is kidding, dahling.*

"Two hundred. Your boss will only make a light snack of you." I had that much in cash. Time enough to hit the ATM before the show.

"Three-fifty." His neck lost a bit of tension. He still looked around, constantly scanning the mingling crowds around the box office.

"Two-fifty." That would drain my wallet. About what I'd planned on having to spend on tickets after searching on line at home.

"Okay, okay. You're signing my death warrant, but I'll let them go for that."

I reached for my wallet inside my belt pack.

Not yet, babe. Make him prove he's got the tickets. I don't like the way he smells.

I trusted Scrap's nose, as long as it wasn't clogged by allergies from Gollum's cat Gandalf. Gollum might be one of my best friends and a convenient lodger, but his cat and my imp had periodic turf wars.

"Show me the tickets."

"Show me the money."

"How do I know they aren't forgeries?" I cocked my

head to the side, giving Scrap a bit of room to do his thing if we needed to fight. My feet took an *en garde* stance automatically, right foot forward, left turned out at a ninety-degree angle, knees bent, balance centered.

"Now would I try to cheat a lady like you?" Mr. Weasel held out his hands palms up in a universal gesture of helplessness.

Helpless, my cute little bum. He's a were. Knew I'd smelled that stench of rotten meat and musk before. You'd think these guys would learn to brush and floss!

"You don't look like a werewolf, little man. Show me the tickets."

Not a werewolf, babe. A wereweasel. Much more dangerous. Sneaky little bastards. But tied to the moon just like their canine cousins.

"That's a new one. We haven't encountered weres before." Time for research.

"We?" Mr. Weasel gasped. His eyes turned yellow and the irises slitted vertically.

Uh-oh.

"We, as in my imp. Ever met a Warrior of the Celestial Blade before?" I held out my palm. Scrap hopped onto it and stretched his neck and bandy legs to make him look taller, ready to transform.

Except he remained firmly in his imp shape and only a pale pink. Normally Scrap became my weapon only in the face of a demon or someone impossibly evil. Then he flushed bright red and stretched easily.

Mr. Weasel's tanned and leathery skin, with a significant brindled-brown five o'clock shadow, blanched. He shifted his weight to the balls of his feet, ready to run.

"Tell me true, Mr. Weasel," I pinned him with my gaze. "Are your tickets forgeries?"

"Y . . . yes."

"And I should fork over good money and risk embarrassing my mother when we are denied entrance to the theater—why?"

"Because Lady Lucia will kill me if I don't come up with a grand by midnight."

"Tell Lady Lucia that I don't care. And the next person in her employ who tries to cheat me will eat my Blade."

I spun on my heel and headed for the taxi stand.

Mom and I would have to settle for the lounge act in the casino of The Crown Jewels.

As I passed a blackjack table, a girl who didn't look older than fifteen, clad in layers of pastel chiffon, pushed a pile of gold chips toward the dealer. Stranger yet, she wore fairy wings in the shape of double oak leaves. I'd seen that girl and her costume on dozens of posters around town advertising the show "Fairy Moon."

Tacky of her to wear her costumes out in public. She even had the mottled pastel body makeup to match the pinks, greens, blues, and yellows of her costume. What was her producer thinking?

Chapter 5

Elvis Presley first played Vegas at the New Frontier Hotel in 1956. He closed after one week of a two week gig.

"I HAVE TO CHECK in with the conference people and get my schedule by five," I grumbled as I got out of the taxi at four thirty.

You will change your clothes, dahling, Scrap insisted.

No sign of Mom back at the room. She must still be with the massage therapist in the spa on the top floor.

"Of course. I'll even look professional." I shook out my layered maroon peasant skirt with the handkerchief hem and the light pink embroidered gauze blouse.

Scrap snorted. *That might look professional at a con, babe. But this is a* writers' *conference. Go for the navy blue suit.*

"Yuck. I didn't even pack it."

But I did!

Scrap's chortle made me cringe. The brat had too much control over my life.

Slacks, pale blue tuxedo front blouse, rope of gray freshwater pearls, and your navy flats, he instructed, pointing to each item in the closet or on the bathroom vanity.

I growled at him, but obeyed. Like most of the gay men I knew, he had a better fashion sense than me. For that matter, most of the straight men I knew had a better fashion sense than me. I loved threadbare jeans and tees. Jeans are neutral. Color combinations didn't matter.

But I always felt better looking my best. Scrap took care of me in more ways than just in battle.

Conference Registration looked like chaos with only a hint of organization. That hint set it above and beyond the normal SF/F cons I attended. Along with the clothing people wore. Scrap was right. These people took professionalism to heart. Lots of suits. An occasional *pressed* golf shirt and khakis. No jeans at all.

At a con, I'd expect any one of these people to work for the hotel.

Tanya, the liaison for the pro writers nabbed me seconds after I stepped off the elevator on the mezzanine. She led me to a small room to our left, away from the knots of attendees waiting for their badges.

"We have a full house this weekend," Tanya bubbled. A tall and leggy woman with *café au lait* skin, she ate up the distance to the Green Room with ease. I had to work my hips almost painfully to keep up; either that or run. Most undignified and unprofessional.

"We sold every single spot three months ago," Tanya continued with hardly a breath for air. "We'd raised the rates to keep the attendance to pro and truly serious prepublished writers. I hope you don't mind that we added a second session of your 'Is It Love or Sex' workshop."

Inwardly I groaned. Outwardly I smiled. "That's fine." I got paid by the hour in the classroom with these people.

"While you're here, we have simple sandwich makings and veggie trays at lunchtime in the Green Room, cold cereals for breakfast, to cut down on your expenses. I understand your mother is with you?"

"Yes. She's prepared to foot her own bills."

"Oh, she's welcome in the Green Room, too. I know how writers have to struggle to stay above water in today's world."

Tanya had no way of knowing that Mom had inherited a considerable fortune from Darren Estevez. The wills he had drawn up at their elopement backfired. He didn't inherit my home (a highly contested piece of real estate among the Powers That Be from other dimensions).

The two hundred seventy five-year-old saltbox rambled with additions and renovations from succeeding generations. It also sat smack dab in the middle of two acres considered neutral since before people came to the area. The energy of the place made it possible to open a new demon portal there. The Powers That Be didn't want a Warrior of the Celestial Blade living on site. Nor did they want a demon turning it into a bed and breakfast retreat for others of his kind.

Darren thought Mom owned the house jointly with me. I owned it outright with no mortgage, thanks to my deceased husband's life insurance. Darren's plan was to murder me so that my half went to Mom, then murder Mom so that he'd inherit the house as sole owner.

Fortunately, an insane witch with a grudge and a criminal history murdered Darren before he could do the same to me and Mom.

"I'll pass on your invitation to Mom," I told Tanya politely.

"Since the conference doesn't officially begin until noon tomorrow, would you and your mother care to join the staff of *Writing Possibilities* for dinner? We and a few of the other professional writers thought we'd sit in the lounge adjacent to the casino. They serve food from the restaurant there and we can catch the first act at seven."

"Sounds like fun." It did, since Mom and I weren't hying off to see "Fairy Moon" tonight. Or ever most likely.

"Excuse me," Tanya stopped a cocktail waitress when she rose from her practiced dip to serve a drink to a spindly man in his mid-forties at the round table for ten.

They had a magnificent air filtration system. I hardly smelled the smoke in the casino at all.

"What can I get ya, sweetie?" the waitress, asked in a friendly drawl. Her accent might have started in Alabama, but decades in the west had given it an edge. She was made up and suitably coiffed for her job, but looked like a fit and firm sixty. Her body had filled out and begun to droop a bit, despite the bright red corset, off-the-shoulder peasant blouse, and short black skirt. The frilly white apron and cap made token reference to the hotel theme. But that corset—some twelve-year-old boy's idea of a wet dream.

"Don't stare, dear," Mom said. "This is like an old folks home for cocktail waitresses and dealers."

Sure enough, a quick glance around the casino showed that most of the staff moved at a reasonable pace and showed more gray hair and plumpness than allowed at the few places on the Strip I'd visited in search of show tickets. Most of the employees at The Crown Jewels Casino were treading water until they could collect Social Security.

"I thought a jazz combo played here tonight," Tanya said. She stared at the karaoke machine on a fold-out metal table at center stage.

"This ain't the Strip, honey. Groups like that get a better paying gig and they don't always bother tellin' us they won't show up for work. What'cha want to drink, dear?"

"Oh." Tanya looked really disappointed. "I guess I'll have a margarita. Can we order food from you, too?"

"Drinks only. I'll send over a gal from the restaurant."

"I'll have a glass of Riesling. What about you, Mom?" I asked as we sat down. I took the place next to Tanya. Mom sat between me and a tall woman in her mid-fifties.

"Whatever you're having, Tess," Mom replied. She busied herself settling the full skirt of her black dress and draping her knitted lace shawl just right. That way, she didn't have to speak to the other woman.

"Hi, I'm Jack Weaver. I write police procedural mysteries," Mr. Tall and Spindly leaned across the table with his hand extended.

I returned his firm handshake. "Tess Noncoiré. I write science fiction and fantasy. This is my mother, Genevieve Noncoiré." (I gave her the preferred Québécois pronunciation of Jahn-vee-ev.) Mom hadn't had time to change her name to Estevez before Darren's murder, so she never bothered.

"And I'm Jocelyn Jones, I used to write historical romance, got burned out, and now I'm ghosting Penny Worth's autobiography," the tall woman next to Mom said. She indicated a well-preserved older woman on her right as Penny Worth.

Ms. Worth took in each of us at the table with an assessing glance, smiled coyly. and said, "My name may be Penny Worth, but I'm valued much higher than that in select circles." She winked at me.

"Huh?" Mom whispered.

How did I tell my mother, a French-Canadian-Catholic-June Cleaver, that Ms. Worth was a prostitute? From the glitter of tasteful diamonds on her hands, ears, and around her neck, I guessed she'd been a high-priced call girl in her day and invested her earnings wisely. She might even still work for the occasional long-term client.

"Penny?" Mom quizzed the other woman. "Penny Haydon, New York City, third-floor walk-up on Eighth in the Village?"

"Yes," Ms. Worth hesitated. "Ginny?"

They squealed in delight and half hugged across Jocelyn Jones. In seconds, Mom and the writer had switched places. The animated conversation changed Mom from quiet, mousy, and depressed, to a younger vibrant version of my mother I'd only glimpsed briefly when I was growing up.

I began talking shop with the two published writers and four unpublished writers, grateful I didn't have to stop and explain vocabulary to both Mom and Ms. Worth. After only half a drink, we busied ourselves with our food—sandwiches and salad, nothing fancy. The conversation lagged.

"Tess," Mom said to the table at large. "You sing. Why don't you try the karaoke machine?"

"Good idea," Tanya jumped in, looking relieved that her party might be saved after all.

Yeah, let's sing! Scrap chimed in. He bounced back to my shoulder from the top of a bank of slot machines halfway across the small casino. *They got any filk on it?*

Filk is the folk music of Science Fiction/Fantasy. A lot of it is parody to familiar tunes, some quite original tributes to favorite authors and characters.

He studied the back of the machine as if he really could operate it. Good trick since he's transparent and only partially in this dimension. Some things, he managed to touch and manipulate. Like his black cherry cheroots and feather boa. Most things he passed right through.

I gave the dreaded machine a long and distrustful stare. My delay earned me a sharp elbow in my ribs.

"Okay." I nervously approached the two steps up to the twelve-by-twelve stage flanked in black curtains. Singing my heart out in a filk circle at a con with twenty other people is one thing. Performing for this group something else entirely.

The last time I'd sung solo had been "Ave Maria" at the wake of a dear friend; followed almost immediately by "There's A Bimbo On The Cover Of My Book," the greatest filk ever.

I studied the long list of songs, mostly from the fifties and sixties. I knew filk words to a lot of them, very few of the original. Would this audience appreciate the parody? I doubted it. Finally, I found one I thought I could vamp my way through as long as the machine gave me the words.

Not as much fun singing about a lonely outlaw with commitment issues when I'd rather tell the story of a popular car with design flaws. I may have slipped on one verse. Jack Weaver's muffled guffaw was my only clue.

Until Mom came up and grabbed the microphone from me. She rolled her eyes at me, then she spotted the song she wanted on the screen.

"Stormy weather," she crooned in her rich contralto. She caressed the words with a velvet tone that hinted at depths of passion.

Mom? Passionate?

Ms. Worth sat up and listened more closely. A hush fell over the tiny lounge. Even the noise from the casino seemed to mute.

You're a projecting empath, too! Junior Sancroix's words came back to me. So, apparently, was my mom.

I sat there, mouth agape in wonderment.

Knew it, knew it, knew it, Scrap giggled. He hung from a ceiling lamp and waggled his wart-bestrewed butt at me.

Settle down! How can you be drunk if I'm not drunk?

We're not drunk, babe, just high on life and music and—and Mom.

I flashed my gaze from Scrap's antics back to Mom. The strap of her little black dress slid slowly down her shoulder in a seductive invitation.

What happens in Vegas stays in Vegas. Whoo—ee, this is going to be fun.

"What happened to my annoying, conservative, fussy, control freak mother?"

Darren Estevez happened to Mom.

"Is she still in demon thrall?" Definitely unstable.

Darren, and his foster son Donovan, had the ability to reach into a mind and lull doubts, anger, and inhibitions. I'd seen Donovan quell a riot with a smile.

No answer. Scrap flitted from chandelier to chandelier, making the imitation flame light bulbs flicker among the faux crystal drips. The already dim lighting faded, making the spotlight on Mom more dominant.

I needed to get her off that stage and back to normal.

"Not yet, dear." Ms. Worth reached across the table and placed her hand atop mine. "Let her finish. She needs to do this."

"Stormy Weather" came to an end, but not my stormy temper. I sat there, alternately seething and applauding my mother as she sang sultry torch song after whimsical show tune after sweet ballad. Each piece ended to rounds of enthusiastic applause. The lounge filled and the casino emptied, just to listen to my mom.

"If she's still in demon thrall, then she's spreading it," I murmured.

"It's a happy thrall," Penny Worth said. "The best singers and working girls have it and know how to use it."

That got my attention.

Chapter 6

In 1967, Nevada passed a law allowing corpora-tions to own casinos. Now it is extremely rare for an individual to own a casino lock, stock, and barrel.

"**W**HAT DO YOU KNOW about demons?" I whispered, wishing that Jocelyn Jones wasn't sitting between us. This conversation needed to be private.

"Oh, sweetie, all men are demons given the right in-centive," she laughed, a soft trilling sound that sent shiv-ers up my spine and raised goose bumps on my arms.

"Or she's a projecting empath, like you are," a new voice said quietly. A male voice, rough around the edges like he didn't use it much.

I turned away from the table to find Breven Sancroix standing just behind my left shoulder. In a lot of folk-lore, this is the place assigned to Death. That's Death as an entity rather than the state of nonbeing.

Fortitude, his huge imp, perched on *his* left shoulder. The nearly invisible beast lifted his long, fully formed wings in an elegant gesture that masked his shifting to a new more aggressive stance. The many warts on his spine and chest seemed to ripple and catch the briefest red glow from the candle lamp on the table. His skin had aged to a dusky patina.

I doubted that chubby Scrap with his stubby wings and bandy legs would ever reach this level of maturity and grace. He was just a scrap of an imp after all, a runt who should have died before his fiftieth birthday. Through sheer determination my imp now boasted a few warts earned in battle as well as nearly one hundred years of life. (Imp years. I had no idea how they converted to human years.)

My face lost heat. "Mr. Sancroix, what are you doing here?"

"My nephew lives here."

He pulled out Mom's chair and sat, careful to let Fortitude whip his tail and wing tips behind the back before settling.

Did the big imp weigh anything in this dimension? When Scrap rode my shoulder, he barely made an impression on my senses. Fortitude might prove a substantial burden, even on Breven Sancroix's broad shoulders.

"Just visiting, then?"

"I may move here. The climate soothes my arthritis. I sold my farm in Pennsylvania. We . . ." He glanced at the uninformed humans about the table. "I'm getting on in years and no longer wish to work the place alone. Junior would rather live and work here."

He didn't look arthritic to me. He moved with the power and suppleness of a much younger man. I found it hard to guess his age. Weathered skin from many years working out of doors, and a tightness about his mouth, suggested late middle age pushing sixty maybe. The scar running from temple to jaw that matched my own, looked old and faded. He'd been a Warrior of the Celestial Blade a long time. Looks can be deceiving, especially in us Warriors.

I stand five feet two inches and barely weigh in at one hundred ten pounds. Most people say I look tiny and frail. I've felled a dozen half-blood (Kajiri) Sasquatch demons twice my size. I've conquered full-blood (Midori) Windago. In a pinch, without any weapons but a set of car keys, I laid out two teenage muggers in a dark parking lot. I run nearly every day and fence three times a week when I'm home.

My scar still looks raw and angry to my eye after three years. So I cover it with makeup even though mundanes can't see it.

"What does your nephew do that he can afford to live in a hotel in Vegas?" I asked.

"He owns the hotel."

That stopped me cold. "He seems very young to own such a . . . prime piece of real estate." Off the Strip, the buildings and businesses wouldn't command the same value as the major operations, but any casino and hotel in Vegas had to be worth a lot more than I could ever dream of making as a writer, even holding on to my place on the best seller lists.

The bellhop hadn't said anything about Junior owning the place. Was he protecting the man, or didn't he know?

"Long story short, he inherited a piece of it and managed to . . . acquire the remaining shares." Breven Sancroix looked almost embarrassed.

"Did he use his talent as a projecting empath to coerce the other owners into selling at a vastly deflated value?" I raised my eyebrows at him.

Breven Sancroix looked away.

"Better question, did Junior tell you about his little problem on the flight here from Chicago?"

Did I say that I don't believe in coincidence? The Sancroixs, uncle and nephew, began to look like the stalker I'd sensed.

"No, he didn't. What happened?"

"Your nephew has a problem." I scanned the bar for eavesdroppers. Every eye and ear concentrated on my mother as she reached into her repertoire for yet another steamy ballad of lust and betrayal.

This time Sancroix lifted his own eyebrows in question.

"This is a conversation best held in private."

"I'll keep an eye on your mom, sweetie," Penny Worth said. She patted my hand again. "She's safe with me."

Even Penny couldn't con Mom into getting into *too* much trouble. Maybe her worldly wisdom would counter Mom's naiveté. I had to trust my mom and her Catholic upbringing.

That trust did not extend to Breven Sancroix.

"There's another bar on the opposite side of the lobby. It's quiet there," Sancroix said. He took my elbow before I'd finished standing and kept me off-balance as we crossed the casino, dodging gamblers, waitresses, and a maze of slot machines. No straight lines and easy exits in a casino. They want you to stop and gamble.

Scrap scrambled to keep up, never getting close enough to alight on my shoulder.

Fortitude remained solidly in place, half asleep, ignoring the world.

"Another white wine?" Sancroix asked, nearly pushing me into the center stool of an unoccupied section around the bar.

I wanted something stronger. I needed my wits about me. "Ginger ale."

"Glenmorangie, straight up."

"A fine single malt scotch. I prefer Lagavulin," I almost smiled. The last time I'd drunk fine whiskey with a man—Gollum—I ended up sleeping with him. Actually sleeping on his couch with him curled up beside me, not making love.

"Anything is better than the homemade brew they served me in the Citadel."

"I spent a year in a Citadel with my Sisterhood. We had the same stuff. Reminiscent of the recipe in the Hammurabi Code. Needed a couple of filters and a less rusty fermentation tank."

We both laughed. A bit of my wariness crumbled.

Scrap dropped onto my shoulder and sank in his talons. I could barely feel his weight or the sharp impression on my skin, but a warning was there. *Don't get too comfortable, babe.*

"The Warriors of the Celestial Blade do take their Spartan living to the extreme," Sancroix said. He smiled, and the lines around his eyes crinkled nicely. He looked younger and less dangerous. "And I think the recipe is as old as the Code of Hammurabi, circa 1780 BC. We've been around a long time. Not a lot changes in the Citadels."

"We have a duty." I nodded. "For centuries, that duty centered around keeping demons from crossing into this dimension through limited access portals. Now the portals are changing. Demons are infiltrating everyday life. The Warriors need to change with the times." Sister Gert had thrown me out rather than accept change.

"Demons are getting more intelligent, gaining more and more human traits as they interbreed. Our duty has to expand into the world at large," he agreed with me.

"Is that why you left your Citadel?" I asked.

"Yes. You, too, I take it."

Our drinks came. No money exchanged hands.

"They kicked me out because I don't take orders well and asked too many questions."

He laughed long and loud, throwing his head back in genuine mirth. Fortitude shifted awkwardly to adjust to the change in balance.

"I bet you gave old Gert a comeupance." He mentioned the leader of the isolated fortress where I'd taken my training.

I'd stumbled on the isolated ravine in the Central Washington desert in a fever delirium. We call the disease the imp flu. Sister Serena, our physician, had to cut the infection out. That's how I got the scar on my face. But since the imp flu is other dimensional, so is the scar. Only other Warriors can see it.

Guilford Van der Hoyden-Smythe, Gollum to his friends, could see the scar: dear friend, researcher, companion, and owner of the dreaded white cat Gandalf.

"You know Sister Gert?"

"Knew. Haven't seen her in years. I think I fathered a child or two on her during shared midsummer festivals." Celebrated on the full moon closest to the Solstice. Demons are at their lowest power at the full moon. The only time it's safe to throw a party in a Citadel that sits atop a demon portal. "But as you know, men are not welcome to linger once the beer is drunk and the willing impregnated. Nor are women welcome to remain in a male Citadel."

"Another good reason to leave."

We clicked our glasses in silent toast. We had more in common than I thought.

"Gert retired last month. Gayla now leads my Citadel," I said.

"Gayla, I don't think I know her." He looked into his scotch as if the answer lay there.

"She's young, a relative newcomer. I pulled her in during a raging thunderstorm; her imp flu was in full fever and festering. She'd have died if I hadn't. Gert wanted to leave her outside, afraid of diminishing resources. Our physician had an injured hand from a demon tag. I cut the infection out of Gayla."

And our bond remained strong. "She's one of the few I can reach through meditation and telepathy when she doesn't answer the telephone she had installed two months ago."

"So, what has Junior been up to?" Sancroix asked after a long pause and one sip of his scotch.

"We hit some bad turbulence while circling Las Vegas. He panicked and nearly caused a riot by projecting his fear into everyone else. He's on a watch list now. Another incident, and Homeland Security won't let him fly again. Ever."

"Damn.

"He needs training to control his talent. Before he panics again and kills innocents."

"I doubt you and your mother had training. It's an isolated incident."

"Mom and I have never caused a near riot aboard an airplane twenty thousand feet in the air. Junior nearly got us all killed."

"I'll speak to him. Where did this happen?"

I shrugged. "We were circling in a holding pattern waiting to land. But he got twitchy and nervous on our first approach."

"The Valley of Fire," he said quietly, gulping a mouthful of the potent scotch.

"What's so special about the Valley of Fire?"

"Local geological wonder. Northeast of town. Worth a day trip. Just don't get caught out there at night. And leave your imp at home."

He rose and left abruptly.

Chapter 7

Average humidity in Las Vegas is 29%.

"*W*AS THAT A CHALLENGE?" I asked Scrap.

"Believe him, lady," the bartender whispered. "Valley of Fire is no place to be after the sun sets. Lots of unexplained stuff. Crosswinds with no source, compasses going berserk. Hoodoos. Even the Indians won't go there after dark unless they are on a vision quest." He looked like he might have some Indian blood in him, a hint of copper in his black skin, thick straight black hair cropped short, and an almost occipital fold around his brown eyes.

"You sound familiar with the place. Is there a tour bus, or should I rent a car?"

"Stay in town and gamble your money away. It's safer." He turned to answer the hail of another customer.

"Scrap, what do you think?"

I like slot machines. I may have figured out how to guarantee a win. He flitted off, strangely subdued.

Time to check on Mom.

I braced myself for the clang and jangle of casino noise. Near silence greeted my ears as I crossed the hotel lobby. Only a few dedicated gamblers maintained possession of preferred places at the slots or a blackjack table. I pushed and shoved my way through the crowd to the table I'd left half empty a short time ago. Three men in their sixties, wearing western-cut suits with bolo ties and huge chunks of turquoise filled my chair, Mom's, and one other. They sat forward, gazes glued to the stage and their mouths half open.

People had dragged stools in from the slot machines to fill the other tables to overflowing. A lot of people stood in every available space around and between tables. The waitresses hopped about with new energy and speed, filling orders, stuffing tips in their cleavages—their cloth bags attached to waistbands all bulged to overflowing.

Penny Worth sat back in her chair appraising the crowd, a small smile on her face.

My eyes followed the gaze of every person in the room. Mom stood spotlighted on the stage. She closed her eyes and stilled her entire being. The last lingering note of a ballad drifted into the shadows, more than a memory, less than audible sound.

Then she opened her eyes, animation and life returning to her face. She broke the spell with her smile—or continued it. I couldn't tell for sure.

"Magic," Penny Worth whispered. "She's absolute magic. I don't think she had that touch when we shared a flat in New York."

Mom in New York? When? She'd married Dad when she was only eighteen.

Without a word, Mom replaced the microphone into the karaoke machine and executed a deep, sweeping bow worthy of presentation at a royal court.

"More!" shouted the man with the biggest chunk of turquoise embedded in his string tie.

"More, more, more," the crowd picked up the chant.

Mom shook her head, gracing them with a huge smile.

"More, more, more." Feet stomped, and the applause took on the rhythm of the repeated demand.

Mom shook her head again. This time she glided the two steps to the edge of the stage. A strong hand reached up to guide her down the single step. She placed her hand atop it and descended with the grace and aplomb of a beauty queen.

"Your mama had good training. Shame to waste it on a karaoke machine," Ms. Worth said.

I barely heard her. All my attention focused tightly on the man who led my mother back to her chair.

Breven Sancroix.

He looked strangely off-balance until I realized Fortitude no longer rode his shoulder.

Scrap, too, had taken a powder.

I couldn't find either of them in any of the usual spots, i.e., hanging from the chandeliers or crouched on the wooden rail rafters. Like cats, imps prefer to perch high and study the surroundings.

Then my gaze lighted on a less welcome sight. A tall man with long black hair caught in a tight braid halfway down his back and shafts of white at his temples surveyed the entire room in one swift glance.

I forgot to breathe as his eyes unerringly found mine.

"No." I think I spoke. I must have because Penny Worth swiveled around and looked in the same direction.

I couldn't move. Couldn't think. Only drink in the superb fitness, grace, and beauty of the man.

Legally, I guess Donovan was my stepbrother. In my blood he was more. So much more.

Not in this lifetime.

No way, no how would I succumb to the power of his charisma. Again.

But that didn't mean I couldn't feast my eyes on him while he hastened to my side as if his life depended upon holding me in his arms.

I longed to hear him tell me how he'd found a way to reveal the truth of his past and his future agenda to me without breaking his covenant with the Powers That Be.

"My, my, my, what do we have here?" Ms. Worth

tracked Donovan's progress across the nearly deserted casino as avidly as I did. "He yours, honey?"

"I sure hope not," Jocelyn Jones said. She straightened her back and smoothed her hair, like a predatory bird preening.

Donovan's smile of welcome turned to a fierce scowl.

Shatter one fantasy.

Oh, wait, he did that months ago.

I think I actually backed away from him. As much as Mom's adoring audience would allow me.

"Well, that explains where Scrap disappeared to," I snapped at the man.

"Not my fault the runt can't come near me. Do you know how much trouble I've had tracking you down!"

"Well, excuse me, I didn't know I was supposed to file my schedule with your secretary."

He broke eye contact and ran his fingers through that fabulously silky black hair. Not fair that a man should have prettier hair than I do. He had more than enough assets to get away with one little flaw.

"Sorry, Tess, that didn't come out right. I have some papers for your mother to sign. It's rather urgent." Then he lifted his gaze to meet mine again.

By that time I'd managed to "gird my loins" so to speak and resist the mind-fogging miasma of beauty he projected.

"Just because you are the executor of your father's estate, doesn't give you the right to stalk me or my mother." That didn't come out right either, but I let it stand. "Can't it wait till we get home on Monday?"

"No. And he was my *foster* father. No blood relation at all."

I'd heard that one before. Over and over again. So how come Donovan looked so much like his half-blood Damiri demon *foster* father and had so much in common with him? Like the ability to stop barroom brawls before they started and lull the inhibitions of the unwary?

"Donovan!" Mom cried. She broke free of her own enthrallment with Sancroix and rushed toward us. She rose up on tiptoe to kiss his cheek. "What brings you to Vegas, dear? Have you been eating right? You look tired. Did you sleep last night?"

"Estate business, Genevieve." He kissed her cheek with genuine affection.

I expected Mom to wince at the Americanized pronunciation of her name.

She surprised me again by patting his broad chest with affection. "I suppose I must do this. You will excuse me." She nodded graciously and vaguely toward me and Sancroix. "Do you have a room, Donovan, or will you be charging off again on the next plane out?"

"I got a room. I have other business in town. But the estate stuff is urgent. I can file the papers with the bank by fax first thing in the morning. I've got the hotel owner waiting to witness your signature in his office." They wandered off together.

"So that's Donovan Estevez," Sancroix whistled through his teeth.

"You know of him?"

"He's famous outside the Citadels."

I raised my eyebrows in question.

"Someone to watch. He has dubious contacts." Meaning with Kajiri demons. I knew that already.

Someone to avoid, Scrap snarled settling back on my shoulder where he belonged. Fortitude joined us as well.

"Do all the imps have a problem staying within ten yards of him?"

"Not all."

Clearly I wasn't getting any more information from him tonight.

A yawn escaped my lungs. "I've had a long day. And tomorrow looks very busy. I think I'll turn in."

"Let me escort you to your room." Sancroix offered me his arm.

"Uh—no, thanks. It's not as if I can't defend myself." I tilted my head to the right where Scrap perched.

"Las Vegas is home to creatures they never taught us about in the Citadels."

"Like wereweasels and vampires?" I joked.

"Precisely."

"Moisturize, moisturize, moisturize," I told myself as I smoothed lotion on my face, hands, and legs beneath my cotton nightie. "One day in the desert and I already feel like a prune."

So I sucked greedily on the bottled water I'd picked up in the convenience store two blocks up the street from the hotel. I predicted I'd go through at least another case before the end of the conference.

A knock on the door interrupted my attempts to mitigate the effects of seven percent humidity aggravated by canned air. Scrap would have a lot of trouble finding any mold, his favored food, anywhere, even in the air conditioners.

Quietly, I crept to the door and peered through the spy hole.

"Tess, I know you're in there," Donovan said. He held up a big bouquet of mixed spring flowers. "I come bearing peace offerings."

"Okay." I opened the door but stood firmly in the doorway, denying him entrance.

"Please accept my apology for my surly mood earlier," he said sweetly, thrusting the bulky bouquet at me, complete with cut glass vase.

I buried my nose in their delicate fragrance. Daisies, and an exotic lily I easily identified. The others I could only guess at the names.

"Can I come in and talk to you?" Donovan looked a bit lost and helpless.

How could I resist him in that mood?

I clamped down on my hormones and backed up enough to let him come in to the modest room with two queen beds, an entertainment center, a worktable—already filled with my laptop, notes, and cell phone charger. Some conferences could afford to give me suites. "Stretching Your Writing Wings" was too new to feel comfortable spending that kind of money.

"What do you want to talk about, and where is my mother?" I set the flowers down on the nightstand between the two beds. Nope, might give him ideas. I switched them to the worktable.

"Genevieve is back at the karaoke machine. A Ms. Penny Worth is keeping an eye on her, making sure none of her adoring fans gets too fresh."

I shook my head in bewilderment. This was so not like my mom. But if singing helped her cope with the posttraumatic stress of Darren, let her keep it up.

I wondered if Breven Sancroix stood among the adoring fans.

And had Mr. Twitchy Junior Sancroix tried to con Mom and Donovan out of anything with his empathic talent.

"What do you need to talk about?"

"This." He gathered me into his arms and lowered his head to capture my lips with his own.

My blood sang. My limbs melted. My mind turned to oatmeal.

For three endless heartbeats I welcomed his touch, gloried in the way our bodies molded together, invited his hands to explore my back and ribs and beneath my breasts.

His callused hands awakened nerve endings. I wanted more. His clothes and my nightgown put too thick a barrier between my skin and his.

His aftershave enticed me with hints of sage and copper.

Whoa, girl. Some tiny niggle of sanity sparked to life. It wiggled to the front of my brain and spread.

Reluctantly, I broke the kiss and pushed him away. I felt cold, empty, and incomplete with three inches of space separating us.

"Tess?" he sounded plaintive and hurt.

"You know my conditions. 'Fess up or get out of my life."

"I have four tickets to 'Fairy Moon' for tomorrow night. VIP circle." He held up four pieces of printed card stock with the whimsical logo of a fairy touching a crescent moon with a magic wand.

He offered me the sun and stars and the universe to go with it.

"Are they real?"

"Only the best for my girl. Think your mother can find a date for the fourth ticket?"

"I'm sure she can." Penny Worth came to mind, not Breven Sancroix. Eagerly, I grabbed the tickets and examined them closely. They looked real enough, heavy paper, printing on both sides; section, row, and seat clearly marked as well as date and time. Embossed logo. Tomorrow night, the seven o'clock show. Thursday night, no obligations to the conference.

Donovan waited expectantly while I scrutinized the gold I held in my hand.

"Thank you."

We looked at each other through a long moment of silence. New heat and awareness rose from my toes to my crown. The invisible scar on my face throbbed.

"Tess," he said with longing.

"Donovan, I . . . you know I want you . . ."

"But . . ." He took a deep breath. Pain flitted across his face. Then a spark of something deeper.

"What happens in Vegas stays in Vegas," I quipped. Goddess, I hadn't had a man in a long time. A very long time. Not since Donovan and I had fallen together last October. And before that? No one since my husband Dill died in an awful motel fire three years ago.

"I need you, Tess." Both our gazes flicked toward the nearest bed. The bed closest to the window I'd staked claim to.

"My mom . . ."

"Will be hours yet. She's found something special she needs to cling to. Like I need to cling to you."

"What the hell."

"No commitment, no guilt, no regrets."

"And no assumptions of a repeat performance." I closed the aching distance between us and kissed him hard, as I'd yearned to do for a very long time.

Chapter 8

*The Golden Nugget has the largest nugget of gold
in the world on display. It weighs sixty-two pounds
and is heavily guarded.*

A LONG TIME later I fell asleep with Donovan's
body wrapped protectively around me and his
heavy arm draped across me, anchoring me against
him.

There is something incredibly intimate about falling
asleep with another person. More so than the act of sex.
It becomes a mingling of minds and dreams.

Air rushed around me, pummeling me from all directions as I fell. I could see no bottom, no place to land,
nothing to cushion my fall. My wings refused to work.

Half a thought reassured me that this was one of
Scrap's adventures. The reality of truly falling took
over.

A blast of anger, outrage, and unrelenting disappointment followed me down, down, and down some more.

"I don't deserve this!" I cried. At the same time, dis-
appointing the one who'd thrown me down weighed
heavily on me, almost like guilt.

"It's not my fault!"

My heart leaped into my throat. Dread formed a tight

knot in my belly. The sheer walls of a deep and twisting shaft sped past me. No handholds. No ledges.

Only the debris of my former body falling looked real.

The anger behind me propelled me around all the convoluted spirals.

Nothing between me and a painful landing that meant the end of my existence.

Something glistened below me. Perhaps, just perhaps I might find enough water down there to absorb my plunge and spit me back out again.

The tiny shimmer grew brighter, more solid. Hard, unforgiving glass. My body and my soul would shatter at the same time as that window into the chamber of the Powers That Be.

This was the end. No recovery. No forgiveness. I had failed in my duty. My own inexperience and cockiness made me reckless to the point of ineptitude. I was the weakness in the wall of defense. Because of me a lot of people died.

I sobbed. Choked on my grief. My heart nearly broke.

Just when I gave myself up to an inevitable and very painful death, something soft and gentle cradled me from behind. It slowed my descent.

The sheer stone walls of a well became tall trees with feathery branches. The hard glass beneath me dissolved into a hidden mountain lake. Grass, moss, and ferns formed a soothing bed that awaited me.

My feet touched down. My knees buckled with relief and strain, unused to supporting my suddenly solid body. Arms encircled me.

"You must still face the Powers That Be for the damage you allowed to happen. But for now you may rest. I will keep you safe. I will teach you what you need to know."

I knew that voice. Dillwyn Bailey Cooper. My beloved Dill. The man I had met at a con and married four days later. Then he had died three months after that in a motel fire set by Darren Estevez and an unknown compatriot. Three short months. All I had with the love of my life was three short months.

My sobs renewed because I knew I must live through the agony of losing him all over again.

He touched my face and wiped away my tears. "This is a true dream. But not yours. Live and thrive in your new self."

And then I woke to the sound of the hotel room door opening.

I was alone in the bed.

"Who brought you flowers?" Mom asked as she breezed in, turning on all the lights and filling the room with vibrancy and the scent of stale tobacco smoke. At three in the morning.

"Huh?" I blinked my eyes in confusion, unsure if this was reality or the horrible dream with the puzzling ending.

I'd fallen asleep with Donovan's arms around my naked body. We'd curled up like two spoons, his breath warm and reassuring against my neck. Now he was gone. And I had dreamed.

This is a true dream. But not yours.

If not mine, was it his? I shuddered at the thought of what he had endured.

He must have left while I slept. I felt his absence more keenly than I wanted to admit.

"Oh, there's a card." Mom dug a tiny white envelope out of the depths of the bouquet and handed it to me. "You read it, I don't have my glasses on."

At home she wore them on a long chain around her neck. Tonight, only her inevitable strand of pearls accented her ample cleavage in her little black dress.

She looked happy and fulfilled for the first time in . . . well . . . forever.

As much as I appreciated the changes, I didn't think I'd ever get used to this mom. The Vegas Mom, more alive than I'd ever known her. Dad had left her for Bill when I was twelve. She was barely thirty-seven then. He'd been unhappy with Mom for a long time before that. She'd been nervous and edgy, afraid of the day he'd leave her. She showed a false and brittle brightness during the two and a half days of her marriage to Darren, a product of his demon glamour rather than true happiness.

"I had such a nice chat with Mr. Sancroix," she mused as she fussed with her toiletry bag.

"Breven or Junior?"

"Both, actually. Junior isn't nearly as nervous as I thought he'd be. Quite charming if a bit immature. Breven says he knows you. Another charming man in a rustic sort of way. I envy him the energy to work a farm all by himself after his wife left him. He raised Junior, you know. I never did quite find out what happened to the boy's parents. But his Uncle Breven is the only father he's ever known."

I let her prattle.

Silently, I read the card, carefully keeping the sheet and light blanket over my shoulders, masking my nudity. I didn't think Mom, even the new Mom, would understand why my prim little nightgown lay in a wadded ball beneath the discarded coverlet.

Did Donovan remember to flush the condoms? Yes, that's plural. Three of them in two hours. The man had stamina, and then some.

My innards tightened in memory of how well, and often, he'd filled me, pushing me to one exploding climax after another.

I yanked my focus back to the card.

"My apologies for trespassing on the goodwill of an honorable Warrior. I hope the four enclosed tickets ensure future good relations. Contessa Lucia Maria Continelli."

The manipulative, cheating, lying bastard!

Chapter 9

Built in the mid 1950s, the fifteen-story Fremont Hotel was the first highrise in downtown Las Vegas.

THE HOUSE LIGHTS BLINKED twice, signaling that "Fairy Moon" was about to begin. I sat between Donovan and Mom. Penny Worth sat beyond her. Donovan made a hunkily handsome man in a fine charcoal suit with a silky, silvery shirt and subtle blue, gray, and silver tie. I didn't want my hormones jumping so high I couldn't concentrate on the show.

Mom's happy smiles and bouncing enthusiasm had convinced me to forgive Donovan. Almost.

That and the limo and the champagne he ordered to transport us to the show. Even Penny Worth seemed impressed, commenting that the champagne was excellent, even if the flutes were plastic—good quality plastic, though.

Can't have everything.

She and Mom had spent a good part of the afternoon talking on the telephone, recounting adventures in New York—I still hadn't figured out when that could have taken place—and shopping for just the right dress for tonight's outing. I was surprised at their joint taste and subdued elegance.

"How'd they do that?" Mom breathed in awe.

An aerial dancer clad in pastel draperies and fairy wings swooped over the audience without visible support. She swung up into the top row, around the full horseshoe of seats and back onto the stage to settle on dainty feet and execute a cute pirouette. The lights made her garb—and her makeup—shift colors randomly. The rainbow morphed around her in time to the live, New Age music. For half a heartbeat I caught a glimpse of bright autumnal rust and green in the mix. Then it faded to softer spring colors.

On a higher level, upstage and beyond the spotlights more bits of action swirled and paused. Costumed beings climbed the walls; fog oozed up from the pit area.

A whisper of something floral drifted past me.

"They look just like real fairies," Mom said, her hand flat on her chest as if trying to calm her heart rate.

"Yeah, they do," I said, more a question to Scrap than a real answer.

My imp pranced around the upper levels of the theater, shadowing the dancers as they flew past him. He couldn't get any closer to me than that with Donovan next to me.

A male dancer took off from the circle of fairies dancing around a huge mock mushroom. A caterpillar smoking a hookah perched on top of the stage prop. That was another, very earthbound dancer in a long green body stocking covered in orange spots. The flying dancer took a different route from the previous one, turning cartwheels in midair and playing loop the loop with Scrap.

Or was Scrap playing loop the loop with the fairy? A human dancer shouldn't be able to see Scrap, let alone play with him.

A few weeks ago, during that dustup with Mom's briefly second husband, I'd heard a few interdimensional rumors that all was not well in Faery, the dimension that centered and anchored a good portion of the rest of the Universe.

More coincidences that weren't really coincidence?

Where were the wires supporting the dancers? How

did the lights make this dancer's pastel costume shift colors in a different pattern from the female?

I didn't really care. Awe and wonder filled me, almost—but not quite—dampening my constant bump of curiosity.

Closer inspection of the dancers on stage showed that each was dressed differently, and their colors changed in different patterns, still keeping in rhythm with the music.

Scrap soon tired of flying around the audience. He settled at the feet of the musicians on a balcony projecting over the stage. They, too, wore similar costumes to the fairy dancers, but I hadn't noticed their colors shifting or their wings flapping.

"No wonder this is the hottest show in town," I said to Mom. "The special effects are fabulous."

"Thank you for sharing the tickets, Donovan," Mom replied. She reached across me to pat his hand, then quickly returned her attention to the stage where individual fairies lifted out of the round dance and dropped back down in an intricate pattern.

I allowed myself to believe that Mom just might recover from her disastrous marriage to Darren.

We gave the fairies a standing ovation as the tinkling music faded along with the stage lights. House lights grew brighter, like a dawning. Mom turned to discuss the show with Penny, her new best friend.

From their animation I guessed that this near stranger—or long lost acquaintance—was dearer to Mom than any of her garden club or church choir friends.

"You going to tell me how you got the flowers and tickets from Lady Lucia?" I whispered to Donovan.

"How did you . . . ?"

"There was a card."

"Oops."

"You bet your sweet ass, oops." A very nicely shaped and tightly muscled ass it was, too. "You're busted. Now tell me." I fixed him with a stern glare.

"Would you believe I encountered the messenger at

the concierge's desk and assumed the duty to deliver them."

I hmfed. "Was he overly pale with blood-red lips and wearing a long black cape?"

"No. She wore faded jeans and a T-shirt with a rock band logo."

"Then Lady Lucia and her minions aren't really vampires."

"How do you know Lady Lucia?" Penny Worth asked. She looked upset, the first strong emotion, other than humor, I'd seen in her.

"Her name came up in conversation," I hedged.

"Don't mess with her. Ever. She's dangerous. People who work with her or socialize with her disappear."

"Have you . . . ?"

"Only once. When I was very young and new to the business. I left before *she* made an appearance at the party at midnight. I didn't like the taste of the drinks."

I didn't dare ask her if Lady Lucia drank blood and shunned daylight.

"Is there a better place for a vampire to hide than Vegas?" Donovan asked. A smile tugged at the corners of his mouth.

"Maybe it's just someone who wants us to think she's a vampire," I said. That's what I wanted to believe. Something creepy shook my convictions, though.

"Think about it. This town operates twenty-four seven. Who questions people who choose to work grave-yard shift and sleep all day with the curtains and blinds pulled tight? Who questions their choice of beverage: *Bloody* Marys." Donovan's smile grew bigger.

"Not a good subject to tease me about." I shifted uneasily, fussing with the chiffon layers of my midnight-blue dress that glittered in the colored lights of the theater. Scrap had found the perfect dress for both the theater and the awards banquet.

As the lights dimmed for the next act, Scrap took off from his perch and flew circles around an area behind us. He trailed a new black-and-silver feather boa behind him like a seductive snake. I did my best to ignore his antics. He was such a queen showing off.

Another, larger imp flew up to join him. Fortitude flapped his wings in long, slow, majestic strokes. The two males contrasted like a pert jay harassing a black swan.

They seemed to converse on a wavelength I could not hear.

If Fortitude was here, then so was Sancroix, and possibly his twitchy nephew. I don't believe in coincidence.

Chapter 10

*Topless dancers became a Las Vegas trademark in
1957 at The Dunes.*

J DIDN'T DARE TRUST Sancroix, even if he did
carry an imp on his shoulder.

In other circumstances I might count him as a potential friend. We had a lot in common, we conversed easily
about our lives as Warriors and our experiences in the
Citadels.

So why did he stalk me? I had no doubts left that Junior had flown from Chicago to Vegas on my flight just
to watch me.

I was as leery of them as I was of Donovan.

Trust has to be earned, Scrap warned me as he settled
back with the musicians where he could watch the show
and keep an eye on me as well.

"You learn anything from Fortitude?" I asked under
the mask of blotting my nose with a tissue.

*Not one damn thing. That imp is more closemouthed
than any I've ever met, including my eldest brother who
barely said three words his first one hundred years.*

Scrap rarely talked about his life before he came to
me. Oblique references only. Just enough to tweak my

curiosity, never enough to satisfy me. Yet I knew I could trust him with my life and my soul.

I also trusted Gollum—Guilford Van der Hoyden-Smythe PhD—with my life and friendship. He, too, had a shadowy past, but I never caught him actually lying to me.

I trusted Donovan with my life. We'd fought demons together twice, and he'd guarded my back admirably. His lies and half truths kept me from trusting him with my heart. The flowers and tickets were just one of many lies.

Didn't stop me from enjoying last night and longing for more. There is something incredibly satisfying about hot monkey sex. Not satisfying enough to go the distance in a relationship.

In that moment I made the decision to contact my Citadel. If they sent Breven Sancroix to help me with Darren, (even if he did arrive too late) they must know something about him.

"How are they going to top the first act finale?" Mom asked. "For dramatic purposes, you end Act One with your second-best piece, saving the best for the Grand Finale."

Hidden depths kept coming out of her mouth. Did I have her demon husband to thank for that, or just time and a growing closeness between us.

Then, too, if Darren hadn't slammed into our lives, would we have torn down some barriers so that we could grow closer?

The house lights blinked once, twice, then doused completely.

The New Age synthesizer music started up on a long slow throb with a light wooden flute flirting with the descant above it. Perfect music to make love to.

Stop that, I admonished myself.

Donovan seemed to have the same idea. He traced sensuous circles along the back of my hand with his thumb.

I jerked it away from him.

A spotlight led our eyes around the perimeter of the theater. A dozen fairy dancers hovered above the audience, disappearing as the light moved on to the next. When each had been highlighted, they converged on silent wings in the center.

I craned my neck to look up to the middle of their circle. They swayed back and forth, hands joined, faces blank and empty. I wondered why, and when, the joy of flying and dancing to beautiful music had drained out of them. They performed by rote, perfectly coordinated in time to the music. Not a flaw revealed itself to me. Except for the total lack of . . . life.

They looked like Mom had when the enormity of Darren's death and his life finally hit her.

The music shifted, became urgent, almost menacing. The fairies broke apart, skittering around the rafters in manic movements.

The light floral scent that had drifted behind them became sharper, spicier with anticipation.

Abruptly everything stopped. Music and dancers. The lights blinked and flashed red.

Movement on stage in the semidarkness drew our eyes. A hint of yellow, suggestive of dawn, brightened the outer edges, partially blocked by a huge set piece that nearly filled the stage.

One by one the fairies converged around the blockage. Moment by moment more details emerged. The set took on the texture of twisted and weathered red rock. Cave openings, big enough for the fairies to enter and disappear, looked like facial features, definition of arms. I stared at a writhing goblin frozen in stone and time.

The dance continued, sometimes sweet, sometimes agonized. Always the intent to enter one of the caves in order to get home. No words. Just the dance and that intense longing.

I didn't have to be an empath to feel the heartbreak of exile.

When the dancers moved above the audience their faces had taken on animation. Anger. Loneliness. Bewilderment.

Maybe the total lack of expression earlier was part of the story.

Their costumes and makeup became uniformly grayer. A trick of the lights. I had to keep reminding myself this was just a story and didn't involve me.

A resounding thunderclap startled us all. Gasps all around. I jumped and found my hand firmly captured by Donovan's. Mom and Penny reached for each other.

Then sighs of relief as the audience realized this, too, was just part of the story.

The thud of raindrops on hard desert sandstone erupted all around the rock formation. A cool breeze wafted through the theater refreshing us. I hadn't noticed how warm the room had become until that tiny chill of sweat drying in the wind.

Lightning zigzagged across the stage. One of the caves, a little one almost invisible in the fold of the goblin's arm, showed a different texture behind the opening.

The clouds thinned and a diffuse glimmer of moonlight—I couldn't tell which quarter—highlighted the opening some more.

The fairies saw it at the same moment I did. They paused for a heartbeat. "Home," they whispered.

Did they really say it aloud or did I imagine it?

Before I could decide, they rose as one into the air on a level with the opening, formed a straight-as-an-arrow line and flitted in. Quickly. The lights changed again. The hint of moonlight was directly behind the opening, then passed on its eternal pathway. The portal darkened, started to close. One last lone fairy had stopped to pluck a fragile desert bloom. The last in line, lagging behind just a bit.

Too late. She'd wasted too many precious moments gathering that lovely memento, the only bright spot in her exile from home. She slammed into the rock wall and dropped like a stone toward the stage.

I gasped in dismay and sadness. The rest of the audience joined in. I felt like that horrible moment near the end of *Peter Pan* when Tinker Bell has drunk the poisoned milk and lies dying in Peter's hand.

Did I begin the slow clap of hands? Someone did. We all did. We clapped as if our lives depended upon it. The fairy's life did depend upon it.

"I believe in fairies," I chanted.

Mom took up the litany. In a heartbeat, twelve hundred voices told the Universe that we believed.

The dancer lying crumpled on the stage slowly changed from dull gray to white to palest pink. As the noise rose to a driving demand, a single yellow arm snaked out of the opening, grabbed the fallen fairy, and yanked her through the portal.

She waved a thank you to the audience and smiled. The entire stage seemed brightened by that tiny uplift of mouth and eyes. Layers of chiffon trailed after her, turning hot and vibrant pink.

We leaped to our feet, rejoicing with our applause and our shouts of "Bravo!" and "Encore!"

I had to wipe a tear from my eye, amazed at the cultural icons at play here. I could use these images, this feeling, the sharing of common goals and desires through the medium of story.

"She made it," Mom sighed. "I'm so glad she made it home safely."

"So am I."

I glanced over to Donovan, to somehow draw him into this wonderful warmth and joy. He stared off at the portal that was now just a shadow on a stage set. His faced creased in some internal pain I could not share.

"I can't ever go home," he whispered. "Never. I'm more in exile than they are."

Chapter 11

Las Vegas averages three thousand weddings on Valentine's Day weekend.

"YOU'RE VERY QUIET," I said to Donovan as we picked our way out of the theater. I wasn't used to seeing his face devoid of animation. It scared me.

Mom and Penny walked a few paces ahead of us, chattering gaily about the magnificent performance.

"I . . . old memories," he stammered. His gaze kept returning to the stage, now in deep shadow, the rock goblin only a vague outline.

It reminded me of the brooding presence of a gargoyle on a cathedral I'd seen in England.

"Sometimes shared pain is lesser pain," I coaxed.

"The fairy falling and crumpling a wing . . ." He shook his head, reached for his cell phone, and busied himself turning it back on.

I needed to pursue this. Donovan actually talking about his past was too rare and important.

Jostling crowds and a line waiting for taxis outside the hotel interrupted any opportunity to speak and expect to be heard, or not overheard.

Donovan's phone chirped discreetly as we pushed

out into the cooling night air. He barked something into it, then cursed.

"The limousine got T-boned at an intersection. We'll have to take a taxi and bill them for the inconvenience," he explained mildly.

"Oh, dear," Mom sighed. "I really need to get back to The Crown Jewels. I'm singing again tonight."

"When did that happen?" I asked. Something akin to disapproval wanted to burst forth. I couldn't express that to Mom. I needed to support her now, help her regain her life after Donovan's foster father had nearly destroyed it.

"Excuse me for buttin' in here," a tall man in his sixties, wearing a white Stetson and an impeccable gray western-cut suit edged between me and my mother. "Name's Ed Stetson, like the hat." He tipped it. "I got a limo heading out to The Crown Jewels. Heard there's this hot new act there." He winked at Mom. "Saw her last night and just have to go back."

"Well, I'll be. Ed Stetson from Austin," Penny said. She hooked her arm through his. "If I remember correctly, and I always do, you drink Bushmills, smoke Cubans, and love strawberries dipped in dark chocolate."

"Only Oregon strawberries in season, sweeter than the California berries. Something about the cold winters sending the plants to sleep. They wake up refreshed and full of sweetness. Like you. How you doing, Penny?" He bent to kiss her cheek.

The conversation went downhill from there. Or uphill. Mom and Penny joined Ed in his big white stretch Cadillac. "He's harmless and rich as a Texan ought to be," Penny reassured me just before the driver closed the wide white door on the dim interior. "Your mama is safe with us."

"Want some supper? I know this lovely place at The Venetian. It's only a few blocks from here." Donovan smiled down at me. He didn't have to say, "Alone at last." It showed in his reinvigorated posture and the way he gazed at me.

A shiver of delight coursed through me. "Let's walk."

Blocks in Vegas can be irrelevant. Some of the bigger venues stretch for half a mile or more. I set a brisk pace, partly to keep warm now that the sun had set. More out of impatience.

Donovan's long legs kept pace with me easily.

Traffic on the sidewalks and streets grew heavier the closer we came to the Strip. We jostled other walkers constantly. Donovan threaded his fingers through mine to keep me close. I enjoyed the warmth and tingles shooting from his palm to mine. He cast an aura of protectiveness around me. For once I let it stand, easing away my need for independence in favor of cultivating his semi-loquacious mood.

The massive facade of The Venetian loomed before us. The ever-present sound system played a synthesized version of a bouncy Italian tune I couldn't name. Its ever-so-slightly off-key rendition—no electronic medium could do it justice—irritated me. I inched closer to Donovan, shying away from the noise.

Inside, the rich carpets, faux marble walls, and pseudo-classical statuary muted the music enough that I relaxed. Our shoulders brushed, and I let my hand linger in his.

We followed the signs around the edge of the smoky casino toward the Grand Canal. The last half flight of stairs opened up into ...

"Wow!" I stopped short, amazed by the lovely blue sky and fluffy white clouds above an open plaza flanked by quaint buildings. The broad painted sky looked too real and gave the impression of a long horizon beyond the rooftops. Nothing felt closed in. A hint of pink just above the roofline suggested we neared sunset. But outside, in Vegas the sky had gone full dark.

A Venetian piazza opened before us with shops and trees and jovial crowds. A group of Renaissance costumed singers performed while a Pierrot clown on stilts in traditional baggy white costume with black-and-white domino makeup manipulated a dancer/puppet in jester green, purple, and red playing the marionette.

I caught a hint of sweet citrus and sharp olive on the warm and gentle breeze, a full ten degrees warmer than the desert chill we'd left behind, but cooler than the hot and crowded casino.

"Have we zipped through the chat room and transported to Italy?"

"Not quite," Donovan chuckled. "Shall we take a gondola ride before we eat?"

"Why not?" I kept turning circles trying to take it all in at once. "I think I need to set my next book in Venice so I can go there for research. If it's half this nice, it will be wonderful."

"The real canal smells of sewage and brine instead of chlorine," he whispered conspiratorially.

"I don't care." I turned in a circle, trying to absorb it all, while still following him toward the canal. My heels caught on a crack in the tiled pavement.

Donovan caught me as I tilted downward. With a laugh, he held me close to his side.

I grinned goofily.

"It will all be here on the way back," he chuckled, tucking my hand into the crook of his arm. "And it will still be just before sunset, no matter what time it is outside."

Comfortably close, we made our way across the arched bridge over the artificial waterway. The incredibly clear, blue water and pristine white stonework sparkled with an invitation to follow it along its twisted pathway, alternately narrow and private and open and jovial.

I resisted the urge to lay my head against Donovan's chest. Even in three-inch heels I couldn't reach that special place on a man's shoulder meant for snuggling.

"Watch your step, my dear." A gentle tug on my hand and I paid enough attention to my feet to walk down the seven white steps lapped by blue water to a waiting boat. A fancy white one with gold trim.

Donovan stepped in first, then held my hand while the gondolier steadied the craft. At the last moment, just before I put both feet firmly on the deck, it rocked and threw me off-balance. Donovan caught me and we tumbled onto the seats laughing and clinging to each other.

The boatman pushed off from his mooring with a long pole. He wore the traditional black knee pants, striped shirt, and flat-crowned skimmer hat. He sang a soft ballad in Italian as he guided us into the center of the narrow waterway.

The subdued lighting caught the shimmer of sequins on my dress. They might have been stars in a midnight-blue sky.

"Thank you for this evening, L'Akita," Donovan said, kissing the back of my hand. His lips lingered and nibbled up my wrist. Then he turned our hands over and kissed my palm.

Delicious flashes of electricity wandered up my arm. Memories of last night came back with renewed intensity.

Coherent thought fled.

"After eight hundred years of watching silently, I need to take action, do things, follow through." His mouth shifted to my brow, my nose, my lips.

Oh, yeah, I was supposed to ask him about those eight hundred years before he became human fifty years ago, though he only looked forty—tops. And a very fit and vibrant forty at that.

The primal energy we shared deepened.

He bent down, reaching beneath the seat, while somehow never removing his mouth from my face. Velvety flower petals trailed along my scar after his caresses.

I managed to look down as the softness met my chin. A single red rosebud, absolutely perfect, with a bit of dew still on it. A matching red ribbon dangled a bright and shiny object from the stem.

A huge, honking, square-cut diamond in an antique gold filigree. The most beautiful and enticing piece of jewelry I'd ever seen.

The diamond flashed. I caught a brief glimpse of a jagged lightning crack in reality.

The ring called to me, begged me to wear it. Forever. If I but touched it, I could rule the Universe.

My heart skipped a beat. Three beats. I forgot to breathe.

"L'Akita, Tess, will you marry me?"

Huh?

I opened my eyes to find myself looking into the dark chocolate depths of his own. Fire sang through my blood.

I wanted to say yes.

Well, my hormones wanted me to say yes.

The ring demanded I say yes.

My brain stretched and snapped awake.

That was the biggest diamond I'd ever seen outside the crown jewels in the Tower of London. Greed reared its nasty head.

"I know I've messed up since we met." He had the grace to look sheepish. "But I figured it out. Well, most of it. And I want things right between us. Will you marry me?"

"You sure did mess up. Like knocking up the wicked little witch who murdered your father right after I refused to have your children without the commitment of marriage."

And he never said the crucial words: "I love you."

"Well, yeah. I really wanted you to be the mother of that child, our child. I want to fill your house with our children. WindScribe was, I don't know, I was just so very angry with you at the moment. I don't love her."

"Good thing since she's locked up in a mental hospital for the rest of her life." And my Aunt MoonFeather, the most honorable person and witch I knew was under orders from the prison warden of the universe to gain custody of that child by hook or by crook.

She'd filed suit in the mundane courts as soon as WindScribe's doctors confirmed her pregnancy. Donovan had countersued. I couldn't help but think that marriage to me might help his case.

He'd seemed obsessed with having children since I met him last autumn.

Children to fill my house. *My house*! The rambling monstrosity on Cape Cod sat smack dab in the middle of neutral ground. A place where peace treaties could be signed in safety. A place where neither demon nor magic ruled.

But a neutral place that lay vulnerable to those seeking to open a new and rogue portal between dimensions.

The most valuable plot of land in Human space to those who knew what it was and how to manipulate it.

Donovan didn't want me. He wanted my children and my house.

My body calmed down and began listening to my head.

The gondolier listened raptly to our conversation as well. Did Scrap?

I suddenly missed his acerbic comments.

"Why can't Scrap come near you? You have to know that I can't marry you until that little issue is resolved." Scrap and I were bound together by magical ties that stretched through several dimensions and the chat room. If he died, I died. If Donovan came between us, I think I'd shrivel up into a mere shadow of myself.

Come to think on it, I hadn't seen Scrap since theater intermission.

Where are you?

Busy.

I felt like a door had slammed in my face.

A wave of loneliness washed over me, chilling any lingering ardor.

"What do you know of Scrap's past?" Donovan asked, so quietly I didn't think our boatman could hear.

"More than I do of yours." Not a whole lot more.

"If the imp is repelled by me, then there must be a darkness in his soul."

"And there isn't in yours? You fell from something. I know that much." And now I also knew he'd been a silent watcher for eight hundred years before that fall.

"What did you fall from? Grace? If that's the case, you have a darkness in your past worse than Scrap's."

His face went still as stone. Redness spread across his cheeks, making them seem sharper than ever and highlighting the faint copper coloring.

"Gondolier, I'm getting out." I stood. The boat rocked.

Donovan steadied me. I slapped his hand away.

"Sorry, ma'am. You have to wait until we reach a landing."

I looked up and down the artificial canal. Tall walls flanked us as we approached a miniature Bridge of Sighs.

"Can't wait that long. *Ciao*." Oblivious to stares and shouts from people watching—including Donovan—I stepped onto the seat with one foot and launched myself upward. I clung to the smooth white faux marble of the bridge and swung one leg up to the railing.

The gondolier kept poling the pretty white-and-gold boat along.

The wedding boat.

All the others were plain black. Donovan had planned well. Too bad I couldn't go along with his plans.

"Tess. Wait," he shouted, half standing on the wobbling gondola.

The boat passed beyond me. He couldn't follow.

Anonymous hands reached down to help me. I scrambled onto the bridge, having flashed only a little too much leg in my precipitous escape. Good thing Scrap color coordinates my undies.

"Thanks, folks." I called and waved to my helpers.

Head high and shoulders straight, I marched for the nearest exit.

Scrap settled on my shoulder and wiggled his tail, lashing my back with its barb. Right where he belonged. Where I belonged.

You didn't ask if your first husband was Damiri demon like Donovan's foster father, he chided me.

"Next time. Want to tell me about the darkness in your soul?"

Next time, babe. I've got unfinished business in Imp Haven.

He disappeared again.

"Damn," I said as I hailed a taxi.

Chapter 12

Slot machines need a complete change of circuit board to affect the percentage of wins.

I HATE LYING to Tess. I had imp business—but not in Imp Haven.

Fortitude bugs me. He's too silent. Too big. Sure he's bonded to a rogue Warrior, but that's no excuse for shunning another imp. I'm bonded to a rogue, too.

Rogue means working outside the confines of a Citadel, not mean or bad or anything like that. I've heard rumors that more and more Warriors of the Celestial Blade are leaving the Citadels.

The portals to other dimensions aren't stable. We need Warriors out in the world, continuing what the secret fraternities and sororities have been doing for centuries in solitude.

Fortitude acts like that's top secret information and I'm not good enough to have access.

Well, I've got my sources, too.

Gayla's imp Ginkgo likes to chat. I think I'll skip through the chat room and over to the Citadel. It's only a thousand miles or so, almost due north. That's a much easier journey than through time. Done that once or twice, don't want to have to do it again.

Since I'm not hopping dimensions, I slip into the big white

room without definition. I close one layer of eyelids to concentrate and visualize my destination. Gotta keep the other three layers open to make sure the scaly faeries on duty don't notice me. Then I slide back into the same dimension but at a different location. Easy as pie.

Except . . .

"Let go of my tail!"

A huge and hairy hand with four digits and an opposable thumb hangs on tight.

This is going to cost me a wart or two.

I twist and yank and send my wings into overtime.

Big fat on steroids laughs, a deep and foreboding expulsion of air that has little to do with humor and a lot to define evil.

I ache to transform. Tess is not here to command me.

What to do? What to do?

I stretch anyway, becoming thinner and sharper. My tail slices the demon's hand.

"Ouch, that hurts," it pouts, sucking dark green blood from its palm.

"That's what you get for detaining an imp on an honest mission," I snarl back. Can't let the beast know how scared I am. That blood was so dark it was almost black.

Faery blood is bright pink or maybe cerulean, never dark. If he's a mutated faery, we're all in trouble. Faeries are the bright and joyful balance of air sprites for the entire universe. They have the only dimension with three demon ghettos because their power of light is so strong. (That's a big secret, so don't tell anyone). Every other dimension has one race of light and one race of dark. (We keep demons in ghettos for a reason. They eat anything and everything in their path). Faeries can flit into many dimensions. Almost as good as imps.

The universe needs faeries.

An imbalance in their domain shakes up the balance across the entire universe.

Humans are weird, though. They don't need a demon ghetto. They kill themselves frequently and with unnatural glee. They are their own victims.

I think maybe I need to take a look in Faery after I talk to Ginkgo. We need more faeries, but not the kind on guard duty in the chat room lately.

"Are we anywhere near the Dragon and St. George?" I asked the skinny taxi driver. I'd come out of The Venetian at a different door and got disoriented.

"Thought you wanted to go to The Crown Jewels," the driver muttered. A longer drive, bigger fare, bigger tip. He looked like one of the many starving performers in town who worked at anything between gigs and tips. I thought I'd seen him before, but who remembers taxi drivers?

"I do. Later. But first I'd like to check on something."

"Tickets to 'Fairy Moon' are scarce as hen's teeth, lady. I know a guy . . ."

"I saw the show earlier this evening."

The muted roar of traffic on the Strip at the other side of the hotel filled the cab as he thought of ways to milk more money out of me.

I took a chance. "Lady Lucia sent me the tickets."

His eyes sparked with interest. And fear. He took a long, assessing look at me through the rearview mirror. I thought his gaze lingered on my scar. Maybe I'm paranoid.

"You a friend of Lady Lucia, you tell her Mickey Mallone take you anywhere in Vegas you want to go." A strange name for a guy with distinct Mediterranean coloring and broken English. "No charge. I wait for you to finish business at the Dragon, then take you to Crown. Anything for a friend of Lady Lucia." He put the car into gear and screeched the tires as he merged into traffic, as if he owned the street.

"I've never met her. She sent me the tickets as a professional courtesy." So I wouldn't go vampire hunting?

My imagination sped into overdrive. I hadn't done enough writing on this trip to control it.

Vampires were myths. No one comes back from the dead. No one.

Not even my husband Dill.

"No one meets Lady Lucia. I gotta go around a cou-

ple of blocks to approach the Dragon from the right."
The barest flick of the turn signal and we were careening
around a corner.

I decided to buckle up.

He pulled into the porte cochere of the Dragon less
than ten minutes later, despite bumper-to-bumper traffic on and off the Strip. This hotel had grown up three
blocks (each the size of a small city) away from the main
action in a slightly less desirable neighborhood. It didn't
have the cachet of a Strip hotel until "Fairy Moon"
brought it to the attention of the masses. Now neon and
glitter had engulfed it.

"I may be a while, Mickey. Get another fare." I
climbed out of the taxi, pressing a ten into his hands.

"No charge, lady. I said no charge for a friend of . . .
you know."

"A tip. Mickey."

He shrugged. The bill disappeared into his jeans
pocket. "You got cell phone? Call me. I come back for
you. You wait for me." He scrawled something on a fast
food bag that smelled of fried fish, tore off the scrap, and
gave it back to me. "You call. Mickey take you anywhere
in Vegas."

"What about the Valley of Fire?"

He gulped and looked away. "Okay," he said
reluctantly.

"What if I rent a car and you drive me?"

A huge smile creased his face. His blindingly white
teeth shone in the dim interior. "That I can do. Forty,
fifty miles each way. Good museum in Overton. When
you want to go?"

I had a morning full of classes for the conference.
"Pack a picnic basket and meet me at The Crown at
noon sharp. I'll have you back in time for the evening
shift." I slammed the door.

"Call Mickey when you ready," he returned as an
overweight, mid-thirties couple wearing matching turquoise shorts and flowered shirts pushed into the taxi
from the other side. They yelled something at each other
and then to Mickey. He took off at a more sedate pace.

These people obviously were not friends of Lady Lucia.

No clocks anywhere inside. I checked the one on my cell phone, forty-five minutes to the next performance of "Fairy Moon." I hadn't spent as much time with Donovan as I thought. The fiasco felt like a lifetime.

Damn. I'd screwed up as much as he had. I wished I'd taken a better look at the ring. Sure, my inborn avarice wanted to own it, wear it, flaunt it. The ring offered me a sense of power and well-being. It needed to grace my hand.

I shook off that notion in a hurry.

The ring looked like it cost as much as my last advance on a two-book contract. If it was real. My first glance gave me the impression of an antique. The cut and setting might give me some clues to where and when Donovan acquired it.

His finances had undergone many ups and downs over the last year. I didn't think he'd recovered enough to buy that ring on the open market.

I edged around the casino, scanning the ranks of slot machines. The metallic music and constant clanking noises set my teeth on edge more than Donovan's proposal. My stomach growled for sustenance. My nerves rejected the idea of food.

Halfway around the small casino I spotted drifting pastel chiffon behind a knot of cocktail waitresses and suited people with discreet gold hotel name badges.

I took a stool at a slot machine between the fairy dancer and the madly whispering staff. I still couldn't understand why the hotel allowed the dancers out in public in costume. This young man's wings drooped and a layer of grime ringed his ragged knee pants and the cuffs of his elbow-length sleeves.

The flowing green, lavender, and blue of his costume looked pale, verging on the gray of the final act. As I watched him slide a gold chip into the machine, the colors of his garb shifted to brighter hues. Then when the rollers came up with another loss, the colors faded again.

This was no trick of the lights.

I looked closer. Narrow exquisite face, pointed ears, delicate grace. A fragile beauty on the verge of shattering.

"I don't understand how anyone could be skimming," one of the staff whispered to his colleagues. Anger made his voice grow louder than he'd intended. "The owners can't sell the hotel out from under us for a little discrepancy in the books."

The faery didn't look or appear to overhear the intense conversation right next to him.

I carefully avoided glancing in either direction. If I wanted to engage the faery or listen in on a private conversation I had to have a reason to linger. The only reason for staying in this section more than half a minute was the slots.

Reluctantly, I dragged my wallet out of my bra—I have to give myself cleavage some way. Cell phone on the left, wallet on the right and I actually look like I have boobs.

When the wasting fever of the imp flu peeled forty-seven pounds off my body and sped up my metabolism to burn every calorie I ingested, I think it took thirty-seven of those pounds off my chest. That's about the only regret I have from that awful experience. After all, the flu gave me Scrap and a whole new purpose in life.

I placed three quarters in the slot and pulled the arm. No mechanical resistance or click, just the smooth engagement of a computer.

The boxes rolled around and around, settling one by one. One double cherry. Two, and then three stalled in front of me. Clangs and whistles. A flashing light. A long shower of quarters dropped into my lap.

"Let me get you a bucket for those," one of the waitresses said, smiling hugely. "And can I get you a drink while I'm at it?"

"Single malt. Straight up. And can I get a turkey sandwich with that?" She moved off.

The knot of staff backed away to the end of the row, almost into the emergency fire exit.

"Lucky you," muttered the faery in a strangely stilted accent. Like he worked to pronounce each word individually and precisely. "My luck has deserted me."

"I'm sorry. Here. Share some of mine." I handed him a fist full of quarters.

He examined the coins as if looking for counterfeit.

"Are these real money?" he asked. "They are not gold. How can they be money?"

Uh-oh. What had I stumbled on to?

Did I say I don't believe in coincidence?

Chapter 13

*Slot machines are negative expectation machines:
the longer you play, the more likely you are to lose.*

"THISTLE, YOU HAVE TO come now," a girl
faery hissed at my puzzled companion. She had
the same stilted accent and the same delicate features.

I'd heard that accent before. Where?

"You know what Lord Gregbaum will do to us if
you're late again." Her flowing draperies had a dominant pale green beneath a film of grimy gray. At the
mention of Lord Gregbaum, the gray became dominant
and the green the barest hint.

Gregbaum? I'd heard that name before.

Thistle handed the quarters back to me. "Thank you,
gracious lady." He bowed formally. "Faery is in your
debt. Mint, wait for me."

Neither one of them touched ground as they hastened through the maze of slot machines.

I gulped.

Anyone but me would dismiss it all as delusion born
of stress, drink, the extra oxygen pumped in so gamblers
got an artificial high, the never ending noise and smoke
in the casino, anything but challenge reality with the notion that faeries could be real.

The waitress appeared with my bucket and sandwich. I dumped my quarters, handed her the bucket, and grabbed the tray.

"Hey, I'm not supposed to serve you if you aren't gambling."

"Keep the quarters. They'll cover the cost." I lifted the scotch in toast and took a quick sip. One does not ever, under any circumstance, waste good single malt scotch, or even mediocre blends, by gulping.

The fragrance opened my senses. A first taste rolled around my mouth with just a hint of a bite. I swallowed and the fire exploded on the back of my tongue and through every nerve ending in my body. "Ah, Lagavulin. The fire of the gods wrapped in velvet." Nothing but the best for a winning gambler. Got to keep them happy and gambling so they eventually lose everything they won and then some.

Another sip, then two more just so I didn't waste the water of life.

Fortified, I turned to dash after the dancers, sandwich and glass in hand. I have my priorities and never miss a chance to eat and drink. With my schedule, the next meal might disappear as fast as faery dust.

"That's the real trouble with this casino. Everyone is obsessed with that stupid show instead of gambling," the waitress muttered. "Except those blasted dancers. They gamble all the time."

"Is that why the casino is being sold?" I came to a screeching halt. "I mean this place is full to overflowing with people. Why sell a profitable resort?"

"Yeah, maybe." She looked embarrassed as she counted the quarters, stuffing every other dollar's worth into her tip bag at her hip.

"What happens to the show if the Dragon and St. George sells? Will the producer move it to another casino?" Judging by the difficulty getting tickets, another hotel should jump at the chance to host a winning show.

"Look, lady, I don't know anything. I'm just a waitress trying to hang on to my job. But if it means so much to you, most times a hotel sells, they implode it—selling tickets to *that* show—and rebuild, bigger and glitzier. And everyone who works there is out of a job until it re-opens, two maybe three years down the road. As for the show? That's up to the producer." She finished counting the money and hurried away.

I tried to find the dancers. They, of course, had disap-peared, probably into the maze of back corridors that serviced the entire hotel/casino/resort.

My spine tingled. Someone watched me. Again.

"Scrap, where are you?"

Silence.

I imagined hidden monsters behind potted plants and rows of gambling machines following my progress across the floor. I'd fought my fair share of monsters. But I needed help to do it.

"Scrap?"

A hazy stirring in the back of my mind.

"What are you doing sleeping on the job?"

Scrap never slept, except right after a fight. He needed rest then to recover from the difficult and draining pro-cess of transforming into the Celestial Blade.

I whipped out my cell phone and called Mickey. As I waited in the busy porte cochere, full of lights and people, I read the twice life-sized digital poster screen advertising "Fairy Moon."

Produced by Gary Gregbaum.

So who made him a lord?

"Who is Gary Gregbaum?" I asked Mickey as he pulled into traffic.

"Bad news."

"Anyone in Vegas who isn't bad news?"

Mickey flashed me his brilliant grin. "Me."

"How'd Gregbaum get a rep like that if he's now the hottest producer of the hottest show in town?"

"He used to be Lady Lucia's lover. Bad blood be-tween those two." He gulped. "I mean . . ."

"Lady Lucia's supposed to be a vampire. There is no bad blood to a vampire." I grinned back at him. This town was getting spooky. Wereweasels, vampires. Faery lords. Someone stalking me.

"Yeah. She threw Gregbaum out on his ear. He's got a grudge. She's got her fangs in a twist 'cause he made a success of the show even after she pulled her financing. Rumor has it that someone else is working with Gregbaum behind the scenes. No one knows who. Maybe another vampire cutting into Lady Lucia's territory. Maybe someone or something else."

"How come you know so much?" I asked suspiciously.

"People talk in cabs. They do not expect the driver to listen. They do not expect driver with broken English to be smart enough to put together stray pieces of information. No one remembers cab drivers." He flashed me a wide grin through the rearview mirror.

Except me. I know I'd seen him before tonight. "So why tell it all to me?"

"Professional courtesy," he mimicked my words in describing Lady Lucia's gift of tickets. He nodded his head in an imitation bow or salute.

I mulled that over for a moment. Any information was better than none. I'd sort out the veracity later.

"What do you hear about the Dragon and St. George being up for sale? Lady Lucia leveraging a buyout so she can close him down?"

"You said it, lady. I didn't."

"My name's Tess."

"Lady Tess."

I rolled my eyes.

"Are you an escapee from Faery, too?"

"Where's Faery? Bulgaria my home." His accent suddenly thickened.

"Okay, so how does Gregbaum treat his dancers?" The look of terror on Mint's face came from somewhere. And she'd said, "You know what he'll do to *us* if you are late again."

"No word. No gossip. None of his dancers speak English. They live in a dormitory in basement of hotel. Never leave building." Mickey sounded bitter.

But they did speak English. Or at least I understood them to speak English.

"How come you know so much?"

"I auditioned and got rejected. Asked around. I'm a good dancer and gymnast. One of the best. They should have hired me. But no, Gregbaum hires each one personally. Brought in the entire cast from somewhere else. Should be some loyalty to people who already live here," he grumbled. His accent grew thicker.

I missed the flash of white teeth in his smile.

"So you are stuck driving a taxi instead of dancing."

"Yeah. Driving taxi for prettiest lady in Las Vegas. You still want to see Valley of Fire tomorrow?"

Did I? Was I connecting dots or following red herrings here. Maybe I needed to wait on that and check out Gary Gregbaum and Lady Lucia instead.

Maybe I needed help.

"Let's wait on that, Mickey. I'll call you."

"No problem. But you really should see the Valley of Fire before you leave. Is most spectacular at sunrise and sunset."

The times of transition in folklore. The times when magic is strongest. When portals to other dimensions open . . . ?

"Two days from now, when the quarter moon is rising and the sun setting. Mickey take you."

A waxing quarter moon, when demons most often breach their portals and invade our dimension.

Whooee! Time travel is such a rush. Back and forth to the Citadel twice without Tess or Ginkgo being aware that I've been gone for *hours* drains me. I really need some beer and OJ. Some mold would be better. Not easily found in the desert. Vegas is drier than the Citadel, if you can believe that. Not given to mold. In Vegas, they have tons of air conditioners that breed my favorite restorative in abundance.

But I don't dare leave Ginkgo while he sleeps off our heavy exertions. Now that he realizes he really likes boys better than girls, I must cement our relationship.

At last I have found the perfect lover. He's younger than I by a good fifty years, and already full sized. Such strength and stamina!

I could wax poetic on my lover's attributes for, like forever. Unfortunately duty calls. Duty in the form of Tess, my beloved Warrior.

Life in the Citadel stifled her. But now that Ginkgo and I are an item, (ooh, I like the sound of that) I wish Tess would visit more often. I'll have to suggest a refresher course in being a Warrior of the Celestial Blade.

"Psst, Ginkgo." I rouse my stud from his snoring slumber. An imp snoring is a beautiful song of love and life affirmation. Yet I must regrettably end it.

"Ginkgo, have you spoken to Gayla?" Gayla is his Warrior.

"Gayla." He smiles dreamily.

"Did you ask her to call Gollum?" Someone has to make use of that telephone she installed at great cost and near rebellion from the ranks of traditionalists. I mean, really, they use very modern pickup trucks to run into town for supplies and make lightning raids on rogue portals. You'd think they'd wake up to changing times and get some electricity and indoor plumbing out here!

"My Gayla made the call. This Gollum person wings his way toward your Tess, though how he can fly in one of those mechanical contraptions I do not understand. Now where were we?" He reaches for me.

He draws circles around the warts on my bum with his talons. Blood wells in the tracks of his tracing. I wrap my tail around his neck. Not quite domination, not quite subjugation with my backside in his face.

I'll check out Faery in a bit.

My cell phone chirped a phrase from "A Night on Bald Mountain," just as I entered the casino across from Mom's stage. The blame thing changed ring tones on its own every day or two. I tried for a discreet and anonymous chirp. The universe wanted to summon me with music geared to the weird.

I glanced at the caller ID and smiled. "Gollum, what's up?" Ten o'clock here. One AM at home on Cape Cod.

"I am. Or I will be in about fifteen minutes."

"Huh?"

"I'm in Chicago, on my way to Vegas."

"Huh? Don't you have classes?"

"None on Friday. Remember, we set up my schedule with the community college so I could have weekends to take you to cons when you need company."

"Oh, yeah. Listen, I'm glad you're coming. I hope you have your laptop with all your interesting databases."

"I figured you might need your archivist when Gayla called me and told me you needed help."

"Gayla?" Either I was missing something or all the smoke and noise of the casinos had fried my brain.

Off to my left, Donovan shuffled in by another door. His eyes looked heavy and his shoulders slumped. He'd been drinking.

Well, what did I expect. I'd be drunk, too, if he'd done to me what I just did to him. I turned my back on him, not ready to deal with that little problem just yet.

That little movement put me in line of sight to Mom crooning her way through "Foggy Day In London Town." No sign of Penny and Ed Stetson.

But Sancroix stood on the fringes of her audience staring at her in fascination.

Or was he studying her like a cat studies its prey? His big imp sat heavily on the man's shoulder. Fortitude had folded his wings, covering his head in sleep.

Except that imps rarely slept.

Was that an imp eye peering out surreptitiously spying on the room for Sancroix? Why the subterfuge if I was the only one in the room who could see the imp?

Because I was the only one in the room who could see the imp.

Junior sat at a table beside him, twisting a paper napkin to shreds. Still nervous and twitchy. A squarely built woman sat beside him, back to me. Something in the angle of her head looked familiar.

I pushed aside the images of stalker and prey. Sancroix had to be one of the good guys, or his imp wouldn't stay with him; Gayla wouldn't have sent him to assist me last month against a little problem with my mother's half-blood Damiri demon husband and a grieving widowed Windago—there was that crazy book title that kept haunting me. Next book. I had two newly under contract already.

"I'll book a room for you here at The Crown Jewels," I told Gollum.

"Already done, love. Don't wait up for me. I'll see you in the morning." He made a kissing sound.

Huh?

Gollum? Guilford Van der Hoyden-Smythe the pedantic professor. My dear friend and archivist. My confidant and the one I trusted almost more than myself.

I really had missed something.

Donovan sloshed up to the bar.

"I'm glad Gollum is coming. He can provide a buffer between me and my ex-stepbrother," I said to myself. I kept reminding myself of all the reasons why I had rejected Donovan. I had to. Otherwise, my hormones and my greed for that diamond might make me do something even more stupid than sleeping with him last night.

Chapter 14

Las Vegas means "The Meadows" in Spanish. The name appears on maps as early as the 1830s. Las Vegas was officially founded in 1905 when the railroad came to town.

MOM ENTERTAINED A LARGE crowd in the lounge with a vibrant rendition of "Seventy-Six Trombones." The song provided a nice balance to the moody torch songs. The audience sang along on the chorus. Some even got up and marched around their tables. She knew how to work an audience.

"Amazing! When did she learn to do that?"

Barely ten thirty. She'd keep them going for hours yet.

I took my cell phone back to our room. No signal.

Back to the lobby. No signal.

Outside in the parking lot. No signal.

I growled something very impolite.

"Is there a problem, Ms. Noncoiré?" a shaky tenor voice asked from behind me.

I whirled about, automatically *en garde*. No sign of Scrap. I sent out a mental call for help.

"Oh, it's you. Junior Sancroix."

He still twitched nervously, his gaze darting right and

left, across the street, and back to my feet. Not my eyes. He looked firmly at the pavement.

"Is there a problem?" He grimaced like he should be embarrassed by my language, but wasn't.

"No cell service."

"That happens sometimes." He shrugged. "You can always use the hotel landlines." His smile turned greedy.

"And pay exorbitant connection fees as well as inflated long-distance charges." I wondered if he had magnets or something inside the building to block service. Or maybe he used his empathic talent to convince people they had no signal when they did. I wouldn't put it past him. He didn't have an imp to lull my distrust.

"Such is life in Vegas." He shrugged again.

"I'm curious. How'd a man in his early thirties come to own a hotel, casino, and convention center?"

"I have connections." He grinned at me. For half a moment in the glaring lights on tall poles his eye teeth looked elongated and extra sharp, his eyes tilted up and his ears pointed on the upward lobes.

"Connections to Lady Lucia?"

"Where'd you hear that name?" Immediately, he clamped his mouth shut, hunched his shoulders defensively, and scanned the skies as well as the parking lot. His hands twitched, and so did his neck.

"The Contessa befriended me with tickets to 'Fairy Moon.' I saw you and your uncle there tonight."

"You will have a full signal on your cell phone by morning." He turned on his heel and fairly ran back into the safety of the casino. He ran as if a vampire followed on his heels.

Stop that! I nearly slapped my face to shake off the imagery. I really needed to get back to work and channel my overactive imagination into my books.

But first, I had another way of contacting my Citadel for information about Breven Sancroix and his nervous nephew.

Too many lights and distractions in my room. I headed to the one place I might find quiet and privacy in this town. The roof.

I didn't obey the "Employees Only" signs on the doors or the chain and padlock across the last bit of stairway. My legs were too short to easily climb over it, but I was limber enough to duck under, even in a fancy dress and heels.

Huge, humming barrel units on the nearly flat roof ran the air-conditioning. I found a shadowed place between two of them, letting their constant and monotonous drone mask the roar of traffic that never ended on the streets. When Scrap decided to come home, he'd find me here, right next to his favorite feeding ground.

I had to clear a space of gravel bits and blown debris before trusting the fine layers of my skirt to the dirty surface. It tilted just a little toward a gutter and filter system to drain the infrequent but heavy rainfall. I suspected somewhere in the maze one of these barrel units contained a cistern for maintaining the extensive landscaping.

Then I sat cross-legged, wiggling a bit to find maximum comfort.

Meditation is not my strong suit. Restlessness and muscles that need to keep moving plagued me as I tried to find an inner stillness. I could almost hear Gollum's voice in my ear, whispering "Breathe. Breathe deeply. Concentrate on breathing."

I smiled inwardly that he was winging his way to me even now. But I didn't let that tiny bit of joy distract me. Instead, I used it to conjure images in my mind of the good times I'd had at the Citadel. There weren't many. But a few.

Sister Serena, laughing with me as she made jokes about our scars. Sister Paige saluting me the first time I felled her in arms practice. Sister Gayla's exuberant shout as she and three pickup loads of Warriors joined me in battle against a band of Sasquatch. We fought for possession of an ancient native artifact, an unfinished blanket that held honor, dignity, honesty, justice, and a few other noble characteristics for all mankind woven into its design.

We Warriors of the Celestial Blade did some good.

My thoughts traveled all the way north to my Citadel and my friends. I imagined a tiny bit of candle flame sparking a light inside any receptive mind within the high stone walls in that hidden ravine between here and there, 'twixt light and shadow, only a part in this dimension and partly in the next.

I felt a connection, another mind rousing from slumber to acknowledge the brush of my thoughts. Serena, always the most sensitive to communication from near or far. She slept lightly, a requirement for a physician.

But this was not a medical emergency and Serena was tired. Her sisters had fought long and hard against another incursion from the Sasquatch trying to open a new portal.

I let her sleep. My questions would wait.

Something awakens me. I'm too groggy to recognize the weak call not directed to anyone in particular.

My Tess.

Duty calls. Duty calls. I can sense Tess getting anxious about me being gone so long. I'm so tired I don't dare manipulate time to return to her earlier in the day.

I can't linger any longer though I want to stay. Sleeping next to my lover has to be one of the greatest joys in life. I cannot imagine such intimacy with any other than my soul mate.

I crawl away from Ginkgo's bed, limp and sated. My legs feel heavy. At the same time, my wings keep carrying me higher and higher.

First, I need to check out Faery. What I left Tess to do in the first place. My visit to Ginkgo and his Warrior Gayla was supposed to be just a quick side trip. But then Ginkgo started throwing pheromones at me like there was no tomorrow.

And for most of the night and half the day, there was no tomorrow. Only us.

Ahhhh!

I duck into the chat room and pause by the doorway back to Earth.

I can see the portal to Faery, just two doors down. A little thing with a haze in front of it. One of the easier barriers to breach, if you know how or have enough willpower. Which I do.

The big, red-scaled monster faeries are still on duty. What is this? The guards are supposed to change every day. Different demon tribes rotate the watches to keep everyone in their proper dimension.

Three days running I've had to dodge these guys.

Maybe, if I make myself real small and keep close to the edge, I can avoid detection. One step. Then two. A third and a flit and I'm right in front of the door I need.

A quick peek inside. The stream that chuckles down the hillside runs clear and clean again. The grass is vividly green and the flowers splash brilliant color. Just like it's supposed to.

Last month, when faeries disputed the succession of their king and that king's murderer still ran loose around Earth, Faery did not look so lovely.

But what is this? The big oak tree with clumps of mistletoe has fallen. The grass beneath its rotting trunk is brown. The upper branches are damming the creek. Water backs up behind it and floods the meadow.

I set my wings in motion to carry me through the portal for further investigation.

And bounce right back into the path of the ugly demons on duty.

"Faery is closed," an ugly male says. "No imps in Faery. No imps outside Imp Haven." He reaches a hairy paw with an opposable thumb for my neck.

Demons with opposable thumbs? Gods and Goddesses, what is this universe coming to? Next thing you know the Powers That Be will give opposable thumbs to cats.

Cats, the most cunning, malicious, and evil of all demons!

I dodge the monster and dive right back to Earth. I need to tell someone about this. But who? Who can help? Who can restore the balance to Faery?

And the balance must be restored. Something is draining energy from Faery. That energy is building up somewhere, raw power an unscrupulous being can tap and manipulate for evil.

Chapter 15

"The Strip" is actually Las Vegas Boulevard, a section of US Highway 91.

A LOT OF THE "WORK" of a conference takes place at the breakfast buffet or in the bar. Since Mom had the main bar tied up most of the evening, writers, agents, and editors congregated in the small dining area adjacent to the casino. Everything is adjacent to or connected to the casino even in small hotels that cater to conventions and conferences.

I'd just settled next to the mystery writer Jack Weaver with a plate full of waffles with strawberries and whipped cream, scrambled eggs, hash browns, bacon, juice, and the watery brown stuff they called coffee in this town when Junior Sancroix elbowed a romance editor aside to take the chair on the opposite side.

Damn. I wanted to talk to that editor. I had some ideas about a contemporary paranormal romance I wanted to discuss with her.

"You're that ringer the conference brought in to draw more people," he announced to the table at large.

"I'm a published writer who has had some success," I corrected him. "So's Mr. Weaver here."

"I want to write a book," Junior said quietly. He looked directly at me.

"The only way to write a book is to write it," I replied.

"Hear, hear!" Jack raised his glass of juice in toast.

Everyone else at the table joined him in the salute, including the editor.

"There's lots of weird things that happen in Vegas, a lot of connections that don't make sense until you start unraveling them, take them back to the source. I need to write about them," Junior insisted. He picked up a stray knife from a cutlery set and began tapping the table with it.

"Then write about them." I tried to ignore him.

"I've never written before. I'll need help. But I think I'll make it a romance. That can't be too hard. After all, bored housewives do it for fun. And make a lot of money at it." He flipped the knife to balance between two fingers and waggled it back and forth.

The temperature around the table dropped below freezing.

"Try it Mr. Sancroix. Just try it and see how 'easy' writing anything is. Romance is one of the hardest to make real and believable." Did I say how annoying this nervous little guy was?

"I'm going to sit in on your classes."

"I believe all my workshops are full. You need to talk to the conference organizers." Pass the buck whenever possible.

"I own this hotel, I can join any damn class I want." He rose abruptly and left. His chair teetered on its rear legs a few seconds before regaining its balance and bumping back to a correct position.

"What was that all about?" the editor asked me.

"I have no idea." But Junior had emphasized "connections." After last night's conversation I suspected he meant Lady Lucia. Or possibly Gregbaum.

I checked my cell phone. Sure enough, I had full signal and a text from Gollum. He'd arrived in the middle of the night and would find me at lunch.

At least one thing in my life was solid and certain.
Gollum.

"Why does every fantasy novel have a medieval setting?" a student in my morning workshop asked. She
looked like she was approaching her fifties reluctantly,
with a too-short sundress, starved-to-thinness body,
and expensively dyed auburn hair. The lines around
her eyes and at the corners of her perpetual frown
gave her away.

"How many fantasies have you read, MaryLynn?" I
asked, seeking the name she'd printed in tiny letters on
her sticky name tag. Last-minute registration. Those of
us who had signed up ahead of time had printed cards
slipped into a badge holder.

"Not many. Every one I pick up is the same as all the
others." She pouted prettily, like a twenty year old.

I'd had experience with women who used that kind of
pout to manipulate people.

"I prefer modern romances. I've sold five and am con-
sidering diversifying." She'd mentioned those five novels
in every comment she'd made in the last hour and a half.

"Seems like you've had bad luck in picking fantasies.
The ones I've read in just the last month have settings
in prehistory, outer space, and contemporary cities. But
the medieval castle is a trope you find quite often, especially in historical romances. Any theories before I give
my explanation—which is only an opinion."

A forest of hands shot up. This was a workshop on
making genre fiction unique while keeping it sellable.
One of the harder topics I had tackled at writer conferences. Registration for this class was supposed to be
limited to those who'd sold at least one short story, pref-
erably a novel.

Unpublished Mr. Twitchy cowered in a back corner.
He didn't appear to be taking notes, contenting himself
with glaring at me.

I turned the discussion toward the longing for older, simpler times when honor and valor could be measured, the romance of historical costumes, the "glamour" of hobnobbing with lords and ladies. Someone also brought up the influence of the Society For Creative Anachronism—the clubs that re-created their own version of the Middle Ages every weekend, the way olden times should have been—where everyone is a lord or lady, and the popularity of Renaissance Faires.

"We could also look at an anthropological explanation," I said. "Some theorize that when an industrialized society is cut off from communication and resources, they will revert to a Medieval level of technology within two generations. A monarchy or oligarchy flows out of that kind of society—strong leaders protecting average people from predatory animals or human enemies—or in some fantasies, alien beings or fantastical creatures like orcs or trolls. If resources are extremely limited, they will fall back to tribal level hunter-gatherers within another three to four generations."

At the moment the words flowed from my mouth, my resident anthropologist, Guilford Van der Hoyden-Smythe, PhD, ducked into the back of the room. About time. The digital clock on my cell phone showed the noon break approaching fast.

He looked freshly showered and shaved in his neat khakis and emerald-green golf shirt. For once his wire-rimmed glasses sat firmly on the bridge of his nose, masking his mild blue eyes. Every silver-gilt hair lay in place.

His professor guise effectively masked the breadth of his shoulders on his tall and lanky frame. I'd sparred with him, rock climbed with him, had him carry me off the field of battle. I knew the strength and power he could deliver.

Thankfully, he sat between me and Mr. Twitchy, blocking the other man's line of sight to me.

Gollum nodded approval of my statement. My heart shimmied for just a second. The windowless conference room seemed a bit brighter and less confined. Mr. Twitchy paled to insignificance.

My real students scribbled notes rapidly. Except for MaryLynn. I had a feeling she really only wanted to rest on the laurels of her five short contemporary romances. A good beginning to a career. But I'd learned early on, languishing in midlist, that building a career requires a new book every year. And each book has to be different, even those written in series. Now that I'd hit a few best seller lists with a new series based upon my time in the Citadel but set in a post-apocalyptic Earth, I had to work harder to constantly improve my prose and keep my readers happy with new adventures and varied settings within the context.

And the next novel was stalled at an outline and three chapters.

Last night I'd fallen asleep over the laptop without writing a word. Mom had put me to bed at two. Then I'd overslept.

No time to call the Citadel. Barely time to grab my notes.

A monitor appeared in the doorway with a five-minute sign.

"Good discussion, people. Any last comments before we break for lunch?"

"What's your next workshop?"

I'd already done two today. "Nine AM tomorrow. I'm spending this afternoon writing. The only way a book gets written is if I apply butt to chair and fingers to keyboard. Conferences are great learning tools, and can jump-start your enthusiasm, but you still have to write the book and I'm on deadline."

"A selling writer is always on deadline," Gollum said quietly when the room had cleared of all but the two of us. Mr. Twitchy was the first to scuttle away.

My friend hugged me lightly and kissed my cheek.

"Tell me about it." That greeting, while not inappropriate between close friends, felt different. Strange. Like I wasn't ready to deal with him after last night's fiasco with Donovan.

And the night before ...

"What are you doing for lunch?" Gollum asked.

"Talking to you about some weird things happening in Las Vegas."

"What about Las Vegas isn't weird?" he chuckled. "I caught the tail end of Genevieve's set last night in the lounge. Took me a while to realize that was really her on stage wearing a red cocktail dress and spike heels. The pearls gave her away, though. I've never seen your mother without them."

"A wedding gift from her mother-in-law. I think they've been in Dad's family for several generations. They go to the person in the bloodline who is supposed to have them. Sometimes I think Mom sleeps with them." I took his arm and led him out of the conference center, a big block of rooms that had once been part of the casino. "The buffet still has breakfast items. Let's eat and then find a private place to talk."

"I love a woman with a healthy appetite."

"What's healthy about waffles with strawberries and whipped cream? And a ton of coffee."

"You don't add chocolate chips to the mess. I'll have an egg white omelet, thank you." He almost shuddered at my food choices. "I did bring you some freshly ground coffee from your favorite kiosk on Cape Cod. We can make a couple of pots in the hotel room machines."

"Bless you, Gollum. How did you know the watered-down dark roast they call coffee here would leave me a walking zombie?"

"Have you thought about buying a syringe and main-lining caffeine?"

"Wouldn't work. The stuff they serve here is too weak to jump-start my heart."

"I'll take on that job," he said so quietly I almost didn't hear.

I let that pass. "So what did you think of Mom's new career? The hotel manager is talking about giving her a contract and hiring her a band." After only two nights.

I still reeled at the idea of my *mother* as a torch singer. In Vegas.

"Would that be a bad thing?"

I had to think about that while we went through the

buffet line. I decided to try their prime rib, fried shrimp, skip the macaroni and cheese to leave room for desert, and the endless salad bar.

"They make a really good cheese cake here," I said when I'd found us a booth near the kitchen door. I hoped the noise and constant traffic would hide our conversation.

The location didn't hide us. MaryLynn walked past to the adjacent booth. She sniffed in my direction. "Second man I've seen her with in as many days. And neither one is registered for the conference." She didn't try to keep her gossip secret.

Gollum's glasses slid down his nose, and he peered at me over the tops. "Who else have you been flirting with?"

I'd hoped to avoid that topic. No way to lie to Gollum when he looked at me like that. "Donovan came to town. He needed Mom's signature on some papers urgently. While he's here, he accompanied us to a show last night." I kept my eyes on cutting the fat off the prime rib.

"Did you get tickets for 'Fairy Moon'? I'd like to see it, too. I'm hearing wonderful things about it on the Internet."

"Good luck getting tickets. Mine came from an unusual source." Okay. Good way to divert attention away from what I had and hadn't done with Donovan in the last forty-eight hours.

"How unusual?"

I tried his egg-white-and-vegetable omelet without looking at it. I wished I hadn't. It tasted as disgusting and inadequate as it looked.

"Ever hear of Lady Lucia?"

He thought a moment. "I have a vague recollection of some kind of organized crime connection. I'd have to look it up, though."

"Spend your afternoon tracking her down. She may be important to another bit of weirdness."

"Oh? Like what?"

"Not here." I looked over my shoulder at MaryLynn and her companion, a stout woman wearing a respectable suit and a preprinted name tag. I knew her from the formal luncheon yesterday. One of the teaching pros, a romance writer breaking into mainstream and on the verge of hitting a major best seller list. She didn't look too happy at MaryLynn's constant stream of negative gossip about the other conference goers.

"Let's take a walk along the Strip. I'll call a taxi as soon as we finish eating."

"You going back for cheesecake?"

"I don't think so. It doesn't sound as good today. I had a bit of tummy upset yesterday afternoon. I wonder if Scrap's lactose intolerance is catching."

"Wouldn't surprise me. Is he here?"

"No. I haven't seen much of him at all since I got here."

"That's unusual. He shouldn't be able to get too far away from you for any length of time."

"That's beginning to worry me." Especially since Fortitude flitted in ahead of Breven Sancroix. Mom had one arm laced with his and the other with Donovan's.

"Let's go. We can slip out this side door."

"Avoiding your mother again? You really need to talk to her about her new career. Maybe she's decided that making friends and trying new things is good. What could happen to her that's worse than marrying a half demon?"

Chapter 16

*The intersection of Flamingo Road and the Strip
mark perfect compass points. A bend in the road
at the Venetian moves the Strip off true north-south
orientation and confuses the unwary.*

MICKEY DROPPED US off at the corner of
Tropicana and Las Vegas Boulevard—the
Strip. I needed some exercise. The one mile plus of walking north to the Dragon and St. George should stretch
my legs and give me time to talk privately with Gollum.
With so much noise and confusion crowding the sidewalks, I doubted even the most avid eavesdropper could
overhear us. If they could find us among the thousands
of people jostling for position away from the bumper-
to-bumper cars.

"They should close off traffic to all but taxis and tour
buses," Gollum grumbled as we dodged six cars running
a red light at the intersection.

"They did that down on Freemont, the downtown
area. I think they roofed part of it, too. I haven't gotten
there yet." I had to turn sideways to avoid being crushed
by a phalanx of Asians dripping camera equipment. My
breasts crushed up against Gollum's arm.

Without a word, he wrapped the arm around my

shoulders and kept me close. For protection, I told myself.

Nothing remotely resembling sexual tension between us. But, oh, it felt good to snuggle next to him and let him guide us through the maze. Standing fourteen inches taller than me, he could see a path blocked to my view of chests and backs.

We goggled and gawked as much as any normal tourist. Each hotel spread out and up, grander than the last monstrosity. Each unique in theme, spectacle, and canned advertisements broadcast to the masses.

"It's much bigger than I thought," Gollum said. "Brighter and happier, too." He turned us in a circle so he could see the miniature Eiffel Tower in the distance and get another look at the sphinxes behind us.

I didn't think they were miniature. And then there was the pyramid.

"I'm told the light shooting out of the top of the pyramid is visible from space as well. When the aliens invade, they'll probably land in Las Vegas, summoned by that beacon," he laughed. "In fact, the elevators are actually inclinators rising at a twenty-nine-degree angle to accommodate the architecture."

I rolled my eyes. Leave it to Gollum to come up with esoteric facts and figures.

A particularly loud advertisement blared at us from one of the animated signs.

"It's a false happiness. It grates on my nerves," I replied, shivering in the desert heat.

"You need to relax and enjoy the carefree spirit of the place." He squeezed my shoulder, pulling me closer yet to his side.

"I need earplugs." We approached the curving bridges, wandering canal, and graceful balconies of The Venetian. I pulled Gollum past the quarter-mile-long hotel front, not wanting to think about my gondola ride last night.

"If you wore earplugs, we couldn't talk. So what do we need to talk about?" he asked. He had to nearly shout for me to hear over the blare of car horns and tinny music blasting out of an old strip mall that had become a tourist gizmo haven.

"Hey, do you want to take a gondola ride? It's not that expensive." He urged me toward the outside portion of the waterway.

I diverted him with the tale of Lady Lucia's wereweasel and her apology of flowers and tickets. I didn't tell him that Donovan had pretended they came from him. Then I told him about the faery at the slot machines and references to *Lord* Gregbaum.

"Hmmmm."

"That's it? No long-winded lectures on the origin of vampire legends? No extended theories on why the dancers never leave the building, and why they wear their costumes into the casino? And, by the way, the costumes look like they need about six sessions at the dry cleaners or complete replacement. What's wrong with you, Gollum?"

"Just thinking. I'll run some questions by my folklore colleagues and Gramps when I get back to the hotel. For now, I think we need to check out the Dragon and St. George. I want to see these gambling faeries myself. Did you know there is a tradition that faeries will bet on anything? Being nearly immortal, they've developed gambling to a fine art, just to pass the time . . ."

Now that's the Gollum I knew and . . . loved. In a way. Best friends. Really.

"I don't believe for a moment that Lady Lucia is a vampire, but if she were, she'd operate on the same principle," I added. "Manipulate us poor mortals into doing her bidding while betting how long it takes us to figure out what she wants."

"By George, I think she's got it!" Gollum laughed, mimicking a British accent.

Speaking of accents . . . "Mr. Master Linguist, where do you think Mickey is from?"

"The cab driver?"

I nodded while trying not to jostle a teenager on a skateboard with a mega cup of soda pop. All I needed was for him to spill it all over my good clothes.

"Couldn't place his accent."

"He says Bulgaria."

"Nope."

"What do you mean. 'Nope'? You speak what, five living languages and read at least three dead ones. Haven't you heard a Bulgarian accent before?"

"You wouldn't have asked me if you honestly believed he was from Bulgaria. I've heard plenty of accents from Bulgaria, Romania, Serbo-Croatia. He's not from there. Trust me on this."

"Okay. Why would he lie while he's trying to be so helpful? Specifically, trying to please Lady Lucia."

"I'll let you know when I know more about Lady Lucia."

We negotiated the sidewalks for the remaining distance to the Dragon and St. George. Once we got off the Strip, traffic lightened a modicum. Then it picked up again around the theater entrance of the hotel.

A lot of people turned away from the desk, shaking their heads in disappointment. Those who picked up previously booked tickets waved them in triumph.

A discreet hand beckoned the next disappointed one from the isolated potted palm near the fire exit.

"I'll try a single ticket. Might be easier than a pair," Gollum said, finally releasing me from his protective grip.

"You stand in line, I see someone I need to talk to." I approached a young couple, probably early twenties. He wore smart casual slacks and a shirt. She wore a graceful sun dress that fell a discreet two inches below the knee. She held her left hand up, flashing an expensive wedding ring and solitaire. Honeymooners. Professionals with some money.

"Never buy a ticket from a guy hiding behind a palm tree. If his tickets are real, he can only legally sell them through a licensed kiosk," I warned the couple.

They wandered off, shaking their heads.

"We'll try for one of the other shows on the Strip," the young man said, kissing his wife's temple.

The wereweasel tried to sidle to the opposite side of

the palm and the exit. I reached behind the plant and grabbed his collar.

"You're still selling forged tickets to innocents," I snarled at him.

"What do you care, lady? Without your imp, you're just another tourist," he sneered back. Only his words came out on a strange lisp. His crooked mustache concealed a barely healed harelip scar. He looked as if he hadn't shaved since I saw him last. Come to think on it, he had the same two-day growth two-days ago.

Weird compounded upon strange.

"Scrap is never far away," I countered. I sure hoped so anyway.

Right here, babe. Scrap settled on my shoulder, the barest hint of dandelion fluff in weight.

The weasely man's eyes grew large. He really did have a vertical pupil instead of round. He must be wearing contacts to give that illusion. I'd seen costumers at cons do the same. And the harelip and mustache could be faked just as easily.

I settled down. No more weird than a Science Fiction/Fantasy convention or con. All of Vegas was a con in a way.

"Tell your mistress I thank her for the flowers and the tickets. Professional courtesy. I respect her territory as long as she stays away from me and mine." That sounded like something I'd write. Therefore, it sounded like what these pretenders expected.

You might want to reconsider that, dahling. We could bet on it. Wanna make a bet. Scrap chomped on a cigar, a big fat one, not his usual black cherry cheroots. He wrapped his tail around my neck. The barbed end had a strange luster to it. So did the rest of him. I was surprised the others in line couldn't see him.

The weasel sure could.

His mouth opened and closed, making strange gasping noises. "Don't feed me to the imp. Please don't feed me to the imp. Say, neat trick with the gondola last night. But you really should have accepted Donovan's proposal. He's one of the good guys."

"Coming from you, that's not a compliment. Sheesh, does the entire town know about last night?"

"Pretty much. Did you get a good look at the size of that ring? That would buy back my marker from Lady Lucia and then some. You really should have said yes."

I rolled my eyes upward in disgust. Or despair. Had I made that big a mistake in turning down Donovan? No way to know now.

"I'll let you go this time, Weasel. But if I ever hear of you scalping forged tickets again, I'll return your head to your mistress, minus your body."

"That's a bit harder than you think, bitch . . ."

"Tell that to the widowed Windago I slew last month." I dropped my grip on his collar.

He stumbled and slinked off. I watched him for a moment to make sure he left the building. When the closest doors whooshed closed on his backside, I returned to Gollum's side.

"Haven't you got anything? Even standing room at the back of the balcony?" my friend asked. He sounded more desperate than disappointed.

"Sold that two months ago. Sorry. The show is sold out for the next six months."

"What about the single tickets in August you had day before yesterday?" I asked.

"Sold those on line right after . . . Oh, it's you. Why didn't you say you were with her?" He reached below his counter and came up with a heavy parchment envelope, the kind wedding invitations come in. He handed it to me. "With Lady Lucia's compliments. Next."

Startled, I slid my finger beneath the envelope's flap and pulled out a piece of notepaper in the same heavy parchment. Gold embossing at the top spelled out "Contessa Lucia Maria Continelli."

"Step aside, ma'am. I've got other people to serve. Please," the clerk said softly. Almost respectfully.

I backed up three steps.

Gollum paced me. "What does it say?" he asked.

"This note will gain you seats tomorrow afternoon at three to a special performance that will be filmed for the upcoming DVD of 'Fairy Moon.' My apologies that I cannot gain you access to the VIP circle. That area will be filled with technical equipment. Respectfully, Contessa Lucia Maria Continelli."

"Wow."

"Wow is right. So why do I feel like I've just been manipulated by the resident vampire crime boss?"

Chapter 17

Poker has the best odds in Vegas as the players play against the skills of each other rather than random spins of a wheel, throw of dice, or computer generated slots. The House still takes a percentage of the pots.

"IF YOU FEEL LIKE you are being manipulated, maybe you are," Gollum said. He took the note paper from me and read it himself. "Interesting handwriting. You don't see the flowing decorations around the capitals much anymore, except in formal calligraphy. But this looks like normal handwriting, not a studied execution of an antique alphabet."

"Scrap, is the weasel anywhere near?" I searched the crowds for signs of Lady Lucia's minion.

Weasel has left the building, he said trying to sound like Elvis. He blew a smoke ring in my face.

I waved it away, choking on the fumes, almost as thick as in the casino.

"What's your schedule tomorrow?" Gollum asked.

I had to stop and think. "Tomorrow's Saturday. Right?" Days tended to run together on the road.

Gollum nodded.

I found my PDA in my belt pack and scanned it. "Critique session nine to eleven. Workshop on adding sensuality to fiction eleven to noon. Formal lunch until two. Awards banquet at six thirty."

"So the only time you have free is late afternoon. Three to five. The exact time of the special performance of 'Fairy Moon.' "

"I've had the feeling of being watched ever since I got here. Do you suppose Contessa Lucia is keeping tabs on me?"

"Possible."

"Let's find Weasel and make him take us to her. Right now."

"It's still daylight, Tess. He couldn't get us in to see Lady Lucia if he wanted to," Gollum said. He looked most professorial as he tugged on his chin.

"Only if she wants us to think she's a vampire."

Both Gollum and Scrap stared at me in silence.

"So we wait until tonight to try to find the lady. For now, we can scout the casino for signs of faery dancers." I marched toward the center of the hotel so fast, Scrap and Gollum had to hurry to catch up.

"Think about it, Tess. What better place for a vampire to hide, than in Vegas?"

"I've heard that argument before. You've said it yourself. No one, absolutely no one, comes back from the dead."

If I believed someone could, I might have gone with the pseudo ghost of my first husband. Turns out I was lucky I did believe no one escapes death's clutches once he's touched you. The ghost turned out to be a demon construct sent to lure me away from my vows as a Warrior of the Celestial Blade and separate me from Scrap.

That would have been the true and final death for both of us. And freed my home from the decidedly non-neutral presence of a Warrior.

The Powers That Be really wanted my home back in neutral hands. Badly.

"Look at all these people," Gollum said. He stared in fascination at the wide variety of sizes, shapes, ages, and clothing. "All economic classes and degrees of education come here to gamble. There is the constant allure of instant wealth, even to the wealthy. The risk, the excitement. I've read some studies . . ." He droned on.

There must be a psychology degree in the alphabet soup that followed his name.

"What's the moon phase?" I asked, trying to bring him back to our topic and mission.

"Waxing new moon," he said, barely pausing in his musing about the human need to gamble. "There must be something in the kinetic connection to the arm of the slot machine. The energy applied and transferred to the gods of chance."

"We're headed toward the waxing quarter moon, the time of greatest demon strength. Are faeries classed as demons in this dimension since they are out of their own universe? Would humans be classed as demons if we entered one of the other worlds?"

"Possibly. Demons are usually classed as violent tribes needing the blood of other sentient beings to nourish themselves." He still didn't look at me, just at the chains of people wandering through the broken aisles—no way to walk a straight line without bumping into an opportunity to lose your money—and those fixated in one spot with card games, dice, or the ubiquitous slot machines.

Not exactly, Scrap said around his cigar. He let go of my ear and my hair to bounce up to a chandelier and peer down at a vacant slot machine. *This one's going to blow, it's primed and ready to pay out. Bet something, Tess. I just know you're gonna win.*

"If portals weaken and demons gain strength at this time of the month allowing crossovers, then the faeries might have growing strength now, too," I said, ignoring Scrap's half correction of my theory.

Screw that idea, Scrap said. He returned to me in disgust. Someone else had sat at the machine, plugged in a bunch a quarters, and lost.

"I wonder if I could win at poker simply by studying the body language and psychology of my opponents," Gollum mused, also ignoring me.

I could fly around and peek at the other player's cards!

Scrap lifted off my shoulder and flew spiraling circles around us.

"Not on your life, Guilford." I yanked on his arm, trying to break his thrall. "We're supposed to be looking for faery dancers."

"Oh. Yes. Certainly." He shoved his glasses back up to the bridge of his nose. "I detect a bit of pastel chiffon over by the bar."

"Which bar? There are six of them."

"The one on our far left. I believe it has a medieval milieu. The bartenders wear tunics and tights. The barmaids have most fetching peasant blouses and bodices with extremely short shirts." He fixed his gaze on a deep cleavage exposed by one of those off-the-shoulder peasant blouses.

Love the way those tights mold to the bartenders' figures. Scrap nearly fell off my shoulder leering at the men when they stepped out from behind their barriers and revealed tunics that barely reached their hips.

I wondered if the guys padded their tights the way women stuffed foam into their bras.

"Totally inaccurate costuming," I said. Though they did present some interesting eye candy for women, and men of Scrap's persuasion. "And the bar specializes in flaming drinks ignited by the mechanical fire-breathing dragon in a cage behind the bar." I sighed. Gimmicks. "The whole town is nothing but one big gimmick."

"The faeries must feel at home here. It has the feel of a Renaissance Faire," Gollum said. His attention kept drifting toward the partially closed off poker rooms.

"Only in this dimension do faeries visit Renaissance Faires," I reminded him sharply. "Let's go see if we can talk to one of them."

I latched a proprietary hand on Gollum's elbow, guiding him toward that hint of pink chiffon. His eyes strayed toward the blackjack tables, then they flicked over one of the cocktail waitresses.

Which bothered me the most?

No time to think. Pink was on the move.

I walked faster.

Ever hear of sightseeing, babe? Scrap grumbled. He wrapped his strangely lustrous tail tighter about my neck to keep him from bouncing off my shoulder. His wings lifted slightly to gather enough air for balance. They looked longer and fuller than they had last time I saw him.

He reminded me of . . . of . . . of me right after Donavon and I had played our own jousting game in bed.

I almost burst out laughing. "Scrap, did you get laid?" I asked under my breath.

And what if I did? He preened, showing off his warts and the extra half inch of wing.

"Just wondering. May I ask who?"

Only if I can ask back.

I didn't want to admit that I'd succumbed to my hormones with the man who kept Scrap away from me with some kind of force field.

Thought so. Obviously not our dear friend Gollum or he'd be looking at you and not that tempting wench bending over the low table inside the bar.

"I think they make those tables that low just so the gals have to flash their cleavage," I said aloud. "It's all padding," I reminded Gollum.

"Oh, yeah. Right. There's our pink chiffon." He bobbed his chin at a bank of slots with whimsical dragon and unicorn décor.

Bells jangled and whistled shrilly. I cringed. So did Scrap.

Off pitch, babe, he grumbled.

"A pitch to make dogs howl."

Bright giggles erupted from one of the unicorn machines. "Sounds like one of our faeries won for a change."

"No such luck. Our winner is just a normal human girl," Gollum stalled our progress.

"Looks like a birthday girl celebrating her twenty-first." I pointed to the bouquet of shiny Mylar above her head and the platoon of "best" friends squealing and clapping their hands around the winner. They all wore similar pastel sundresses in layers of ruffled floral prints.

"So what do we do now?" Gollum asked. His eyes strayed toward a closed poker room.

"We find Mickey and figure out how to get an audience with Lady Lucia."

"Hadn't we better wait until after we see the show tomorrow?"

"Afraid I'll tick her off and she'll rescind the tickets?"

"Yes."

He's got your number, babe. Scrap nearly fell off my shoulder laughing.

They had a point. I did have a temper, easily roused in the face of evil manipulating people.

"Okay. Let's get out of here and put the word out on the street that I want an interview with Lady Lucia at midnight tomorrow. After the awards banquet."

Done. And done.

"How?" I looked at Scrap to make sure he was still with me.

Just a word in the right ear.

Chapter 18

Due to racial prejudice, when Sammy Davis Jr. first played Vegas, he had to enter and leave the hotel by the back entrance through the kitchen.

WE MADE IT OUT of the casino into the theater lobby, aiming for the exit nearest there.

Suddenly, two big men grabbed my elbows from behind and turned me back toward the now closed and empty theater area. I saw muscle on candy-cane-red skin and black leather and not much else.

"Scrap, what is happening?"

You sure you want to know? He spat out his cigar. The faint glow left his skin as he stretched and thinned.

Uh-oh. Time to gear up for a fight.

"Tess, I don't like this," Gollum warned, too late. "Too much of a coincidence that these guys show up so soon after we request an interview . . ."

"Shaddup," growled one of the brutes.

Strangely, Gollum did. First time I'd known that to happen.

We passed under the archway to the theater lobby. A black curtain swooshed across the opening, giving us the illusion of privacy.

Then a steel gate slid across on well-oiled tracks, seal-

ing us in. I heard the lock close in an ominous clack and
clang. At the same time, the quadruple doors into the
theater opened outward slowly, by unseen hands. A phalanx of human figures stood in the dark portal, none of
them touching the doors. It looked like it opened into
another world.

How'd they do that?

Hidden electronics must open and close doors and
gates and curtains. Had to be remote controls.

The bad guys pulled so hard on my arms, my feet left
the floor.

I relaxed my shoulders. My arms flew up and my
feet flew down. The polished tile blocks, each a yard
square, in a discreet and sophisticated green swirl imitation marble, had no traction. My professional-looking
wedge-heeled pumps slid like an onion through sizzling
butter in a fry pan.

The brutes tightened their grips on my arms, fighting
to keep me under their control. I kept sliding, letting go
of my balance, further separating me from my captors.

A rough spot in the tiles. My feet found traction.
I threw myself forward, leaving the big and uglies
behind.

"Scrap, to me!"

He landed heavily on my right hand, already halfway
through his transformation.

Two of the leather-clad guys still held Gollum in grips
that might break his upper arms. My two stalked forward
intent on recapturing me. Three more hung around the
edges, making sure none of us escaped.

Gulp. They all wore long broadswords in plain black
leather scabbards to match their knickers and vests.
Their exposed skin looked like fresh blood over muscles
layered upon muscles. Just barely, I noted pointy ears
and a flash of energy across their backs that might have
been wings they left behind in their home dimension.

Faeries on steroids, Scrap whispered as he continued
to change. *I've met these guys before.*

"At least they don't have bat wings," I grumbled as I
twirled the staff that Scrap had become. The centrifugal

force helped him elongate. His ears grew together and curved, becoming a half-moon blade. His bandy legs and tail became its twin blade at the other end. Each blade extruded long, hair-fine spikes on the outside curve, mimicking the star and Milky Way configuration of the Goddess of the Celestial Blade Warriors.

I drew strength from my memories of seeing the Goddess rise in the sky, of the unity with the universe, and the power pulsing from the heavens into me.

The brutes drew their swords. Seven against one. If they were just normal demons, I'd say the odds were even. But they had those monstrous long swords that must weigh ten pounds apiece. Even wielding the Celestial Blade like a sword, they had me on reach alone.

I kicked off my shoes. "Shit!" A string of more violent curses exploded from my gut. I'd worn knee-high nylons. Worse traction. No time to find the shoes and slip back into them.

"Okay, guys. Who's first?" I shifted my grip and swung the blade over my head, at knee level, and straight ahead, keeping it constantly in motion in no particular pattern.

They looked at my twirling blade, then at each other.

"Drop the blade, or we kill your boyfriend," a quiet voice said from the direction of the theater.

I chanced a glance in Gollum's direction. His two captors both held the tips of their swords at his throat.

"Fuck!"

"Don't listen to him, Tess. I can take care of myself," Gollum said quietly.

Right. That coming from the most nonviolent person I'd ever met.

Still, I did have a vague memory of waking up from a tazer-induced coma to find three Marines down with bruises on their throats and Gollum leaning protectively over me.

"What do you want, Gregbaum?" I asked the newcomer. He had to be the producer. No one else had authority in this area.

"I want you to leave Las Vegas on the next plane."

"No can do." I slashed at the goon edging over to my

left side. He backed off. "I'm contracted to the writers' conference. I'm also sworn to protect the innocent from demons. These guys look like demons, and you are holding a dance troupe of innocent faeries hostage."

I parried a sword that crept too close. Without thinking, I slid into a long lunge and aimed for my attacker's bare chest. He yelped and arched away from the tip of the curved blade, sword held off to the side.

My feet continued sliding forward. My thighs burned and pulled. I flipped the blade and raked him with the tines. A dozen parallel scratches oozed dark green, almost black blood—it matched their clothes.

At the same moment, Gollum's attackers flew across the lobby and bounced against the ticket desk. Their heads hit the edge with matching resounding cracks. They slid to the ground, mouths open in surprise as their eyes closed and bodies grew limp.

Gollum went to his knees. His face twisted in agony. He mewled something incomprehensible and buried his head in his hands.

The remaining four monsters backed off, taking up positions between me and Gregbaum. I recovered forward from the lunge, not sure my inner thigh muscles hadn't separated from the bone. They screamed at me. A groin pull. One of the hardest injuries to recover from, and I'd done it to myself.

Stupid, stupid, stupid.

"Get out of here, Guilford." I used his real name to break through whatever emotions tangled his mind in that awful grimace.

"I . . . can't . . . leave . . . you," he choked.

"Sure you can. You just get to your feet and walk out the fire exit." I edged closer to my enemies. I had to finish this quick before real pain set in and kept me anchored in place.

The guy I'd nicked still bled. Rivulets streamed down his chest to disappear beneath his pants.

"The alarms will sound if you open that door," Gregbaum said.

"And your point would be?"

For the first time, I got a good look at the hottest producer in Las Vegas. Medium height and build, he looked like the slime lord of lounge lizards: slick sharkskin suit and a black shirt open nearly to the waist, revealing a bit of a hairy paunch. Five gold chains of varying length encircled his neck and another his right wrist. The left wrist sported a watch nearly the size of the school clocks in Paul Revere Elementary, where I'd attended kindergarten through sixth grade.

The kicker was the diamond pinky ring. It looked like a miniature version of the one Donovan offered with his proposal.

What in the hell was going on here?

"You may stay until your scheduled flight home. But do not enter my theater again. Do not, under penalty of death, try to contact any of my employees."

"Agreed, as long as you do nothing to harm any of the dancers." Just because I couldn't complete this mission didn't mean I couldn't pass it off to another Warrior. Breven Sancroix had taken the same vows I had.

"The blade." Gregbaum snapped his fingers

"Scrap has tasted blood. He can retract as soon as I'm clear." I jerked my chin toward the steel gate and black curtain.

Gregbaum waved his hand. The lock clicked open and the gate withdrew about eighteen inches; just enough for Gollum and me to slip through.

"How'd you open that?" I asked, turning back toward Gregbaum.

He and his minions faded into the theater darkness. Concealing fog swirled around them. The doors closed quickly but silently.

On the last breath of air before the portal sealed, I heard a whisper. "Get back to the Valley of Fire. We can't let her near the place."

Nasty, nasty, nasty. Those brutes taste like they just crawled out of a toxic waste dump. Come to think on it, maybe they did.

But where is that dump and who put what into it to spawn these ugly thugs? Stolen energy from Faery for sure. But what else?

Imps used to offer a bounty on identification of new monsters not assigned a ghetto. Lots of credit with the Powers That Be and prestige all over the universes. I could parlay that into a new artifact of power for my dahling Tess.

Or break through the barrier between me and Donovan.

Gonna take some homework to figure out if these guys are mutated faeries or something entirely new. Their connection to Gregbaum and the "Fairy Moon" show means something.

If the dancers are real faeries . . . hmmmmm.

I'll have a nice long chat about this with my babe and Gollum. Later.

Right now I have to rest. And eat. The air conditioner atop this casino is jammed full of mold. That will sustain me long enough to follow Tess back to our hotel. She'll order OJ and beer for me. Then I can sleep.

Maybe. I shrink back to my normal cute self (Hey, there's a new wart on my chest!) as Tess begins limping toward the exit. Gollum drags himself out of his own inner misery and supports her with an arm about her waist.

They look like lovers, but this is not an intimate embrace. This is one friend helping another.

Oh, no! My babe hurts. I can't leave her. But this is no ordinary wound that I can make all better with a bit of imp spit to counter demon venom and infection. This is something deep inside her muscles.

Sharp burning pains run up and down my legs in sympathy. My back aches, and my wings are numb. I need to curl up into a fetal ball and nurse my hurts. I can't. I have to stay close to Tess. I have to help her. But I can't. I must eat. NOW.

Useless. I feel so useless. Just a scrap of an imp who can't help his Warrior. And I'm so tired.

What to do? What to do? I can't even run home to Mum and Imp Haven. The freeze-dried-garbage-dump-of-the-universe offers me no comfort. No love. No sanctuary.

Tess drops into Mickey's taxi. Gollum follows. I can only fall into her lap and hope my body heat helps her pain.

Her pain is my pain. I can't heal myself because I cannot heal her. I cannot recover from the strain of transformation because I cannot leave her while she hurts.

We are more than vulnerable.

Chapter 19

*A High Roller Suite at the MGM Grand has three
thouand square feet and comes with a private butler
and chef.*

THANK THE GODDESS FOR ELEVATORS.
My normal bouncing up eight flights of stairs in
lieu of jogging five miles every morning would have
done permanent damage to my groin muscles. Gollum
acting as a crutch helped some. Still I fell facedown
through the door of my room and onto the closest
bed.

Mom's bed. Full of clothes. My face tangled with dirty
underclothes inside her suitcase.

Ewww! Enough to push me to a sitting position. "Ice,"
I croaked to Gollum.

He left with the ice bucket and my key card.

"Mom, what are you doing? We don't go home until
Monday morning." I held my injured right leg up with
both hands while she extricated her red party dress from
beneath me.

"I'm not going home." She tsked as she surveyed a
crease in the georgette draperies.

"What?"

"You used to be more articulate, dear."

"Can't you see I'm suffering? Words elude me when I'm in pain."

"What did you do this time?"

"Fencing. Long lunge." I sank back onto her pillows. "Would you call room service and order me two beers and two glasses of orange juice?"

Scrap sighed from his fetal ball in the crook of my arm. I couldn't tell if he slumbered or had gone comatose.

That sounded good to me right now. A couple of ibuprofen and about twenty-four hours of sleep ought to help.

Gotta keep movin 'r it'll stiff up, Scrap mumbled. His mental speech came through slurred. He was in worse shape than I.

"I told you years ago that you'd get hurt in a most unladylike manner with that horrible sport."

Now that was the mother I knew and loved.

"Let me see, dear." She held up my leg and probed gently. "Hmmm. Big knot forming. Might just be a strain instead of a true pull. I'll order you an immediate massage. That will keep the blood flowing and prevent it from stiffening."

Huh?

"You still didn't answer my question. If you aren't going home, why are you packing?"

"I've signed a contract to sing at the hotel Wednesday through Sunday nights. They're hiring me a band and giving me a wardrobe allowance, not that I need one. I'm moving in with Penny."

"Uh, Mom, you do know that she's a hooker."

"Not anymore. We had a long talk. She's retired. That Joyce woman is writing her memoirs. Pretty steamy stuff." She waggled her eyebrows.

"How can you be sure she's retired. She seemed pretty tight with that Stetson fellow."

"Penny is tired. Flirting is second nature with her. Always has been. But she's no longer serious. And she needs my help."

"You? Mom, you've barely stepped off Cape Cod for fifteen years or more. Your life is the Garden Club and church choir—and picking up after me." I gave Mom room and board in the mother-in-law apartment attached to the house. I didn't think she'd survive on her own. She barely knew how to balance a checkbook or pay her bills. Dad and I did that for her.

"Penny made a bunch of money, but she didn't keep it. Her jewelry is paste and her very small two-bedroom house is heavily mortgaged. She really needs money from that tell-all book. I can at least give her a little something extra each month for the mortgage payment."

"Mom, what is going on? This isn't you. You've always been suspicious of strangers. Disapproved of new friends. And I still don't believe you ever spent time in New York." No more stalling. Looked like this was the time to talk to her, even if I didn't really want to.

"But it is me, Teresa. This is the me I dreamed of being when I was in high school." She sat on the edge of the bed and gave me a long soulful look.

"I've never heard this story." I scooched over to make room for her. Girl chat, like I had with my friend Allie back home. Never with my mom.

Unthinkable with the old mom. Quite natural with this vibrant woman with the whole world opening before her.

"Your Grandmother Maria forbade us to talk about it." She caressed the silky fabric of the dress she held.

"Was it Grandma Maria or Grandpa Al who forbade you to talk about wanting to sing for a living?" Feisty and forgetful Grandma Maria was the only family member who cheered me on when I launched into the risky career of a professional novelist.

I hadn't known my grandfather well. He died when I was six. Either that or he left town. No one talked much about him. And I hadn't found a headstone for him in the local cemetery, at least nowhere near his parents.

"I thought I was ready to tackle New York my senior year in high school." Mom fumbled with her pearls, an old and comforting habit. "I ran away at the end of January, right after my eighteenth birthday, with a few hundred dollars I'd been saving since ... since grade school.

But I wasn't ready for New York. The competition, the dirt, the noise, the scathing critiques from really nasty people." Tears flooded her eyes. She turned her head away.

"That's when you met Penny!"

She nodded. "We shared a flat for a short time. We met at an audition and hit it off. Sometimes I think she was the only person in all of New York who had a kind word for me."

I pulled her down into a hug. "I know how bad rejection from strangers can be. When my first short story was rejected, I thought my writing career had ended before it started. The editor told me I should forget about ever putting pen to paper again. It wasn't even a professional level magazine. Just a paid-in-copies low-budget rag. Thank goodness my friend Bob . . ."

Here I had to pause. Bob had died last autumn while helping me on my first mission as a Warrior of the Celestial Blade.

"Bob convinced me to send the story to professional publications until it sold. He nagged me if I let a rejected copy sit on my desk more than twenty-four hours before mailing it to the next editor. You didn't have friends in the city to encourage and support you."

"I had Penny. Even she wasn't enough. I was so energetic and full of hope. But it didn't last long. You had a few positive rejections right off the bat. 'Good writing but not right for us. What else do you have?' I had only 'Get off the stage. Next.' "

"Friends make all the difference when you try something new." My thoughts turned to Bob, and then to Gollum and Allie, and yes, even to Donovan. Most of all I had Scrap. No matter how bad things got, I'd never be alone.

"And look at you now. On the best seller lists and making good money. You have done with your life what I wanted to do with mine. Instead, I crawled home with my tail between my legs and accepted a marriage to your father that my father arranged. A nice Catholic man with a good job as an accountant. And we all know what a disaster that turned out to be. I didn't even finish high school."

My father hadn't married by the age of twenty-six, very late for a good Catholic man from a French Canadian family. He accepted the arranged marriage under pressure from his parents. He'd needed another fifteen years to come to terms with his alternative sexual preferences.

"Was the whole marriage a disaster?" I know Dad had hurt Mom terribly when he moved in with Bill. Looking back, that was just one more rejection in Mom's life. One more person telling her she wasn't good enough at anything she tried.

I knew I couldn't be the next person to tell her not to bother trying because she would fail. She couldn't know she'd failed until she tried.

I had to let her do this.

"My marriage wasn't all bad. We had some good times. I have three wonderful children, even though your brother Stephen lives in Chicago and rarely calls home."

I talked to Steve more often than he talked to either of our parents.

"What will I do without you, Mom? I mean, you organize my house and my life. You keep me fed when I forget to eat because I'm on deadline . . ."

"You'll manage, dear. You'll manage because you have to. And because you have friends. I can't be your crutch forever." Mom gave me a wicked wink, like she knew how Dad and I took care of her because she let us.

Then she straightened up and began pulling more outfits out of the closet. Mostly cocktail dresses. I didn't remember her packing so many. She must have gone shopping. "You have Gollum living in the cottage, and your father and Bill close by. And Allie. Best friends are more valuable than gold. Though I wish she'd find some nice man and give up being a policewoman. Most unladylike."

We both laughed at the idea of my best friend doing

anything but be a cop. She'd saved my ass a couple of times when the going got tough with demons and escapees from the prison warden of the universe.

"And don't forget MoonFeather."

"Yes. Your father's sister does seem to have more in common with you than my side of the family. I don't approve of her being a witch, or living with Josh without the benefit of marriage, or her three divorces, but she is a good friend to you."

Wow. A compliment about MoonFeather. That was almost more than I could imagine. Mom really had undergone a major attitude adjustment.

"I worry about you, Mom. This is a big step. Something totally different from what you are used to."

"I know. Isn't it exciting!" She gave a little girl laugh. Then she sobered. "Marrying Darren was a disaster that taught me I have to live every day as if it were my last. When I found out that he only married me to get to you, and something weird about inheriting your house, I thought I'd never recover. I thought about killing myself. But that would only have given him what he wanted. Now I'm doing what *I* want to do for the first time in a very long time. I need to do this."

"If it doesn't work out," and I couldn't see how it could, "you can always come home. I'll keep a spare bed for you. I'm only a phone call away." We hugged again. "Now about that contract . . ."

"Don't worry. I had Donovan look it over. He's good about that sort of thing. But he seemed upset. Did you two have another fight?"

Gulp. "Yeah, sorta."

"You going to tell me about it?"

"No."

"Make it up soon. I don't like my kids fighting."

"He's not . . ."

"Yes, he is. He's my stepson and I care for him. He needs a mother. He's also executor of Darren's estate. Now I updated my will before we left home. I've left lump sums for Cecilia and Stephen, the rest goes to you. You gave me a home when no one else would. You took care of me when I should have taken care of you. If anything happens to me, you'll have to work with Donovan on the estate business. So apologize and get back to being friends. That's an order."

"Nothing is going to happen to you, Mom. You're still young and healthy . . ."

"Oh, good, Gollum is back with your ice. He can carry my bags down to the lobby. I'll order your massage through the concierge. Are you sure all you want is beer and orange juice? You've got my cell phone number and I've left Penny's number and address on the notepad by the phone. Call me." She bustled out, organized and efficient and in charge of her life.

I wish I could say the same for myself.

I dozed off and on for the rest of the afternoon. So did Scrap. The beer and OJ arrived. We slurped it down. I added some ibuprofen to mine, and nodded off again.

Gollum stayed with me, changing ice packs, coming up with a heating pad to alternate with them, taking phone calls from my mom, declining offers to dine with other writers from the conference, rejecting a last-minute request for me to critique a manuscript.

How many times in the past few months had he camped out in my hotel room helping me cope with a mission?

Around five, Gollum stuck a room service menu in front of me. "You have to eat to keep your strength up. Protein to rebuild muscle tissue."

"The chicken Alfredo is the only thing that looks good," I mumbled.

"Are you sure? You said at lunch that you thought you might have acquired Scrap's lactose intolerance." He frowned at me.

"I was only joking. Buffet cheesecake probably sat out a little too long. Honestly, I don't feel much like eating. Must be the beer and OJ. But the chicken Alfredo sounds good. And coffee. The coffee you brought me, not the watered-down generic beans they serve in this town."

"Okay. If you say so." He placed the order.

Food arrived nearly an hour later. The aroma of garlic and chicken woke up my appetite. My leg felt a lot better. Even Scrap roused enough to pop out in search of mold.

"You have a massage scheduled for seven," Gollum said, setting a tray on my lap. I hadn't moved from where I'd collapsed on the bed.

We ate companionably, chatting and rehashing what I'd seen and done since arriving. A music station played something soft on the television.

The chicken Alfredo didn't sit well. Maybe I ate too much. Maybe the pain pills had upset my digestion. I rarely take them. Since surviving the imp flu, my body doesn't succumb to viruses and disease. I heal quickly from wounds, and react strangely to any kind of drugs. Maybe my nerves had finally caught up with me after refusing Donovan's proposal.

Had I done the right thing?

Of course I had. How could I marry a man I didn't trust?

Donovan had sunk too much time, money, and energy into establishing a homeland for Kajiri demons—half-bloods. Any man with that much sympathy for beings that existed only to breed and eat—and eat anything including human flesh and blood—needed careful watching. I'd seen some of Donovan's buddies in the Sasquatch tribe do just that.

On the other hand, I had met a few Kajiri who truly wanted only to blend in and let their human genetics dominate. Their demon relatives cast them out. And heaven help them in the human world if any of their demon characteristics showed through, even for a moment.

No easy answers.

If I questioned the rightness of the match, then it wasn't right. I couldn't imagine sharing the emotional intimacy of friendship with Donovan like I did with Gollum.

Walking to the elevator and then to the hotel spa on the top floor wasn't easy. "Thanks for being my crutch," I said to Gollum when he left me at the door.

"That's what I'm here for. I'll get on the Internet while you're here and follow up on some research." He kissed my cheek and ducked back into the elevator.

"Gollum, can you do a background check on Sancroix?" I finally remembered my failed attempt to contact the Citadel.

He waved to acknowledge that he heard me. The doors closed on him and whisked him away. I sighed. He helped me more than he knew just by being my friend.

Massages are the best thing ever invented by humans. Maybe they were invented by the gods and passed down to us in heavenly visions. I don't know.

Raoul knew precisely how to manipulate, rotate, and stretch my injury, all the while applying proper compression. It was merely a strain and not a pull. Because I got treatment right away, it shouldn't bother me for too long. But it needed rest tonight and tomorrow. He worked my entire body to get everything back into line and balanced.

I came out of the spa feeling fifty percent back to normal. I could put weight on my right leg without wincing. It carried me all the way down to the room—via the elevator. I'm not stubborn enough or dumb enough to tackle stairs at this stage.

Two feet inside my door, I dashed to the bathroom and lost my lovely chicken Alfredo to the porcelain throne.

You don't want to know the details.

"Lactose intolerance," Gollum muttered through the closed door. "I'll get you some dry toast and tea."

"Yuck."

"It will help. I promise. And some acidophilus."

"And I've got some oceanfront property for sale, only two blocks from here."

I brushed my teeth and took a quick shower. Much better.

When I emerged from the bathroom in my royal blue terry robe, I found Mickey, in the doorway, with the door wide open. He and Gollum stared at each other in bewilderment.

Was that Junior scuttling toward the elevator, head down, fists clenched, looking about furtively?

Mickey carried a huge bouquet of white roses. His swarthy face looked as pale as the flowers.

"What?" I demanded.

He handed me a thick parchment envelope bearing Lady Lucia's crest.

I read the note inside, holding my breath. "The bearer will escort you to a rendezvous point at nine of the clock this evening."

"Crap." I felt like it, too.

Chapter 20

El Rancho Vegas was the first hotel/casino built on the Strip in 1941. The venerable hotel and its trademark windmill burned to the ground in 1960. The lot across from the Sahara, in the shadow of the Stratosphere, remains empty, and, some say, haunted.

"SO, WHAT DO WE KNOW?" I asked Gollum at eight thirty. My tummy had recovered enough that I could eat a roast beef sandwich and a ginger ale. I had some persistent bloating, like the day before my period, only worse.

Familiarity with Scrap's lactose intolerance led me to hope I wouldn't let loose the bloating at an inappropriate moment.

The groin pull still presented problems. I could walk with only a little limp, stand if I had to with my weight off it. Moving was better than standing. I hoped I wouldn't have to fight.

Scrap was still out of it. That meant mundane weapons at best. Should I steal a wooden kabob skewer from the kitchen? Or was it silver vampires were sensitive to? No, that's werewolves. I definitely needed a wooden stake, if for no other reason than intimidation.

I gazed at Scrap fondly. Usually he made his recovery elsewhere. Because of my injury, he couldn't get very far from me. For the first time I understood Gollum's attachment to his wretched cat. Having Scrap's body, insubstantial as it was, curled up beside me comforted me, reassured me that I wasn't alone.

"We know that a Contessa Lucia Maria Continelli, wife of Italian Count Antonio Bertrand Continelli died in 1818 along with her husband and small son. Their fortified Tuscan villa was burned to the ground. The count was not liked. Hints of taking prisoners during the Napoleonic invasions for the sole purpose of torture. He didn't discriminate as to which side they fought for."

I gulped. This sounded very like the blood-and-gore stories surrounding Vlad the Impaler.

"No modern driver's license, Social Security number, or telephone listing for Lucia." Gollum peered at his computer screen over the top of his glasses. Which had slid to the end of his nose, as usual.

I wanted to grab a miniature screwdriver kit and tighten the frames.

"So, whoever this woman is, she's maintaining a profile that would fit a vampire," I mused.

"Folklore around the ancestral estate in Italy claims she was repeatedly milked by a local vampire. A long wasting illness that prevented her from appearing in public during the sunlight hours. The villagers didn't trust her. I'm guessing she was foreign to them at the time of the marriage. Never discount the value of folklore."

"She's a charlatan. I bet we find she ran away from a farm in Iowa twenty years ago and has manipulated a mini empire based on a kinky reputation."

"The elastic bandage will help support the thigh muscles, and will be invisible under slacks," he added.

I'd learned months ago to blink and then try to follow the rapid twists and turns of his mind.

"Should I show up with a wooden stake tucked in my pocket?"

No answer. Gollum, at least, had the grace to almost blush.

"As for Gregbaum, he started as a stage magician, working small clubs and bars. Mostly for tips. Never made it big. Hung around the fringes of legitimate stage productions. Then, suddenly, two years ago he shows up with enormous backing for a real show. Launches it almost overnight, no auditions, already has sets and costumes. He signs a contract one day with a hotel on the skids. Puts up a few fliers around town the next, and opens 'Fairy Moon' on the third. Instantly, the Dragon and St. George is saved from forced sale and implosion."

"Where'd he get the money?" I thought back on the rumor that the hotel was on the verge of selling again. Apparently, "Fairy Moon" wasn't enough to bail the owners out of whatever hole they'd dug themselves into.

"I find no list of investors."

"He had to come up with it somewhere. That is not a cheap show to put on, even if he isn't paying his dancers and is keeping them locked in a dormitory in the basement, as if they were white slaves."

"Interesting simile."

"Why." I gave up trying to get my hair to do something sophisticated. The total lack of humidity kept it from frizzing, but that's the best I can say about it. I limped over to his station in the armchair by the windows, laptop perched on his long thighs, big feet propped on the table.

"There is an arrest record, no conviction, for Gary Gregbaum: illegally importing underage girls from Eastern Bloc nations for immoral purposes."

"What? Why wasn't he convicted?"

"Court records do not say. His lawyer of record is Gerard Moncrieff."

I whistled. "Very expensive bastard."

"Very tricky bastard. He wins all his cases on technical errors rather than on the evidence. I'm guessing the DA dismissed shaky charges rather than face Moncrieff in court."

A discreet knock on the door.

I looked at Gollum to see if he'd walk all the way across the room to answer it.

He continued to stare at his laptop, an occasional key stroke occupied all of his attention. "Nothing on San-croix yet."

I sighed and limped over to find Mickey quaking in the hallway.

"You ready?" he asked, wringing his hands. He looked incredibly young, with his skinny shoulders and lean frame. Then he raised his eyes to me. He had big brown eyes that held an eternity of sorrow and grief. Age and frown lines radiated out from those soulful orbs, belying his youthful countenance.

"I'm ready." As ready as I'd ever be. I'd gone for classy casual (the same tone as the conference) with dove-gray slacks and a pink knit top, black lace-up shoes not much more substantial than sneakers but with good traction. A cable knit sweater in gray with pink flecks thrown over my shoulders completed the outfit. Scrap had, of course, picked it out and coordinated it for me.

"Gollum?"

"This is a scouting mission, you can handle it." He waved at me, never taking his eyes off his computer.

"Like hell, I can. Get your ass out of *my* armchair." A long-standing argument approaching joke status. "I need backup. I need you to listen to accents. I need you to whisper advice in the face of an unknown enemy." I was a schoolteacher before I began writing full time. I'd handled reluctant teenagers and quarrelsome five year olds alike.

Gollum responded to the same authoritative voice.

"Of course." He blinked at me as if seeing me for the first time.

"What about me?" Mickey asked. He kept his eyes on the carpet. He'd dropped the phony Slavic accent.

"No need to risk yourself."

"One such as you must know that I have to go." He didn't look happy about it.

"Do I get to ask why?"

"Not yet." He looked up finally and flashed me a win-

some grin. For half a moment I caught an afterimage
of pointed ears peeking through his jaw-length straight
hair. Then it was gone.

"Did you bring the comb? I think you're going to
need it," Gollum said. He referred to a magical artifact
that allowed me to see through demon glamour and
decipher auras. I hated wearing it as it turned bits and
pieces of my hair crystal clear and brittle. It also gave
me headaches.

"No."

I'll get it. Scrap surged up from his sleeping ball looking refreshed and eager. He popped out. Three eye
blinks later, he dropped onto my shoulder, the precious
antique gold filigree piece in his chubby hand.

Mickey followed his movements unerringly.

"You aren't from Bulgaria, are you?"

"My guess, he's from Faery." Gollum yawned and
held the door open for us.

I held my breath and my temper for about as long as
you'd expect. Exactly half of one heartbeat.

"And just when did you plan to share this information with me?" I was surprised steam didn't roil out my
ears.

"When you needed to know." Gollum smiled.

"Which is when?"

"About three seconds after I figured it out."

"Oh." My righteous indignation drained out of
me, like a slow leak in a hot air balloon. "Is this true,
Mickey?"

"I am not allowed to say, but if a human figures it out,
I do not have to deny it. That is the rule of the Powers
That Be."

Hmmm. Something to consider when dealing with
Donovan. Now I just had to figure out what he was
hiding.

"I noticed the moment he stopped faking an accent
that certain inflections reminded me of the speech patterns of the coven of witches that went missing to Faery
for twenty-eight years . . ." Gollum droned on about nuances of accents and how much difference could occur

in relatively small geographic distances all the way down the elevator and into Mickey's taxi.

The portal to Faery is closed, Scrap said. He leaned on top of my head to peer closely at Mickey. *Ask him when and how he got here. He might be a spy for the other side.*

I asked.

"Closed?" Mickey looked truly bewildered and frightened. "No one can get in or out of Faery?" A single tear leaked out of the corner of his eye.

"That's what Scrap says."

"I came through the chat room right after we noticed the dancers missing. A brightness and a luster vanished from our lives; from the goodness that is Faery. A trail of energy followed them and continued to leak. The Powers That Be must have sealed it off to prevent further leakage. I have to get my people back home soon!"

"I know you do. We'll help," I promised.

"May I take out my colored contacts now?" Mickey asked as he settled behind the wheel.

"As long as you don't need them to see clearly . . ."

"I see better without them. Necessary for disguise." He bent his head and pressed fingertips to eye corners. When he looked up again the bright lights of the hotel porte cochere revealed the greenest irises I'd ever seen.

"Faery green," I breathed.

Mickey nodded and smiled shyly. "Too distinctive for blending in with humans."

Gollum and I rode in the back, as if we were paying passengers. I took the opportunity to test the comb. My hair tangled around it instantly, like iron filings reaching for a magnet.

Gollum looked his usual pensive self with layers and layers of energy radiating out from him; every color imaginable, some warm and inviting, others cold and calculated, even a few dark and brooding—or guilty.

We all have our secrets.

He kept talking.

Mickey, on the other hand, appeared royal blue with

wings and pointed ears shadowing his body. I caught a hint of gold around his brow, then it vanished.

Ah-ha! Our spy from Faery had royal connections. Not just any normal volunteer for a do-or-die mission. I hoped no one had to die.

Part of me wanted to reach out and hug him in reassurance.

"He always this verbose?" Mickey asked as he pulled into traffic.

His words shattered my musing. So I snagged the comb out of my hair, pulling several crystalline strands with it. My scalp hurt where it had lodged.

I liked his new accent, his real accent. Some of his words came out with an almost Latin inflection, as in Classic Latin rather than Latino, and he tended to clip off the last sound.

"Get enough single malt scotch into Gollum and he spouts in tongues. But he always spouts," I laughed.

Gollum glared at me over the top of his glasses.

Mickey wound through traffic, right and left, left and right, circling buildings, and returning to the Strip in different locations. We passed the vacant lot where the El Rancho Vegas had burned. No one ever built on that lot, prime real estate though it was. I got a creepy feeling there.

Ghosts, Scrap whispered to me. *Not happy ones.*

We passed it by, almost glad that the raucous noise and glaring lights of the Stratosphere drew our attention away from the dark shadows.

After a half hour Mickey cruised into an underground parking garage and jerked to a stop beside a long black hearse with tinted windows.

"Why the convoluted route to get us beneath the Dragon and St. George?" I asked before touching the door handle. I wasn't getting in that dark monster of a deathmobile.

"Just following orders," Mickey said. He looked abashed as he held up a page of printed instructions. He sounded defiant. Quite an actor this guy. No telling what he really felt.

"Probably to disorient you," Gollum said. He opened his door and unfolded his long limbs.

"Whoever gave you the directions didn't count on Scrap." My buddy preened. "I can't get lost as long as he's with me."

Gollum froze halfway to standing.

Instantly, I looked for danger.

"Mickey," Gollum said with deep seriousness. "Did you choose the route?" He snatched the printed directions from Mickey's hand almost too quickly to follow.

I think if I'd still worn the comb I would have seen a strange energy pattern follow his arm in both directions.

"I . . . I . . ." Mickey blushed and looked down.

"Ritual maze," Gollum muttered and threw the directions back at Mickey. "What kind of magic did we just weave?"

"The . . . the pattern will bind Lady Tess to the mission of rescuing the dancers from Faery," he whispered.

"What else?" Gollum pushed up his glasses and peered around us, examining each and every shadow minutely.

"Nothing. I swear."

Gollum fixed his gaze firmly upon Mickey, glasses slipping, nothing between his eyes and his prey.

I shuddered at the image of nonviolent Gollum unleashing his pent-up energy.

"I wove protection for Lady Tess around the edges," Mickey said after a long silence, as if compelled by Gollum.

"Good. She needs it. She's too reckless," Gollum said, almost casually as he unfolded himself completely and got out of the car. "She'd complete the mission without the spell. She's stubborn like that."

I took umbrage and started to spout a protest. There's a difference between dedication and stubbornness. Not much, but a difference.

"We appreciate the protection. Did you know she can't get lost as long as Scrap is with her?"

"I did. But don't tell that, or the ritual route to Lady

Lucia. You need some secrets to come out of this alive," Mickey warned. "The Lady said to get you lost. Not how I was to go about it."

Gregbaum hangs out at this hotel. Is he involved in Lady Lucia picking this place for a meet up?

Tess described Donovan's little love token to me. If it does match Gregbaum's pinky ring, then the two are connected in some way. Near twin rings of antique design and great value are no coincidence.

I'm not going to comment on keeping Tess informed of where and when we are and which way is north. I'm good at that. Have to be to get around the chat room and other dimensions. I've got anchors all over the place that help me orient myself.

Except for those awful moments in the Valley of Fire. The magnetics there screwed up every one of my senses and blocked access to my pole points. For a bit, I couldn't even get back to the chat room.

I think I'm going to squash all ideas about Tess going there. Can't take a chance on either or both of us getting lost.

Now let's see what Lady Lucia has in store for us.

"The hearse is clean, babe. A bit morose, but a great bit of atmosphere. This fake countessa has a wonderful sense for stage management. Maybe she helped design the 'Fairy Moon' sets."

Chapter 21

Las Vegas has no mosquitoes. Due to the dry climate, there are no stagnant pools of water for them to breed.

WE APPROACHED THE HEARSE cautiously. I kept my senses open, listening to any sound behind our footfalls. My training at the Citadel had taught me not to stare at any one point for very long.

"Keep your eyes moving. Memorize every detail and note things that have moved or change on the next pass," I heard Sister Gert's words in my mind.

And I saw her off in a corner, shadowed by support pillars and classy cars.

I shook my head. Looked again. She was gone. A figment of my imagination?

I smell imp, Scrap said. His attention riveted toward the same corner. *Gone now. Running away. They know we are here, but don't want to say hello. How rude.*

An uneasy feeling crept up my spine.

The driver's side window of the hearse slid open an inch.

"My orders say only the Warrior," an androgynous voice said from the region of the driver's seat. It could have come from a male tenor or a husky female alto. Either one had been darkened by smoke and harsh whiskey.

"I bring my advisers or I don't come," I replied.

A moment of silence. I got the feeling from the shape of the shadow within a shadow behind the glass that the driver consulted on a cell phone.

"They may come." A passenger door behind the driver opened by unseen hands. Or remote control.

I was getting tired of the special effects.

Gollum held the door open for me. I looked around carefully, making note of where Mickey had parked.

A flicker of movement over by the elevator bank drew my gaze like a compass homing in on magnetic north. Fortitude flew a wide loop around the lot, just above the roofs of the parked cars. Breven Sancroix whistled sharply and held out his arm, like a falconer calling his bird.

Junior stood beside him, tapping his foot. He and Fortitude exchanged a long silent gaze, like they communicated, excluding Breven, Fortitude's Warrior. "We have to get out of here before someone sees us," he hissed.

"What?" Breven looked around hastily, eyes gliding right over us as if he didn't notice a party of three and an imp hanging around a hearse.

Junior assumed a more relaxed pose and disengaged his attention from Fortitude, and us. "Mom's going to kill us if she doesn't get in to see the show. She can't get in without my pass."

How come they got tickets two nights running? He said pass, not tickets. That meant he had an important relationship to Gregbaum. And who was his mother? I thought he was an orphan. Or did Breven want the world to think Junior was an orphan to hide his parentage?

A bright pop of intuition lit my mind. I thought I'd seen Gert. Breven admitted to a long-standing relationship with her.

Could Junior be theirs? If so, why hide it?

Curiouser and curiouser.

The elevator came, and the two figures disappeared into its maw. Where had the third gone?

No more time to puzzle on it. The driver tapped his steering wheel impatiently.

I climbed into the hearse and sank onto wide red velvet seats, two and two facing each other. Real silk velvet, not upholstery velour. A single red rose rested in a gold vase attached to the panel between the windows. A magnum of champagne rested in an ice bucket on the console between the seats. A single crystal flute awaited the touch of wine. Real crystal, not the plastic Donovan provided in his limo.

I inspected the label. It looked expensive. I don't know wine. With single malt scotch, I could tell if I should be impressed.

Gollum whistled silently and raised his eyebrows. His glasses nearly slid off his nose.

Mickey reached for the glass. "We can share," he said. He looked like he needed a drink.

"No." Gollum stayed his hand. "Rules of hospitality. Same here as in Faery. Once you accept food or drink from an otherworldly creature you are bound to them. By obligation or magic. Depends on the realm."

Mickey sat back, arms crossed. His eyes kept straying to the wine.

We drove for over an hour. A dark partition separated us from the driver. Another from the long bed where a coffin could sit. Dark windows separated us from reality. The bright lights of the Strip disappeared quickly. So did ordinary streetlights. Traffic thinned to an occasional car coming form the other direction across a wide divide. Our speed felt freeway fast.

I began feeling closed in, suffocated, as if the hearse was a coffin instead of the conveyance for one. And my stomach hurt.

Gollum pulled my feet into his lap and placed the ice bucket against my inner thigh. "Might as well get some use out of it." He grinned and began massaging my calves.

I was too tense to appreciate how good his long fingers felt.

"He's taking us out into the desert. To dump us?" I tried to assess my resources. Could I walk out if we suddenly found ourselves in the middle of nowhere?

That idea made the closed stuffiness of the hearse feel less confining, more protective.

Maybe Scrap could whisk us through the chat room and back to civilization. If he'd recovered enough from transforming. He loves to fight, but the change process drains him terribly.

"I doubt it. Lady Lucia sent the champagne and the rose as a peace offering," Mickey said. He sat with his back to the driver, facing me. "She only does that if she intends to let you live. Otherwise, why waste the money?"

"To lull my suspicions. Scrap, can you get a bead on who or what is driving us?"

Human. Male. Deliciously male in tight black leather and a snap brim cap. Good pecs under the jacket. He works out.

I translated the important part. Scrap must be feeling back to normal if he bothered to size up the man's attractive qualities.

We fell into silence, not knowing if Lady Lucia had planted listening bugs or not.

Eventually, a swath of light cut through the desert blackness.

Looks like a town. Just a little place, tractor dealer, feed store, and a huge resort. Ooh, they have a pool with waterfalls and palm trees. Looks like an oasis.

"Pinyon," Mickey muttered without waiting for translation. Had he heard Scrap? "Fifty miles or so northeast of Vegas."

"Not far from the Valley of Fire," I mused, imagining the local map in my head.

"Side road fifteen miles behind us," Mickey confirmed.

"The resort is now the prime employer in this area," Gollum chimed in. "Agriculture is drying up—along with the underground lake and artesian springs that water this entire area. They have to drill deeper every year and import more water from other sources to provide enough for the city. Less and less for the farms. I've read estimates that Vegas will run out of water in as little as fifty years. Other so-called experts estimate one hundred fifty. The city has instituted state-of-the-art recycling systems—the most advanced in the world—to forestall the inevitable. Either way, the city is floating on borrowed water."

Our hearse glided to a stop, and our doors opened. Again by remote control. I peered out before exiting.

"We're at the back entrance to the spa rather than the front door of the resort."

"The contessa doesn't want to attract undue attention," Gollum muttered. "Let's see what the lady wants." He climbed out first and reached back to help me. Like a fine gentleman. Someone in his past had drilled manners into him until they came naturally.

I always felt like Donovan's courtesies were forced. Just a second's delay as if he had to pause and think about what he should do. Same way with his emotions. He had to think about what he was feeling, examine it from all angles, never truly understanding what was going on.

As I stood, the lactose-intolerance–induced bloating released. Not pleasant.

"Feel better?" Gollum grinned.

"Actually I do. Not so much pressure on my injury."

Our driver remained inside and unseen by any but Scrap. The door into the spa opened, inviting us in. Again, untended by human hands.

Scrap clung to my shoulder, stretching a bit, his nose twitching and his tail swishing across my back.

I don't like this place. Beneath the chlorine and antiseptic, it smells of blood. Human blood. He turned pink, and his talons pierced my top almost to my skin.

Nothing downstairs but two massages, a blow job, and a pedicure that's going to get kinky real fast. Wanna watch, babe? Scrap retracted his talons and flitted through the heavy fire door on the ground floor and back out again.

His normal gray/green translucency returned. The blood was no threat to us.

That didn't mean I had to like it.

"I vote we go upstairs," I replied—the only other egress from the landing just inside the exterior door.

You might learn something for when you finally decide to seduce Gollum. Not that he needs much seducing, dahling. If you know what I mean. Scrap waggled his unlit cigar at me.

"Sounds like a party up there," Gollum muttered. "Maybe we should look for an elevator." He stared me in the eyes as if daring me to walk up those stairs.

I glanced from him to the stairs and back again.

Watch da birdie in da camera, babe. Scrap pointed to a miniscule red light at the first turn of the stairs.

"I don't want to get trapped in an enclosed box at the mercy of electronics and the whims of Murphy's Law," I told Gollum, gesturing slightly with my head toward the camera.

He knew me well enough to catch on quickly and nodded. "Would you care to take the point?" He gestured me up the stair ahead of him. "We'll watch your back."

"You'd better." I jammed the comb back into my hair. Then I took my time, judging each step carefully, trying not to limp obviously or lean too heavily on the banister. If I showed any signs of weakness at this point, I made myself vulnerable.

When I hurt, Scrap hurt. He might not be able to transform.

True to his word, Gollum stayed one step below me. Close enough to give me a boost up if I needed it, or catch me if I fell.

Mickey came behind him, turning around and around, keeping everything in sight at once.

Eventually, we mastered the two sets of thirteen steps. I wondered who had a hand in designing that little bit of bad luck. The fire door stood propped wide open by a skull with the top hacked off raggedly and a black candle stub jammed inside. It gave off a creepy light, creating more shadows than it banished. It looked like real bone. I kept telling myself it had to be ceramic or good quality plastic. It just had to be. I refused to think about the possibility of it being a real skull, from a real human being.

"Dramatic Halloween nonsense I can do without," I muttered.

"Effective atmosphere if you're feeling vulnerable, though," Gollum replied.

"I'm feeling vulnerable," Mickey whispered.

"Don't show it," I hissed back.

He shrugged his shoulders and settled his back before putting on a brave, and totally false, smile.

I muttered something more and stepped across the threshold of the local lady vampire mob boss.

I had a fleeting impression of sparse and graceful furniture in pale wood and muted upholstery with far too many bodies vying for the few seats. More bodies stood around in listless, muted conversation. Black candles—mostly in antique brass-and-silver candelabra rather than skulls—barely lit the room. High ceilings robbed the lower reaches of light. I almost had the feeling of being out of doors.

How to tell if the room had tasteful appointments or impoverished scarcity?

This was how people lived in the "good old days" before electricity. They couldn't see anything after sunset unless they spent a fortune on smelly fish oil lamps or candles. They huddled together in the immediate circle of light cast by clusters of fixtures leaving the rest of the world in spooky shadow.

"Andiamo," a sultry feminine voice called. A lovely blonde in her early forties floated forward. A few streaks of white highlighted her hair nicely. She either paid someone a lot of money for those highlights or she had fantastic genes.

She linked her arm in mine and drew me deeper into the room.

A bevy of pale hangers-on edged closer to us. No sign of the wereweasel.

The magical comb I'd stuck in my short hair showed me nothing special in the auras. Just ordinary people.

Except Lady Lucia had no radiant energy at all. That scared me more than if she took bat form.

If you haven't heard already, I have a thing about bats. I'll fight a dozen Sasquatch and Windago any day before I'll face down even one little insect-eating bat.

Gollum looked like he wanted to take notes. Mickey looked numb and overwhelmed. They followed close on my heels.

"Nice gown, Lady Lucia," I said, taking in the delicate cream-and-terra-cotta silk that looked like it walked off a costume rack labeled 1835. Something about the cut and clean lines suggested a Florentine designer.

Her guests at least had kept up with the times with a preponderance of black silky fabrics and tight jeans.

"Introduce me to your friends, Signora Tess," she said with a frown. Her accent sounded thick, as if her English was newly learned.

I raised an eyebrow to Gollum. He shrugged, still studying cadence and inflection.

"Contessa, allow me to present Dr. Guilford Van der Hoyden-Smythe and Mickey Mallone, our local guide and driver." I thought I'd be polite and formal, play along with her game a bit before I decided to expose her.

From the looks of her cleavage, it wouldn't take much to expose a lot more of her than acceptable in polite society. But then, this was Vegas, or the outskirts thereof. Who knew what was acceptable.

Even as I thought about it, a hint of dusky skin peeked above her tightly corseted décolletage, the same shade as the terra cotta in said gown's trim.

Gollum's eyes riveted right where she'd intended.

Okay. Gloves off. I was tired of being polite.

"You'd think someone who'd left Tuscany almost two hundred years ago, and who had prided herself on keeping up with the height of fashion would update her dress occasionally," I said. "Your headlights are showing and it's not a good look in mixed company."

She scowled at me, keeping her mouth firmly closed.

"Oh, and the accent is too thick." I thought fast and furious about what Gollum had said about how rapidly accents mutated. The details had gone in one ear and out the other eye.

"Tess . . ." Gollum warned.

I shrugged. "If she's really a vampire, you'd think she'd keep up with the times, try to blend in, stay under the radar. But then she'd have established a legal identity as Lady Lucia."

This time the lady sneered, revealing two very long and pointed eye teeth. Still no aura. She could have been masking it. Some people can do that—Donovan among them, just another reason not to trust him. But anger cracks any mask, and some energy should have leaked out.

"I've seen better implants and prosthetics at every con I've attended." I almost yawned. Then decided that reaction was too over the top.

A short lad drifted forward carrying a tray filled with silver goblets, brimming with dry ice mist. My height—which isn't saying much—he looked to be about twelve. Until he got close and the frown lines around his mouth and eyes added a couple of decades, or centuries, to his face.

He didn't have an aura either.

This was getting spooky.

"We party tonight, Signora Tess," Lucia said. Some of the accent faded, some—not all. "Time for word games and shadow boxing later. When we know what we both want." She lifted one of the goblets from the tray and handed it to me. "The specialty of the house. Goats from my beloved Tuscany contributed the milk. The blood came from a different donor. Whipped together into a froth with secret spices." She flashed more of the elongated teeth.

"We call it 'Smoothie Mary,' " the lad said with an evil grin that showed the same orthodontia as the Contessa.

"Um, thanks to Mary, whomever she may be, but no thanks. I'm allergic to milk. The animal casein." I trotted out an old high school biology lesson. The guy I'd dated my sophomore year had that allergy. Not just intolerant, allergic. He couldn't have cheese or cream or butter. Eggs were out of the question as well. "I think the blood falls into the same category as the goat milk."

I put the drink cup back on the tray. The icy stem burned my fingers. I wanted my hands fully functioning in case I had to fight my way out of here.

Scrap had remained strangely silent. I spotted him sitting on a chandelier, hanging almost upside down and spying on one of the men in jeans so tight they had to cut off circulation to vital parts. So far no comments about the legitimacy of our hostess' claims to being a vampire.

If she were truly evil, he'd have turned bright red and stretched halfway into transformation by now.

Wouldn't he?

"Tell me, Lady Lucia, are vampires in the same classification as demons? And if so, which ghetto did you escape from?"

The entire room went utterly still. Not even the candle flames flickered.

Chapter 22

The inland sea that covered much of SW North America began to recede 200 million years ago.

"E R, TESS," GOLLUM STAMMERED. He hastily scanned the room for signs of trouble.

I'd already sized up the mass of bodies and dismissed them as useless wannabes.

Lady Lucia presented the only real threat. And maybe the pseudo child with the tray of drinks.

"Actually, vampires can't be classed as demons in this dimension," I blathered on. "Earth is their home world. Or is death a home world? If so, they'd be demons, if you use the 'out of dimension' definition, but I'm told that's not accurate." Gee I sounded a lot like Gollum there. I hate it when I babble. "So, what remains is the question of which dimensional ghetto did vampires crawl out of?"

At least Scrap diverted his attention back to me for about two heartbeats. Then he returned to ogling the shirtless males in black jeans that outlined every crack and protrusion on their bodies. Ordinary males. From the way their auras fluctuated, I guessed they found other men as attractive as females.

"Anyway, a vampire by definition is evil," I continued

seemingly oblivious to the way the hangers-on pressed closer. "So if, Lady Lucia really is a vampire, then Scrap would have transformed the moment we walked in the door, I'd have killed her and we'd be on our way home."

A gasp of outrage ran around the room. I saw a lot of teeth in my peripheral vision. My attention remained on Lady Lucia.

She threw back her head and laughed long and loud. More of her bosom escaped the corset and lace. "Very good logic, *cara mía* Signora Tess. Very good indeed. However, your little friend cannot react to my inherent evil, because I offer no evil intentions toward you. Tonight." She looked long and hard at Scrap.

He flashed her a toothy grin. He had longer and sharper ones than she did. And a lot more of them.

And his were real.

How could she see him?

"I can see your imp, Signora Tess, because I can see the aura of blackness about him. He has many secrets, this one."

Now I felt more than a little uneasy. Did I really begin edging toward the door?

If I did, she came right along with me, and five of her minions slid between me and Gollum. Mickey stood isolated by another group of five to my left.

I couldn't leave them. They were defenseless, mostly. I was not.

"You brought me here for a reason, Lady Lucia. I want to know what it is."

"Is my little party not enough for you?" She reached out and grabbed by her leather vest a listless and anemic looking girl in her early twenties. She wasn't wearing anything beneath the vest except a micromini leather skirt that shifted upward to reveal wisps of blonde pubic hair.

She had an aura, barely. Mostly she'd been drained of so much energy—or blood—there wasn't a lot left to show.

The twin puncture wounds on her neck, right over the jugular, grabbed my attention.

Gollum looked a little sick. Mickey more so.

"This is Mary," Lady Lucia continued. "You may thank her for mixing the drinks tonight."

I gulped. "Um, thanks, Mary. I'm sure they were delish." I tried looking away. I really did.

Mary lifted her mouth in a feeble attempt at a smile.

"What's your point, Lady Lucia?" I still couldn't look away from Mary. Call it fascinated horror.

It felt a lot like fear.

Lady Lucia had taken my preconceived notions and juggled them, keeping them all in the air at the same time.

"My point is, that I have a lot of power in this region. I have many followers, many who will do my bidding without question. But I cannot bring down Gary Gregbaum."

"You have my attention. I do not like what that man is doing."

"His show is lovely, isn't it?" Lady Lucia dropped her grip on Mary and pushed her away. She stumbled toward a chair and fell into it like the rag doll she had become.

"Lovely. And disturbing," I said. "Tell me, does the audience clap for the dying faery at every performance? That has become a tradition in our world, to bring Tinker Bell back to life."

"No. You began that tradition for 'Fairy Moon.' Amazing that the performance touched you so deeply, you who are so jaded and contemptuous of that which you do not understand." She glided toward the center of the room.

My feet followed her of their own volition. The crowd shifted around us. I noticed the knots of people around Mickey and Gollum also moved, keeping the same distance between us.

Directly beneath Scrap's chandelier, Lady Lucia took the stage, bathed in gentle candlelight from the fifty or more flames above her head. One of them threatened Scrap's tail. I wondered when, or if, he'd notice.

"You, *cara mia* Tess, have the power to do what I cannot," Lady Lucia pronounced.

"Which is?"

"Free the faery dancers and ruin Gary Gregbaum."

"And how am I supposed to do that?"

"You must go where I and my kind cannot. You must find the portal in the Valley of Fire and lead the faeries to it."

No way no how, Babe. I am not going to the Valley of Fire. Never again. Not in this lifetime or any other. It will be the death of me. And that means it's the death of you, too.

When I die, you die. When you die, I die.

You aren't going there either. Much too dangerous. Mountains of iron-laden sandstone with twisted and looping canyons screw with the senses and challenge the balance of life.

Get Mr. Holier Than Thou Breven Sancroix and snooty Fortitude to do it.

Or get Mr. Stinky Donovan Estevez to do it.

Anyone but you and me, babe. Abso-fucking-lutely anyone but us.

"Glad to see something could grab your attention, Scrap," I muttered. The more I heard about this Valley of Fire, the more curious I became. And the more scared.

Scrap's aura sparked, or maybe that was just his tail catching fire. Normally, I couldn't detect his aura at all. I didn't need to. His body color told me what I needed to know of his emotions. Right now he was so pale, even I had trouble seeing him.

And I never detected the darkness Lady Lucia claimed to see around him. The king of the Orculli Trolls had told me about that darkness, too.

I looked to Gollum for inspiration. His eyes had glazed over in his need to get on the Internet and do some research.

"What do I get out of this venture?" I asked Lady Lucia. "I'm figuring it's as dangerous for me as for you."

A moment of silence as she looked me up and down, assessing, weighing her options. And mine.

"You fulfill your vows as a Warrior of the Celestial Blade, you restore balance to the dimensions. But you must hurry. My sources tell me the rogue portal is unstable and will close within days. If that happens, then Faery is forever damaged. The good energy that flows there, balancing many evils, will be lost to the universe." She looked serious. "You will gain much credit with the Powers That Be. Something you will need if you ever hope to survive outside a Citadel."

Believe her, babe. The good energy in Faery already turns bad. Think about those mutant faeries on steroids that Gregbaum employs.

"Okay, and what do you get, Lady Lucia?"

"I see Gary Gregbaum writhe in disgrace and poverty."

"If the portal closes, can't we get the faeries back to their homeland through the chat room?" I looked to Scrap for confirmation. He claimed to know the chat room as well as anyone.

Not a good idea, dahling. It's one thing for me to slip you in and out upon occasion when the demons on guard are particularly dumb. Quite another to take an entire troupe through. Besides, last time I flitted through, the door to Faery was sealed. Both directions.

"You need to know that I have purchased the Dragon and St. George," Lady Lucia continued. "My first act upon taking over in four days will be to fire all the managers who are skimming gambling profits and implode the hotel. Gregbaum will never produce another show in Las Vegas, no matter who has the audacity to back him. I will see to that."

There is nothing so great as the wrath of a woman scorned.

The skinny lad without an aura tugged on the flounce at the end of her three-quarter sleeve. "Do not forget the curse."

"Do I want to know?"

More bad news, babe. This does not look good, or like fun. We're gonna need help, maybe of the Donovan kind.

"Gregbaum has placed a curse upon his dancers. If any one of them leaves the building, they all become living torches."

Mickey nodded, confirming the existence of the curse.

"You must break the curse and lead the faeries to freedom before I take possession and the portal closes. I cannot be responsible for what will become of this world should you fail," Lucia continued.

Mickey fainted.

Chapter 23

Boulder City is the only town in Nevada where gambling is not legal.

NOW I RECOGNIZE Mickey! With his defenses down, his real self shines through like a beacon in the dark. That's what Faery should be and has lost.

Let me back up just a tad—like a month or two our time. See there's this psycho chick named WindScribe. She's one of the coven that went missing twenty-eight years ago, only they think they were only in Faery about a month. Got news for them. Time runs different in Faery.

Anyway, WindScribe got caught doing something more than a little naugty and very very dangerous. She tried setting free a bunch of Cthulhu demons from their ghetto in the back of Faery.

Naturally, the king of Faery was pissed. WindScribe snapped his neck. Now this little escapade led to all kinds of trouble that Tess and I dealt with already.

But back in Faery, life didn't return to normal. There was a big fight between our boy Mickey, who's something like the crown prince of Faery, and his stepmom the queen. Queeny won and now rules Faery. But there's a whole lot of things wrong. So wrong the chat room portal is closed until they get things right.

Mickey must be here to get back the faery dancers who got kidnapped while no one was in charge and life was chaotic. Until he does that, Faery can't heal.

He's a true prince. He should be ruling.

"Time to get our boy home," Gollum said. He broke through his guards and Mickey's to crouch beside him. He tested Mickey's pulse and touched his brow with the back of his hand.

"Is he okay?" I asked, elbowing my way over to them.

Scrap descended to my shoulder like a good little imp. He'd gained a little color, back to his normal gray/green with just a hint of yellow concern. Not a bit of pink or red on him. We were still safe.

But for how long?

"Hard to tell what's okay for him," Gollum whispered. "Pulse too rapid and skin too cold and clammy."

Not good, Scrap said. He shifted to the top of my head, claws grasping the comb. I didn't know if he used its powers or merely kept it in place. *Faeries have a higher heart rate than humans, but that makes their skin warmer.*

I shook my head at Gollum, hoping he'd understand that we had to get him out of here. No sense in betraying his origins to Lady Lucia and her gang if we didn't have to.

Mickey's eyes fluttered. Again, I got the impression of something off in their tilt and placement in his pinched and narrow face. He moaned and tried to roll over.

Gollum steadied his movements. "Catch your bearings, boy, before you try to stand."

"I'll have you know I am no 'boy,' " Mickey sneered with the disdain of a true aristocrat. All traces of the bouncy youth vanished.

Then the familiar Mickey returned in a flash. "I'm okay. Just get me out of here. The heat, and the candles, and too much perfume overcame me."

Yeah, right.

I'd seen his eyes roll up the moment Lady Lucia mentioned the consequences of Gregbaum's curse. If any of the faery dancers left the building, they'd go up in flames. A horrible death for anyone. Might be especially tormenting to faeries.

"Lady Lucia." I turned and faced our hostess-cum-ally-cum-adversary. "May we trouble you for the use of your car for our return to the city?"

"Of course." She snapped her fingers.

The lad scuttled out. Then I heard footsteps clattering on a staircase at the opposite end of the building from our entrance.

"The car will meet you out front. It will take a few minutes to retrieve it from the garage. If you come this way, you may walk by the pool and wander the hotel gift shop for a moment. Feel free to gamble." She ushered us out of the party room, down a short hallway.

We passed a tiny kitchenette, a bath nearly as large a my hotel room. The luxurious tub had water jets, deep enough for ten to swim in. Three partially closed doors looked like they might be guest rooms, smaller than the bath. Couples were engaged in heavy make out sessions there, mostly unclothed and oblivious to us.

Then the hallway ended. To our left lay the master (or mistress) bedroom with a huge circular bed, sitting area, and access to another bath. I couldn't see the details but guessed it to be more utilitarian. To our right a broad green marble staircase curved downward.

But it was the painting on the end wall that grabbed my attention. A masterful oil portrait of Lady Lucia in her late teens. She wore a white gown, of the late Napoleonic period, with a full, flowing mantilla of white chantilly lace—very rare and costly; chantilly is usually black silk. She could have been pregnant, hard to tell in those high-waisted gowns. The painted image displayed her left hand quite prominently. On her heart finger, she wore a gold filigree ring with a huge square-cut diamond.

I'd seen that ring before, tied to a rose stem as Donovan offered it to me with his proposal.

Gary Gregbaum wore a duplicate on his pinky finger.

I checked. Lady Lucia did not wear that ring; several other very expensive ones, but not that one.

Who had the original? Donovan or Gregbaum? And how did they come to possess such a valuable and cherished antique?

I'm off to Mum's for a nice little chat about how to trace that ring. I'm surprised it didn't end up in Mum's front yard, the freeze-dried-garbage-dump-of-the-universe. That's where I found Tess' comb, and the brooch that signifies leadership of all the Sisterhoods of the Celestial Blade—maybe Brotherhoods, too. We'll see when she's defeated her thirteen enemies and earned a precious stone for each of the settings in the brooch. I also found a dragon skull there that now sits atop Tess' back door. No one ever uses the front door and it's sealed during bad weather. That skull works better than any stone gargoyle for repelling nasties from the house. And since it's from a real dragon and not a gargoyle, it doesn't keep me out.

No one special guarding the chat room tonight. Guess Gregbaum has called in all of his faeries on steroids for some other project. Just some giant fleas hanging around jumping hither, thither, and yon, biting at the air. They look like tiny dots against the endless white that stretches on and on and on forever. No color, no break in the vastness except an occasional doorway. Those fleas all seem to be congregating around the black splotch in front of Faery.

That used to be a clear opening, inviting any and all to share in the hospitality, the peace, and the joy of living. Anyone could get into Faery, if they could find their way into the chat room. Now Faery is closed to all until the balance is restored. Uh-oh! The seal used to be a perfect circle. Now it's distorted and ugly.

Things are getting worse, and time is running out. I've got to get to Mum's quick.

I slide toward the leather curtain that covers Imp Haven. A

single flea nips at my tail. Ow, that itches. At least it didn't take off any of my warts. I worked hard to earn those beauty spots, I'm not giving them up to some *flea*!

Mum stands in front of her hovel, broom in hand. The broom has seen better days. Pretty useless now as a broom, still effective at swatting my cute little tush—now covered in six, count 'em six, lovely warts. She frowns the moment I come into view.

I drop down in front of her in an almost graceful flight just like a good little imp. Her frown deepens.

"What are you doing here?" she shouts. "I thought for sure somewhat would have killed you by now."

"Wishful thinking, Mum?" I bow, just like Tess taught me. Always good to be respectful of one's elders. Especially if you want something from them.

"Get out, ungrateful, thieving, murdering runt!" She swipes with her broom.

I flit out of reach, ever so grateful my wings have grown enough to do that. "Mum, wait, please, before you kick me out on my own again; I need to know how to track the magical trail of an artifact of power."

"If you don't know how to do that by now, you are even more useless than when you left the first time." Another swat with the broom.

Ow! That hurt. And it, sniff, cost me the wart on the tip of my tail!

I hope it was the broom that took it off and not the flea. Too, too humiliating to lose it to a flea.

Chapter 24

The Desert Inn opened in 1950 with a color scheme of Bermuda pink and emerald green that carried onto the golf course with green grass and pink flags.

*M*ICKEY LED THE WAY out of Lady Lucia's apartment, hastening down the green marble steps with reckless speed.

Some of his need to be away from this place, and our hostess, infected me.

Before I could comment on the ring, or the portrait for that matter, Gollum grabbed my arm and ushered me down the sweeping stairway. "Watch your step," he said quietly. "The marble may be slick."

I braced myself between him and the banister. Not until I tried to take the first step down on my right leg, did I realize how tired and aching that strained muscle had become.

Lady Lucia remained at the top, watching us through narrowed and speculative eyes.

I used my limping pace to give me time to survey as much of the area as possible, wondering why a formal entrance to the suite above opened into the bedrooms, and the back way gave access to the salon.

"The place is bass-ackwards," I muttered when we finally reached a fenced-in covered patio at the side of the building. Pale flagstones floored the area. Terra cotta tubs overflowed with flowering vines. A single circular table and lounge chair were placed at the center with an umbrella for additional shade. A four-foot-high split log fence and a hedge of some spiky desert plant offered scant separation from the rest of the resort. From the chair, one could watch the waterfall cascade down the artificial volcano at the center of the oddly shaped pool. Ah, Lady Lucia's private garden, protected from the desert sun.

Mickey held open a rough plank gate reminiscent of a rustic ranch. His feet twitched, and his hands clenched spasmodically.

Without saying a word, we followed a meandering path through the oasis-styled gardens, along back corridors of the hotel, with more than a few hints of Morocco in the décor—including some flamingo pink and desert green decorative tiles, to the front porte cochére. No telling who was listening.

A black, full-sized Hummer awaited us, the driver already secreted behind the wheel. Thank the Goddess it wasn't the hearse. I wasn't in the mood for mind games.

I crammed myself in the middle of the back seat, with Gollum on the right, stretching his long legs, and Mickey on my left, huddled in on himself, still fidgeting nervously. No discreet panel separating us from the front seat this time. None of us seemed inclined to talk anyway.

My leg wanted to curl up, but it cramped when I pulled my feet onto the seat and wrapped my arms about my legs. So I stretched them out again and lolled my head back against the seat. Eyes closed, I blanked the drive through the desert night, thinking furiously.

The rings. Donovan. Gregbaum. Lady Lucia. All connected. Maybe Sancroix and his nephew, too. All wanting different and conflicting things from me.

Danger lurked in following any course of action. How could I decide until I had more information?

I trusted Gollum to research Lady Lucia, now that we had a vital clue. As the new owner of the Dragon and St. George, she had to have a corporate registry somewhere, funding, investors, something.

Only I could approach Donovan and find out about that ring.

Could I trust Mickey to investigate the faery dancers and the curse upon them?

At last we stopped next to Mickey's taxi in the underground parking lot.

"What time is it?" I asked, coming out of my meditation with nothing resolved. "There aren't any clocks anywhere in this town."

"Past midnight," Gollum said, checking his illuminated watch with more dials and functions than I could count.

Eighteen minutes past, Scrap corrected him. He'd popped out for a few moments on the long ride home. Now he was back.

"Tonight's show is over. I need to talk to those dancers," I mumbled.

"Not tonight." Gollum forcefully steered me into the taxi. "You are in no shape to defend yourself."

Enough said. I knew he was right.

Mickey still hadn't said a word. He expertly pulled into the nighttime traffic on the Strip, no less dense than at noon. The Strip didn't need noon sunshine. Enough neon flashed, blinked, and scrolled to keep it bright twenty-four/seven.

"Mickey, what do you know about magic?"

"Not enough," he muttered. "I know faery magic. I do not know Gregbaum's. I sensed the spell around the building. I can go in and out. It must contain only the lost dancers. I came on the scene later and so it does not stretch to me, or any other faery. Only the dancers."

"Can you find out what kind of spell he's used?" I leaned forward and squeezed his shoulder, hoping to offer comfort and support.

He flinched away from my touch, as if it burned his skin through his light shirt.

"I have to. You may go home now, Lady Tess. I know what I must do. You cannot help me." His words came out tight and strained.

"Mickey, you bound me to the mission. My vows to my Sisterhood bind me to the mission. I'm not leaving."

"We'll talk about this tomorrow, when we've all had a chance to rest and do some research. Do you understand, Mickey?" Gollum asked in his sternest school-teacher voice. "You will do nothing without consulting us. We have skills and knowledge you don't."

Mickey seemed to collapse in on himself, as if only his anger, or his fear, had kept him upright. "I understand. I will wait to rescue my people until I talk to you."

He paused then looked at me through the mirror, engaging my gaze. "Lady Tess, I am not sorry I wove magic around your mother to help her sing. I needed you to feel safe leaving her alone to help me. I saw you at the airport. I recognized your scar and your imp. I watched you take the shuttle to The Crown Jewels and followed."

"You may have done Mom a tremendous favor, Mickey. Don't apologize for that. I need to see the show again," I said decisively. "We'll use Lady Lucia's letter to get us in to the special performance tomorrow afternoon. There are clues there. I know it."

You bet there are! The whole show is a road map, Scrap added solemnly. *I wish it led somewhere else.*

"If I may, I would like to accompany you, Lady Tess. I may recognize something you do not."

"We'll all go. But for now, we rest. Mickey, pick us up tomorrow at two thirty." Gollum put an end to any arguments at the same moment Mickey drew his cab to a stop outside The Crown Jewels.

"Scrap, keep an eye on Mickey. Make sure he doesn't do anything stupid," Tess whispered as soon as she was out of the taxi.

Babe, you're hurt, I can't . . .

"I'm going to bed. You can scout around until I fall out of bed ten minutes before my first conference session in the morning."

Gotcha, babe. Rest, secure in the knowledge . . .

"Yadda, yadda, yadda. Get going. Mickey's already three blocks away and burning rubber."

I mark Mickey with an anchor that leads back to the chat room. He won't get far without me knowing.

I can get from where I'm going back to Mickey or over to Tess and they won't know how long I've really been gone.

Time, after all, is just another dimension. If you know how to use it. And, thanks to my babe and her adventures, I'm getting better and better at manipulating that dimension.

There are nuances to the chat room not everyone knows. Imps learn some of them at their mum's knee.

Me, I had to listen to other imps whispering in corners when they thought I wasn't around.

Being only a scrap of an imp, I wasn't supposed to survive my first fifty years. I did. My siblings attacked me for my audacity.

I survived that, too. Though some of them didn't. Mum has never forgiven me. I don't care. I have never forgiven them.

Survival of the fittest. I may not be the biggest imp ever, or the most dignified. But I'm clever, and because of my small size, I can get in and out of places unseen and unheard that my bigger comrades overlook.

Like the side corridor off the chat room. It's hard to see. Harder to fit through. Only those flea demons can follow me. Well maybe a j'appel dragon can. They are only palm-sized until you call their true name. Then they grow and grow and grow to fill the chat room with smelly scales and sulfur-ridden breath.

Easy to avoid using a j'appel dragon's real name, you think? Not if they change it every hour. Not if they choose names like "Because" or "Help" as their true name.

Anyway, they avoid this tiny little corridor because if they suddenly grow to full size in there, they'll suffocate or get squeezed to death.

I skip along the dimensionless white that stretches into infinity. Good idea to trail my fingers along one wall, just to keep my bearings. Easy to get lost in here without landmarks. Even for an imp.

Ah, there, that's what I need. That magic ring Gregbaum wears so proudly bulges through the walls like the inside of a pimple. I told you it isn't firmly set in any one dimension. Therefore, part of it is always in the chat room.

Mum said I should know how to track it. I guess this is the right place. I stand on tiptoe and peer at the gold filigree and that beautiful, perfect diamond with just a hint of yellow in the coloration, or maybe a reflection of the gold setting. I could get lost in that stone, staring into its depths, seeing the tiny black spot in the middle that is an echo of the blackness in my own soul.

Back out. Back out. Can't afford to do that. If I look too closely, I might regret some of the things I've done in order to stay alive and grow big enough to companion my dahling Tess.

I memorize every twist and scroll and how the metal cradles the stone. Now I know I can pick this ring out anywhere. So all I have to do is track it back in time.

Where is the energy signature? An object this powerful always wants to go back to its origins. Just like me. I always want to go back to Mum even when she hates me.

A wisp of smoke, almost clear, hard to see except for that very faint yellow tinge. Now I've got it. Follow the trail. Don't take any side turns. Just follow it back, back, back, nearly back to the beginning of time.

At least to the beginning of Faery.

Chapter 25

Casino floor layouts deliberately route customers past slot machines on the way to showrooms, restaurants, and other attractions.

REST WAS NOT in the cards, or the dice, or the slots, for me that night. At least not yet.

Mom finished another torch song on a lingering, wistful note, just as we walked into the casino. (We had to go through the casino to get anywhere in the hotel.)

"Ladies and gentlemen, let me introduce you to my daughter, a better nightingale than me!" she crooned into her mike.

The packed audience erupted in applause.

"Come up here, Tess, and join me in a song," Mom invited. She wore emerald green that sparkled and draped her full figure admirably. I don't think it was all faery glamour. My mom showed through, a bright, vibrant woman who'd finally found fulfillment of a youthful dream.

If I wasn't mistaken, she'd lost more than a few pounds since the fiasco of her brief marriage to Donovan's foster father. Either that or she wore a tightly laced corset that would make Lady Lucia's look baggy.

I went limp inside, too tired to sing, too tired to fight

my mom. In her current enthusiasm, I'd not best her with arguments. Faster to give in, sing one song, and retreat.

But when I stood beside my mother, she handed me the mike and withdrew.

What to sing?

I looked to the lanky man with ebony skin and long black hair slicked into a tight ponytail who sat at an electric keyboard with an impressive array of controls.

Then it came to me. I knew precisely the song that fit my mood and the situation. I'd first heard Gwen Knighten perform her whimsical song solo with a harp at a science fiction convention. She kept us laughing and crying at the same time.

"Vamp along with something light and harpish," I told the musician quietly, giving him the rhythm and key. "This piece is called 'My Fairytale.' It sort of says it all."

> *"Oh, the day is warm, and sunlight is streaming*
> *Through slotted windows on the battlements today*
> *And the stone walls are holding so fast*
> *But they always seem sturdy when you are away.*
> *The spring flags are flying, the merry maidens dance,*
> *The portents in magicland point to romance,*
> *And it was a day like today, not so very long ago,*
> *I lived in this castle, and you were my beau.*
> *Or was that the time when I lived in the forest,*
> *And you met me halfway to grandmother's place?*
> *I forget, I forget; it all runs together,*
> *But open the storybook, put on that face."*

As I started in on the chorus, I spotted Donovan off to the side of the room. He was trying to blend in with a pillar, but my heart could find him anywhere. This song was as much for him as it was for me, or my mom, or all of us together.

> *"Take me in, yes, I'll be your victim,*
> *I'll be the matchgirl, and you be the wind.*
> *Take me in, yes, I'll be your victim,*
> *I'll be Red Riding Hood, you be the wolf.*

I'll be the girl who gets burned in the oven,
and you'll be the baker who serves me for pie.
I won't expect any boring old woodcutters
coming to save me at the end of the day—
In the end, yes, I'll be your victim
You'll be my frog and I won't be a princess.
In the end, no curtain, no laughter,
no pumpkin, no coachman, no happily ever after."

That got a round of laughter from the audience, including Gollum. It only earned a deep frown from Donovan. He wasn't about to forgive me. I didn't know how I
was going to approach him with questions about the ring.
But I had to. If not tonight, then tomorrow.

"Oh, the woods are deep, and yet it's still sunny,
The birds are all singing along with me now
As I walk on my way—don't know where I'm going,
But wherever it is, I'll end up villain-chow.
Oh, what's that behind me, that scurry, that scamper,
That rustle of movement just under the trees?
It's a bird, it's a pigeon, it's eating my breadcrumbs
Don't know my way home; now I feel ill at ease.
Is this the one where you're the fox in the suitcoat
Who spellbinds me, then carves me up for a snack?
I don't know, I don't know; but these plots never vary,
So I'll skip on along while you plan your attack."

This time the audience joined me in the chorus—at
Gollum's prompting—just like a filk session at an SF
con. My mood brightened, and I added a little gusto to
the music.

"Oh, the night is dark, and my neck is aching:
The prince climbing up my hair is pulling too hard,
And I can't move an inch! This position is painful,
But I don't want my head to be down in the yard.
When you reach the window, your boots on the
      stonework,
You lean up to kiss me, I'm gasping for air,

*And you shake your head sharply, say, 'Sorry, wrong
    tower,'*
Then slide down while pulling out half of my hair.
I think you're supposed to be charming and handsome,
I think I'm supposed to be winsome and sweet,
But it all gets confusing, and right now I'm cursing—
I can't get these glass slippers onto my feet."

This time I ventured out among the audience, belting the chorus, and getting them to clap along with me in rhythm. Using the song as a cover, I wound my way to where Donovan still clung to his pillar. His forlorn expression almost tugged at my heartstrings.

Almost.

I knew some of the blackness deep inside him. He wouldn't hurt for long. I was sure he'd already lined up a bedmate for tonight.

"I need to talk to you," I whispered while catching my breath for the next line."

"We have nothing to talk about." He tried turning his back on me.

Oh, how I longed to reach out and smooth the strain away from his well muscled shoulders.

"What about Lady Lucia's heirloom ring?"

I ambled back to the center of the room, still singing.

*"Now it's just before dawn, and you know I'm not
    sleeping,*
For you stuck that pea way down under my bed.
*I would never have said that I'd go through with this
    one*
*If that damned poisoned apple weren't clouding my
    head.*
Oh, you'll be the spindle that pricks the girl's finger,
And I'll be asleep for the next hundred years,
And while you're out riding your horse on the wold,
I'm stuck here spinning this flax into gold.
*And when you struck me dumb and then made me
    knit sweaters*
Of nettles for seven boys turned into swans,

Oh, I thought I would kill you; I did, but I couldn't,
We both know that I fall for all of your cons."

One last round of the chorus as I returned to the stage, ready to hand the mike back to Mom and make my escape. I didn't need to worry about Donovan. I could feel him heading toward the elevators.

"Take me in, yes, I'll be your victim,
I'll be Red Riding Hood, you be the wolf."

Please, oh please, don't let that part of the story be true this time.

But Donovan wasn't waiting for me at the elevators, or at the door to my room.

I dialed his room and was told he had checked out.

Now what?

Um, Tess?

"Now what?" I snapped at Scrap.

I can't find Mickey.

What do you mean? You've got instant radar. You can find anything or anyone." Anxiety began burning up from my gut to my throat.

He's dropped off the radar. Fortitude can't find him either.

"Where did you see him last?"

Three blocks from here. He just—vanished.

I called Gollum's cell phone. "We have to find Mickey before he kills Gregbaum."

"Wait . . . what . . ." he stammered. I hadn't even given him a chance to say hello.

So I told him what Scrap reported. "If he kills Gregbaum, the curse will die with him. That's what Mickey's going to do. And he'll get killed in trying!"

"Ask Scrap if he can find Gregbaum."

"Good idea." I shouted into the ether.

Yeah, he's in his penthouse wining and dining. Looking for a new home for "Fairy Moon." Scrap yawned, sounding bored.

"Is Mickey with Gregbaum?" Gollum asked.

I relayed the question, hating the delays.

Nope. I checked that first thing Mickey went missing. I'm not stupid.

"The curse may not die with the magician," Gollum said. He yawned himself.

I loosed my own. This sleepiness was catching. Well, it was almost two in the morning.

"Mickey has to investigate the spell before he does anything," Gollum continued.

"Is he smart enough to calm down and take the time to do that?" I wouldn't. I'd have charged right in with blade swirling.

"Mickey knows a lot more about magic than we do."

"I'm not so sure ..." I heard a brief knock on the door. Before I could get up to answer it, Gollum let himself in with my spare keycard.

He folded his phone and spoke to me directly. "He's from Faery. He knows magic. He knows the limitations. Trust me, Tess. Mickey is not a fool."

"Scrap, where are the dancers?" If Mickey was going to try a rescue, he might just go there directly.

All tucked up in their little beds, fast asleep. A bit of a pause. *Tess, they've cried themselves to sleep. I've got to go in there and give them some hope.* He sounded as if he wanted to cry, too.

My heart nearly broke. I'd never known Scrap to care for anything so deeply, except for himself—and me.

"Stop him, Tess," Gollum shouted, looking up as if he might espy Scrap. "If the dancers perform as if they have hope, Gregbaum will get wise to us and change his spell."

Ooops! Scrap bounced out of the air into my lap with a whoosh and a thud. For half a heartbeat he took solid form.

"Damn, but you are heavy." I started to shove Scrap away when he faded to his normal insubstantial translucence.

Gollum stared gape-jawed at the space where Scrap appeared.

Sorry, babe. Rebounded off Gregbaum's protections.

"Must be a strong web of interdimensional weaving around the dancers' dormitory," Gollum mused.

"Wait, did you hear Scrap as well as see him?" A spell strong enough to do that really scared me.

"I just heard bits of his words. Enough to piece together what happened. Then he faded. We're up against some pretty powerful stuff here, Tess. We need help."

"What kind of help?" I thought I knew where he was headed with this and didn't like it. "MoonFeather?" My aunt was a witch of the Wicca variety and knew more about real magic than I wanted to admit.

Gollum shook his head. "Donovan. He's got connections in all kinds of strange places."

"Including to Lady Lucia *and* to Gregbaum."

Gollum's glasses slid to the end of his nose.

I ordered a bottle of single malt scotch from room service. The price made me blanch. "What about a blend?"

The waiter rattled off a list and their prices.

"I think we'll try the Muirhead." That scotch had a decent reputation and they used to sponsor a top notch bagpipe band.

"Ma'am, if price is your consideration, I've got a bottle of Sheep Dip I can't give away. I'll let you have the whole bottle for half the price of the Muirhead," the waiter said.

"Sold."

I'd heard stories about that scotch. Farmers in England used to deduct it from their taxes as necessary agricultural supplies.

"Let's hope it tastes better than its namesake."

Chapter 26

*Some of the best educated people in Las Vegas work
as bartenders. The tips are better than schoolteacher
salaries.*

IF TESS IS GOING TO SPEND TIME with Mr. Stinky
Man, I've got to get out of here. Might as well use the
time to my advantage.

I zip into the side corridor of the chat room, noting that
Mickey's beacon is blinking again. He's brooding in a tiny one-
room apartment. Okay to leave him for a while.

I stand in front of a window into the past. The beings flitting
about on the other side of the glass pane, or deep inside like a
TV, I can't tell for sure, are faeries. Or the distant ancestors of
them. I see subtle differences, more pointed ears, longer noses
that almost resemble animal snouts. And they are bigger.

They frown more, too. Not since WindScribe killed the last
king of the faeries and tried to loose a whole horde of full-
blooded demons on all the dimensions, has anyone, I mean
anyone, in living memory seen a faery frown. But here they
stand in a big circle around a forge. They have linked hands
to seal whatever is inside. No one escapes a circle of faery
magic.

A very large human smith pounds his hammer against an
anvil. He works a strip of gold thinner and thinner.

A dwarf, sitting at a tall bench beside the brightly burning hearth, chips away at a rock.

Bound in braided ropes of holly, mistletoe, and ivy sits an imp at the exact center of the circle. My heart reels in shock. The knots and twists in those ropes have turned three innocuous plants into imp's bane, the most dreaded form of punishment for my kind. At least the poor prisoner won't care what they do to him, until they do it. He's powerless, has no judgment, and cannot connect to those who love him. Worse of all, he can't duck into the chat room or through any portal to escape.

If you haven't guessed already, I've spent some time under the influence of imp's bane. Last autumn, when Sasquatch, masquerading as terrorists, kidnapped my Tess and filled their headquarters with imp's bane. I spent the entire time swinging from the rafters, making friends with a bat, and disconnected from Tess. If she hadn't discovered the purpose of the imp's bane and started burning it bit by bit, we would have died from the separation.

And I couldn't hop into the chat room for relief. The arcane knots anchored me in one dimension. Most beings can only get into one or two dimensions, if they can get beyond the demons in the chat room. Imps can go anywhere. We have to in order to do our jobs as Celestial Blades. We have to catalog as many demon forms we can. Can't fight them if you don't know what they are.

Then I noticed that this is no ordinary imp. He's big. The biggest imp I've ever seen. Which means he's old. And cranky. Imps change color to reflect their mood. Normally we're sort of gray-green, go blue with pleasure, purple with desire, yellow with laughter, green with curiosity. Vermilion just before we transform into a weapon.

This imp, beneath his deep orange anger—I'd be angry, too, with that much imp's bane coiled around me, and sick with it, too—is black. I have never seen a black imp before. His bat-wing ears are shaped wrong, too, more like pointy rat ears. And there's not a single wart to soften his ugliness.

The tap, tap, tap of the dwarf's tools changes to a softer, more hesitant rhythm.

I see the precious stone emerge from the rock. Little tiny

chips fly away, revealing the biggest diamond I've ever seen. A few more taps of the chisel and he begins shaping the jewel, adding facets—lots of them—polishing it.

By this time, the smith has done something to the gold to turn it into wire. He hands it off to a lady faery who wears a gold filigree crown. She shapes and twists the wire into a ring to match her crown.

Much chanting and dancing in circles. Then, finally, the diamond is ready to mate with the gold.

And a true mating it is. For the ring that is born of both gold and diamond becomes something more, something special.

I can't see what they are doing; they close ranks and block my view. But I can smell the magic. Strong magic. Not black and evil, but not entirely white and healing either. Something more sinister than normal Faery Blessings.

The faeries back away. The imp is gone. The ropes of imp's bane lie limp and withering on the bright green grass.

The faery queen holds the ring up for all to see, The dark flaw at the very center of the diamond is no imperfection. It is the imp, imprisoned forever. Forced to stare at his own black reflection for eternity. No flaw or crack in the diamond for the black imp to communicate with the outside world. The faery magic keeps him from opening a portal to the chat room.

He can only open a portal under the direction of the ring wearer. This ring will open the portal to Faery so we can send the dancers home.

Then Queenie slips the ring on the thumb of her left hand.

I nearly faint with shock.

There is only one ring. Not two, as we thought. The ring flexes to fit the hand of the wearer.

But if Gregbaum just got the ring, and Donovan had it only days ago, how did he get the dancers over to Earth?

I move on. More to learn. I just hope I can get back to Tess before she needs me. These windows in time distort my senses and I'm not certain when I was when I entered the chat room.

I filled the water glass from the bathroom with scotch and handed it to Gollum. "Drink it down, language guy."

He stared at the amber liquid. "A terrible waste of good scotch to just drink it."

"I know. But this is necessary. And not necessarily good scotch," I busied myself fishing a tiny digital recorder out of my computer bag. The memory chip was empty. I hadn't had a single idea for the novel to record since leaving Providence on Wednesday morning.

Gollum closed his eyes and drank. A grimace almost formed on his face. "Tastes like burned butterscotch filtered through Groundskeeper Willie's moth-eaten kilt." He took another gulp. "You aren't joining me?"

"You bet your sweet ass I am. I'm not wasting all of that water of life on your ability to speak in tongues when you're drunk." I poured myself a healthy belt and topped off his glass.

"What legend am I supposed to channel this time?" He settled into the armchair and put his big feet up on the side of the bed. This could take some time.

Time I felt pressing close against my chest like a two-hundred-pound imp.

"I don't know what's going to come out of your subconscious or the ether. But last time you did this, you pointed us in the right direction based on local legends. Let's see what local spirits choose your brain as a vehicle to enlighten me." I sat cross-legged on the bed and stuffed pillows behind my back. Nope, the strained muscles in my thigh didn't like that. So I stretched out, my feet atop his ankles. A small connection. A familiar and comfortable connection.

The recorder sat on the table next to Gollum's left elbow. He took another deep swallow, grimaced at the burn, and turned on the gadget.

"If I have to guzzle alcohol, beer would go down easier." He took another belt. This time his face twisted only a little bit. He already grew a bit numb.

"Beer isn't strong enough. It would take too long." I sipped my own glass, respecting the miracle of decent whiskey as it should be. I don't know about filtering through a moth-eaten kilt, but I caught the burned butterscotch and the essence of heather in the blend. "And if you have to get stone-cold drunk, you might as well have the water of life." I saluted him with my glass.

He refilled his to the brim.

"And *if* I recite some obscure legend in an ancient and unspeakable tongue, who will translate for you while I sleep off the drunk? Presuming, of course, I could figure it out."

"I have my sources. Now drink up. It's getting late, and I'd like to get a little sleep tonight."

He downed his glass. His hands shook as he reached for the bottle. I took it from him and poured a steady stream. No sense in slopping good whiskey on the table.

One more glassful—I was still on my first, and he tipped his head back. His eyes crossed and he smiled while his glasses slipped all the way off his hawk nose into his lap.

"Did I ever tell you how much I love you, Tess?" he mumbled.

"Um ... not in so many words." What had I done to him? This was not my Gollum. But maybe it was. I took a long drink of my scotch. A new set of possibilities opened in my liquor-loosened brain.

What would it be like to have his long-fingered hands caress me with intimate care.

Shivers of delight ran up and down my spine, further numbing my mind.

Before I could pursue those thoughts, Gollum mumbled something I couldn't understand.

Anxiously, I leaned forward and held the recorder close to his mouth. I had to catch every word and nuance.

Without warning, he sat up straight, planting his feet firmly on the floor. I had to roll for balance as he dislodged my feet. His empty glass dangled from his hand.

His abrupt movement knocked the recorder out of

my hand. He kept talking. Nonsense syllables to my ear.
But I'm not a linguist.

"Shit! I hope we get all this." I fumbled around on
the floor until I found the recorder under the lion's claw
table leg support. Carefully I positioned it close to his
mouth.

He stopped talking. His head rolled to the side, and
he let out a snore.

Chapter 27

The highest recorded dealer tip in Las Vegas was $120,000 out of a $2 million pot.

I LEFT GOLLUM sprawled on the armchair, head lolling, drunken snores erupting from his mouth. I paused a moment to look back at him fondly.

Seemed like I was always postponing things with Gollum. Always the press of time on our missions when our emotions surged to the surface. On a normal day we walked politely around each other, careful not to tread on each other's toes or turf.

With the digital recorder in hand, I sought the bartender in the quiet bar on the opposite side of the lobby from the lounge. He looked up from polishing the bar as I entered.

Only one patron here at this late hour. The noise from the casino had dulled but kept going. With its convention-oriented customer base, this hotel did slow down in the wee small hours of the morning, unlike the bigger hotels closer to the Strip.

"I'm just going off shift, ma'am. My replacement will serve you in a moment." He looked tired, as if his night had been as long and fraught with emergencies as mine.

"Actually, I need to talk to you."

His eyebrows perked up, and he lost some of the look of fatigue.

"You said the other night that only local Native Americans venture into the Valley of Fire at night when they are on vision quest . . ."

"Yes," he replied slowly. A wall grew up between us, almost visible in the way his face lost all animation and his gaze found other places to rest away from me.

"I'm guessing you are at least part Native American."

He nodded.

"Do you speak or understand any of the local dialects?"

The relief bartender sidled into place beside him. "What can I get you ma'am?" she asked politely.

"We're just leaving. Together," my bartender said. He stashed his polishing towel and slid beneath a bar that blocked an opening between patrons and servers. "I'm not fluent. But I can at least recognize if it's Modoc or Paiute."

"Can you listen to a recording? It may be a local dialect or possibly something older." I held up the digital gadget.

He took it from me as he led me to a bench seat behind a potted palm in the lobby. "I'm not supposed to fraternize with customers, so let's keep this short and discreet." He looked around, barely acknowledging the sleepy desk clerks.

He turned on the recorder. Gollum's voice came out sounding strangely soft and lilting.

"I'm missing part of it," my bartender shook his head. Then he listened again.

"Please. This could be very important."

"It's very old. The language my great-grandfather used when he told the ancient legends of my people. He was the last full-blooded Paiute in my family."

"Do you recognize it?"

"Yeah. Even with the missing part in the middle."

I waited expectantly.

"You aren't a member of the tribe. You have no right to be in the places where you might have heard this."

"Believe me. I came by it legitimately. It's important."

"I'm guessing you aren't the normal Las Vegas tourist out for a weekend of fun and games."

"No, I'm not. I have connections in places you would not believe. Spiritual places." Dared I say more?

He nodded. "I won't give you my name, and I won't ask yours. This is between Warriors, though I've never met your kind before."

I nodded agreement. "I'll not repeat this to anyone who doesn't absolutely have to know in order to save their lives."

"Okay. It's a kind of riddle. I don't know the meaning. Only that it's connected to the vision quest my great-grandfather had when he became a man." He paused and gulped. "It translates loosely—very loosely as there are no modern equivalent words to a lot of it."

"Does it makes sense in English?" It wouldn't do me a lot of good if it only made sense in archaic Paiute.

"Maybe to you. It says: The moon awakes from a little sleep. It becomes a key held in the arm of a . . . a Guardian who is also a monster. That word is really not right, but it's the closest I can come."

"What does this moon key open?" A portal. It had to be a clue to a portal.

"It opens a path to twilight lands of peace and plenty, lands that a Warrior may glimpse but never enter. Only one Warrior will rise above the ties that bind him to this earth to walk between." He sat back and closed his eyes. The look of exhaustion returned, as if he'd channeled that bit of information instead of repeating a memory.

"Anything else?"

"Yeah. This recording cuts off before the end. My great-grandfather said that this key only works once in ten lifetimes."

I touched his hand briefly in thanks, and sympathy. "This was your vision quest, too, wasn't it."

"Yeah. Does it mean anything to you?"

"Not yet. But it will. The Powers that Be will let me know when I need to know."

"The Powers That Be?" he mused more than asked. "Do you fight alongside Breven Sancroix?"

Something in his guarded expression made me wary. "We trained in the same tradition, but I have never fought beside him."

"My instincts tell me that he is not to be trusted." He kept his eyes lowered to the recorder in his hands.

"Even though his nephew owns this hotel?"

"Especially because his nephew owns this hotel. He did not come by the majority shares honestly. He . . . he is not normal. His . . . you white folks call it an aura . . . his aura is not fully human."

He only confirmed my suspicions.

My informant lowered his voice further. "He doesn't talk about it, but I believe there is another stockholder. One who does not walk before twilight."

Abruptly, he dropped the recorder into my lap and left without looking back."

Gollum had left my room by the time I returned. I noticed he'd taken four bottles of water from the case in the bathroom. The best hangover remedy I've discovered is lots of cool clear water and as many aspirin as my tummy will handle, followed by orange juice or tomato juice in the morning.

As enticing as my bed looked, I couldn't rest yet. Still one more chore.

I tried Donovan's cell phone with another shot of scotch courage in me—the last of the bottle.

"What?" he growled.

"Sorry if I woke you. We need to talk."

"I have nothing to say to you. You've made it quite clear what you think of me."

"Don't hang up," I begged hastily. "Please. It's about the ring." I let that hang between us a moment, hoping he'd think I meant a possible engagement so he'd pause long enough to let me continue.

"What about it?"

"I saw the same ring in Lady Lucia's wedding portrait." I still hadn't convinced myself she really was a vampire and had lived during the Napoleonic Wars.

"You sure it's the same ring?" He sounded interested. Or suspicious.

"Pretty sure. It looked a lot like Gregbaum's pinky ring."

"You still at the hotel?" he asked.

I heard a rustle of clothing in the background and tried hard to rid my mind of the image of Donovan in the nude. Such a beautiful man on the outside. Why couldn't he be as beautiful on the inside? Or at least trustworthy where my heart was concerned.

"In my room."

"Alone? You don't need to answer that. The nerd is there, too. Harder to separate you from him than it is from that imp of yours."

I didn't want to think about those implications. "Actually, I am alone."

Seconds later Donovan tapped at my door.

"You didn't check out of the hotel after all," I greeted him. "You just bribed the front desk to divert your calls."

"Nice to see you too, Tess." He bent to kiss my cheek as he pushed past me into the room. "What's this all about, and why do you have anything to do with Lady Lucia? She's more dangerous to you than you can imagine."

I swallowed my defensiveness. As long as Donovan had information I needed, I couldn't let my emotions lead us into another fight.

"Lady Lucia summoned us."

"Not good." Donovan took Gollum's place in the armchair. "Start at the beginning," he ordered me.

"You already know the part about the flowers and the tickets to 'Fairy Moon.' "

"But not why she sent them." I suspected a lie there. He knew, or at least knew part of it. I could tell by the narrowing of his pupils. "Talk, Tess."

My back bristled at his orders. I wanted to slap him.

Or kiss him. I didn't know which. So I stood with my back to him and stared out at the lights of Las Vegas. After too many long moments I told him everything, from the beginning, from my first encounter with the wereweasel to Mickey disappearing.

"He's gone back to Faery for more information," Donovan muttered.

"Scrap says the entrance to Faery from the chat room is closed."

"Then how are you supposed to get the dancers back home?"

"Apparently there's a rogue portal in the Valley of Fire. Gregbaum's goons are guarding it. Lady Lucia thinks I can find it." And the nameless bartender had given me clues if I only knew how to follow them.

"You may be the only *human* who can find it," Donovan mused. He stared longingly at the empty bottle of scotch.

"Are you implying that Gregbaum isn't human?" I shuddered. Kajiri demons could transform into a human body in this dimension. Midori, or full-blood demons, could only shape-change in their home dimension.

"I didn't think Gregbaum was Kajiri, but from the way you describe him, he might be," Donovan mused. "How else does he have the strength to cast true magic?"

"What's his other half?"

Donovan shrugged.

"What about the ring?" I asked. "Does it have any special significance?"

"According to Tuscan legends, the Continelli family are magicians. But that talent died out around the time of Lady Lucia's 'death,' " Donovan said. "Perhaps the ring gave them the powers, and she took it with her when she um . . . left."

"Lady Lucia died. The family castle was burned to the ground in 1818, the entire family trapped inside. This lady is a fraud," I insisted.

"Are you sure about that, Tess?" Donovan asked. "Did they ever find *all* the bodies?"

"What do you know?" I rounded on him.

"Too much and not enough."

"Where'd you get the ring, Donovan? Why'd you choose that ring to propose to me with?"

"Marry me, and I'll tell you all I know." Donovan fixed me with a steady glare, daring me to refuse.

"You cheating bastard, that's blackmail!" I suppressed the excitement that warred with my anger.

Now what did I do?

Chapter 28

The Strip became the nickname of Las Vegas Boulevard because all the glitzy neon signs reminded a casino owner of Sunset Boulevard, also known as Sunset Strip.

"DON'T DO IT, TESS. Don't give in. I can tell you want the ring. It calls to you. You lust after it more than you lust after Mr. Stinky. And that is saying a lot." I call to her from my perch outside her door. I got back from my investigations just in time.

I can tell the ring must come to my Tess; if for no other reason than she could help me free the trapped imp from his diamond prison.

His fate scares me more than Mum does. I can't let him stay there any longer than necessary.

"Scrap, is the ring my next artifact of power?" she asks on a tight mental connection that Donovan will never intercept.

"Maybe, babe," I hedge. "Maybe not. Too soon to tell."

But I know. I know faery magic will make it fit her hand perfectly. I know it will safely guide her wherever she needs to go.

I don't know its history well enough to guess further. I only know it was meant for Tess.

But if she gives in to Donovan, he will be the death of me.

When I die, Tess dies.

I cannot let that happen. But how can I protect her when Donovan's presence pushes me away from my babe with a stronger spell than the protective web around the faery dancers?

I must find a way to separate Tess from Donovan. Maybe Lady Lucia can help. She wants the ring, too. She seems to favor Tess.

Hmmmm, I wonder why.

"If I married you tonight, what's to keep me from filing for annulment on grounds of coercion the moment you tell me everything?" I asked. Try as I might, I couldn't keep my face and voice bland.

There was more to this ring business than either Donovan or Scrap wanted to tell me.

"You have too much honor bred into you, Tess, to ever do that to me. And if you did plan on that, I'd still have a night in which to persuade you that you and I are meant to be together." Donovan stood up in one smooth movement. A step brought him to my side.

He didn't touch me. Yet he was so close, his warmth enfolded me in an aura that blotted out the rest of the world. His breath on my neck tingled all the way to my toes. My body tensed in anticipation of something wild and wonderful.

"You're right. I won't go through another quicky marriage in a drive-by wedding chapel. When I marry again, I'll do it right, in a church, with flowers and music, and hundreds of guests and a huge reception that costs the earth."

I had to step away from him. My head already spun with desire. I needed all my strength of will to keep from wrapping my arms around him and kissing his socks off.

"You'll never find out what you need to know . . ."

"I'll just have to ask Lady Lucia."

"Tess, no. She's dangerous. Even if she weren't a vampire, she controls criminal elements in this town that

won't hesitate to eliminate those who get too curious."
He reached a hand out to me.

I skipped away, as fearful of him as I was of any horde
of demons.

Demons, I knew how to fight.

"The rules still stand. I can't marry you until I trust
you. I can't trust you until I know the truth about what
you are."

"I am a man."

"Now. What were you fifty years ago when you
'fell'?"

"How'd you . . . ?"

"King Scazzy, the prison warden of the universe, told
me that you fell. What did you fall from?" That oh-so-
real dream when I lay cradled in his arms rushed through
me faster than I/we fell in that dream.

Something . . .

And Dill. What did my deceased husband have to do
with his fall?

"A believer falls from grace," he offered, holding his hands out, palms up, in a universal gesture of
supplication.

"That sounds close, but not the truth. Maybe you
fell . . .

A flash of inspiration or memory or something very
like a vision rocked me. Maybe something from the
dream. The half-remembered sensation of wings falling
off, the debris of a solid body shattering, the rush of fear
and joy at the first sensation of movement after ever so
long sitting and watching. Ever watching, never doing.

Failing in my/his/our mission because I/he/we couldn't
move, could only sit and watch and let other powers
overwhelm me/him/us.

And then another memory. This one was really mine.
I had to grab hold of the entertainment cabinet to remain upright.

An autumnal rain in the middle of the high desert
of central Washington State. I stood in the central yard
of the Citadel surrounded by my Sisters of the Celestial Blade. A dedication ceremony for the newly re-

paired roof of the refectory. A line of copper-and-stone gargoyles on the edges, spouting streams of rain onto carefully placed plant groupings. One missing gargoyle failed to channel water off the roof. Instead, the empty place dumped a river of water onto Sister Gert's head. The rest of the Sisterhood had to suppress our giggles. Even then, three years ago, Sister Gert barely held on to the reins of leadership.

The broken gargoyle had been a bat.

The second time I'd seen Donovan, before we officially met, he'd been with a family group at a convention. All of them dressed very realistically as bats.

I shuddered in revulsion. Anything but a bat.

Donovan's foster father, my short-lived stepfather, had been a Damiri demon who took bat form.

Donovan had told me once that he was given to Darren for fostering because of a resemblance.

Dear Goddess, anything but a bat.

"Gargoyles are more than decorative rain spouts," I whispered.

Donovan blanched.

That told me all I needed to know.

"Which cathedral did you fall from?" I asked in fascinated horror.

"In a strange coincidence, Lincoln Cathedral, the home of the iconic depiction of all imps. I'll have to take you there sometime to show you the statue of Scrap's distant ancestor."

"Gargoyles are supposed to repel evil spirits. But you came to sympathize with them. You let them overwhelm you and invade a vital place!"

"I didn't consciously allow enemies into a sacred place. I was too young and inexperienced when I took the job. Gargoyles don't grow and change and learn after they assume a solid body."

"Is that why you are so dedicated to providing the Kajiri with a homeland? Because you sympathize with them, want to be one of them?" I really shuddered then. My teeth chattered with the ice that spread from my belly outward.

"No. I have other reasons for providing refuge to Kajiri."

"A refuge? A place where they can take their natural forms without prejudice. A place where they can eat what they need to sustain their lives—including human blood."

Blood drained from my head. Now I had to sit down. I wrapped my arms around myself and rocked back and forth on the edge of the bed.

How could I ever have thought I could have a future with this man?

How could I have ever let him touch me?

"You fell, all right. Fell from a noble calling, from honor and dignity. You have betrayed the very purpose of your creation! You have defiled your mission in life."

"I was ugly and reviled. Just like the ones I was supposed to banish."

"So the Powers That Be gave you physical beauty to teach you that there are things more important." I shifted so I didn't have to look at him. "How does Dill fit into this? I shared your dream of falling, only to be caught by Dillwyn Bailey Cooper."

"You shared my dream? Do you know how rare that is? How special? Doesn't that tell you that we belong together?"

"Answer my question, Donovan."

He sighed and ran his hands through his hair. The braid loosened and softened the lines around his face. I had to look away or get caught in his mesmerizing trap again.

"Dill was there, an innocent who observed my fall, because he was attuned to changes in atmosphere and dimensional distortions. He transformed and rose up through a natural surrounding into a well of souls to catch me before I crashed. He sheltered me; gave me my first lessons in what it's like to be human. He and his family wanted desperately to foster me. But Darren Estevez got to the Powers That Be first. He convinced them that his stern chastisement was a better education for me than love and nurture."

I gasped and thought my heart would break. We'd waltzed all around the issue of Dill for months. I'd suspected his Kajiri origins but never had them confirmed. I still held out hope that this was just one more lie of Donovan's. That hope was mighty thin and fragile at this moment.

"Were ... were you with Darren when he started the fire in our motel room that killed Dill? You owned the motel and profited from over-insurance." I knew Darren was guilty. Scrap had helped me travel through time to relive those awful moments. I'd watched Darren pull Dill back into the heart of the fire and knock him unconscious just as he was about to escape. But I couldn't identify Darren's shadowy companion.

If Donovan had been involved, I'd kill him right here and now. With or without Scrap's help.

"No. I was not a part of that conspiracy. Dill chose that motel because he knew I owned it. He wanted to spend some time with me before moving permanently to Cape Cod with you. Darren followed him there without my knowledge or consent."

I didn't believe him.

"Tess, I loved Dill like a brother. He and his family were the only bright spots in my life. Their love and friendship, even after Darren took me, gave me the courage to continue living; the courage to want to live as a human rather than a demon."

"Dill denied his demon ancestry," I said, as much to convince myself as Donovan. "He moved to Cape Cod with me to get away from his family, away from everything they stood for. Why can't you honor that part of his memory?"

"Because I watched him get physically ill, feverish, and aching in every joint when he refused to transform. Kajiri need to change on the night of the waxing quarter moon. It's a natural and necessary biological imperative with them if they have a demon ancestor within ten generations. But Dill wouldn't do it. He never felt safe doing it. He loved being human and loving a human woman. You. I want to build a sanctuary for mixed-blood de-

mons so they don't have to make themselves ill denying who and what they truly are. Even the ones whose
demon ancestry is so diluted they are barely aware of it.
They *need* what I can give them."

"Dill risked everything to catch you in your fall."

"Out in the deep forest of Mount Hood. He was
backpacking in the wilderness, collecting rock samples.
No one around for miles. He could briefly transform and
save me, or watch me die. He risked transformation."

The lights of Las Vegas blurred as I blinked away
tears. That was my Dill. He took a small risk to save a
stranger. He took a much bigger risk to save me during
that fire.

"Tess, don't shut me out." Donovan knelt in front of
me. He tried to take my hands.

I slapped him away.

"Go," I croaked.

"I suppose you're going to call Van der Hoyden-
Smythe to comfort you in this new knowledge," he
sneered.

"Just go."

I rocked and rocked some more, trapped in my own
revulsion of him.

I barely heard the door snick closed behind him.

My mom wasn't there to help me through the tears.

Shaking with the knowledge of the power within the ring, and
the horror of trapping an imp inside it for all time, I sneak
back to the chat room.

There is a blackness within me. I could so easily have
shared a similar fate with the black imp.

TRAPPED, held hostage, no way out. Forced to face his
crimes day in and day out without respite.

With that much imp's bane in his system, and the magic of
the diamond holding it in him, he'd probably forgotten how to
open a portal even if he broke through. He has to be directed
by the wearer of the ring.

If I had not found Tess and guided her to the Citadel, the one place that could save us both, I would have been banished from impkind, maybe given to the faeries so they could trap me, too.

I saved Tess from grief at the untimely death (murder) of her beloved husband Dill. Her anguish bordered on suicide.

She saved me from punishment for doing what I had to do to survive. According to imp law, I had no right to survive.

I probe deeper into the side corridor of the chat room.

The next window the ring takes me to is Earth. Medieval France to be specific. Another blacksmith. But this is no ordinary blacksmith. He plays with metal combinations and chemical formulae, seeking the Philosopher's Stone—that which will turn iron into gold, that which will answer all the questions of the Universe. Had he taken the route of a cleric and book learning, they'd have called him an alchemist.

By either name, he seeks to remove impurities from the ordinary to make it divine.

But he does not believe in the Church's teaching. He believes he can find God within iron and turn it to gold.

At this time and place, faith and religion are not separated. So they call him Noncoiré, the unbeliever.

I know all this the moment I see him. His blood sings with the essence of Tess. I read him as well as I read my dahling.

What is this? He gathers arcane herbs in the woodland, seeking poisons that will eat away at the metal, alter it, purify it, force it to transmute. In his primitive learning he believes that gold is pure. Iron is not. The concept of elements (the periodic table kind, not Earth, Air, Fire, and Water) has not surfaced.

His cat—a black male of course—that has become his familiar, stalks insects, tiny lizards, and mice. It bounds back to him with each new treasure. Monsieur Noncoiré exclaims with pleasure and caresses the cat with long and firm strokes.

I hate that cat already. I know it will do something awful. I just know it. Cats are only capable of inflicting horrible torture on other beings. And they purr while they do it.

But this is no ordinary woodland. The colors are a little too bright. Outlines and images just a bit too well defined.

I smell Faery.

Sure enough, just as this blacksmith yanks a mandrake out of the dirt by its roots, the plant screams. The preternatural screech obscures the sound of a faery popping into this dimension.

I don't need to hear it. I can smell it. Like cinnamon and lavender and warm comfort.

The cat smells it also and pounces. It comes up with a tiny white-and-gold faery in its mouth.

"Now, now, Balthazar," the man says in his ancient French. "Let the poor beastie go. You won't like the taste of him."

Gently, he pries the cat's mouth open and catches the wounded faery as it tumbles free.

"Well, well, well, what do we have here?"

"You have a king of the faeries, and I command you to release me!" the imperious little squirt says. He makes a big show of straightening his expensive clothes. They look a bit ragged and slimy from the ravages of the cat's mouth.

"I could let you go, inside my hungry cat."

"No, no, no. You don't want to do that." Kingy sounds scared. He's probably new to the job and hasn't learned how to outsmart a cat. (It ain't easy, friend.)

"Or I could let you go where you can get safely back to your own home before the cat nabs you."

Ah, Noncoiré is smart, or he's had dealings with faeries before. He knows how to bargain with them.

"I'd prefer the latter, sir." Kingy sounds scared.

"But my cat is hungry and I've naught to feed him. Except you."

The cat looks very sleek and well fed to me. Good thing there is a barrier of time between it and me, or I'd be sneezing my tail off by now. Funny how well-fed cats give off more allergens than skinny, stinky, mangy ones. At least for imps.

"Um . . . I could give you something valuable. You could sell it to *buy* food for the monster."

"Well, that would be nice. But even the village idiot knows that faery gold turns to dross the moment it leaves faery hands. No, no, I'd better just feed you to the cat."

"I have something else. Something more valuable than all the gold in France." Kingy is desperate now.

"And what would that be? I'll have to see it, hold it, and know it's not going to disappear before I can let you go."

Kingy frowns and drops his head. Then slowly he draws a ring from his finger and drops it into Noncoiré's hand. It grows to human size as it falls, landing solidly against the palm.

The stone winks and scintillates in the dappled sunshine. I hear a tiny crack in the Universe. The transfer of ownership of the ring has created a flaw in the diamond. A bit of the black imp's essence sends out a greedy probe.

Noncoiré gasps and opens his palm a bit to get a better look. A cunning smile replaces his astonishment. The power within the ring calls to him. But he doesn't know how to use it.

The faery flits away—on a drunken path because his wings are a bit torn—then pops back into Faery a whisker's width away from the cat's nose. He's lost the ring, he can't go anywhere but home, and only by the portal he came in on.

Maybe he didn't know the power of the ring. A long time has passed since its making. I'm thinking Kingy thought it was a symbol of his authority, sort of like the crown. Just part of the regalia.

So now the ring is in human hands. And no one knows what it can do.

And then I hear something else, the tiniest of sounds. Like a crack in the Universe opening. Just a little one. But enough for me to hear the black imp's scream of mental anguish. I must save him.

Chapter 29

As of 2000, because of the buffet, Circus Circus serves more meals than any other hotel in the world, 13,000 per day.

AFTER DONOVAN LEFT, I made my way back to the quiet bar and drank three more Scotches. The alcohol barely made a dent in my inner pain and turmoil.

At some point I must have moved on autopilot to brush my teeth, change to a nightgown, and crawl into bed. Scrap nudged me awake in time to shower and gather my supplies for classes and workshops.

By the time I joined my fellow writers at the breakfast buffet, I'd recovered enough to smile and reply politely to random comments. Mostly, I was numb. Numb in body and mind. Not even a hangover.

Gollum showed up as I pushed my scrambled eggs and ham around the plate, pretending to eat. He pulled an extra chair up to the round table filled with eager conference attendees. He straddled it and grabbed my toast off my plate.

"I had a productive evening after I left you," he said quietly. "Answers to a bunch of queries. You find anything interesting?"

"Oh, are you a writer, too?" one of the perky and eager writers at the table gushed. I'd forgotten her name. She had a couple of short fiction credits and her entry in the critique workshop for a full-length fantasy novel showed promise.

"Only academic papers," Gollum replied seriously. "Very boring stuff. Mostly I do research for Tess."

This set off a discussion on the value of research to the writer. I let the conversation flow around me, still avoiding thinking, avoiding eating, avoiding the fact that sooner or later I'd have to face Donovan again.

"Would you check to see if any gargoyles broke or fell from Lincoln Cathedral about fifty years ago?" I whispered.

Gollum's eyebrows shot nearly to his hairline.

Miss Perky heard me. "Oooooh, are you going to have gargoyles in your next book?"

"Maybe the book after the current work in progress." I hadn't thought about it, but yes, I could work gargoyles into my post apocalyptic fantasy novels involving a version of the Sisterhood of the Celestial Blade Warriors.

My best writing happens when my life sucks. I work through my inner pain by pushing it all onto my characters. That way I can examine it from all sides, find a compromise, dismiss it, whatever I need to do. Yes, I needed to work some very nasty gargoyles into my fiction.

Feeling began to return to my mind and my body. Good feeling, a need to work and be active again.

Maybe it was the fourth cup of coffee.

"Gramps got a line on the ring," Gollum said. "Go do your classes. I'll meet you in the lobby at two." He pulled out his ever-present laptop and logged onto the Internet.

"Any word from Mickey?"

"Not yet. But I think he'll be on time. He really wants to see that show." He let out a low whistle and clicked through several links.

"What have you found?"

"No record of a gargoyle falling at Lincoln Cathedral."

"Hmm, so he told another lie."

"Who?"

"Donovan." I had to change the subject here and now before my table mates asked too many awkward questions. "Any legends about the Valley of Fire and vision quests show up on your radar?"

No, Tess. Don't do it. Don't even think about going there. Scrap jumped off his perch on top of my head and flew an agitated pattern from one light fixture to the next.

"Strangely enough, very little. Mostly academic explanations of the petroglyphs. Very PC and mundane. If there are local legends of a more spiritual nature, no one repeats them to outsiders," Gollum said, following his gargoyle links around the Internet.

"Keep looking." I shoved my chair back and collected my folders of papers.

"Mind if I finish your breakfast first?" Gollum asked, only half joking.

"Be my guest."

"Never known you to turn away from food before," he muttered, grabbing clean cutlery from an empty table.

I grumbled something and left him to my leavings.

A thought hit me square in the middle of my chest, strong enough to rob me of breath. Gollum deserved better.

His tongue loosened by alcohol, he'd confessed to loving me.

He deserved more of me than just friendship.

My first husband had died over three years ago, after a whirlwind courtship of four days and three months of marriage. I'd banished his ghost for good last month. Part of me knew I needed to move on. Part of me still felt attached to Dill.

A part of my heart had broken off last night when I sent Donovan packing. I felt betrayed; leery of trusting my heart again.

Was there anything left for Gollum? Could I give him, or any man, more than friendship right now?

I really needed to talk to my mom.

Strange, I'd never wanted to turn to her with my emotional problems when she hovered around me like an overprotective mother hen. For nearly two decades she'd tried to live her life through me. But now that she'd flown the coop to find a life of her own, the one person who'd understand my dilemma wasn't there. Talking to her by phone wasn't enough.

Junior showed up at my morning class. "Is It Love Or Just Sex" was about the very fine line dividing a sensuous romance from erotica, and keeping either from slipping into porn. If Junior did indeed want to write a romance involving the inner workings of Las Vegas, he might need this workshop.

I spent a lot of time emphasizing verbs and emotions. A couple of men in the group wanted more graphic details. I pointed out the difference between experiencing love and reading an engineering text. I had more than a few memories of my night with Donovan to remind me.

"Some people get off on observing from a distance," I said, toward the end of the two-hour period. That idea came from my visualization of Donovan as a hideous bat gargoyle sitting silently and watching the sordid details of life for eight hundred years.

"The modern reader of genre fiction," and Donovan too, "wants to experience the emotions as well as the sensations. If we just want anatomical details, we can get a vibrator and rent some porn."

Donovan had the experiencing sensations down pat. I doubted he had mastered allowing emotions into the equations. One or the other, but not both at the same time. His humanity was incomplete. He hadn't spent enough time with Dill.

Neither had I.

Feeling better about myself and a lot of other things from this weekend, I dismissed the class to their lunches.

Junior lingered behind, grabbing me as I passed him to leave the room. I stared at his tight grip on my upper arm with all of the disdain I could muster.

Scrap landed on top of my head, glowing hot pink. He blew smoke into Mr. Twitchy's face.

Belatedly, Junior removed his hand, wiping it on his slacks as if stained or soiled. Maybe just sweaty. He looked as nervous as ever.

Let me at him, Tess. Let me give him a taste of his own violence.

I muttered something.

Scrap faded, still pink, still grumbling, but less ready to transform.

"I've got a couple of chapters of my book ready for you to look over," Junior said.

"I never agreed . . ."

"Doesn't matter what you agreed to . . ."

"Junior, mind your manners," Mom said, coming up behind him.

Only Mom could make this guy think about anything but his own self. Yeah for Mom.

"No one invited you, demon whore."

Mom gasped and reached for her pearls, a talisman.

Scrap turned vermilion and stretched.

Before Junior finished the phrase, I had my hands around his throat and his back against the wall. I didn't need Scrap for this. I wanted to inflict violence myself.

His skin paled to near perfect sculpted marble, his ears elongated to a point and the slant of his eyes shifted. The exquisite beauty had twisted to something terrible, angry, vengeful, more frightening than Gregbaum's mutant faeries. And as with those blood-red goons in black leather, I caught an energy signature of wings.

Changeling, Scrap gasped.

An old legend. Faeries are near immortal and rarely have children of their own. But their desire to raise a child and experience the joy of seeing it grow and learn approaches desperation. So they will, upon occasion, substitute one of their own, shape-changed into an infant—for a human child.

I can taste his magic. He set the spell around the faery dancers!

And I bet he was extremely bitter about his exile from Faery. He had to have arranged the kidnapping of the dancers and the enlistment of the mutants. Gregbaum, the *mortal* magician with no talent was Junior's puppet and front man.

That was why he had a pass to the show for himself, Breven and ... and Sister Gert, the woman he *called* Mom.

As if he'd heard Scrap, Junior snapped back to normal mortal appearance.

"Apologize to my mother, you slimy worm," I said through gritted teeth. My mind spun with implications. He must be the shadow investor in the show.

"It's what she is," he whined. His eyes darted back and forth, lighted briefly above me on Scrap, then returned to face me with something akin to bravado.

"Despite your *opinion,* which I do not value at all, my mother brings a lot of customers into this establishment. You should at least respect the money she makes for you and keep your mouth shut!"

He gulped and I felt his Adam's apple bob beneath my hands.

"Now, are you going to apologize or do I squeeze the life out of your miserable hide."

This guy needs to go back to Faery, fast, Scrap decided. *Too bad the portal is closed. You and I could zip him through the chat room faster than he can think.*

"Genevieve signed a contract. I don't have to ..."

I squeezed harder until he barely breathed. "Her name is pronounced Jahn-vee-ev."

Couldn't do better myself, Scrap chortled. He blew more smoke, making Junior's breathing even more difficult.

"Tess, you can remember your manners as well. You, at least, had the advantage of a loving mother to beat some sense into you," Mom said mildly. Almost too much calm in her voice. If she'd been me, I'd start looking for a place to hide.

"His mother abandoned him to relatives when he was a baby," she continued. "That's no excuse I realize, but . . . no daughter of mine will stoop to his level of boorishness."

Now that was the mother I knew and loved. And respected.

"Remember, Junior, verbal abuse is grounds to invalidate that contract. Also grounds to sue you for your shares of stock in this hotel. I think about now that your silent partner would be more than happy to get rid of you." I eased up on my grip, but kept him pinned with my malevolent gaze.

I'm surprised a silent partner has put up with him this long.

"If you could just get me in to see Lady Lucia . . ."

"If she's your partner, why do *I* have to get you in to see her?"

"She stopped taking my calls months ago. She's trying to leverage me out."

"Then I'd think you'd bend over backward to be polite to my mother, the woman who is bringing in extra revenue and solidifying your position. And me, since Lady Lucia provided me with VIP tickets to sold-out 'Fairy Moon,' invited me to a private party, and *wants* me to see the show again."

I shook my hands and then wiped them on my slacks.

"She's waiting for that apology."

Junior's gaze darted about again, looking for an escape, from me as well as the apology.

Scrap and I hemmed him in. I took one step closer, hands raised.

He looked like he'd vomit.

"I . . . I apologize, Ms. Noncoiré, for repeating the opinion of others without thinking."

"That will do for now," I sighed. "Want to have lunch, Mom? Junior's buying."

I might even put up with his presence just to find out who dripped the venom of that opinion and why he got tickets to "Fairy Moon" for his mother if she deserted him when he was a baby, leaving him with Breven San-croix to drag him through childhood any way he could.

I wondered if Breven knew he'd raised a changeling. And what happened to his real child?

Scrap, if we send Junior back to Faery, will his other self be returned?

How in the six hundred sixty-six hells am I supposed to know? That's a faery secret and they have never talked to anyone about it. Ever.

One more thing to talk to Mickey about.

Chapter 30

Prostitution is legal, and highly taxed, in much of Nevada; however, it is not legal in Las Vegas.

IF LADY LUCIA is Junior's silent partner, then I need to know what she plans. I zip through the chat room, barely lingering long enough to flutter my wings twice let alone get noticed by whoever is on guard duty today.

I come out in Lucia's parlor. It's deserted and totally tidy. I smell pine cleaner, the same brand Mom uses—used—on Tess' house. The place is silent, so I prowl, keeping to the ceiling—no one ever looks up.

The ageless and ancient lad servant sleeps like the dead in one of the little interior, windowless rooms. His bed is a coffin with a handful of dirt from his native land scattered on the bottom. Maybe he really is a vampire. I can't be sure since I've never met one before or had them confirmed in imp demon chronicles.

The sound of water gently lapping against tile draws me to the central bathroom and that huge hot tub meant for six. But only two occupy it this morning.

Donovan and Lucia.

Not a stitch of clothing on them. Her sun-deprived whiter-than-white skin is firm and smooth with only a little acceptance of gravity on her lovely, rose-tipped breasts. She's so beautiful she could almost tempt me to start loving females.

His muscles ripple sleekly beneath his nearly hairless coppery skin. A magnificent reminder of why I find men so enticing.

They make a couple that look good together. I bet their personalities fit, too—opposing strengths, weaknesses, and tempers.

The bubbling chlorine-filled water that reflects the deep blue tile in the tub can't mask the scent of their recent joining. The musk lingers in the air like a gentle aftertaste.

They are both pushing out hot and heavy pheromones that tell me there is more to come.

I'm quite happy to hang around the outside of the open door and watch.

But their conversation is what draws me as close as I can get.

"You don't seem so weary of your humanity now as you did at dawn," Lucia whispers. She runs a big toe up his inner thigh, letting it caress him in his most sensitive parts.

"I don't know, Contessa. The delights of a body, or your body aside, I just don't know what I'm doing right and what I'm doing wrong. It's all so confusing." He grabs her foot and brings it up to his mouth, sucking on each of her toes. His free hand drifts toward her ample breast, just barely breaking the water's surface.

"You are doing that precisely right," she gasps, very near to coming. "What is so confusing about enjoying every sensation the Universe inflicts upon us? The good as well as the pain." She purrs in response to his tugs on her toes followed by a vicious little bite.

"The emotions," he sighs. "There is no logic. I don't know if I feel anger, or fear, or jealousy, or love. I don't know *how* I'm supposed to feel when, or with whom."

Lady Lucia throws back her head and laughs loudly. "Welcome to being human, my lovely Donovan. No one can figure out emotions. That's what makes life so delicious."

"As delicious as you." His hands move around her breasts, nipping and kneading fiercely.

"If you are truly ready to give up all this . . ." She scoots closer to him, pulling her foot free from his mouth and draping her leg across his lap. Her hand caresses between his legs and gains instant and elegant response. "The Powers That Be owe me a few favors, or they will when I right the balances in Las Vegas. I can get you returned to your hideous gargoyle existence. You can sit and watch and do your job silently rather than have to figure out how to properly interact."

"I'm not that much of a coward," he growls. He's responding to her ministrations with enthusiasm.

"You wouldn't have to go back to that boring old Citadel and the copper body of a bat. I'd get you a new position, a prized one at Notre Dame de Paris. Perhaps somewhere in Florence and a dragon body beckons you more?"

What!

Donovan was previously a copper bat overlooking a Citadel?

I grow faint with this discovery.

No wonder he makes his human home on Half Moon Lake in Central Washington State. His magnificent glass-and-cedar house that lets him look out on the world from a private island is only twenty-five miles from the place where he looked out and watched the world from the refectory roof of my babe's Citadel.

This is too rich to keep secret. But now is not the time to tell Tess. Maybe later, when it's all over, she'll appreciate the irony.

I leave them to their activities that begin to grow violent. He bites her nipple hard. She shoves his face away with a fierce grasp of his chin. He pulls her hair back. She pinions his hands against the pool.

"Again, so soon?" she laughs as she yanks him up and onto his back on the tile floor with more than human strength.

"I'm never satisfied. Not even by you." Then he whispers or broadcasts telepathically, I'm not sure which. I have to strain to listen. "Except by Tess."

He flips Lucia over, capturing both her hands in one of his as he prepares to enter her most vigorously.

"Don't tell her that," Lucia giggles. Her ears are better than mine; that makes her otherworldly if not a vampire. "If you do, she'll never let you off her leash long enough for you come back to me or any of your other companions."

He seems most determined to banish his frustrations in this act. I hope it works and keeps him away from my babe for a while.

This would be fun to watch if I had the patience. Maybe I'll just nip over to that Citadel and enjoy a little of these dominance games with my own Ginkgo.

At five minutes to three, Gollum, Mickey, and I entered the Dragon and St. George and headed directly toward the theater.

Watch your back, babe, Scrap nearly screamed in my ear as he darted up to the ceiling of the adjacent casino. *Mr. Stinky is in the building.*

Sure enough, Donovan stood tall and steadfast in front of the curtain separating the casino from the theater entrance.

"You can't keep calling him Mr. Stinky, Scrap. We know what he is now, so he doesn't smell wrong. He smells of what he was, combined with what he is," I replied.

Whatever. I still say he stinks.

"What are you doing here?" Gollum snarled at his rival.

Mickey hung back, hollow-eyed and silent, as he'd been since he picked us up at The Crown Jewels twenty minutes ago.

"Lady Lucia's orders," Donovan spat back. He turned and threw the curtain to one side.

"Since when do you take orders from anyone?" I asked, squeezing through the slight opening in the metal gate.

Donovan muttered something. His face remained dark and resentful. His five o'clock shadow had expired and reached well beyond the wee hours of the morning.

How long since he'd slept, eaten, or shaved?

Too long by the angry set of his shoulders and clenching fists. Maybe Scrap was right. He did carry a certain unwashed quality.

I didn't need the magical comb, which lay hidden in my pocket, to know he hurt deeply.

My heart skipped a beat in the knowledge that my rejection of him had brought him this low.

It's all an act, dahling. Believe me, he's not as depressed as he wants you to think.

I had to remind myself that he had *betrayed* his life mission and his creator. He'd been *condemned* to being human raised by a Kajiri demon for his crimes.

Would he have turned out more complete, less ruthless, with a different purpose in life if my Dill had raised him instead of Darren Estevez?

He might have more morals, Scrap laughed, reading my thoughts.

I'd never know.

The curtain dropped behind us, shutting out the clang and clatter of the casino. The sudden silence and dim lighting of the theater lobby distorted my perceptions. I instinctively took up an *en garde* position. Only a little pull on my thigh warned me I hadn't completely healed yet.

At least I'd worn decent shoes this time.

But I had no weapon today. Scrap was exiled a good ten yards from me as long as Donovan was anywhere near. Or until overwhelming demon evil threatened me.

Did Lady Lucia know that when she ordered Donovan here?

More important, what sort of blackmail had she used against him? Nothing less would coerce him into doing something he didn't want to do, or didn't earn him a great advantage, or a great deal of money.

A phalanx of six mutant faeries in black leather greeted us. I jammed the comb into my hair, letting the tight curls grab hold of it.

Instantly a dark mist enveloped the faeries. I saw the

energy signature of wings on their backs; great leathery and ragged-edged things. Normal eyes couldn't see them. They used up a lot of energy concealing those wings. I had a small advantage in that knowledge.

If these guys weren't evil, I didn't know what was. Scrap should be able to break through Donovan's force field if things got nasty. Or is that nastier?

Not until they threaten you, babe.

Then Gregbaum emerged from the center of his palace guard, dwarfed by them, but radiating a confidence that diminished them.

My gaze zeroed in on his pinky ring.

Gollum followed the track of my eyes and raised his eyebrows in question.

"It's a fake," I said dismissively. At least it didn't radiate an aura of magic as I expected. It just sat on his finger, but something . . . pulled at me, demanded I take the ring from him, use it as it was intended.

Gregbaum didn't have the power or talent to activate whatever it was. It wanted me, knew I'd use it to its full capacity.

I don't know if it existed entirely in this dimension.

Looking at the producer's pudgy fingers, I judged it could be the same size as the ring Donovan offered me. Was it the same ring, a duplicate, or just a fake?

There are no coincidences, Scrap reminded me from his perch atop the curtain rod behind me. *That ring keeps cropping up. You may need it to finish this adventure.*

Gregbaum bristled.

"He's a fake. No wonder Lady Lucia dominates him," I added with a derisive smile. I needed to keep him slightly off-balance.

"Tess, don't," Donovan warned.

"You have your agenda, Donovan. I have mine. Right now I want to see the show. I have Lady Lucia's private invitation for me and my entourage. Are you part of that?" With a slight gesture, I drew Gollum and Mickey closer.

"Lady Lucia called me an hour ago to inform me that

I let you in or face her wrath. I admit you with extreme prejudice and reluctance." Gregbaum stepped aside a half step. His guards remained sternly in place.

"Noted. I won't engage a weapon unless they do," I stated the terms of this temporary truce.

A brief nod from Gregbaum and a narrow passage opened for us into the theater.

My skin crawled as I passed through the ranks of dumb muscle. Gollum and Mickey kept as close to me as they could without actually sharing the same skin. Donovan entered the theater a distant fourth.

Inside, the VIP circle was filled with cameras, lights, sound equipment, and crews. More of the same had taken up positions on the musicians' ledge and the varied levels of the stage. A quality production.

If Lady Lucia closed down the show in three more days, Gregbaum still had a money maker in the DVD.

Three days to negate any spells the smarmy producer and Junior had placed on the dancers, find the portal, and return them to Faery.

"This isn't your fight, Tess Noncoiré," Gregbaum said.

"If not my fight, then whose?"

But Gregbaum had already disappeared into the bowels of the backstage.

I wanted a different perspective from my first viewing of the show. So I took a seat in the third row to the left of the cameras.

Mickey and Gollum sat on either side of me. Donovan pointedly walked around to the opposite side, where he could watch me as well as the show.

Scrap breathed a sigh of relief and flitted back to me.

Within seconds the cameras began rolling and the music came up. Once more the story, the dance, the music, and the magic of "Fairy Moon" sucked me in. My hair comb revealed the special magic of Faery shining through the performance, giving me glimpses of laughter, beauty, kindness, and joy. Qualities all the other dimensions needed to share.

If the human dimension had twisted Junior to the

polar opposite of true Faery, then Donovan was right. We didn't need a demon ghetto to balance our goodness and light. We were often our own demons.

For endless moments I became a part of it all. I knew that if even a small amount of Faery's brightness dimmed, all the dimensions became poorer. The Juniors and the mutants would have a free rein to wreak havoc.

The action never stopped for camera or lights or tech problems. A true performance from beginning to end.

About halfway into the first act I jolted back to reality. The faces of the dancers were absolutely blank. They performed by rote.

My attention wandered to the set; an open garden, an oasis set in the middle of a forbidding desert, complete with tinkling fountains and false gaiety. A metaphor for the city of Las Vegas. The caterpillar on the mushroom reminded me of the hookah-smoking character in *Alice in Wonderland*. Another metaphor for the addiction of gambling, bright lights, glamorous shows, and more gambling.

The full moon set on the action as the lights faded for the end of the first act. My attention pricked. Full moon was the time demons' strength waned and portals closed.

We waited a scant ten minutes for the dancers to rest and gulp gallons of water. They lounged about the stage, watching the set and lights change. Gregbaum stalked around, shouting orders, growing angrier by the minute. Change this, adjust that.

"No," the dancers said as one. They flowed upright and into position between Gregbaum and the set piece of the rock goblin. "We dance as before or we do not dance at all."

Mickey tensed beside me. "Gregbaum does not want you to see the truth within the set," he whispered.

Across from me, I watched Donovan jerk out of his slouch. He, too, noted that something was up.

More shouts. Some dancers slunk off stage. Others held their ground.

Scrap flitted about, invisibly tweaking hair and blowing cigar smoke in the faces of the stagehands who stood about in indecision.

"This theater is haunted," one of the hands said, waving smoke out of his nose. He made the sign of the cross and looked around nervously.

Gregbaum threw up his hands and contented himself with shifting camera angles. The DVD probably would show very vague impressions of the set rather than details.

"I've got to get closer," I whispered to Gollum.

He stayed me with a hand on my knee. "He'll notice and use that as an excuse to throw us out."

"I'm not on his radar," Mickey whispered. As he spoke, he slithered down to crawl along the narrow aisle between rows of high-backed seats. He really did have acrobatic talents. Quickly, he disappeared into the shadows. A hint of movement at the edge of the pit showed his progress.

The theater grew black.

Music drifted to life on a slow eerie flute note. Lights came up on the stage. Cameras fixed on the red rock goblin. Faeries crept out of holes in the stage.

A waxing quarter moon rose behind them all. The time when the walls between worlds thinned and portals could be unlocked. If you had a key.

Only at that time did the Celestial Goddess reveal herself in the heavens: the quarter moon defined her cheek, starscapes became her eyes and mouth, the Milky Way streamed away from her as her hair blown in the celestial wind. When Scrap became my blade, he mimicked that configuration.

Everything glittered in the coruscated light. My eyes refused to focus, trying to follow the randomly blinking and scattered lights rather then settle on any one object. A blank spot appeared beneath the goblin's arm. That tiny circle absorbed the light rather than reflecting it so that it appeared a black hole.

"Gollum, what's the moon phase?" I gripped his hand tightly where it rested on my knee.

Waxing quarter on Monday night, Scrap answered for him.

This was Saturday. Not much time. A lot to do before then. I could only lead the faeries to safety on Monday night when the moon revealed the portal within the rocks.

I still needed Donovan to complete the task.

Chapter 31

A fire raced through the MGM Grand on November 21, 1980, claiming eighty-five lives.

TOO SOON, we reached the climax of the show. I held my breath as the little girl faery paused one last moment to drink in the awesome majesty of the desert embodied in one tiny yellow flower; so different from her home and yet so very beautiful in its own right.

As the portal grew smaller and smaller, I wanted to shout to her to hurry. My heart nearly broke when she tried to fly through and hit solid rock.

Once more I *had* to stand and clap, slowly, methodically. I had to let the world know that I believed in faeries and my belief gave them life. Gollum rose beside me, tall and determined. He increased the pulse of our clapping. Then Mickey added his own applause from the pit area, and Donovan, and the camera men, and the stage crew. We all made this a truly live performance for those who would only share the magic by DVD.

At long last, the portal opened a fraction and one long arm reached through to help the lost faery go home.

One huge group sigh of relief and it was over. I felt restored by the show. At the same time I knew sadness because it was the last time I would see it live. There could only be a few more performances before the show closed forever, and the dancers either died or I led them home.

I knew what I had to do next.

"Mickey, can you examine the spell on the dormitory and somehow find its weak spots?" He nodded. "Gollum, rent us a car, probably something with four wheel drive. Noon tomorrow. We're going to the Valley Of Fire."

"What are you going to do?"

"Besides the awards banquet tonight and my final class tomorrow morning?" I smiled sweetly.

They exited the theater ahead of me, heads bent in consultation.

I hung back, fading into the shadows beside the exit.

Sometimes I can become a chameleon. With a shift in facial muscles and posture, and a tug on clothing to alter its shape, I lose my distinctiveness. With Scrap's help, I can even adjust the shade of my clothes.

No Scrap this time. I set him to watch from the musicians' ledge.

"You can't hide from me, Tess," Donovan said as he came abreast of me.

"I don't want to hide, I just didn't want you to notice me until you were too close to avoid me." I took his arm possessively and walked beside him into the lobby. He didn't pull away from my grasp. Good. I knew he could. He had lots of honed muscle beneath his black polo shirt. He'd bested me more than once on the fencing strip.

He paused in the center. "What do you want?"

"I don't suppose you'd let me borrow that ring?" I tried to look innocent.

He scowled. "Why?" He wasn't going to make it easy on me.

"It has properties I need to complete my mission." I turned to face him, keeping my hand in the crook of his elbow.

"I don't have it anymore."

Damn!

"Then I'll just have to tell Lady Lucia you lost her

treasured wedding ring." I stepped back and withdrew the slight connection of my hand on his arm.

"Lady Lucia!" he exploded. "I bought that ring in Paris last December. From a reputable antique dealer. I have provenance back to 1850."

Interesting. He had the ring a month ago when I refused to mother his children without love and marriage first. He had it when he ran from my rejection into bed with WindScribe, who now carried his child.

"Did you give the ring to Gregbaum after I refused your proposal?"

"I sold it to him. At a handsome profit."

"He used to be close to Lady Lucia, possibly intimate with her. He had to have seen her portrait wearing that ring and recognized it," I mused out loud. "What made you buy that particular ring besides its beauty and value? There must have been others offered in the auction."

"There were. But I knew at first glance that ring was special. I catch glimpses of power in it, but I can't access it. Can you?"

I shrugged. "I only know that it begs me to wear it."

"If I thought he'd give it up, I'd buy it back and give it to Lady Lucia." Donovan turned as if to leave.

I grabbed his arm once more. "Please, Donovan, buy it back. I'll reimburse the money. I'll give it to Lady Lucia when I'm done with it. Please. I really need the ring to save the faeries."

"How? How does it work?"

"I don't know yet. I only know I need it."

Scrap, talk to me, tell me everything you've found out! I knew he'd been investigating, not how far he'd ranged in doing so.

Donovan stood there, challenging me to say more.

I met him glare for glare, equal in stubbornness and determination.

We stood there so long, Gregbaum slithered out of the theater, stopping short within a yard of us.

"Why are you still here?" he snarled. His face grew red. A sure symptom of high blood pressure. Maybe he'd keel over with a heart attack and I could just grab the ring off his hand.

"Sell me the ring, Gregbaum," I demanded.

"No. Why should I?"

Because it is an artifact of power. It only partially exists in this dimension. You can't control it. If you try, it will burn you up. That last was just a guess. But I couldn't say any of that out loud.

"Because I'll tell Lady Lucia you have it if you don't sell it to me or let me borrow it," I said. "She might even invent a new drink in your honor: Bloody Gary. Or do you prefer Gregbaum smoothie?"

The pudgy man blanched beneath his high color.

"I don't have to keep it from Lady Lucia. I might even make a present of it to her. With the proviso that you never get your hands on it." He folded his arms across his chest, calm again, face a more normal shade.

"What if I tell Junior Sancroix you have it?" I smiled sweetly.

He grew white again but held firm. "Go ahead. He can't do anything more to me once Lucia closes down my show."

"Can't he?" I tried to raise one eyebrow and only succeeded in twisting my face into a grimace.

Donovan quirked his left eyebrow up. I'm sure he did it just to best me. He was in that kind of mood.

"Fifty thousand, cash. Now. Otherwise I'll bury it out in the desert where you'll never find it."

I blanched this time. I might be able to lay my hands on that kind of cash given a week to liquidate some savings and stocks. A lot of stocks. Maybe raid my IRA.

"That's twice what I sold it to you for," Donovan snarled.

"Fifty large is half what it's worth," Gregbaum returned.

"I'll give you thirty in an hour. That's five grand in profit in two days. I'd say a pretty good return on your money," Donovan snapped back.

Thank you, I mouthed.

"I'm not doing it for you. I want credit with Lady Lucia for giving it back to her. It's a whole lot safer for her to owe me favors than the other way around." He stalked off, leaving me to face Gregbaum on my own.

If I could get it back to Lucia, she just might let me borrow it Monday night. She wanted me to rescue the faery dancers.

"You'll never get your hands on this little treasure now. I know Donovan. In fact, I may just let him have it for the twenty-five grand I bought it for. Just so's he'll let me open a new show in his new casino up in Half Moon Lake."

"He abandoned plans for a casino and is building a much smaller spa." I'd witnessed his signature (in blood) on the refinancing after his original casino building collapsed into a rogue portal when I closed it last autumn.

"Did he? I hear he's in Vegas looking for new investors. Why do you think he's talking to Lady Lucia? She doesn't care who—or rather *what*—patronizes his 'spa,' " Gregbaum tossed over his shoulder as he turned to leave.

"You can't open a new show without new dancers," I called after him.

"I've got access to dozens more." His disembodied voice echoed ominously around the tile and marble lobby.

I need to do more research on that ring. Tess won't need me at the awards banquet, though I do love to watch her glow with satisfaction when she wins.

Maybe I'd better postpone my trip until I help her get all gussied up. She is absolutely helpless when it comes to clothes. She'll mix gold with silver jewelry, cover her shoulders with a shawl that clashes with her gown, and put on mismatched shoes. She's even been known to forget to brush her hair. A total fashion disaster.

Once she's set, I'll flit off to track that ring from Tess' ancestors to Lady Lucia. Then I'll find a way to get it back to her.

Hmmm, if it's only partially in this dimension, maybe I can grab it right off of Gregbaum's hand from inside the chat room.

After I know more. Can't drop it in Tess' lap and have it burn her up because she doesn't know how to use it.

Now for some fun dressing dahling Tess. That midnight blue number will have to do. No time to shop for something new and it is quite suitable for the occasion. the strappy black sandals with two inch heels—she's never comfortable in anything higher—will set it off and not strain her pulled muscle. Silver jewelry, I think. And I might be able to add some more sparkle to the chiffon. She lost some of the original sequins and beads climbing out of the gondola and the remainder are too subtle and already dimming in luster.

Yes! Silver glitter. Too bad I can't get back into Faery for some sparkle. Who else has some?

Pixies?

Tricky. They aren't as giving as faeries. There's always a cost and hidden condition with a pixie. I'll have to call in some favors and make promises with my fingers crossed. Might even have to let them tie my tail in a knot.

But my Tess is worth every bit of it. She'll look marvelous tonight.

She'll look even better when I get that ring for her.

So how did it get from the Noncoiré family of blacksmiths to Lady Lucia?

Once more I stand looking through a window in time. We've moved forward a lot of centuries to eighteen fourteen. The same remote village, on the slopes of the French Alps where the first Noncoiré tricked a faery out of the ring. Italy is just over the pass of the mountain visible in the distance. I bet the local language has as much Italian as French in it.

My lock on the ring takes me back to the same woodland. Another Noncoiré blacksmith reclines against a tree, powerful legs stretched out into the grass.

And he's naked. Magnificently, rawly naked except for the ring on a leather lacing around his neck. Oh, my. I have to mop up a little drool. This youth's muscles ripple cleanly beneath his sleek skin. And the way he stretches promises much prolonged delight. His blond curls look like gold in the dappled sunshine.

He glows with health and energy and optimism. He should. A young Lucia nestles beside him, equally naked. Her skin is smooth with pampering. No ugly calluses on her hands or feet. She doesn't work, or walk much, and her shoes must be custom made. Her black hair is sleek and tossed up into a casual do that probably took her maid hours to achieve.

Hey, isn't she a blonde now? Oohh, the secrets only her hairdresser knows for sure.

Nearby, an elegant palfrey nibbles at the greenery. She rides everywhere. Must have some noble blood and money in the family.

So this is an illicit love affair. The daughter of the local lord slipping out to tryst with a commoner. And not a bit of protection between them. Doesn't she know the consequences?

She whispers sweet nothings into the blacksmith's ear. As she speaks, she wiggles her body along his, enticing him to new—um—lengths of passion.

She is well practiced in these arts and probably not a virgin for all of her maybe fifteen years. At least that's how young she looks. I'm beginning to believe that looks are deceiving.

I notice that she speaks good French, hardly a hint of the thick Italian accent she affects in modern society.

Our young man responds with enthusiasm if not exactly gentleness.

Lucia matches him in passion and eagerness. I could watch these two lovers all day. Their passion is raw, not violent like she indulges with Donovan now. They remind me of my precious moments with Ginkgo.

When they finally finish and lie back all sweaty, panting, and satisfied—me, too, for that matter—Lucia dallies with the ring on its chain.

"A good luck charm. Been wit' me family for generations," the young man explains. His accent is thick, local and uneducated.

"Does it bring you luck?" she asks coyly. Her long dark hair dangles across his chest, tickling him.

He wraps a curl around his finger and tugs gently until her

mouth reaches his. They kiss, openmouthed, devouring each other for endless moments.

I sigh. Young love is so sweet.

But I'm not convinced Lucia is entirely sweet. Her left hand has never left the ring.

"I call it luck that you favor me," young Noncoiré says. He's breathing hard again.

Oh, the stamina of the young. I may get another show.

"This ring should be a token of our love. As long as *we* have it, we can find ways to be together," she replies. "This ring is special. Magic."

"I'm off to war soon. Emperor Napoleon needs all Frenchmen to rally for his next campaign. France will rule the world again." He sounds as if he believes that claptrap.

How else can ambitious generals con men into following them into hell and death?

"I hate the thought of you leaving me! You could be captured. You could die. And I'd never see you again." She pouts prettily, a practiced look. Her hand clamps tighter around the ring.

If he takes the ring with him and dies, she's lost more than just a lover. And she knows it.

"That's the cost of bringing France back to her rightful place on top of the world."

I snort in derision.

"Perhaps I'd better keep the ring for you. Just in case." She clasps the ring tightly, keeping her hand and her body in close contact with him.

Deep in my mind I hear a chortle of triumph. That is a new voice, neither Lucia or the young blacksmith.

"*Oui*, ma sweet. It is my gift to you, so that you never forget me." He slips the leather thong from his neck and places it around hers.

Gods and Goddesses! It's the imp within the ring. He's using the tiny crack from the last transfer of ownership to leak power and enticement. He needs Lucia to own the ring because . . . I'm not sure why. But she offers him more hope than the peasant blacksmith.

Again she holds it tightly, covetously.

A tiny niggle of doubt wiggles into my mind. I'm not as sure as I was before that I should release that imp.

And then they are at it again. Their hands and mouths explore, nip, pinch, taste, and stroke. I watch them avidly, forgetting all about the black imp and the ring.

Their world goes transparent on me. I have nothing else to learn here.

Except in my last quick glimpse, I know that Lucia will never forget her strong blacksmith. Her first true love. The father of her child.

Does she know that Tess includes the son of that blacksmith in her family tree?

I bet she does. The name alone should give away the connection. No wonder she favors Tess with flowers and tickets to "Fairy Moon." I bet she also knows all about the Sisterhood of the Celestial Blade. She knows about me. She knows that Tess and I are the only ones who can rescue the faery dancers.

But we need the ring to do it.

Chapter 32

Downtown Las Vegas (Freemont Street as opposed to the Strip) is sometimes called Glitter Gulch because of the proliferation of big neon signs.

GOLLUM MET ME at the elevator on the convention floor. His dark blue suit with the crisp white shirt fit him perfectly. For once, his glasses sat firmly on his nose, where they belonged. He'd even combed his soft blond hair. The only mar on his perfect demeanor was the blinding tie filled with cartoon space aliens.

"I've gotta have some fun," he said, blushing.

"I like it. Sometimes these award ceremonies get a little too tense: as if they are more important than the books they honor."

He nodded. "Academic stuff is a lot more pretentious. The competition cutthroat. You look wonderful by the way."

I twirled in my sparkling cocktail dress. Who knows where Scrap found the extra glitter, or how he affixed it to the chiffon,(I'd lost more than a few sequins climbing out of the gondola and over the bridge at the Venetian) but it added just that extra dimension that made me feel special.

Gollum offered me his arm in escort.

Shyly, I took it, acutely aware of his masculine scent, his lean body, and a new layer we added to our friendship.

He stood a foot taller than me, even with heels. Still, we managed to match our strides and fit together.

For once I didn't want to talk about our mission. I just wanted to spend time with my friend.

We took our places at a round table for ten. A female mystery editor I didn't know and a male agent who specialized in Romance fiction already sat there. She was into her third drink and fidgeting anxiously, looking longingly into her purse. Probably at a pack of cigarettes.

She pulled out a cell phone and stared at the screen, willing it to ring.

So much for clichés. I wondered if she had a sick child at home and needed to check in with the family.

The male agent might not look like a romantic hero with his spindly frame, balding head, and ill-fitting suit, but he certainly knew how to market them.

I expected the other six places to fill up rapidly with conference attendees who wanted a chance to chat with our table mates.

Within moments, my mother floated in, looking elegant in a cream-and-gold outfit, with gold clips in her graying blonde hair—which had new highlights. Behind her walked her housemate Penny and the tall man with a Stetson we'd encountered outside the theater a few nights ago. The agent and editor looked grateful when I introduced them. They'd probably been inundated all weekend with unpublished writers seeking an "in" in the publishing industry.

"I wanted to share a moment of triumph with you, Tess," Mom said kissing my cheek. "I haven't supported you very well in your career."

"You kept house for me for three years so I could get on with the work." I kissed her back. "That was more help than you can imagine."

"But I didn't give you the emotional support. Now I understand the necessity of that. I want to be the first to hug you when you win this award." She preened a bit as if my triumph was all her doing.

"I haven't won yet." I didn't go on to say that this regional writers conference award didn't carry a lot of prestige. Yet. If they continued to put on a top quality conference like this weekend, it would gain in importance.

"Who's your competition, Tess?" Penny asked. Her eyes moved constantly, weighing and assessing everyone in the noisy crowd. She looked a little more careworn and dowdy than the first time I met her, more like the aging woman with more bills than income that Mom had described.

"A mystery writer and a historical romance writer," I replied, pointing out the man and woman in question at different tables.

"Lightweight stuff," Gollum muttered.

I tilted my head in silent question.

"I read them both. You're a shoo-in."

"When did you read them?" I asked. He hadn't known he was coming until Thursday.

"On the plane Thursday night. I read yours, of course, when it first came out. Got my first edition hardcover autographed, too." He cocked me a grin that warmed my heart.

And suddenly I knew that I loved him. My heart seemed to swell until surely it would burst. My gaze locked on his, and the room faded to insignificance.

I just knew that my heart was safe with Gollum. Donovan could back me up in a fight, to keep me from physical harm. But Gollum protected *me*.

I squeezed his hand beneath the table, promising . . . I didn't know what precisely I promised, only that we would talk.

My heart skipped a beat. But not from Gollum's gentle caress of his thumb across my palm.

My body knew before my mind did, that Donovan walked into the room.

He looked magnificent, as always, freshly showered and shaved, wearing a custom tailored black suit, gray shirt, and silvery tie. The white slashes at his temples added distinction to his already noble profile. Every woman in the room, and quite a few men, riveted their attention on him as he wove through the tables. Quiet and calm followed in his wake.

Gollum immediately withdrew his hand from mine. He seemed to shrink inside himself as well.

I grew cold inside.

Mom didn't need to wave to catch Donovan's attention. He zeroed in on us—or me—the moment he passed through the door.

I heard a few sighs of disappointment as he bent to hug my mother with one arm. "You look lovely, Genevieve. I hope I get to hear you sing later." His eyes met mine above her head. Cold, yet burning with resentment.

Penny and her date shifted to allow Donovan to sit next to Mom. At least I didn't have to look at him across the table. Or feel his body heat beside me.

Instinctively, I edged my chair closer to Gollum so that our thighs touched. Our hands found each other again like magnets to iron.

Only two places left to fill at our table. The pretentious romance writer who wanted to rest on her laurels claimed the seat next to the agent. "I'm thinking of changing agents for my next project. Are you interested?" she demanded before she finished sitting.

"Talk about rude," Penny said, rolling her eyes.

The writer didn't seem to hear anything but the agent's mumbled comments about needing a formal query and proposal.

"I'm an established writer. You need only look at my previous success," she humphed and shifted her chair.

"In this business you are only as good as the next book," the agent insisted and turned his attention to a writer at the table behind him.

The editor waved over Jack Weaver, the gentleman I'd met the first night who wrote police procedural mysteries. Obviously a friend, or client.

Did we have enough critical mass to overcome the

negative vibes coming off Donovan and the romance writer?

Any further discussion was interrupted by waiters in formal livery bringing salads and taking drink orders.

Fortitude flew in, scouting the room. I didn't dare follow his progress by turning my head and looking up. No one else could see him.

But I did check out the door, a normal action. Both Sancroix men stood, waiting and assessing. They wore suits that needed pressing with their ties loosened. From the flush on Junior's face, I wondered if he'd been drinking.

Then I spotted a squarely built woman behind them. She wore an ill-fitting and dated gray taffeta dress that matched her bluntly cut short hair.

Sister Gert. Sancroix had suggested an old relationship with her. I thought I'd seen her in the distance at the St. George and Dragon. Something was up. Something strange.

And Scrap wasn't around to scout for me.

Gert's imp, Juniper, remained firmly on her shoulder. Maybe it was just the shadows but he looked darker than I remembered.

"I'd go greet Breven and his new wife, but I really don't want to talk to Junior," Mom whispered.

"New wife?" I nearly choked.

"At first I thought he was courting me, very attentive. Then I realized he was merely making me more comfortable singing in Junior's hotel."

"Hey, Tess, you going to sing tonight?" Jack Weaver interrupted. "I really enjoyed that victim song."

His question distracted me from the newcomers. They took seats in the corner, their backs defensively to the walls. The two imps took up positions near the ceiling, two dark smudges against the white-and-gold scrollwork decorations.

"*My Fairytale*," I corrected Jack, forcing my attention to my immediate companions. I gave him enough information to find the CD on-line.

"Yeah. That was really fun. I've been doing some web searches. I may have to change genres just so I can go to SF conventions and do more filk."

"Actually," his editor interrupted. "We're starting a new imprint of SF/F mysteries. If you could set one of your usual styled stories on a space station and extrapolate forward some forensics gadgets, we might be able to open you to a new market and keep the old one."

"I've been wanting to try out a scanner that would pick up from an eyeball the last thing a victim saw . . ." Jack mused. "I'd have to find a way to prove it's reliable. Then I could get someone to screw with the settings or implant the wrong image . . ."

"SF readers tend to be pretty omnivorous," I added. "Once they discover you, they are likely to cross over and read your backlist."

"Then I can legitimately go to cons and enjoy more filk!"

Gollum took up the thread. He had a nice light baritone and filked with me at cons.

Donovan, however, avoided the free-for-all song fests. Though we'd met at High Desert Con last autumn, and he professed to be a fan, I'd only seen him at one other, in the Bay area when he and a family group dressed as bats.

At that fateful con in the high desert, my best friend from college had died tragically and unnecessarily. Gollum had stayed with me and helped me deal with the aftermath. Donovan had gone off to coddle and hide the children of some half-demon clients who had actually struck the killing blow on my friend.

I was better off with Donovan out of my life.

But I still needed his help getting that ring, and maybe the extra body to rescue the dancers.

The rest of the evening passed in a blur of animated conversation and decent food. It was an awards banquet, after all. The food was standard fare, but nicely prepared and not overcooked.

Then Tanya, the organizer, took her place behind the podium. A nervous hush fell over the crowd. After the usual speeches and introductions, the guest editors began handing out the awards: cover art, short fiction, small press fiction, and lastly "Best Genre Book of the Year."

Mom took my hand and held on tight.

Gollum took my other hand and pointedly kissed my palm.

Donovan continued to glower.

I lost to the historical romance writer. This was largely a romance-oriented crowd after all. Resignation rather than disappointment filled me. Fatigue crept up my spine.

"Well, now I can get back to work," I muttered. I flicked my gaze to both Donovan and Gollum, so they'd know which job I intended to get back to.

They both nodded.

"After I listen to my mom sing, of course," I added.

We all laughed and adjourned to the lounge.

Tess has settled in with Gollum. I am so happy. He's the man she belongs with, not Mr. Stinky who never has smelled right, even for a fallen gargoyle. Stone and copper and desert sage and something rotten at the core don't add up. I knew those scents never came from Lincoln Cathedral like he claimed. Now I know they come from the Citadel. There is more. Much, much more to learn.

I'd also like to know what Fortitude and Juniper are up to. Somehow, they don't belong here, and not together.

The next window in time I find in the chat room, only a few years have passed since Lucia bartered sex for the ring. As I look over an ancient villa in Tuscany, I sense that the young blacksmith is no longer in the picture, either as far as the ring is concerned, or in Lady Lucia's life.

I zero in on a walled garden. A gnarled old tree props up the western wall. Graceful benches of sunwashed stone rest beneath the shady boughs. A central fountain shows a nude nymph pouring water from an urn.

Long shadows fill the garden as the sun drops behind the western hills.

Lady Lucia, now a more mature and full-figured woman (she's about twenty now by my calculations) plays with a blond toddler, probably a boy. A strand of pearls graces her neck—a typical wedding gift. Most pearls look alike to me, I haven't studied them like I have that diamond on her hand. Something in this strand whispers to me that I should recognize them.

The little boy screams in delight and chases dandelion fluff she has blown for him. I guess he might be three. I do not know human children. They grow more quickly than imps. But they die sooner than we do, too. Unless the imp faces a murderous sibling. Then we die quite young.

Or should, if the murder goes as planned and doesn't backfire.

But I digress.

A very angry count paces the garden. His dark hair and olive skin have little or nothing in common with the child. He's at least forty, maybe older.

Lucia seems very unconcerned for the amount of rage pouring out of her husband.

"Send the child away. I will not look on him."

"I prefer to keep your son close." Lucia brings the child into a tight hug that ends in a tickle. He laughs delightedly, finding much joy in life and in his mama.

Oh, that I had ever known such joy and love!

"That is not *my* son," the count spits. He is in a towering rage now. Spittle forms at the corners of his mouth. His swarthy skin takes on red hues from too much blood. He looks like he could stroke out at any moment.

"You acknowledged the boy at his birth," Lucy reminds him.

"I did not know then what I know now. Who is his father?"

"I have slept with no man since our marriage," Lucia spits back. I think she's actually telling the truth. "Not that you have taken me to your bed very often. You seem to find the boys in the scullery more to your taste!" Now she's mad, too.

Ah, he's a man after my own heart, but a bit too long in the tooth for me. I like my men young and firm and strong. He might have been a soldier once, but now he's had too many years of soft living and frequent loving. His belly sags and his jowls flop when he walks.

The babe senses the anger and begins to cry. Both parents ignore him. He runs to his mama and beats on her lap, demanding she fix this upset.

"But what of before our marriage?" the count yells. "You pushed for a quick wedding after your father and I agreed on the marriage contract."

"I will not dignify this discussion by answering you." She rises gracefully and gathers the child to her bosom. He cries pitifully against her shoulder.

"The villagers already whisper that I am cuckold," the count sneers.

"Better a live cuckold than a dead vampire. They also whisper of that. They compare you to some ancient Carpathian who dined on the blood of his enemies."

The count has the grace to grow pale with fear. " 'Tis not me they call vampire—but you. You and the changeling child!"

"Only because you feed their fears and direct them away from yourself toward me."

Before he can respond, angry shouts from the front gates spill into the closed courtyard. There is only one escape from here, through the villa. While they argue, the sun sets and the quarter moon rises.

I smell fire. Fire within and fire without. The villagers surround the villa. The walls may be of stone, but the floors and ceilings are old wood. Rotting wood. The once rich furnishings are brittle with age. One torch thrown through a window left open to catch the evening breeze begins an inferno.

The count tries climbing a wall.

The villagers catch him and drive a stake through his heart. Then they pour over the wall in search of his mate.

Lady Lucia twists the diamond-and-filigree ring on her finger. She twists and twists as she prays for deliverance.

A door opens in the air. She does not question it, does not look back. She takes with her only the clothes on her back, the pearls around her neck, and the child in her arms.

And just before she steps through, I see the pointed ears, elongated teeth and folds of bat wings beneath her arms.

Some distant, very distant, ancestor of hers was a Damiri demon; the same as Donovan's foster father Darren, and apparently Tess' husband Dill.

Chapter 33

Even though summer temperatures soar to 110F for days on end the average daily temperature in Las Vegas is only 66.3F degrees, due to relatively cool winters.

*T*HE AWARDS CEREMONY seemed to adjourn *en masse* to the lounge. The winner and her friends needed to celebrate. The losers and their friends needed to commiserate. Drinks flowed fast and furious.

Mom ran through a series of upbeat show tunes before crooning a trilogy of bluesy torch songs. Once again, she managed to make her last note a long, haunting, melancholy memory. This was more than faery magic. It was Mom magic. My mom.

Her audience seemed almost in shock, on the verge of poignant tears. They'd go home with that note lingering in their minds for a long time.

I wished I knew how to do that with words at the end of a novel.

While Mom took a breath and a sip of water, my table mates pushed me toward the stage. "What do I sing?" I asked Gollum.

" 'Bimbo.' What else?" We both laughed. The crowd

was well populated with book people. They'd appreciate the greatest filk song ever written.

Easy enough to get Mom's accompanist to play "She'll Be Coming 'Round the Mountain." Looks of puzzlement passed around the crowd.

And then I sang, soft and jazzy, imitating my mother's caress of the microphone, "There's a bimbo on the cover of my book."

A slow ripple of laughter beginning with Gollum and Jack Weaver spread outward in ever wider ripples.

By the time I got to the verse about a rocket ship on the cover that isn't in the book, I had them all laughing and clapping.

Good thing the audience picked up the chorus for me. I nearly choked at the sight of Lady Lucia, resplendent in a fringed red sheath straight out of the Roaring Twenties. She sparkled and glittered, the waving fronds of her dress shifting like waves on the sand. Her entourage of pale young things in black leather faded into the background. Lucia's fangs gleamed in the spotty light almost as bright as the long strand of pearls dangling from her neck.

But those modern cultured pearls couldn't hold a candle to the luster of the shorter strand of older, Mediterranean pearls on my mother's throat, about an inch and a half from Lucia's mouth.

In three steps I was at my mother's side, thrusting the mike into her hands and pushing her back to the stage, away from the red menace.

"Stay away from my mother," I snarled. "She's innocent and off-limits to your games."

"What about you, *cara mia*? Are you off-limits, too? What about your boyfriend?" Her gaze lingered on the angry pulse in Gollum's throat.

"I'll complete your mission on time. Then we are done."

"If thinking that makes it easier for you to do as I requested, then go ahead and believe it." Lucia pouted prettily and left abruptly. Her followers had to hastily down their drinks, or place them unfinished on tables to keep up with her aggressive stride.

"How have you managed to avoid getting killed in a car accident?" I asked Gollum as I clung to the hand rest above the passenger door of the SUV he'd rented.

"What do you mean? I've never had a ticket. I'm a good driver!" he said as he drifted across the center line of the northbound freeway to the accompaniment of honking horns and flipping fingers.

"When you pay attention and don't speed." This relationship might go nowhere fast if he got us both killed. "Scrap's not around to whisk me out if you crash this thing."

"Oh, okay." Dutifully, Gollum checked his mirrors, put on his turn signal and crossed over to the righthand lane of I 15. Within a few minutes his speed had crept back up to fifteen miles an hour over the speed limit.

I sighed and made sure my seat belt was snug.

"You can come back anytime, Scrap. Donovan's not with us," I called into the ether.

Um, babe, how badly do you want that ring?

"Why? What did you find out?" I translated for Gollum.

Um, only that it's yours by right of inheritance according to some very ancient laws. Lady Lucia had no right to sell the ring to feed herself and her child.

"Scrap, if she was totally broke and starving, I think that's an excellent excuse to sell the ring, especially to feed her child."

"Wait, a minute, did he say Lucia had a baby? Vampires can't have children," Gollum interjected.

"Depends on the timing," I said. "If she had the child before she became a vampire."

"Scrap, did you find out if the ring will help me complete this mission?"

No answer.

"What did he say?" Gollum asked. This time he slowed down to half turn toward me.

"Nothing. He's gone again."

"The turnoff to the Valley of Fire is just up here. Scrap's view of the place would really be helpful."

I sat in silence, gawking at the undulating landscape. At one time, something like two hundred million years ago—you'd have to ask my deceased husband the geologist for more exact details—this entire area had been under an inland sea that cut the North American continent in two. Gently rounded layers of multicolored sandstone flowed up and down with ripples revealing ancient tidal and current action. Mostly creams and yellows with occasional hints of rust and brown didn't show the promise of the fiery landscape I expected. Some of the hilltops and mountain peaks twisted into jagged outcroppings born of volcanic action and earthquake upthrust.

Towering clouds built up from the south, casting it all in weird yellowish light. I picked out sharp details on one rock formation and lost the next in shadow.

"I didn't expect so much plant life in the desert." I shifted back and forth looking at new green foliage and bright yellow, pink, and red flowers.

"End of April. Two-week window for wildflowers when the winter rains are balanced with the increasing spring sunshine. Not that there's that much sunlight today. We might get some rain out of those clouds," he muttered as he slowed to a crawl onto the access road. The narrow two-lane (more like one and a half in places, no shoulder) pavement wandered around following a natural depression.

"Look at all those cairns! Stop, I want to take a picture." I was out of the car, camera in hand, almost before he finished pulling up the emergency brake.

This was a scouting expedition, after all; never know when something weird that attracts my attention might turn out useful.

I knelt before a two-foot-high pile of stones. Someone had carefully balanced each rock atop another into a kind of memorial. I'd read about rock cairns in Celtic lands many times, marking the location of the death of a loved one, a special romantic tryst, a sacred spring, or even an ancient peace treaty.

"I wonder if Scottish sheepherders brought the custom with them?" Snap, snap. A bunch of pictures loaded onto the memory chip. Strange, the automatic flash came on for one but not the next.

"According to my source, the locals call them Hoodoos," Gollum said. Of course he'd read all he could about this area before coming with me. He was an anthropologist. He'd left me at the door to my room last night with just a gentle peck on the cheek so that he could bone up on this place. "No one will tell me what the cairns are for or why they call them Hoodoos. It's possible they trap evil spirits, or ward against them. Perhaps they commemorate successful vision quests. There are certainly a lot of them."

Long lines of rock piles, ranging from tiny to several feet high, marched off into the distance, mostly lining the road.

"I like to think some of them at least mark the moment a couple fell in love. Some of the ones in Britain do that." I sighed, remembering fondly each and every one of the men I'd loved, from Bobby Smith in third grade up to my husband Dill, and then, in a strange erotic needful way, Donovan.

And now . . .

"I like that tradition."

Quickly, Gollum wrapped an arm around my waist and drew me close. His mouth hovered over mine.

I held my breath, savoring the quick intensity of the moment.

And then I rose up on tiptoe, he bent his head, and we met in an explosive kiss that chilled and warmed me from crown to heel. We melted together, arms and bodies entwined. Our lips melded, then parted to allow tongues a more intimate exploration.

"Wow," I whispered several long minutes later.

"I've wanted to do that since the moment I met you, back on that hillside in Alder Hill in the aftermath of an attack on adolescents by a hell hound last September." His breath brushed my cheek.

Passion flared in me again. The two inches that separated us was too much. We kissed again, slower this time, sweetly and gently, exploring possibilities.

Chapter 34

Card counting, while not illegal, is highly frowned upon. Not many casinos use fewer than three decks to discourage the practice.

TESS NEEDS THAT RING to open the portal for the faery dancers. I'm the only one who can get it for her. Once she's completed this mission, I have to find a way to free the imp inside. No creatures, no matter how bad they are, no matter what crimes against the universe they have committed, should be trapped forever inside a diamond prison.

The facets reflect only that imp's image. He must examine his crimes over and over again until he goes insane or repents. Even then there is no escape.

Only more insanity.

He calls to me through the cracks in the diamond. He tells me of his agony. I share it. I have to free him.

Since I'm already in the chat room, tracing the ring, I'll just pop along to see where it is now.

Gregbaum still has it on his pinky finger. He hasn't sold it back to Donovan, nor has he given it to Lady Lucia.

For once the slimy lounge lizard is alone. Actually he's sitting on the john, just like any normal human being. PeeeUUuuuuu. He stinks worse than I do. Wonder if he knows about milk and what it does to a sensitive tummy. He probably doesn't care. He's so angry at the world he must think his indigestion is the result of a conspiracy against him fostered by Lady Lucia.

The ring bulges through the fabric of time and dimension, as much in the chat room as it is on his hand. That's because of the imp inside. Now if I can just wiggle my body into that translucent fabric of woven energy, sort of half merge with it as if I'm about to pop into that stinky bathroom with Gregbaum.

I have to stay right on top of the ring and slide my talons around it.

Nope, that won't work. It slips out of my grasp, moving partially into another dimension of time and space.

Hmmmm.

I catch my claws into the elaborate filigree, making my energy part and parcel with it.

YES!

Now I just wiggle it downward, ever so slowly, pausing at the swollen knuckle. A second talon pulling on the other side of the ring activates the bit of faery magic in the metal. Inside Faery, everyone is the same size. So I have to let the ring know it needs to change size to fit the next recipient.

Gregbaum gives off another smelly grunt. He clenches his fists.

Ugh. This is one of the most unpleasant jobs I've ever done. I'll take Mum's freeze-dried dump any day. Nothing smells when frozen that deeply.

Oooh, ahhh, I kind of grunt along with Gregbaum to encourage him.

At last he relaxes his fingers and the ring pops off his hand and into mine.

Before he can notice it's gone, I'm fully back into the chat room in firm possession of the key to any dimension.

Oh, crap. Which rhymes with Scrap. My claws scratched Gregbaum and drew blood and smeared the ring. Now—if he knows how—he can track me or the ring through any dimension.

I'm betting that Junior knows how.

No time to think, or gloat. I've got to get this thing to Tess, the rightful owner now. It's hers, both as a descendant of the first Noncoiré and a descendant of Lady Lucia's son. I've checked the family tree Tess' sister Cecilia keeps. The first Noncoiré to leave France for Quebec was indeed the fair-haired boy. Somehow, Lucia must have taken him back to his grandparents where he grew up not knowing his true heritage—human or demon.

Tess isn't going to like that little bit of information. I can only hope that the demon in her is so diluted with human blood that she can't accidentally transform into a bat under extreme duress or anger. I don't think Lucia knew her own heritage when she escaped Tuscany. If she did, then she would have transformed and flown over the wall and out of harm's way.

Tess' blood is almost two hundred years more dilute. She should be safe. I hope. She's never ached to transform at the quarter waxing moon like other mixed bloods.

I think Lucia knows her connection to Tess. The name is not common. And she has this fondness for my babe. If she knows, then I doubt she'll harm her descendant. After all, she went to great lengths to protect her child. The family ties are blood ties. Tess' blood calls to her great, great, multigreat grandmother.

Not harming Tess doesn't mean she will go out of her way to protect Tess.

I pray my babe is safe.

I can't smell any demon in her, and I bonded with her like any good imp will bond with a human Warrior. Never heard even a whisper of imp and Kajiri pairing up.

So let's just keep that a secret from her for now. She really hates bats. Fears them, too.

Cecilia has a lot to answer for. It was she who scared three-year-old Tess out of her wits in a bat Halloween costume. Scared her so much that she quakes in fear and goes all sweaty at the mere mention of a bat.

Gulp. Maybe her phobia really stems from knowing deep in her hind brain that part of her wants to take on the natural bat form of a Damiri demon.

Later. I'll deal with all that later.

Right now, I'm going to drop this ring in her lap just to see how she reacts.

Now, where is Tess?

A sharp wind swirled around us.

"That storm is likely to dump rain soon. We'd best get going," Gollum said, sounding as reluctant to separate from our kiss as I.

"The sooner we see what we need to see, the sooner we can return to the hotel." I swallowed my smile. We both knew what would happen back at the hotel. Tingles ran all through me like champagne bubbles in my blood.

"Right." He kept looking into my eyes, almost reading my mind.

Well, my thoughts were pretty close to the surface.

Before he could tug me back to the car, I bent and placed two loose stones together, the little one atop the other. "Ours."

Laughing and holding hands, we climbed back aboard the huge SUV.

"What do you think the Hoodoos are for?"

"I don't know. No one wants to talk folklore about this place, though they'll talk forever about the stories depicted in the rock paintings," Gollum rambled on, much as Gollum was wont to ramble about favored subjects. Just one of the things I love about him. He's a wellspring of information.

"There's one string of images of a steam train and a trestle that depicts an actual wreck in the late 1800s. Another very ancient one shows a tragic fall of a young man from a high place and the ordeal he and his father went through getting him back home. The obvious truth behind these incidents leads anthropologists to think the others are more than random graffiti."

"I'd like to see some of those paintings. Maybe they'll give us some insight, or directions."

"First stop is the Visitor Center. The best petroglyphs are beyond it."

The road climbed a slight hill and turned a corner . . .

"Oh, my God!" My mouth fell open. Towering walls

of red filled the valley below. Single weathered rock formations stood out in a barren plain of brown. Clusters of rocks nestled together in fanciful outlines. Tall mountains with rounded slopes and sheer cliffs. Cave openings, arches, everywhere signs of time's slow erosion.

All red.

As if the rocks themselves burned with an unholy fire.

Chapter 35

*No reliable dating process exists for petroglyphs. In
cases where the images were created by scraping off
the black patina, regrowth of a new patina suggests
approximate time spans.*

GOLLUM DRONED ON ABOUT iron in the
rock. I didn't care. I twisted and turned, afraid I'd
miss something.

"We've got to find the Goblin Rock. Just like the one
in the show," I said over and over.

"This valley stretches for miles. There are side roads
and trails. People get lost hiking around here. And
there's no water."

"Then look for activity of the mutant faery on steroids kind. I'm sure Gregbaum has set them to guard his
private portal."

"Maps at the Visitor Center. And photos. We'll find
the goblin, but it's going to take some time."

"We only have today. Waxing quarter moon tomorrow night."

"And a fierce storm building. Looks like enough
water in those clouds to cause flash flooding." Gollum
sped up, taking the twisting road a little too fast for my

taste. But he got us to the Visitor Center in only a few moments.

Inside, native art, sculpture, and baskets tempted me. CDs of music and books made my fingers itch and my credit card burn. Lots and lots of books. I needed to examine each and every one. I needed to talk to the people who worked here. If only I had the time to totally immerse myself in the magic of this beautiful valley.

"Have you ever seen a rock formation that looks like a goblin?" I finally asked one of the guides.

"Um. Describing a particular formation is very subjective." The young woman wearing the gray-green ranger uniform cast a wary glance at a large group of people milling around. With jet-black hair pulled into a ponytail and a coppery cast to her skin, I guessed that more than one indigenous aboriginal lurked in her family tree.

All the people in the group she indicated wore badges that boasted a large cross in each corner with barely enough room for the name in the center.

How politically correct of her. Don't use the goblin word in front of church-going tourists.

Gnashing my teeth, I turned my attention to a rack of postcards. Lots of different views naming the rocks innocuous things like "Lion" or "Turtle."

"I've got a line on some petroglyphs that might help us," Gollum said. He tugged on my arm and handed me a stack of maps, books, fliers, postcards.

"Spend your entire expense account?"

"Not quite. But I may come back for some of those baskets worked around deer horns. Magnificent examples of symbolism for my classes."

I liked the way he placed a firm hand at the small of my back and leaned close to speak to me. He radiated clear signals that we belonged together. I envisioned us going on together like this, working closely, sharing ideas and careers and goals, for a long, long time.

Funny I never had thought of a distant future with Donovan, only a passion-filled present.

Hot monkey sex isn't everything.

"I don't suppose you fence?" I asked as we climbed back into the car.

"I know the principles and can quote the rule book, but no, I do not engage in that violent sport." He looked sad.

I wanted to reach out to him comfortingly. "Oh, well, we'll find other things to do together." Damn, I was hoping to replace Donovan as a sparring partner.

The next stop in our quest was an area called "Mouse's Tank." We drove north from the Visitor Center along a two-lane paved track imitating a road. Buses and cars filled the tiny parking lot. As we drove in, three buses hastily loaded their passengers, all of them anxiously looking at the sky.

Luminous white clouds with black underbellies roiled higher and higher. Rain soon. I hoped we had time. An intense storm could wash out the roads. Good thing we'd opted for four-wheel drive.

"Late 1800s, an outlaw Indian hid out here for months. It's the only reliable water source at the surface in the entire valley," Gollum paraphrased the pamphlet he read. "It's rich in petroglyphs."

"And there's an interpretive sign." I pointed at a large set of drawings covered in plexiglass and mounted at eye level.

Gollum opened the back hatch and retrieved a hefty looking backpack.

"What?"

"Two years in the African bush. I learned to never venture into an unknown area without supplies." He clamped his mouth closed.

"The two years you spent in the Peace Corps?" Those years had come into question before—by Homeland Security and the Marines no less. I wondered what secrets he guarded regarding the dark continent.

"Yeah, the Peace Corps." He slung his arms through the pack straps, and walked to the sign.

He looked over the top of his glasses at drawings and nicely lettered translations. "Some of these are okay. Some of them have been whitewashed to make them politically correct—but no one will admit that. We'll be better off taking a bunch of digitals and downloading them into the laptop. Then we can interpret them ourselves." He set off down the marked path with long strides, too absorbed in the anthropological treasure to remember me.

I shrugged and followed. Good thing I run five miles most mornings when I'm at home. I had to pump my legs double time to catch up with his long strides. A sharpness in the stretch of my inner thigh reminded me I'd hurt myself, badly, only a few days ago.

If we did indeed become a couple, would my life be one long catch-up with his brain and his long legs?

"The footing is tricky here." He paused at a slight drop-off, holding out his hand to me with a grin.

He hadn't forgotten me after all. I clasped his fingers. My world brightened far more than the gloomy cloud cover should have allowed. The three metal stairs installed by the parks department—or whoever maintained the trail—were covered in sand and looked a bit rickety. The jumble of rocks beside them didn't look any steadier. We balanced each other and jumped to safety.

We walked about one hundred yards hand in hand, comfortable together. We fell into a rhythm of steps that almost matched.

"This place is truly ancient," I whispered. "I feel like an intruder into sacred space."

"Me, too. It's something akin to the atmosphere inside a cathedral. Something waiting and observing."

Like a gargoyle. Like Donovan.

I looked around anxiously. No sign of anything *visible*.

"We won't linger," Gollum reassured me. He wrapped an arm about my shoulders. "And remember, we're here to learn, not to desecrate."

"Every place is sacred. It's the actions of people that desecrate it," I quoted a half-remembered book.

More people returned to their cars than traveled in our direction. The twisting canyon channeled a chill wind. I was glad I'd worn a sweater over my jeans and T-shirt.

"I thought this area was supposed to be covered in rock art," Gollum said. He looked all around him with a puzzled frown.

I searched, too. "Look up." I pointed.

"How come I didn't see that?" he gasped, taking in the black on red, or beige on black handprints, stick figures, and squiggly lines that marched across the rock face twenty or more feet above us.

"Because you're too tall. You have to look down to keep from stepping on other people. I have to look up to see around you."

"Being five foot nothing has its advantages." He peered down at me. Then closed the difference in our heights for a quick kiss. Sweet and affectionate.

It ended too soon.

"That's five foot two," I countered, still gazing fondly into his eyes. "Grandma Maria is five foot nothing."

"Camera?" He broke the moment.

I hauled it out of my pocket, one-handed, reluctant to let go of him with the other.

Between the two of us, we snapped over one hundred photos. A growing awareness of isolation and the freshening wind drew us closer together. We progressed along the trail more rapidly than we expected.

"That looks like a family dancing together," I whispered, pointing to a line of stick figures holding hands. Snap, snap.

"I think that one next to them is a shaman, see the antlers on his head?"

"The squiggle lines could be water. See there's a break where they spread out, a river crossing."

"I'd almost bet the single squiggle is the course of a journey, each bend could represent a day's travel."

My eyes kept returning to the groups of human figures dancing in a circle. Faint smudges, an almost round "head" with triangular shoulders and long body trailing off, above them looked ominous. But they could be just smudges, not necessarily spirits or predators.

My vision tilted and rocked. For half a moment the images and symbols came alive. "Guardians protecting an important shaman," I whispered. "Worshipers coming here in respect, offering food and water to the spirits. Another man who doesn't respect anyone, not even himself, is cast out."

The world reeled around me clockwise, then reversed and halted back at the beginning, bringing me back into myself, in the here and now.

"Interesting idea," Gollum mused. He took more pictures.

"What about the cross—recent Christian missionaries?" I asked, pointing to another image near the family.

"Judging from the patina that has regrown, I think it's older. More likely it represents the four directions. See how the top doesn't point straight up? It goes off to the side a bit; could be aimed at true north. Hard to tell. My sense of direction is twisted around."

"Mine, too." I stopped for a moment and closed my eyes, trying to feel the tug of the north pole, just like Scrap taught me. The increasing wind tugged at me from all directions. I had no sense of where I was. Or when I was.

"Scrap?" I called, hoping he'd help me out.

Silence.

Swallows chirping and swooping about signaled water. We searched further. The trail ended.

The birds showed us the recess that held a miniature reservoir. Hidden beneath another of the ubiquitous arches, I had to lean precariously over the top of a boulder to catch a glimpse of the clear pool. If Gollum hadn't steadied my balance, I might have fallen in. The air inside the chamber—roofed to slow evaporation, and open on two sides and part of a third—smelled damp, but not rank. I guessed the sandstone filtered the water clear as it seeped from above.

"Easy to get trapped in there." I shuddered and withdrew quickly. Drowning in the desert seemed a particularly horrible way to go. I was certain some villain in my next book would meet his justly deserved end that way.

"No wonder Mouse was able to hide out for months. Unless you know this 'tank' is here, you'd never find it," Gollum said. His voice echoed in the water chamber as he took his own turn looking in.

"We'd better start back. That storm is getting closer. This trail looks like a flood channel and I don't want to get caught here when the rain hits," I warned.

We spotted more petroglyphs and arched caves on the way back, taking yet more pictures.

The parking lot was empty by the time we reached our car.

Something ominous crawled up my back.

"I don't like this," I said. "Something smells wrong."

"It's just the electricity in the air. Extra ozone. We'll get thunder and a lightning show before long," Gollum reassured me, stowing the backpack.

"If Scrap were here, he could scout ahead for us."

"Where is he?"

"I don't know. He refused to come. Something about weird magnetics among the rocks scare him." I saw again the drawing of the disrespectful man being cast out of the valley.

"I don't like the sound of that. Let's start back. Keep your eyes peeled."

We headed back the way we'd come. Having learned my lesson with the rock symbols, I looked up as well as all around.

"There!" I pointed to some unusually large birds circling an area south of the road, west of the Visitor Center. They flew an ever-changing spiral, moving west and then south, never getting too far off one central point. The silhouettes were wrong, proportions distorted. Nothing sleek and aerodynamic about those airborne beasts.

Once more, I thought of gargoyles watching and waiting.

"I don't think those are birds," I said.

"But they are predators," Gollum agreed.

A flash of lightning left black spots in my vision and strange afterimages. But I'd seen the distinctive ragged bat shape of the wings of Gregbaum's mutant faeries.

Chapter 36

Rock, one of the hardest substances in nature is gently shaped and molded by water, one of the most pliable and flexible substances.

THE RING BURNS HOT and heavy in my hand. I've got to drop it. But I can't. Tess is nowhere near. She has to have it on her finger to invoke universal laws of possession.

I seek in a wider and wider circle for her. We are so tightly bonded I should be able to just follow the threads of love tinged with her unique colors of gold and yellow and topaz. They are faint. Something masks them from my perceptions.

There is only one place that I know of that can do that.

The Valley of Fire.

My blood runs cold with fear.

She needs me. Trouble looms on her horizon. The mutant faeries circle and swarm. Their flight plan brings them closer and closer to her. They draw their swords and fold their wings to dive.

I have to go to Tess. Now

Cautiously, I circle her essence, avoiding the flea demons on guard in the chat room. They nip at me, over and over, never satisfied with just a little bit of blood. Always needing more. Just like a vampire. Or a demon.

Then, at last, I find a faint echo of my Warrior. That tentative signature is weaker than the ring when it bulged through the dimensions.

I have to trust my instincts and my love for Tess to break through the barriers. With a deep breath, I close my eyes and plunge.

I fall and fall through time and space. I keep falling until I sense air around my wings. At the last instant they snap open and slow my descent to Tess' shoulders.

I rub my cheek against her hair, grateful to be back with her. I am complete now. We have a mission.

She commands me to her hand, needing me to transform and fight those awful red-and-black faeries.

My blood runs hot now. I flash from fog to flamingo to poppy in an instant. I stretch and thin. My ears start to curve into one blade, my tail sharpens into the other.

Before I lose it, I drop the ring onto her finger.

And then, just as I am almost complete, Tess twirling me like a baton to help me, something reaches out and grabs my essence.

I am yanked away from my Tess into blackness.

"What!" I screeched. Scrap was here, in my hands, fast becoming a weapon to fight those horrible beasts. And then he disappeared. Just winked out . . . no, more like continued to stretch wire-thin and rush through the air to someplace . . .

Someplace like that towering rock formation about a half mile from the small parking lot and picnic ground where we've pulled over. A boulder on top looked like a round hay bale resting on its side. Below it a tower with protrusions and arches and openings just like . . .

"Gollum, look at those rocks."

"Which rocks? There are dozens of them." Again he focused at foot- and eye-level as he shrugged into his backpack and pulled a collapsible walking stick from a side pouch.

"Look *up*. And out."

And then he spotted it and his jaw dropped. There,

in the near distance was the side profile of the Goblin Rock we sought.

"Why didn't we see it on the way in?"

"Because the angle and the light were wrong. The sun was behind the clouds. Now it's below them, coming at us sideways."

I took off running. I had to see more of that rock, test it, probe it, make certain this was the one we wanted and that a portal truly did exist.

Eight winged forms, with blood-red scaly skin, wearing black leather knickers and vests to match their wings, alit between me and the formation. The last remnants of sunlight glinted on the blue-black steel of their broadswords.

"What better signal that this is what I'm looking for than you guys guarding it," I sneered at them.

Where in the hell was Scrap when I truly needed him?

"Tess, catch," Gollum called. I reached up, only half daring to turn.

His aim was true. The walking stick sailed into my hand, fully extended. It had a cork knob on one end, and a small point on the other.

Not exactly a Celestial Blade, but something. I grasped it like a quarterstaff and faced my opponents.

Gollum's ragged breathing sounded in my ear. Crap. Now I'd have to protect him as well as myself and get us out of here.

"I'll watch your back," he said.

I didn't have time to snort. The first of the mob lunged at me with his four-foot blade.

I blocked it with the staff, heavy metal ringing against lightweight metal. The staff bent but didn't break.

A quick series of attacks and parries. My ears clanged from the noise.

Movement on my periphery. Scrap? Please, oh, please, let it be Scrap.

No such luck. Just the bad guys trying to circle us.

I kept the attacker in my center focus, trying to maneuver him around so I only had to battle on one front.

Gollum's body warmth against my back didn't reassure me much.

Then a whoosh of air and a black-and-red form slammed against a small outcropping five yards away. Air rushed out of his lungs and his neck bent unnaturally.

"What?"

"Aikido. I used his own energy against him. Quite an interesting phenomenon . . ."

"Not now, Gollum. Just get me his sword."

"Oh. Yes. Of course."

The bad guys backed off a bit, suddenly wary of us. Easy prey had turned into nasty cats. I was madder than a wet cat—mad at Scrap for disappearing and mad at myself for dashing into this situation.

Mad made me mean. I'm not proud of it, but it is a fact.

I swung the staff like a club, aiming for the gut of my nearest opponent. He skipped back, confused.

These guys weren't terribly bright, didn't know how to think on their feet.

A fat raindrop hit my forehead with a splat. Then another. The dry sandy soil sopped up the first drops thirstily. But it came too fast, drenching me in seconds. The ground beneath my feet became a slurry.

Once more, I faced these guys with treacherous footing.

Shit! Actually I said something a lot stronger and less polite.

But if I had trouble finding traction in hiking boots, they weren't doing any better in bare feet.

The next thing I knew Gollum slid a sword grip into my left hand. I'd been too busy watching red-faced bad faeries watch me to notice how he got it.

"I'll love you forever for getting this," I whispered, dropping the staff as I gripped the sword.

"I'll hold you to that."

Using both hands on the big grip, I lifted it high over my head. Not exactly a fourteen-ounce fencing foil. But thanks to my training with the Sisterhood of the Celestial Blade, I knew how to use it.

My shoulders groaned. I'd skipped weight training over the last few months.

My closest opponent opened his eyes wide. I saw fear reflected there.

I swung the blade and felt it connect with muscle and bone.

An unearthly screech pierced my eardrums. I didn't dare cover them to block out some of the pain.

Another, more daring (or desperate) bad guy jumped toward me, using his wings to get him close. Too close.

He should have read the rule book. If you are close enough to kiss, you are too close to fence.

I wasn't fencing. I was fighting for my life.

An upper cut of the sword connected between his legs and bounced back. Damn, he must have been wearing a cup.

He grinned at me, showing far too many razor-sharp teeth, not unlike Scrap's multiple rows.

A quick spin and I backkicked into his gut.

He doubled over with a whoosh. I used my momentum to get the sword up and slashed his neck. The rain turned his black blood gray. It joined the small river forming at my feet and disappeared downslope—into the base of the goblin rock.

I smelled sulfur and rotting garbage tinged with black licorice.

They'd had enough. With another unearthly screech, they all lifted into the air, grabbed their fallen comrades, and sped off to the south, trying to outrun the storm.

I tracked them as they disappeared into the lowering clouds. For the first time in my life I wished I had bat wings to help me fly after them.

"Tess, we've got to get out of here." Gollum sounded frantic. "We're standing in the middle of a wash. It's going to flood!"

As if to emphasize his words, lightning seared across the sky. Thunder boomed before the jagged fork had completely disappeared. For half an instant everything in my path showed sharp and clear in the too bright light.

Afterimages nearly blinded me.

Still holding the sword—don't ask me why I didn't throw down the extra weight—I grabbed his outstretched hand. He scooped up the backpack by one strap with the other and we dragged each other uphill, toward the SUV.

Another flash and boom. This time I spotted a black winged image at the lower edge of the clouds. One of the black faeries pointed his sword toward us. The next bolt of lightning channeled down the blue-black blade directly into the gas tank of the SUV.

Flames and heat erupted in a tower of black smoke. The blast sent me reeling backward. I lost my balance and fell into a gush of water at the edge of the wash.

Where am I?

I want to choke and sob in fear. I can't find my body.

Total blackness surrounds me, robs me of all my senses. No smell, no sight, not even a hint of a taste on my forked tongue.

Do I still have a tongue?

Tess! I scream with my mind. The words echo back to me, without sound.

Okay, officially time to panic.

Tess, help me!

Nothing.

I am nothing.

My Tess will die because I am nothing.

Chapter 37

Rain is scarce in the Valley of Fire, but when it comes, it can cause torrential flash floods that alter the landscape in a moment.

"*O*FF YOUR ASS, sweetheart. We've got to get to higher ground." Gollum hauled me to my feet, one-handed. The muscles in his arm strained and stood out.

A sudden deep lethargy washed through me, stronger than the waters swirling at my feet, reaching for my knees.

Sharp pain on my cheek.

"Snap out of it, Tess. This is no time to go all weak and girlie on me."

"What? How dare you!" Anger heated my blood. I still felt heavy, but enough strength trickled through me to follow Gollum. As long as he held my hand.

I felt like a psychic vampire, feeding off his energy just to stay alive.

We scrambled and reached. Stepped and slid. Eventually, he hauled me over the lip of a rock into a cave opening. This time he needed both arms to get me up.

"Is it safe?" I choked out through chattering teeth.

My wet underwear clung to me like a second skin of snow. Jeans and sweaters did little to ward off the chill.

"As safe as anywhere. Water formed the cave, trickling through here over aeons. I don't think we'll get inundated. The walls are still pretty thick.

I checked them out skeptically.

"Trust me on this, Tess. I know how to survive in the bush."

"You also know some pretty esoteric martial arts." Memory of the battle returned to me. Memories of waking to find U.S. Marines passed out on the floor with bruises on their throats chilled me more than the rain.

"Well, yes. I had to switch from some more aggressive and lethal forms after I took a vow of nonviolence. But that was before I met you and learned I might need to more actively defend myself upon occasion." He chattered on, filling the cave with calm words as nature raged outside.

A fierce wind howled through the canyons, adding its voice to the thunder, the pounding rain, and the rushing floods.

"Nonviolence?" I had to back up a bit, having lost my thoughts while he pulled a tiny camp stove out of his pack and lit it. The acrid scent of canned fuel burning sharpened my wandering focus. "Is that part of the Peace Corps?"

"Well, not exactly. I wasn't in the Peace Corps. Or at least, not what you think of as the Peace Corps. But we did keep the peace in a way."

"You're rambling, Gollum. Covering the truth with so many words I can't find the lie. You're very good at that."

I left hanging my primary, and frequently vocalized, objection to Donovan: the fact that he lied, often, glibly, and with convincing acting.

"Well, um, I guess I have to tell you the truth, don't I?"

"If we want to build on that kiss we shared, yes, you do. My life is an open book to you. About time you shared a bit of yours."

By this time, he'd filled a pot with rainwater and set it on the stove to boil. Packets of instant coffee came out of the pack next, along with sugar. Lots and lots of sugar.

"No, cream. Sorry. But then you shouldn't have real cream anymore."

"You're stalling." I dug into the pack myself this time. Meals Ready to Eat. A silvery space blanket. A sleeping bag. First aid kit. And more. The thing must have weighed fifty pounds, and he hauled it around like I did my purse.

"I ran away from home and became a mercenary for two years."

Something? Anything is better than this nothingness. Sort of like having five full-sized imps jump me and land on my chest. Then one gets off to beat me in the face. Still a pressure choking the life from me but not quite so heavy.

A ray of hope. Who said that as long as there is hope, there is life?

Now that the deep oppression has eased, my panic lessens as well.

Now I can think beyond gibbering.

Now I must face the darkness within me as well as without.

I need a cigar.

"A mercenary? I just don't see it," I said, sitting cross-legged in front of Gollum's stove. Its tiny warmth wasn't enough (I was almost surprised I felt no trace of the muscle pull). Chills made my entire body shake and tremble.

"Get out of those wet clothes and wrap the space blanket around you," Gollum ordered. He began peeling off his own sweatshirt and polo shirt.

We both looked at his clothes as they came away in pieces.

"Wait." I cast aside my drenched sweater. Too bad it was acrylic and not wool. Wool would have insulated me wet or dry. "Where did that cut come from?" I tentatively ran my hands across a long bloody slash that started in his left bicep—a very nicely formed and firm bicep at that—and continued down his chest to disappear beneath the belt of his jeans.

"Oh." He stared at the blood oozing out of the cut. It looked raw and angry, ripe for infection. His face paled and his glasses slipped off.

I caught them before they hit the ground and smashed.

"Scrap, get your ass back here. We've got a demon wound."

Nothing.

"Imp spit won't help this," Gollum muttered, just barely remaining upright. "It's a sword cut, not a demon bite."

"Good thing you brought a first aid kit and started water to heat. I'll need to clean the wound. Lie down on the blanket while I patch you up."

"I'm fine."

"No, you aren't. If you were fine, you'd still be sitting and not falling over." A gentle shove to his good shoulder got him flat on his back.

During my years as a schoolteacher I'd learned basic first aid. I'd helped Sister Serena in the clinic back at the Citadel. I wished she was here to help. She'd know if the wound was deep enough to need stitches.

After basic cleaning with soapy water—he'd brought along one of those miniature bars you get in hotel bathrooms—and a liberal dose of basic antiseptic, I used every adhesive strip and gauze pad I could ferret out of the kit. I was about to start ripping up his T-shirt (the same dark maroon as the polo) when he stayed my hand.

"I'll be fine. I wasn't even aware that the demon managed to slash me. It was just the shock of seeing my own blood. Heaven knows I've seen enough of other people's and demon blood to numb my sensibilities." He placed his glasses firmly back on his nose and struggled to sit.

I got a shoulder under him and heaved.

"Speaking of which, I still don't see you as a mercenary in Africa." I draped the space blanket around his shoulders and set about reading the directions on the MREs. He needed food and liquid to heal the wound and fight infection.

"You have to understand, I suffered a great deal of rage at the time."

"You?"

"I'd just turned twenty-one. I'd graduated from Yale at nineteen, completed the course work at Columbia for my first masters and was halfway through the research for my thesis. Yet I was still reduced to working for the company that handles my mother's family finances. Entire financial empires built on lies, deceit, manipulation, and beating down the competition at any cost. I lived in New York and hated every minute of it."

Okay. I knew he was smart and that his family had money. This sounded like three or four steps above what I'd imagined.

I sat back and listened, hoping that once he got started, he wouldn't stop until I'd learned everything I could about him.

"Then my dad died and a bunch of other crap happened. Gramps was the only one I could talk to, and then he had a heart attack. Mother ordered me not to upset him with my trivial problems. I left New York and didn't stop for a long time. Somewhere in my head I had the idea I'd become a Warrior of the Celestial Blade, if I could only find a Citadel and an imp. Africa seemed as good a place as any. The army wouldn't take me because of my vision. Mercenary companies aren't quite so picky."

He swallowed the barely warm coffee I handed him. His eyes remained focused on the inside of the empty cup.

"I made it through basic still angry. Then my sergeant

handed me a uniform, a gun, and a backpack." He fell into a deep contemplative silence.

"Surely your rage ran out before two years," I whispered.

"It did. But I'd signed a contract. The day it was up, I went home. I didn't know what I was going to do, only I wasn't going back to the financial firm. My first night back in New York, some kid tried to mug me for thirty-five bucks in my wallet."

Another long silence.

I knew I couldn't break it. He had to speak on his own. The hurt on his face told me more than words.

"I killed him with my bare hands. Then I looked at him, really looked at him. He was a runaway, literally starving to death. I'd seen enough starving kids in Africa to know what it looks like. He needed my few bucks to buy food."

I pulled his head down into my lap, caressing his fine silver-gilt hair and let him sob out his guilt and grief.

"At that moment, I took a vow of nonviolence. I intend to keep it, Tess," he finally said into the darkness. "I will defend myself, and you, to a point. But I will never kill again."

Chapter 38

Little evidence exists to indicate any group of people have lived permanently in the Valley of Fire.

"CAN YOU EVER FORGIVE ME for killing an innocent?" Gollum asked quietly in the darkness. The cave shrouded us and muffled the sound of the rain outside. We might be the only two people in the world.

"I'm probably the one person in the world who understands," I said quietly.

"Those kids who mugged you last month." A glimmer of hope came through his voice.

"They weren't starving, but they were so young. They had their whole lives ahead of them. Except I broke the boy's trachea. And I enjoyed the release of all my pent-up frustrations and anger and aggression."

This time I fell into a silence only I could break. The vivid image of the feel of the boy's throat beneath my fingers. The satisfying crunch as I slammed my hand into him.

Then the horrifying knowledge that I'd killed him. With my bare hands.

"If Allie and her partner hadn't showed up when they

did, if Joe hadn't known how to perform a tracheotomy in the field, I'd have murdered a fifteen-year-old child."

He squeezed my hand and sat up. "We'd better get some hot food into us, and cold clothes off of us."

We set about getting ourselves fed and warm. Gollum proved quite skilled at survival camping. In moments I had the sleeping bag wrapped around my nearly naked body and my hands wrapped around a steaming cup of sweet coffee. He wore the space blanket like a toga, his long limbs sticking out awkwardly. Only he wasn't awkward or nerdy now. He was magnificently alpha male taking care of me.

Somehow I always knew he'd be a plaid boxer shorts kind of guy. Nothing pretentious about him. Unlike Donovan who wore black and tight and trendy.

Finally, I had time to worry about insurance for the rental car, worry about my mom, worry about the book I needed to write, worry about how to save the faery dancers, worry about Scrap.

I lifted the cup to my mouth, avoiding the hard thinking with the anticipation of the hot liquid trickling down my throat into my tummy and spreading out from there.

Something glistened in the dim firelight. I stopped and stared.

"Gollum, where did this come from?" I couldn't look away from the diamond-and-gold filigree that adorned my right hand. It had no weight, fit me as if made for my hand, and acted as if it had been with me for a lifetime.

"Gregbaum has fat hands. Even his pinky finger is bigger than my thumb. Lady Lucia is taller than me, she has bigger hands. How come this fits so well when it was made for her?"

"We already know it's no ordinary ring." Gollum took my hand and twisted it to better catch the light. "It belongs to you now, it fits you. It suits you." He kissed my fingers. "I wish I could offer you something quite so fine."

"I think you'll manage, once we get back to civilization." His kiss warmed me more than coffee and food ever could.

"The rain is letting up. We really should do something about getting out of here." He didn't look anxious to return to reality. Our little cave seemed quite snug and comfortable.

"I think I lost my cell phone in the fight." As good an excuse as any. I'd look to make sure. Later. Much, much later.

"And mine got drowned in the rain. It needs to dry out. Maybe get a new battery before it will work again."

As if we needed excuses.

"Scrap's been gone a long time. He must have given me the ring before he took off again. I've never known him to run from a fight before."

"Maybe he knew you didn't need a lot of help this time. Imp business has always been a mystery." He looked like he might say more, but didn't.

I remembered the time I asked Gollum if he ever turned off the professorial lectures. He replied, "When I make love to a beautiful woman."

He wasn't talking now. He turned my hand over and kissed the palm. Then the wrist. When his lips met my elbow, I thought I'd jump through the cave ceiling from the intensity.

"Scrap knows enough to give me privacy when I need it," I reassured us both. "But are you sure you're not too injured for this?"

His mouth reaching the hollow at the top of my shoulder was answer enough. Every muscle in my body turned to liquid. The sleeping bag fell away.

"Still wearing red underwear, I see," he murmured on a chuckle.

I couldn't comment on the habit developed during my year at the Citadel. Red reminded us of the blood demons spilled and we needed to avenge.

My thoughts skittered far, far away from that time.

We both came to our knees, hands and mouths exploring skin textures and tastes. I tangled my fingers in the light hair of his chest that spread out at the waist band of his shorts. I followed the enticing arrow down and down, relishing every inch of him, smooth and rough. Salty and sweet.

Then, finally, we could contain ourselves no longer. His mouth latched onto mine, open with a tentatively questing tongue.

I responded, like to like. We molded and blended together.

The last remnants of our clothing fell away. We needed no blankets. We made our own heat.

Slowly, tenderly, we touched again. Fire followed his fingertips as they traced my nipples. I nipped at his. His tongue circled my belly button.

I arched my back, willing him lower.

"Not yet, my love," he whispered. "Time. Tonight we've got time."

We took our time, learning each other's bodies, drinking in each new sensation. Dimly I noted as I covered him with a condom (smart men always have one, or a couple, in their wallet) that he'd been circumcised. Neither Donovan nor my husband had. It made no difference in the end.

At last, skin tingling, heat filling us, every nerve ending on fire, we came together in an explosion of passion. I'd never known such completeness; such a feeling of rightness.

I saw stars and knew we must have burst into a million pieces that unified the Universe. I didn't know where I left off and he began.

We affirmed life.

All too soon, the chill night and our growling stomachs brought us back to the mundane realities. I wanted nothing more than to nestle alongside my love; my one true love.

Why are you still alive? The booming voice echoed and rattled around my empty skull.

"Why indeed?"

You should not have survived.

"Tell me about it. Snatching me right out of my Warrior's hand at the moment of transformation hurt."

You dared trespass.

"So?"

Silence. Just when I thought something might show me a way out, it disappears again.

"Why am I here?" I shout into the nothingness.

You know.

"No, I don't! I was trying to do my job. A job I do very well by the way, helping my Warrior of the Celestial Blade send some nasty demons back where they belong. We restore the balance."

Small atonement for the balance you destroyed.

Oops.

I cover for my deep guilt by imagining the euphoria of tobacco smoke, hot and raw in my throat, then the rush of pleasure in my brain. Almost as good as sex.

Now how am I going to explain to Ginkgo why I didn't make our next rendezvous?

You should think instead on why you will not return to your Warrior. As long as you live here, she will live. But she will not fight demons again with the Celestial Blade.

"Now wait just one minute . . ."

We have waited many millennia. We can wait longer. But can you?

Gulp.

I really need that cigar.

We ask again, why are you alive?

"I'm alive because my Warrior needs me."

You have lied to your Warrior.

"No, I haven't. I'm always truthful with Tess."

You commit the lie of omission. Your silence puts her in danger.

"She doesn't need to know everything about me!"

You neglected to inform her when you learned the truth of the Fallen One; long before she discovered it on her own.

Ouch. That experience was so humiliating I blocked it from

my memory. I actually lost a wart in a mud puddle when the gargoyles of York Minster cast me out.

More silence, a deepening of the oppressive blackness. That fifth imp is back on top of my chest.

"I'm alive because I was more cunning than my siblings."

Imp law required your death.

"Imp law is unfair! So what if I'm a runt? So what if I'm half the size I should be? I'm cunning and I'm smart. I'm the best imp for Tess. We fit together well. We work together well. Together we have taken out a tribe of rogue Sasquatch. We have battled vengeful Windago who broke the rules of King Scazzy. We've subdued those mutant faeries on steroids. Show me any other full-sized imp who has done that much and lived to tell about it."

Another silence. I get the feeling whoever or whatever judges me is thinking about that.

You survived those who were sent to murder you—to carry out imp justice. But you did not stop there.

Now I'm in real trouble.

I watched the dawn burst above the horizon. No lingering glimmer while the birds woke up. I'd grown used to a gradual lighting further north. But here, in the desert with a long, long horizon, one moment a bare hint of sun, then the fiery orb appeared and filled the valley outside our cave with morning freshness.

The floods had passed. A few droplets sparkled on plant leaves, then evaporated in the desert air.

I sat fully dressed and cross-legged on the lip of the cave, rocking back and forth. Only a tiny pull on my inner thigh remained of my previous injury.

"Where are you, Scrap?" I whispered, not wanting to wake Gollum.

"Hasn't he returned?" Gollum asked. He propped himself up on one elbow and blinked at me.

I handed him his glasses. They'd gotten buried in the jumble of his discarded clothing. Wonderful memories

of last night wanted to settle peacefully all through me.
Worry pushed them aside.

"He's never been gone this long. I think he's in trouble." I returned to my vigil at the cave mouth.

"He's clever . . ."

"Something has gone terribly wrong. I can feel it." My
eyes kept returning to the Goblin Rock fifty yards away.
Long shadows made it look black, robbing it of dimension and texture. Only its distinct silhouette stood out.

"Park rangers will be coming around soon. We should
be out by the car when they arrive," Gollum said. He set
about folding up our camp and returning it to his backpack. "You should eat."

"I can't."

He sat beside me. I had to scooch over to make room
for him in the narrow opening.

"Something is terribly wrong if you can't eat. Let me
at least make you coffee."

"Whatever. I'm going to hunt for my cell phone and
get a better look at that rock."

Without waiting for him, I slid down the five-feet-high cliff face. Finding Scrap was something I had to do
on my own. That goblin cave looked like the best place
to start.

Over and over I heard Scrap whisper in my ear. *If you
die, I die. If I die, you die.*

Back at the Citadel we'd sat death watch over a Sister. Her imp, Tulip, had taken a demon tag to protect her.
Sister Jenny suffered no injury, yet she died by inches
because her imp suffered. Neither one would let the
other go. Finally, Tulip had succumbed and Sister Jenny
died with a sigh of relief.

I suspected Scrap had delivered a *coup de grâce* for
them. Who would do that for us?

I hoped that Gollum loved me enough to break
through his vow of nonviolence for that one last mercy.

Chapter 39

In 1935 the Valley of Fire became Nevada's first state park.

*W*E ARE THE GUARDIANS *of this sacred place. We cannot allow your murderous ways to desecrate our valley.*

"Self-defense is not murder." This could get dicey. I have to choose my words carefully or lose everything.

If I die, Tess dies. I cannot allow that to happen to my babe. She's mine and deserves the best imp possible.

That's me. One way or another, I'm going to get back to her.

"I killed those who attacked me. That is allowed."

They had a lawful warrant for your execution.

"They didn't tell me that. They just jumped me. I fought back the only way I could, as would you, or any self-respecting imp."

You did not stop there.

A cigar would really help me think right now. When did I ever let that stop me?

"Good imps have to give in to the bloodlust. That's how we continue to fight demons when all looks lost."

Bloodlust must be controlled.

"But that goes against the definition of bloodlust. We

lose control and keep swinging until there is no one left to swing at."

Even the innocent?

There's that "I" word. Gods, I hate it when people throw that at me.

"When I am the Celestial Blade, Tess controls me. I can only kill those she decides must die."

You had not yet bonded with your Warrior when you murdered five innocent imps, three of them your siblings.

"Yeah, well, they were standing around watching, and cheering on my vicious siblings with their compounded bloodlust. One brother with a grudge fed his hate to another and another. They let that anger compound, bouncing back and forth until it became a living entity that would not rest until they killed someone. The watchers fed that bloodlust as well. They weren't totally innocent."

Silence.

This is it. This is the moment when these Guardians decide my fate.

"Tess, no, you can't climb that rock." Gollum lifted me down from where I clung to the sandstone precariously. The soft surface crumbled when I put my weight on it.

"I've got to. Can't you see, that's Scrap's face up there." I pointed at the round hay bale that had taken on a full face twisted into a grimace, more than just the suggestion of eyes, nose, and mouth. Intelligence dimmed by pain peeked out from those cavernous eyes.

"I don't know Scrap like you do, Tess. All I see is eroded red sandstone. I can't let you risk yourself on a treacherous climb. If the rangers find you up there, we'll be in big trouble. Bigger trouble than from the burned-out car and staying past closing. Maybe in jail so we can't make tonight's deadline with the moon." He sounded so practical, and so very concerned.

I knew he stopped me because it was the best thing. But if Scrap were somehow trapped inside that formation ...

I collapsed in a heap at the base, sobbing and pounding out my frustration. I could not banish the emptiness in my gut where Scrap used to be. That annoying, preening, sarcastic, cigar-smoking brat! Not even Gollum's love could fill that void.

"Come back to me, Scrap. Please come back to me."

Do you consider the deaths of the bystanders necessary?

"Well, when you put it that way . . . in a way, yeah. I needed to teach all of Imp Haven that I'm not just a useless runt. I'm someone to contend with. I count. I'm just as important as they are."

Did you not prove that when you killed your attackers?

"Well, yeah. I guess."

Can you bring yourself to regret those deaths?

"Can I have a cigar while I think about it?"

Instantly, the darkness grows thicker. I feel my cute little bottom sagging deeper and deeper into the hell this nothingness becomes. My hearts slow. My thoughts drift.

Who knows how long I've been here. Who knows how long I must stay. No light, no sound. This is worse than the diamond prison of the rogue imp.

Tess must be worried. I ache all over that my actions cause her pain. I regret that if I die, she must die. She deserves better.

"I do regret that I needlessly killed." Maybe not for the reasons these Guardians wanted to hear, but if in any way I have done something that will come back to hurt my dahling Tess, then yes, I do regret it.

For once I keep my thoughts to myself and my voice silent. I owe Tess that much.

You have much left to give. You and your Warrior have a destiny to fulfill. Remember the darkness within you and learn from it.

The imp within the diamond didn't have that chance.

"Tess, someone's coming. I can see a dust trail on the road. We have to flag them down or we'll never get out of here in time to rescue the faery dancers." Gollum tugged at my shoulder.

He could have picked me up and carried me. I think he knew that I had to come of my own volition. Abandoning Scrap had to be my decision alone.

I wasn't ready to do that. But I had to. I had to trust that if he ever broke free, he'd find me.

Maybe when I came back to open the portal, I could get him out.

The rising sun glimmered against the diamond in the ring.

I twisted it, trying to get it off. I hated it. I hated that it was the last artifact of power Scrap gave me. Perhaps stealing it from Gregbaum had caused him to get trapped here in the Valley of Fire.

The ring wouldn't come off. It just kept turning around and around my finger.

I glanced up, looking for inspiration.

Elongated streams of smoke with oval, faceless heads and triangular bodies that trailed off into thin wisps seeped from the rock. Just like in the petroglyphs. They flew around and around me, swooping to include me in their widening spiral around the Goblin Rock.

I ducked, but kept staring at them, entranced by their awesome beauty.

Then in clouds of black, copper, sage, and deep purple they separated to the far corners of the park.

Or was that just dawn light catching a mist?

Hiya, babe. Miss me? Scrap landed on my shoulder with a poof of displaced air.

"You've got some explaining to do, young man." My tremendous relief came out in anger. I couldn't help it.

Later, babe. Right now you've got some explaining to do to those rangers looking over the mess of a car. What'd you do to it anyway?

"Those black faeries channeled lightning into it because you weren't here to help me defeat them." I scrambled to my feet and hastened after Gollum.

Don't suppose he's got a cigar in that backpack ...

I rolled my eyes. The almost sensation of Scrap on my shoulder felt good. I wanted to hug him, smother him in kisses, and spank his bottom all at the same time.

"Say, how come you lost all your warts?"

He hung his head in humiliation and faded until all I could see of him was his little pug nose and the outline of his bat-wing ears.

"You'll have plenty of opportunity to earn them back. Maybe tonight," I reassured him.

He brightened at that.

"You can go get a cigar if you want."

Nah, not yet. I don't want to leave you in this valley alone. There's all kinds of nasties hanging around.

"Like those forms that preceded you out of the rock formation?"

He looked back over his shoulder, wrapping his tail around my neck in a near choke hold.

Actually those are the good guys. The Guardians of all that is sacred within the valley.

I didn't quite hear him mutter something else. Something like "I'm one of the bad guys."

By the time I caught up with Gollum, he'd already explained with heated gestures how we got trapped in the park overnight.

"A gang of five teens were climbing the rocks. We stopped to explain to them why they shouldn't and they took offense. They torched the car! And then the storm hit and the few streetlights went out. We were trapped here. All night."

"You really need better security," I added. A trick I'd learned from schoolchildren when I taught: always make the accuser look guiltier than you are.

"Cell phones?" the fair-haired young man asked. His tanned skin flushed and he looked embarrassed.

"Out here?" I pulled mine out of my pocket and showed him the half-full battery and no bars of signal. Actually, I was a bit surprised to find it intact.

"I hope you took full insurance on the rental," said the second ranger, the same dark-haired woman I'd talked to at the Visitor Center yesterday. She nodded her head slightly in the direction of the Goblin Rock, acknowledging that I'd found it.

She probably knew something about it. And maybe something about the misty forms that had streamed out and away from it.

"Of course," Gollum replied to the insurance question, pretending affront. From the glint in his eye, I guessed he enjoyed playing this role.

A forest green SUV pulled up behind the beige park service pickup. Breven Sancroix leaned out of the driver's side window. "Thought you two might need a ride when you didn't show last night. Flash floods closed a bunch of roads. I came as soon as they bulldozed them free of debris."

I saw no sign of Fortitude. Scrap's pug nose worked overtime, seeking the big imp.

Now that's one of the bad guys. Fortitude is so bad he doesn't dare enter the valley, Scrap said. He shifted around so that his back was to the newcomer. *I dare you to ask Mr. Holier Than Thou Sancroix why his dark-skinned imp is waiting for him, safely back at the entrance.*

Chapter 40

There is a one in thirty-five chance that rain will fall in Las Vegas on any given day.

"HOW DID YOU KNOW we needed a ride?" I asked Sancroix as soon as he put his truck in gear and headed toward Las Vegas. Scrap occupied my right shoulder, looking out the window and away from our driver.

Gollum and his monster backpack stretched across the back seat. He half reclined with his feet up and the backpack in his lap, as if he didn't trust it in the rear compartment.

"Fortitude told me you were in trouble." Sancroix stared straight ahead, seemingly concentrating on the road.

Small construction vehicles with front loaders scooped gravel and sand from the pavement where washes and arroyos had overflowed their banks. We might not have been able to get out of the park last night, even with four wheel drive.

A mountain of paperwork awaited us, from both the rental agency and the park.

"I hope you have a story to tell the rental agency," Sancroix said.

"Did Fortitude tell you about our battle?"

"Yeah. He also told me your imp deserted you. No wonder you two had to go rogue. I'm surprised the imps let him live to adulthood."

Angry words of defense jumped to my lips. I swallowed them. No sense aggravating this man when he'd come to our rescue.

"How'd the imp allow your mother to marry a demon?" he asked when we reached the freeway and he could engage cruise control. "That should have brought a full herd of them down on you."

I looked over my shoulder to Gollum in the back seat. No comment from him, just a shrug of his shoulders.

"I didn't let her do anything. She eloped. I don't know how you work, but we aren't in Citadels. We have to appear to work within the law. Darren Estevez was a prominent and wealthy citizen. He paid taxes and, as far as I know, voted regularly. I couldn't just kill him and leave the body for someone else to clean up. As it was, I spent most of a day in jail, accused of his murder." And missed an important combat challenge because of it.

"How'd you know about Estevez?" Gollum finally asked. He sounded as if he didn't really care. I could tell by the way his eyes flicked about behind his glasses, that he thought furiously, weighing and assessing information.

"What he really wants to know is why you don't have an archivist assigned to you," I added.

"Had one. Didn't like the guy." Sancroix closed his mouth with a snap. No more discussion on that subject.

I looked to Gollum again for more information.

Another shrug. He didn't know any more about that than I did. Then he froze, mouth half open. "Gramps' brother," he mouthed.

His grimace told me that man had not died comfortably in bed, at home, surrounded by his loved ones.

"Mom's marriage to Darren only lasted thirty-six hours. He's dead now. We don't have to worry about it anymore."

"Don't we? Do you know how much damage a Damiri demon can do in thirty-six hours?"

I had a good idea. For weeks I wondered if Mom would ever recover. She seemed to have found her feet along with her new career. With a little help from a faery. I figured I owed Mickey and his clan a lot, even if my vows to the Sisterhood didn't compel me to rescue the dancers.

Somehow we filled the hour-long drive with boring and mundane conversation. Mostly about the storm and power outages in the city.

First thing I did back at the hotel was book the room for three extra nights. Gollum winked at me and did not engage his room beyond noon.

"Do we have time for a shower?" I asked.

"A quick one. We've got to connect with Mickey and you have to have a long conversation with Scrap about that ring."

And a longer conversation with my mom. Just to talk and share and make sure she was all right off on her own. But it wasn't even ten in the morning. She sang last night until after two, so she wouldn't be up yet.

I'd take that shower first.

Well, I can see I'm not needed for a few moments—make that an hour. I've got some errands to run. Mickey needs to know where and when to find us.

I need to know if Lady Lucia knows that Tess is her great, great, multi-great granddaughter. And if she does, is she going to tell Tess?

If she does know, there is more than a little bit of kink in her, screwing Donovan, the same man who lusts after her descendant. (I'm tired of figuring the number of greats in that relationship.)

I can't allow that. I may have atoned for some of the darkness in my soul. But when it comes to my babe, I'll kill and kill again to protect her. Even from her own ancestor.

I pop in on Lady Lucia's parlor. Empty. Dirty glasses, spilled snack trays, scattered used napkins all over the place. Cleaning services haven't arrived yet.

So I creep silently, and as invisibly as possible, toward the back of the suite. At the top of the marble stairs, I hear muted voices. A quick check leads me down to the covered patio.

The contessa wears a black caftan that covers her from neck to ankle. Only the very tips of her fingers reach beyond the heavily embroidered sleeves. A huge black straw hat with a cartwheel of a brim shelters her head and face. Smoky dark glasses with lenses that cover her from above her sculpted eyebrows to her cheekbone add to the protection.

I can smell sunscreen with an spf of about 200 on her. It almost masks the odor of stale blood. She fed last night.

The bored driver of the hearse, not the wizened boy who served drinks at the party—he's asleep in his coffin—attends her at her elbow, placing sheaves of papers on the round table before her. He's as covered as she is, and the table's umbrella shades them both.

I don't think I could pick up an aura on either of them from the numbers of layers between them and the sun. But something is leaking from Lady Lucia. Something warm and gentle that seems totally alien to her vampire image.

I sneak a little closer, very slowly, keeping to the darkest of the numerous shadows. At last, I'm on top of the hat and peek at the framed drawing that captures nearly all of Lucia's attention. Her fingers trace the image of a child's face. A blond child dressed in antique breeches, shirt, and short coat. Her son.

More than that, I see an image of a very young Tess creeping through the pencil lines.

Oh, yeah, Lucia knows that Tess is her relative. She knows and she cherishes.

Feeling good and safe from her, I flit off to my other errands.

The shower took longer than we planned since we took it together. By the light of day we delighted in relearning each other's body through the exquisite mediums of soap and water. For the first time in a long time, I felt cherished and protected without any agenda except mutual affection. I nestled my head in the hollow of his chest and just listened to the rhythm of his heart while hot water poured over us.

By the time we finished, room service had arrived with full breakfasts for us both, including beer and OJ for Scrap. He really did know how to leave us alone when we needed privacy.

Caught up with Mickey, he announced around a huge cigar. He flicked ash out the open window where he perched.

"What does Mickey have to say?" I ground out the cigar and pointed him toward nourishment.

Strangely obedient, he refrained from complaining about his lost cigar.

I stared at him, wondering what had brought about this abrupt attitude adjustment.

Mickey says that Gregbaum's magic net around the dormitory is pretty strong hoodoo. Partly faery in origin—which explains Junior's participation—partly something else he can't figure out. No way to break it without knowing everything Gregbaum and Junior know about magic. But he thinks you can break the spell around the hotel with the ring. Scrap slurped up half his breakfast in one long pull on a straw.

I relayed that message to Gollum. He dressed and munched bacon while he thought long and hard. "I need to call Gramps. I also need to get someone to cover my classes tomorrow. Do you suppose MoonFeather would talk about something Wiccan that can pass as Anthro 101?" He fished in his overnight bag. "Damn, I don't have any spare batteries for the cell phone."

I tossed him mine. He took it to his laptop to look up phone numbers, still working on breakfast and pulling on his shirt at the same time.

Easily, we fell into a familiar routine. I had my tasks, he had his. We worked comfortably together.

Between my cell phone and the hotel's exorbitant long-distance charges, we managed to cover some of the bases.

"Ask Scrap about the ring," Gollum said between calls.

The imp snoozed on my shoulder, clinging to my hair. At the sound of his name, he roused. *Yeah, wadda ya want*, he growled in his Chicago gangster voice. He leaned away, clinging to my hair for balance to grab his cigar from the windowsill.

"Ow, I felt that," I complained, reclaiming possession of my hair with a tug.

Time to close the window and turn on the AC. A proper imp can only take so much, ya know. The clear blue sky was rapidly paling to white in the desert heat.

"Nice to see some of your spark and disrespect has returned," I replied. I don't think I'd know how to work with a docile and obedient imp.

Mickey's at the door.

I got up to answer it before I heard the knock. "We need to know about the ring," I reminded Scrap.

Um—It opens any portal into any dimension. He lapsed into silence as Mickey entered the room and we all exchanged pleasantries.

"Something is wrong with Scrap," Mickey whispered.

Hey, I heard ya! I'm right here. He still hadn't moved from my shoulder. His insubstantial tail tightened on my throat again.

Strange. I shouldn't be able to feel that much of him. Was he more in this dimension than before, or was he more intense in his need to stay with me?

"I need to know how the ring works to be able to use it," I said to Scrap.

No, you don't. You just have to twist it, round and round your finger, willing a doorway to appear. Oh, yeah, and it helps if you twist it widdershins, toward the thumb.

"What aren't you telling me, Scrap?" Anger tinged my voice, masking my deep concern.

Ask Mr Bloody Sancroix and his black imp. He popped out with a whoosh of cigar smoke.

Twenty minutes later we wandered the outer aisles of the Dragon and St. George Casino, searching for access to the backstage.

"How are we going to get twenty dancers out to the Valley of Fire?" I asked. "Supposing we can get them out of here alive."

"Can't they fly?" Gollum asked. His glasses slid as he looked up from examining the lock on a fire door.

I thought the door should lead where we wanted to go even though it stated in plain letters across it: "Fire Exit. Alarm will sound if opened." My sense of direction faltered under the barrage of flashing lights, loud music, and animated shouts from gamblers.

Something about the assault on my senses made me want to let the machines make decisions for me. I should plug in some quarters and gamble. . . .

Scrap was of little help. He kept dangling over the slot machines, still trying to figure out how to hack into one.

"The dancers may be too weak to fly that distance," I argued. "They are fading from too long a separation from Faery."

"I will get a bus," Mickey affirmed. "From the taxi company." He looked grim. His leaf-green eyes looked dull.

His time in this dimension also stretched too long.

"Scrap, get your ass back here."

Have I told you today how beautiful you look with the glow of love about you? He waggled his cigar at me in a poor imitation of Groucho Marx. Then he circled above me, relishing the stretch of his wings.

"Can the crap, Scrap. What's on the other side of this door?"

Your wish is my command, babe. He popped out, leaving me wreathed in cigar smoke.

I coughed and waved the noxious fumes out of my face.

Mickey laughed. Mickey laughing worked better and thought more clearly than grim and frightened Mickey.

At least Scrap was good for something.

It's just a long corridor. Scrap whooshed back in. He tangled my hair in his talons and buried his nose against my scalp.

"I just washed my hair, it's clean, I promise." This clinginess, alternating with distraction was getting annoying. "Now tell me where that long corridor leads and does it really have an alarm on it?"

You didn't ask that, Scrap pouted.

I rolled my eyes. He was worse than a kindergartener on the first day of school.

Three doors off the corridor going left, back toward the theater. One goes down. One goes up, and one zigzags around to the dressing rooms, he sighed. He must have noticed my lack of patience. *And yes, this door is wired with alarms.*

"I wish you'd go back to being your normal sarcastic self," I muttered under my breath.

He heard me. I knew he did because he blew a smoke ring that completely circled my head, like a halo drifting down and tilting.

I'd seen that cartoon too many times.

Mickey and Gollum, at least, thought it funny.

"Upward staircase must lead to the theater control booth," Gollum mused when I'd translated Scrap's report.

"Down goes to the dormitory," Mickey added.

"Scrap, is there an exit to the outside at the end of that corridor?"

Yes, dahling. And it is also wired into the alarm system.

"Alarms can be cut or hacked." I looked hopefully toward Gollum.

But it was Mickey who nodded with a grin. "This I know how to do."

Scrap twisted my curls around his claws some more. *I'm thinking we grab the dancers backstage and take them out that exit.*

"I'm thinking the same thing. But there's no show tonight. We'll have to gather them up from the casino and the dormitory. Now how do we negate the magic around the building that keeps the dancers from igniting into faery torches?"

We all looked at each other blankly.

Gollum led us back to the center of the casino action. "We don't want anyone to notice us hanging out in any one location too long," he whispered.

"So, Mr. Professor-who-knows-everything, how do we break that spell?"

"We ask Lady Lucia. She set us onto the project. She must have some idea how Gregbaum works."

"It's not even noon. She won't be up yet."

I think she can be roused. Try her telephone. Scrap bounced a bit, like he was excited. I couldn't see him to tell what color he'd turned.

"And where do I find her telephone number?"

Scrap rattled off a string of numbers. Gollum already had out his new super-duper cell phone that does everything but breathe and entered the number.

"How'd you get the number, Scrap?" Maybe he'd actually been scouting around while AWOL.

I memorized it when I visited. She's got a nice blood-red landline phone next to her bed.

"That is also the number listed on the incorporation documents registered with the escrow office handling the sale of this casino," Gollum mused as he dialed.

Chapter 41

*There are more churches per capita in Las Vegas
than any other US city representing some sixty-five
faiths and denominations.*

"OKAY, SCRAP, WE'VE GOT AN HOUR to kill before
we can meet Lady Lucia at her office," Tess says.
She hangs on to my tail just so. I can't fade out of her grip or
escape to the chat room when she does that.

I'm as trapped here as I was in the Goblin Rock by the
Guardians. This is a little less unpleasant though.

We're in a back corner booth of a café on the end of a
horseshoe-shaped strip mall. Lucia's office is in the center of
the long block. This place serves breakfast twenty-four/seven.
Gollum and Mickey are slurping coffee like it's going out of
style. Tess toys with her second breakfast of pancakes with fresh
strawberries. No more whipped cream for either of us.

She lets her coffee sit. A sure sign that she means business.
Even if she is sitting so close to Gollum they might as well be
one person.

About time. I've known all along that Gollum is her soul
mate. But no, she had to dally with Donovan because he's
beautiful. She had to succumb to lust that clouded her good
sense.

Now she knows better. She's distracted with the newness of their love. Maybe I can get her all the way off the subject of Lady Lucia and the ring long enough for her to let go of my tail.

"I'm hungry." Being trapped in sensory deprivation will do that to a body. "There's no mold in this town, even after a rain. If you don't mind letting go of my tail, I'll just pop back home, check on MoonFeather and your dad and grab some mold from around the washing machine in the basement."

"Nope. Not until you tell me everything you know about the ring and how to use it." Her grip becomes firmer.

My tummy growls.

She doesn't listen to it.

"You want to eat, you've got to talk first."

"Ask him the origins of the ring," Gollum says. He's peering at me like he can almost see me. Now that he and Tess have gotten so close, maybe he can. He can see her scar and it comes from the same place I do.

"The faeries made it," I admit.

Mickey brightens. "I know how to use faery magic."

"Not this magic. Your ancestors forgot its essence a long time ago. That's why they lost it," I growl back at him.

Then I have to unfold the story of how alchemist/blacksmith Noncoiré got the ring.

"So it really is mine by inheritance." Tess stared at the ring on her right hand as if diving into the diamond.

"Um . . . Tess, I wouldn't do that if I were you." I can feel the black imp leaking power, manipulating, urging Tess to meld her mind to his, give him a way to slip through the crack that got bigger when I stole the ring from Gregbaum.

"Do what?" She's still mesmerized and going deeper.

"Don't get lost in that diamond." I yank on her hair.

"What's in there that's so dangerous?" Mickey asks. He sounds really stern . . . like maybe he has an idea what lurks within those facets.

"A rogue imp," I admit quietly. I hope that only Mickey hears me. I should know better. Tess is attuned to me and my thought patterns. "An imp so evil he's turned black."

Maybe that will get her thinking about Fortitude instead of the ring.

"An imp can go anywhere," she breathes.

Nope, my ruse didn't work.

"What could an imp do that the faeries imprisoned him like that. Was it voluntary or is it being punished?" Gollum asks.

"I don't know. I only saw that his skin had turned black from his misdeeds." I emphasize the black to make sure she hears it this time.

"Your skin changes color with your emotions," Tess offers. Small comfort.

"I cannot turn black."

"Have you ever been as completely enraged, hopeless, and helpless as that imp?" she asks. I know she's trying to help.

"Yes." I cannot say more. I look her dead in the eye, begging her not to pursue it.

"Tess, when this is all done, I have to free that imp. I cannot condemn him to that bleak existence that is no existence. Not any longer than he's already endured."

"Scrap," Gollum addresses me directly once Tess has relayed my words. "Scrap, after all these millennia, that imp has to have gone completely insane. If he was black and rogue before, he will be more so now. You don't dare loose him."

"I have to!"

"We'll discuss this later. Tell me how Lady Lucia got the ring."

"She stole it from one of your ancestors, then he went off to Napoleon's war and got killed." That's all Tess really needs to know. I can't tell her that the young blond blacksmith with the godlike beautiful body fathered Lucia's child. So I fall into storytelling mode and make that final scene in the Continelli garden as exciting as possible, adding a few nuances to make the count the villain of the piece—maybe a vampire—and how Lucia used the ring to escape with her child. I also suggest that she might be a Kajiri demon rather than a vampire.

"We know sometime after that escape Lucia sold the ring. From that point, it's traceable to the auction house in Paris last December when Donovan bought it," Tess muses. If she noticed that I left out some bits, she doesn't push the issue.

"Then Donovan sold it to Gregbaum," Gollum adds.

"So how did you get it back for me, Scrap?"

"I stole it, like any self-respecting imp."

They all laugh at that.

"Can I go find some real food now?"

Tess lets go of my tail and I'm off before I have to reveal any more secrets.

Something rattled around my hind brain, demanding attention but sliding away whenever I tried to get close to it. It would hit me when I really needed it.

"For a woman wealthy enough to own the Pinyon outright, and be sole stockholder of the corporation buying the Dragon and St. George, you'd think she could afford an office in a more prestigious part of town," Gollum muttered.

We sat in that back café booth staring across the parking lot at the plain glass door. It was tucked between two storefronts in a strip mall at the corner of a residential intersection. A coffee shop that served only specialty coffee and pastries stood to the left of her door and had a constant stream of patrons. A hair salon occupied a large space on the right. For a Monday just after noon both places seemed very active.

"You'd think she'd have one of those mansions out in the hills overlooking the city instead of living in an apartment above the spa at the Pinyon," Mickey added. "She'd have more privacy out there."

"It's two minutes to one. Let's go in." I slid out of the booth. Scrap returned to my shoulder and burped. I was suddenly enfolded in a cloud of damp, musty air. He'd only been gone a minute. Long enough to gorge on his favored food. He'd also grabbed his new black-and-silver boa on the trip. He tossed it over his shoulder dramatically.

Gollum threw some money down. He's good about that. We approached the office door slowly, looking all around and taking note of those who took note of us.

At the last minute I slipped the ring off my hand and onto a key chain in my belt pack. I didn't want Lucia to know I had it yet. If the time came when I needed a major bribe, I'd tell her.

A thick layer of paint on the inside of the glass blocked any chance that daylight might filter in.

"We're being watched. I can feel it," Mickey whispered.

"From inside or out?" Gollum asked, also peering around.

Mickey shrugged.

Camera above the door. Scrap preened and mugged, flashing the boa in front of the lens.

"Scrap says we're safe." I replied.

Gollum opened the door and ushered me in with a gentle hand at my waist. Have I mentioned how much I enjoyed his little courtesies that come so naturally?

A dim electric bulb gave off enough light to see a narrow landing and a staircase leading up. No space between the stairs and the walls. No way to get behind the stairs. I couldn't see if maybe the coffee shop and salon jutted into the area behind.

"At least there's no place for an attacker to hide," Mickey added. He twitched and started as a heavy truck drove past on the through street.

"Scrap, please scout ahead."

Do I have ta?

I rolled my eyes. "You can leave me alone for ten seconds."

That's a long time in demonland. Time enough to get us both killed.

"Scrap, stop stalling and scout ahead."

He popped out. Two seconds later he landed on my shoulder again, flapping the boa in my face. *All clear for us, dahling, but there's a fierce argument going on behind closed doors*. He sang the last phrase, only slightly off key.

"Remind me not to ask you to join in next time Mom drags me up to the stage."

He blew a smoke ring in my face.

I coughed and waved it away. But I didn't need to. The air-conditioning sucked the smoke away so fast I almost didn't see it.

"What does this place smell like, Scrap?"

Car air freshener. Pine. Fading. He wrinkled his snub nose in distaste. *No character at all*.

"Would the air conditioner at the Pinyon account for Lady Lucia's lack of demon odor?"

"Shouldn't," Gollum answered for the imp.

Something clicked in my mind. Then it slid away again.

"I'm thinking, that if Lucia has been poor, so poor she sold a valuable and treasured heirloom, that maybe the habit of saving money is how she gained so much. She doesn't spend where she doesn't have to."

"And she doesn't share. I couldn't find a single list of stockholders in any of the multitude of shadow corporations. Layers and Layers of secrecy."

"Just like Darren Estevez," I added.

Damiri demons are all richer than Bill Gates, Scrap laughed.

"No one is richer than Bill Gates."

Wanna make a bet? Lucia's got assets upon assets that no one knows about. Darren, too, but not as many. That's why his kids are fighting so hard to get your Mom's half of the fortune.

"Hmmmmm." I had to think a moment and paused on the last step, one foot in the air. "The estate is tied up in probate. Mom's getting an allowance from his liquid assets. Donovan can't cash in on the capital yet, except the exorbitant fees he collects as executor of the estate."

That's when I heard the raised voices behind the closed wooden door to the left of the landing. Fancy scrollwork detailed the door, avoiding the traditional cross-shaped reinforcing panels. The wall straight ahead and to the right was cement blocks painted a boring and unobtrusive gray.

"I have to own at least fifty-one percent!" Donovan nearly screamed. "A haven for the Kajiri is useless if I don't control it!"

"I will not invest in your great enterprise. But I will own one haven and pay you to manage it," Lucia replied, a little too loudly for the sweetness in her tone to be convincing. "I'm thinking an entire town built around a resort. No one lives there unless they work there and we screen all employees to make certain they contain at least one drop of demon blood in their veins."

"You, of all people, should recognize the wisdom of diversifying. You own too much in and around Vegas. The SEC and the IRS are going to start investigating your corporations sooner or later. Experience tells me the haven should be elsewhere."

"Like Half Moon Lake, Washington?" Lucia lowered her voice enough that I almost couldn't hear her through the thick door.

"Precisely. Invest the forty percent I need to start building, and I'll either buy you out in five years or you'll start earning handsome dividends." I recognized the subtle magic of Donovan's ability to persuade creeping into his voice.

"I do not like dividends. I like profits. I control the entire enterprise or it does not happen." Lucia bit each word off precisely, adding steel to her determination.

I sensed they'd reached a major impasse. They'd repeated these arguments over and over and gotten nowhere.

"I can go elsewhere for the money." Donovan slammed something, maybe his fist, against the desk. He had a temper, worse than mine. I'd been on the receiving end of it when he let his emotions get the better of his good sense during a fencing match. I still bore the scar on my right forearm. It would heal eventually. Not soon enough to my mind.

"Where?" Lucia asked sweetly. "I have made certain that no one in Las Vegas will lend you anything."

"Gary Gregbaum owes me. Therefore, his silent partner Junior Sancroix also owes me. I'll give them a theater designed for the show. Junior doesn't have to compromise The Crown Jewels and his financial arrangements with you. We'll attract people away from Vegas just to see the show, let alone every Kajiri in Vegas just trying to blend in. I'm helping him move his dancers tonight."

Mickey, Gollum, and I shared frightened glances at that. "We have to get the dancers first," I mouthed.

They nodded.

"Gregbaum wouldn't dare," Lucia hissed.

"What has he got to lose?"

In the moment of silence that followed, I decided to knock on the door. It was already five past one.

"Enter!" Lucia ordered.

"I'll be leaving you to your other business," Donovan said angrily. "This discussion is not over yet."

"You will stay," Lucia replied. "This discussion requires your cooperation. I will owe you a favor. Perhaps a forty percent favor. Perhaps less."

I pushed open the door to find Donovan leaning over a massive ebony desk, both fists planted on the glossy top. Lady Lucia sat across from him in a high-backed chair that molded to her frame. Today she wore a long red skirt and a black silk shirt. A red suede blazer was draped across one end of the massive desk.

Every one of the six windows in the wall behind her had been painted black. The only illumination came from wall sconces with electrified candles that flickered like real flame.

As I walked across the ten feet that separated us, I expected Scrap to disappear. He remained firmly on my shoulder, tail wrapped around my neck, in Donovan's presence.

"Either Lucia's evil overcomes Donovan's power to push you away, or you've overcome some darkness in your soul so that gargoyles don't repel you any longer," I whispered to my buddy.

You got that right, babe. Almost worth the price of my warts to know you and me can take this cheater down together. He's sleeping with Lucia by the way.

"Tell me something I didn't already suspect. He's not picky about his bed partners."

Chapter 42

Gambling debts are now legally enforceable in all states.

DONOVAN CURSED LOUDLY and fluently when he saw me enter the room. He slammed his fist into the desk again, this time leaving a dent.

"Tsk, tsk," Lucia clucked. "Temper, temper."

Donovan jerked upright. "I'm outta here."

"No," Lucia ordered.

Everyone in the room stilled, even Scrap.

"You will stay, Donovan. You will listen, and in the end, if you want any help with your great enterprise, you will assist me in any way I deem appropriate." Her accent slid toward French and away from Italian. Natural, I guess since I now knew it to be her birth language. Like my mother. I knew the inflections and the tendency to emphasize the last syllable well.

Funny, my mom hadn't lapsed into her own baby talk version of Québécois since coming to Vegas. She'd found herself on this journey. She no longer needed to cling to a past she couldn't reclaim. At least some part of this trip was a success.

Thinking about my mom, I wondered at Lucia's interest in her the other night.

The lady flashed a bit of fang at Donovan. I figured I'd probably confront her in private. Later. Mom wasn't singing tonight, so Lucia couldn't approach her in the lounge.

"You aren't taking the dancers tonight, Donovan," I said crisply. I braced my feet and held my hands loosely at my sides ready to command Scrap into weapon form.

I sensed Gollum and Mickey moving behind and beside me, to give me space and watch my back if necessary.

"Who's going to stop me?" Donovan sneered.

"I am. Because I'm taking them back to Faery tonight." I wished Scrap would turn red as a precursor to transforming.

Instead, he moved to the top of my head and hissed. A lot of good that would do. But also a signal that neither Donovan nor Lucia posed a serious threat to me at this moment.

"Good one, Tess. In case you didn't get the memo, Faery is closed until they restore the balance within." Donovan threw back his head and laughed.

"The only way to restore the balance is to return the dancers to their home. While they are here, they drain energy and faery gold into this dimension."

"Faery gold?" Lucia asked.

"They gamble with it," Gollum said.

"The gold remains gold as long as it is inside the building. But it turns to dross the moment it leaves." Mickey quirked a mischievous smile at our hostess.

Now it was her turn to laugh. "So that is why the accounting is always short. The managers aren't skimming and the owners are losing money at gaming because they host 'Fairy Moon,' drawing ticket holders away from the slots." Lucia almost wept with mirth. "They didn't have to sell. They merely needed to cancel the show and evict Gregbaum."

"That doesn't change anything. The faeries can't get home," Donovan said. "That's the Powers That Be wielding their power for power's sake and not thinking through the consequences. They're good at that."

"You'd enjoy making the Powers That Be look foolish, wouldn't you, Donovan," I said. I almost smiled, too, but didn't want to play my ace too quickly.

"Damned right I would. They haven't done me any favors lately." He began to pace, a sure sign of his discomfort. He had an amazing quality of stillness when he needed it; a leftover from the centuries he'd spent watching the world pass by. Most of the time he made up for those centuries of watching and waiting with vigorous action, pacing when there was nothing else he could do.

"I've got news for you." I smiled as sweetly as I could. "There's a back way in. But I'm the only one who can find it. Help me tonight, and I'm sure the Powers That Be will make note in their scorekeeping."

"I'm not going to help you do anything." Donovan aimed his restless steps toward the door.

"You will help her," Lucia insisted. Her quiet voice filled the room with authority. She half stood and leaned forward, revealing just a hint of fang. In the uncertain light, the white streaks of hair at her temples showed clearly—like a hereditary birthmark among the Damiri. Except those were artificial sun streaks in blonde hair. Weren't they?

Scrap, explain.

Expensive dye job. Underneath, her hair is as black as Donovan's heart or Fortitude's skin.

Donovan had those wings of silver hair, as did his foster father Darren. My deceased husband Dill had the beginnings of white at his temples. But then, he was a lot younger than Donovan.

But the Damiri always give their children names that began with D and usually ended with N. I sent that thought to Scrap.

Dunno. He lit up a new black cherry cheroot with a bit of flame at the tip of his finger. *The demon blood is pretty much diluted in her. Maybe her folks didn't know.*

Or maybe it's a more modern custom.

I felt a shrug from Scrap. Maybe, maybe not.

"Why do I have to help? You've already turned me

down on financing." Donovan faced her, fists clenched, shoulders hunched. I half expected him to lift his arms and spread bat wings.

Quickly, I banished that image from my mind before it made me curl into a fetal ball in a corner gibbering in panic.

"With this new proposition on the table, financing can be renegotiated." She sat again, the atmosphere around her fading from menace to sweetness and possibilities.

"Sixty-forty split, we build in Half Moon Lake, and the new corporation is in the name of my choosing," he spat back at her.

"Gaming laws?" she countered.

"Nominal tribal affiliation on the spa. This is an extension of that project."

"Have your lawyer call my lawyer. They will draw up the contracts. Usual signature practices." Meaning they signed in blood. If either of them broke faith with the contract their blood would burn in their bodies, as if the contracts burned, too.

"Can we get back to the dancers?" I interrupted.

"Easy. I drive the bus. You three ambush us and take the dancers to the destination of your choice." Donovan dismissed us.

"What about his soldiers? What about the magic net around the Dragon and St. George? What's to keep him from extending that net to include the bus?"

"What magic net?" Donovan asked.

I looked to Lucia. She seemed disinclined to meet anyone's gaze. Okay. So she knew about the net, but she didn't want to talk about it.

Why?

So I told Donovan about the spell that would immolate the faery dancers the moment they left the building, and about the stronger one around the dormitory.

"You've got to be kidding. No one in this dimension can work that kind of magic. Other dimensions, yes. But the energy fields are all wrong on Earth."

"Are they? Are you forgetting about the energy leaks out of Faery?" I asked. A wave of weariness washed through me. The better part of valor seemed to be for me to take the visitor's chair resting at an odd angle across from Lucia. It looked like Donovan had thrust it out of the way, hard, at some point in the earlier argument.

Good move, babe. Puts you in a position of authority. Scrap chuckled. He hopped onto the desk and waggled his ears at Lucia.

She didn't seem to notice him. I hoped she couldn't see his disrespectful strutting. We still didn't know the extent of her power or her deadliness.

"You know how the net was set," I addressed Lucia.

"How would I know such a thing?" She gestured expansively, reverting to her fake Italian accent.

"You were intimate with Gregbaum at the time he started the show. I suspect you financed him as part of the relationship. He did something to split you up, now you want revenge, to destroy him. The thing he values most is that show. You have to close it."

The ring in my belt pack nearly burned with the need to be back on my hand. Or I lusted to show off that diamond. I don't know which.

"I may have watched Gregbaum dance around the building, setting candles and chanting strange words that Junior Sancroix dictated," she conceded.

"I think you know more than that." Somewhere in horror fiction I'd read that one must never give a vampire control by engaging their gaze. I ignored it. All vampire fiction anyway.

Lucia squirmed. "How would I know anything of magic?"

"Because when you escaped from the fire that destroyed Castello Continelli, you ran to Faery." That had to be the default setting on the ring. Faeries made it for a reason. A way to always return home no matter where they were trapped.

"How did you . . ."

I smiled sweetly and gestured toward Scrap. The brat continued to prance and make ugly faces at her.

She didn't get my meaning. So Scrap blew smoke in her face. She choked and waved it away.

"The imp," she said matter-of-factly.

"The imp," I confirmed. "Imps can go anywhere, anywhen. He watched you. Learned something of your history."

"Something but not all?" she asked archly.

"This is all fascinating, but it's getting us nowhere," Donovan interrupted.

"Oh, but it is," I replied. "I have something you want, Lady Lucia. Something you want very badly. In return, you will give Gollum and Mickey a detailed account of the setting of the spell so that they can find a way to reverse it."

I toyed with my key chain. The ring was half hidden between my car key and my house key.

Lucia leaned forward a bit. A spark gave life to her overly dilated eyes. She truly was quite beautiful when she wasn't playing vampire crime boss. Lustrous hair and flawless skin, and a face with symmetrical features and high cheekbones. In human terms she'd reached her prime. In demon terms . . . well I didn't know what Kajiri considered prime.

"Where did you find it?" Lucia asked breathlessly.

"Do you know the most recent history of the . . . um . . . artifact?"

She shook her head, still leaning forward. If she pushed her reach to the fullest extent, she could snatch the ring from my hand.

I shoved my chair back two inches.

Gollum moved to stand behind me, one hand on my shoulder. More importantly, he stood between me and Donovan. Two days ago I thought Donovan could swat Gollum aside like a pesky fly. Now I wasn't so sure. Gollum had pushed those mutant faeries a goodly distance with his esoteric martial arts. Donovan coiled enough energy within him, that if used against him, it might knock him through those painted glass panes.

"Donovan, please leave the room," I said.

"That is not necessary," Lucia dismissed my request.

"Can you control him when he loses his temper?" I looked only to Lucia.

"How'd you get it?" Donovan snarled, half angry, half amazed. He looked like he wanted to grab the ring, taking my arm off at the shoulder if he had to. His perpetual anger rose off him in hot waves. But he had to go through Gollum to get to me.

I sat back easily, unworried.

"Professional secret. Can you control him?" I repeated.

"Donovan will remain calm." Lucia sent him to the far corner of the office with a glimpse of her pointed teeth.

"You must understand that this artifact will be returned to you only when the faeries are back home and I have survived the mission," I hedged. Something deep inside me did not want to share the ring. It kept shouting in my mind that it was *MINE*.

I tried to believe the imp inside was still coherent enough to understand that Scrap would try to free it. That could only happen if the ring remained in my possession.

If Scrap was bloodthirsty, irreverent, and sarcastic, the trapped imp must be completely evil and insane by this time.

Lucia looked disappointed, but she nodded.

Reluctantly, I flipped the keys so that they nestled in my palm, the ring between them. It caught each nuance of the flickering light and reflected it in a dozen colored shafts. The entire office seemed filled with dancing rainbows.

Lucia's hand reached for it.

I closed my fist.

She sat back sighing in disappointment. A wistful look of longing and nostalgia crossed her face. (More evidence to me that she wasn't a vampire. She showed too much emotion for the soulless undead.) "You know it is genuine?" she asked.

"It damned well better be. How'd you get it away from Gregbaum?" Donovan snarled.

"Gary Gregbaum had it all this time?" Feral hunger snarled from her lips.

"Gregbaum only had it a few days. Donovan bought it at auction last December in Paris. He claims to have provenance back to 1850." Something about the date bothered me.

Scrap had said that Lucia sold the ring to buy food for her child. But the child had been about three in 1819 when she escaped Tuscany to Faery. In human years he'd have been an adult by 1850. Maybe they spent a couple of decades in Faery. Time runs differently there.

"Donovan sold the ring to Gregbaum on Friday, I believe. Or possibly Thursday night," I returned to the topic at hand. I left out the interlude when the ring could have been mine in the rocking gondola at The Venetian Hotel. No need to revisit that fiasco.

"And you acquired it . . . how?" Lucia asked more politely.

Donovan started pacing again.

He made me nervous. I clasped the ring tightly, then returned it to the inside pouch of the pack.

"I claim the ring by right of inheritance. It belonged to the Noncoiré family for many generations before it came to you, Lady Lucia."

"How much of that . . . um . . . episode do you know?" she asked arching an eyebrow.

I shrugged. "Only what Scrap told me. That you seduced my ancestor just to get the ring, then hightailed it over the border to marry Continelli, while your lover went off to Napoleon's war and got himself killed."

She looked squarely at Scrap. He turned his back to me and some silent communication passed between them.

Instant jealousy rose up in me.

"Very well. You know that the ring was a gift of love; honorable, and genuine."

I nodded.

"It was mine to keep or sell as I needed."

"Yes."

"Gregbaum doesn't have enough power in him to retain the ring," Lucia said, glaring at Donovan. "I declare it Tess' rightful possession for the time being. Spoils of war. When this is all over, Tess will return it to me as a gesture of thanks for my help."

"Agreed," Donovan sighed.

"Before the alchemist tricked a faery king to gain possession of the ring, it belonged to my people. It should come to me," Mickey insisted. For the first time he looked avaricious, bordering on turning into one of the black-and-red faeries if thwarted.

Time to end this.

"Lady Lucia, you have only to give Mickey and Gollum a detailed account of Gregbaum setting the spell and order Donovan to assist me tonight in getting the faeries home. Then the ring is yours."

"You've got to sign a promissory note to help finance *my* casino before I'll help Tess do anything," Donovan said. His color ran high, and his muscles tensed. His temper rode very close to the surface.

Gollum's new phone chirped an airy waltz. He glanced at the screen. All color drained out of his face. He looked a little unsteady on his feet. "Excuse me, I've got to take this."

He fled.

Donovan smiled wickedly. "Looks to me, Tess, like you might be on the receiving end of rejection this time."

"What are you talking about?"

"Let's just say, I've done my fair share of background checks. Made more than a few phone calls, too. You're in for quite a surprise. But that has nothing to do with our agreement for tonight. Just don't come running back to me afterward."

Chapter 43

In Spanish, Nevada means snowcapped.

I DON'T LIKE the clipped New York accent that slides into Gollum's words. He sounds terse and angry through the heavy door. He also sounds a bit sad.

This could be bad news for Tess.

So I slip away from her and hover around Gollum's left ear trying to hear both sides of his conversation.

Drat, I'm too late. He's closing the phone that does everything just as I pop through. I count to ten then ten more as he sucks in air and lets it out again verrrrrry slowly. That's his martial arts training. He's got to regain control over his emotions before he faces Tess again.

This does not bode well.

I never thought to probe his secrets before. He's so right for my dahling I figured he'd come clean honestly, without manipulation when the time was right. Tess says he did that last night when they were in that cave becoming a couple. A lasting and important couple.

Ouch, he nearly closes the door on my tail. Good thing I'm only partly in this dimension and can slide through the dense wood with little problem. Still it reminds me too much of the nothing place between here and there where the Guardians trapped me.

I do not like dark and dense anymore, even though it does provide nice hiding places from the too-perceptive. I'll just have to be better at camouflage.

This may call for another feather boa, or some makeup.

First things first. Gollum's gearing up to say something.

"Tess, let's figure out this spell. Now. We haven't a lot of time and there's no repeat performance," Gollum ground out the moment he reentered Lady Lucia's office. His face was bland, but he bit off the last syllable of his words and his gaze would not meet mine.

"What's wrong?" I reached out to touch his hand.

He jerked away from me as if burned.

"Later. We'll talk later. I promise. Just not right now." Each of those last four words sounded like a separate sentence. Maybe even a full paragraph.

Something twisted in my belly. I'm not usually prescient. Gollum's tense shoulders and board stiff fingers—like he was afraid if he clenched them he'd smash his fist into something, or someone—told me more than I wanted to know.

Then there was Donovan's satisfied smirk marring his handsome face. If I ever doubted my decision to sever an intimate relationship with him, I didn't now. This man could be cruel.

The conversation turned to esoteric circles, pentagrams, incense, candle placement, and chants. My cursory reading in ceremonial magic for my books wasn't deep enough to fathom the importance of the details Gollum pried out of Lady Lucia's memory.

"I am certain that the black candles belonged in the center of each triangle that formed the points of the pentagram," she insisted for the third time. "The red ones went inside the pentagon at the center and the white ones between the points but inside the circle marking the pentangle."

That caught my attention. "In white magic, Moon-

Feather always places the white candles representing
Air at the center, the red for Fire at the points, blue for
Water goes between the points, and the black or brown
for Earth outside the circle." My aunt always used multiple symbolism. I knew that in her pentagrams the
white center represented purity of spirit. Any darkness
that might creep into the spell had to remain outside
the circle. Dark Earth also represented a grounding or
anchor to reality.

She used a much lighter incense, blending the ingre-
dients from her own herb garden as much as possible.

"This is not white magic," Lucia reminded me. "Gregbaum needed something very dark, but not truly black."
Hence the heavy, artificial incense and the burning blood.
He cut one of his mutant faeries to get that blood. He set
plain incense smudge pots at the cardinal direction points
around the building. The ones containing blood went
around the dormitory in the basement of the building.

If MoonFeather needed blood, she'd use her own
menstrual blood or take a little from a goat or chicken,
but only an animal that was destined to die anyway to
fill her table later.

"I think you should use green candles for Earth.
Green the same color as Mickey's eyes, faery green."

Gollum nodded assent and made a note on his new
cell phone that replaced his PDA and laptop.

"This is not like any magic I know of." Mickey shook
his head. "We are creatures of the Air. Trapping the
dancers in the basement, beneath the Earth is draining
them of strength more than being away from home for
so long."

"I know this as much as anyone," Lucia said proudly.
She looked as if she intended to say more but bit off the
last words.

"You designed the spell." I kept my voice matter-of-
fact, avoiding any hint of accusation.

Her silence said it all.

"I advised Junior on some of the symbolism. How did
you guess?" she asked sweetly.

"Because I don't think Gregbaum or Junior is smart

enough to layer symbolism on top of symbolism and re-arrange those symbols so subtly."

Lucia's smile grew bigger. She almost bared her fangs.

Did all Damiri have those fangs? I didn't think so. Darren hadn't, not when he was in human form anyway. Dill had never showed evidence of them, other than prominent eye teeth.

"You are correct." She nodded her head regally.

"If you set it, then you know how to reverse it," I said.

"That is just the point, my dear Tess. I do not know how to reverse it. I planned it as a one-time trap, never needed again. Then Gregbaum betrayed me, and I sev-ered our relationship. Now I need to finish severing every connection I ever had to the man."

Uh-oh. Gregbaum's blood is on the ring. When it goes back to Lucia, she'll be able to track him.

Huh?

Trust me, babe. She'll trace the scent through three di-mensions before giving up. Even cleaning it with bleach won't help.

I didn't want to think about what Lady Lucia would consider betrayal.

Did Gregbaum take another to his bed? Eee-wwwwww!

Or had the slimy lounge lizard deprived Lucia of a meal? Double eeewwwww!

I hoped, I really, really hoped, that he had just cheated her out of some money.

And to think, nine months ago I didn't believe in any of this crap. Now I easily envisioned Junior bent over a bowl of water, scrying our conversation through magic, tracing us through a drop of Gregbaum's blood in the water to call to the blood on the ring.

"We're out of here," I said. "Gollum, you and Mickey go back to the hotel and put your heads together on this."

"What are you going to do?" Gollum looked up, meeting my eyes for the first time since his phone call.

He'd banished the strong emotions and now showed only a deep interest in something bizarre.

"What any self-respecting woman would do. I'm going to call my mom. And if that doesn't work, I'll contact the Citadel. Someone, somewhere has to know how to get those faeries back home."

Don't bet on it, dahling. Can't we go shopping instead?

"Tess, before we go to our separate tasks, I have to talk to you." Gollum didn't look happy about that. He didn't touch my back as he escorted me down the stairs, away from Lady Lucia.

"So talk."

"Alone." He looked pointedly at Mickey.

Oooh, one of those talks. I'll leave you to it while I check out the mall. Scrap popped out. I barely noticed.

"I'll drop you at The Crown Jewels. Then I'll check local magic shops for supplies while you talk," Mickey said distractedly.

"Thank you, Mickey. What are we going to do about the blood . . . ?" I didn't want to finish that thought.

"You may have some of mine," Mickey said proudly. "Good faery blood to balance the wrongness of the changed ones."

We said nothing more until Gollum closed the door of our hotel room. He went immediately to the long windows and stared at the mountains in the distance. A tiny bit of snow glistened on the high peaks, left over from last night's storm.

"So what is so important?" I asked, making myself comfortable on the bed with pillows propped behind my back. I had a bad feeling about this. Our relationship was so new, still fragile, I didn't want to risk it just yet. Give it time to grow and strengthen. Then we could weather any storm together.

As we had last night.

Inwardly, I smiled at the specialness of making love with Gollum.

"Tess . . . I . . ." He gulped and swallowed. Then he hung his head, reluctant to turn and meet my gaze.

"Spit it out. One sentence at a time, stripped bare of emotion." That's what I did in my books when I didn't quite know how to get from here to there.

He straightened and stared through the window. His eyes clouded and I knew he looked deeply into his past. A shadowy past I had not shared with him.

"Tess, I'm married."

The world went white. I grew hot with chill pricking the edges.

"How . . . why didn't you tell me last autumn when we first met? Why isn't *she* with you?" I could write a better *fictional* excuse to get out of a relationship.

My temper threatened to boil over.

I had to remind myself, this was Gollum, my Gollum.

Well, maybe he wasn't mine after all. Maybe I should listen more closely.

"We were very young. I was nineteen and had just finished the course work for my first masters. Julia had just graduated from high school. Our parents had known each other forever. They'd planned for us to marry since we were infants. And I do love her. I'll always love her. She's special. But in a different way from you. You are my soul mate. She's a sprite from my childhood."

He sank onto the edge of the bed opposite me. Finally, he dropped his eyes to mine.

"I know now that Julia and her mother never got along because they are both bipolar. Bridget—that's my mother-in-law—always saw raising a daughter as a competition. Almost a blood sport. She decided it was time for us to marry because she wanted to put on the social event of the season. I agreed because I thought I could rescue Julia from an emotionally abusive situation."

I gulped. Living on Cape Cod where some of the wealthiest people in the country had summer homes,

I'd seen the same thing happen over and over. I'd even
taught some of those girls in school.

"The wedding was a disaster, I take it?" I prodded.

"Yeah. Bridget couldn't allow Julia to outshine her.
She even wore white and commandeered the photog-
rapher to follow her around, ignoring the bride and
groom." He said that as if he was an observer and not
the groom in question. He suddenly looked younger and
more vulnerable. At the same time, his eyes became care-
hardened. "My mother wasn't much better. She, at least,
had the decency to wear ice blue—not quite white."

I thought I understood why he'd taken the job with
the financial advisers in New York even though he hated
the city. "What happened to send you off to Africa two
years later?"

"Three miscarriages." He had to stop and blink rapidly. He took off his glasses and rubbed his eyes. "Julia
grew more and more depressed. I got her to therapists,
specialists, anyone who might help her. She flushed her
meds, certain they'd caused her to lose our babies." He
winced. "Maybe they did. Maybe she just wasn't healthy
enough to carry a baby to term."

Damn, damn, damn.

"After the third one, her mother convinced her she
was a total failure as a human being. Julia tried to slit
her wrists. Her doctors recommended a stay in a very
expensive, very exclusive sanitarium." He recited each
word methodically, without emotion. Just spitting it out.

"Like the one where we stashed WindScribe?"
WindScribe, the witch who'd started the imbalance in
Faery by killing the king. She'd also murdered Darren
Estevez. Her violent tendencies and ravings about demons and beings from other worlds guaranteed she'd
never convince the authorities she was sane enough to
stand trial or ever earn release. If she'd just kept her
mouth shut, Donovan might have married her just to
gain custody of the child she carried.

"Actually, they are in the same facility, different wings.
Julia isn't violent, but she does tend to wander. She's
been there for fifteen years. That phone call . . . she es-

caped and jumped into the river. She . . . Oh, God, Tess, she can't swim."

"Did . . . did she drown?"

"No. Her nurse dragged her out in time." Another long pause.

I didn't know what to say or how to say it. He looked as if he'd reject any attempt to touch him. So I wrapped my arms around myself and held on tight. If I kept it up, maybe I could keep my heart from breaking.

"When she regained consciousness, she came back to reality, quite lucid and sane. She does that sometimes. The first thing she asks for is me. I'm her only anchor, her only link to happiness. She made the phone call. She wept and asked that I take her back home, to our apartment in New York."

"Are you going to do that?"

"I doubt her episode of clarity will last long enough to fill out the release papers. But I have to go see her."

"Yes, you do."

"I always thought that once I fell in love again, found the right woman, I'd just divorce Julia so I could remarry. Now that I've found you . . . now that I know that you and I could have a future together, this happens and I know I can't divorce her. I can't abandon her like that."

"And I'd be a complete heel to ask you to."

Chapter 44

*Las Vegas receives on average 4.13 inches of rainfall
a year. Their extensive water management program
uses more recycled water than any other. Nothing
is wasted.*

AFTER SEVERAL LONG MOMENTS of absolute silence, Gollum left.

What could we say? Our emotions rode so close to
the surface, any careless word or inflection could shatter
us both. Irrevocably.

We both had chores to do before he could return to
his wife. Before he could walk out of my life forever.

Maybe he didn't have to leave forever. Julia existed
behind locked doors, incapable of leading a normal life
with her husband.

Could I live with a married man, and continue to love
him?

I did the only thing I was capable of doing. I went for a
walk. The moment I stepped out into the afternoon heat
I called my mom. Not that I could tell her anything over
the phone. I just needed to connect to her, know that
when I needed to talk, she'd be there for me.

"I'm not singing tonight, why don't we have dinner
together," Mom said on a yawn.

"If it's early. I have a . . . a date tonight," I replied.

Off the Strip, Las Vegas was just another city. I walked past homes with desert landscaping—lots of crushed rock and succulent plants and cacti. An occasional cottonwood offered shade from the unrelenting sun. Nearly every corner had a convenience shop, drugstore, or small strip of shops. No different from any other residential neighborhood.

"I hope you and Donovan are finally getting together," Mom said showing more interest in the conversation than in her yawns.

Not bloody likely.

"He'll be there tonight. It's sort of a group thing. But I'm not dating him." Never again. After one night with Gollum I had little interest in Donovan. Even though . . .

Did I have to give up Gollum because of his youthful commitment to Julia? She need never know. Even if someone told her that her husband had chosen another, she might not understand in her few moments of sanity.

I knew what my mother would advise before she left New England. But this new mom, the Las Vegas mom, might have a different perspective on my love life.

My heart twisted with guilt.

"How early is early?" Mom asked.

There was something unusual in Mom's voice. But then nothing about this trip had been ordinary for her.

"Before sunset, like around five. Six at the latest."

"Sorry. I'm having brunch right now with friends. I won't be ready to eat that early. Call me in the morning or when you get back from your date. I'll be up until about two. That's my new schedule." I heard a doorbell ring in the background.

"Mom, last night you spoke with a woman in a red dress and a long strand of pearls," I continued before she could hang up.

"Oh, her. She wanted me to break my contract with Junior and sing at her club. I don't remember which one." The doorbell rang again in the background. "Tess, I've got to go . . ."

"Just tell me if she sounded in any way threatening."

"Threatening? I don't think so."

"She looked like she wanted to bite you."

"Oh, that," Mom laughed. "I think she's a lesbian. But it was awful noisy with the whole lounge singing along with you. She had to bend quite close so I could hear her."

"If you say so."

She hung up without saying good-bye.

Before I could decide what to do, the phone chirped out the opening phrase of "In The Hall Of The Mountain King."

"Mom?" I asked hopefully, not bothering to look at the caller ID.

"Have you lost your mother, Tess? I can't let you two out of my sight for a minute," said Allie Engstrom on a chuckle. She'd been my best friend since kindergarten.

"Not really lost her, just misplaced the Québécois June Cleaver and replaced her with Auntie Mame," I replied.

"Wow! That must be some weekend getaway."

"You wouldn't believe half of it." Well, maybe Allie would believe half of it. She'd helped me out with some pesky garden gnomes with teeth last month and knew about Darren being a demon. "What's up?"

"Do I still need to pick you up at midnight in Providence?"

"Gosh, Allie, sorry, I forgot, I'll be staying over an extra day or maybe two." Picture me pounding fist to forehead.

"What about your mom?"

"Well, actually, she's not coming home."

"Did you kill her?" Only half a joke. I'd threatened to strangle my mother upon occasion. She'd frustrated me beyond words until last Wednesday night when she broke free of her chrysalis.

"No, Mom has taken a job as a lounge singer. She's moved in with an ex-hooker, and I think she's found a new boyfriend."

"That's the premise of your next book, right?"

"No. That's what really happened."

"Wow! And what about you? How are you handling this?"

"I don't know yet. I'm happy for her, but I'm still processing the changes. Gollum is helping." I winced. After tonight Gollum might not be around to help. Too much unknown about *us* to tell at the moment.

"You finally did it!"

"Yeah, we did." I started melting a bit. I could talk about anything with Allie. We knew everything about each other, right down to the inflection of voice that said more than words.

I could cry with her and find a balance as well as exult with her over my one night of joy.

"How was it? Is he as gentle and caring as he comes across? Or is he secretly wild and abandoned?" she asked breathlessly.

"Both!"

We laughed out loud together. Remember the good times. Hold them close against the pain to come.

Make decisions when the emotions are under control.

"Maybe I need to come to Vegas to change my life," Allie finally said a bit wistfully.

"I really wish you were here right now." How could I convey the depth of my need for her friendship now. Telling her everything over a cell phone wasn't enough. Wasn't right. I needed her to hold my hand and offer her shoulder for me to cry on when the truth spilled out of me.

I needed her to help me work through the dilemma of Julia.

Scrap came back and rubbed his cheek against my hair. I'd never be truly alone. As much as I missed Gollum already, Scrap would comfort me. I slipped the ring off the key chain and back onto my hand where it belonged.

"Anything I can do to help, long distance?"

"Not really." I reached up and tweaked Scrap's tail affectionately. I didn't need to talk to him. He knew everything and understood my hurt.

I didn't dare tell Allie about Lady Lucia pretending to be a vampire. She'd be on the next plane. She loved vampire fiction and secretly longed to meet one.

"Say, remember last month when you asked me to do a background check on Breven Sancroix?"

I paused in the middle of the sidewalk. The sun beat down on my neck and head, reminding me I hadn't put on sunscreen or worn a hat. That's how stupid and distracted I was after Gollum's confession.

I moved to the shade of a cottonwood overhanging someone's yard. "Did you find anything unusual?"

"Not much. He's lived quietly for the most part on a farm in western Pennsylvania for about twenty years. The deed is held jointly by him and Gertrud—no e on the end—Sancroix née Jarwoski. What flagged my interest was that, before then, neither of them exists—she still doesn't. No birth records, no Social Security number, no driver's license. Nada. Nothing. And no one has ever seen her."

"You said he lived *mostly* quietly."

"Except for periodic reports of violence—taking apart a bar that didn't have his favorite beer, road rage, and shooting a trespasser on his land. Luckily, he didn't kill the teenager breaking into his barn. And since the kid was high on drugs, his parents got him into rehab and didn't press charges."

I shuddered. Would I become so used to killing demons with the Celestial Blade that I let it spill over into ordinary life?

For the first time I truly understood Gollum's vow of nonviolence.

Oh, God. Gollum!

"That's what made me think he had a prison record under a different name," Allie continued, unaware of my mental digression. "If you could get me a sample of his fingerprints I could cross-check."

"I'll see what I can do." We chatted a few more minutes and said our good-byes with promises of a long catch-up chat when I got home. My mind had already jumped ahead into more useful patterns than crying over my lost lover.

Breven Sancroix had an imp. Therefore, he had to have spent some time in a Citadel. And that's where his wife Gertrud Jarwoski had holed up for just as long. Hence the blank spot before the farm in Pennsylvania. His conversation led me to believe he'd lived in the Citadel quite a while. Longer than I had. Fortitude had a lot of warts earned in battle. Scrap kept losing his due to some strange law of impland so that I couldn't tell how many he was supposed to have, or if an imp gained some of those beauty marks in the normal aging process.

My deductions led me to believe that Sancroix had battled more than a few demons since living in the real world. (Citadel life is quite surreal.)

By this time I'd looped around the block and returned to the hotel. I hurried back to my room. Then I hid the ring inside my computer bag. I also turned on the shower and the television. I didn't want any eavesdroppers, mundane or magical.

I'll keep a lookout, Scrap promised and flew back out to the hallway.

With as much privacy as I could manage surrounding me, I hit my speed dial for Gayla, leader of my Sisterhood.

Chapter 45

*Of the men who died building the Hoover Dam, the
first and the last were father and son.*

"SISTER SERENA?" I queried the voice that answered my call. I hadn't expected the Sisterhood's
physician to pick up the landline.

"Tess, so good to hear from you," she cried. A moment of rapid exchange in the background. I could well
imagine a half-dozen women gathering around for the
thrill of an infrequent phone call. Those who chose the
Citadel life didn't have much outside contact.

I made small talk for a few sentences, heard about
this Sister's ailment, that Sister's retirement, and the on-
going pressure against the portal they guarded.

Tonight, of all nights, they needed to prepare for battle in a good mood, with reminders of what they fought
for and why. The good times among themselves, and the
innocents outside their walls.

Tonight, when the moon waxed one quarter full,
demons were at their strongest and portals at their
weakest.

Tonight, when I fought to get innocent faeries through
a rogue portal, my Sisterhood would fight to keep a stable portal closed.

"But you do not call to gossip," Serena said quietly. "Our imps can pass that information back and forth."

"Yes." I wondered why Scrap hadn't acted as messenger very often. But then, as the runt of the pack, and gay at that, he hadn't made friends among his kind. Until recently. I remembered a certain glow about him and the name Ginkgo on his mind.

"About a month ago I requested help from any other rogue Warrior you could contact."

"I remember that." Serena sounded thoughtful. "Did someone come?"

"He came too late to help. I managed on my own. With the help of some friends."

"Oh, Tess, you haven't violated your vow of secrecy," Serena said, disappointment dripping from her words.

"Not really. My friends are either involved in our lifestyle or figured it out when I got attacked in broad daylight by the Orculli trolls." I almost laughed at that. King Scazzy of the garden gnomes with teeth, was actually the prison warden of the universe. He'd been on a mission at the time. No one had thought to clue me in until after we'd exchanged blows and blood had been drawn. MoonFeather's blood. I was still hard-put to forgive Scazzy for that.

"I called to find out what you know about the rogue Warrior. Breven Sancroix is still hanging around."

"Sancroix?" Sister Serena paused a moment. She probably drummed her fingers on her thigh, a habitual gesture—she had to constantly work the fingers of her right hand to keep them supple after a demon tag. "Sancroix! I remember him from long ago. He and his Brotherhood visited one Summer Solstice. It was quite a party. I'd just come back from my residency. So I got to deliver a bunch of babies around the Vernal Equinox. Gert had a boy, I think, and sent it to Sancroix for raising once he'd been weaned."

Junior was too old to be that baby, perhaps thirty-five. No reason he couldn't be the child of a previous Solstice celebration, though. Unusual that Sancroix referred to his *nephew* as Junior.

"No wonder Sancroix remembers Sister Gert quite fondly," I prompted.

"Gert's not here at the moment, or I'd ask her."

"Where'd she get to?" As if I didn't know.

Sister Gert had a lot invested in maintaining the status quo. A status quo outdated about one hundred years ago.

"Um." Serena dropped her voice to a barely audible whisper. "She's talking about going rogue, something about a farm in Pennsylvania."

Uh-oh.

Did I say I don't believe in coincidences?

I needed to keep an eye on Sancroix and Gert. The best way to do that was to include them in tonight's activities—let him burn off a little of his reported violence constructively. I had no doubt that Gregbaum had a dozen or more minions guarding both the dormitory and the portal at Goblin Rock. Two extra Celestial Blades would help.

I've got better ways to glean the truth from gossip. Time for a quick trip to visit my lover Ginkgo.

Imp memory goes back a long way.

He'll know everything there is to know about Juniper, companion to Sister Gert. If the good sister did give birth to a kid or two by Sancroix, then her imp probably loosed a couple of litters by Fortitude.

Once I know Fortitude's character, I'll know a lot about Breven Sancroix.

I don't trust either one of them. Interesting to find out if anyone else does.

More interesting to find out why Sancroix left his Citadel. Did he go voluntarily or was he kicked out?

Sunset came late, around seven thirty. Moonrise was scheduled for nine fifty-seven. Not a lot of time to break into the Dragon and St. George, free the dancers, get them on a bus and drive them for a full hour out to the Valley Of Fire.

Timing was everything.

The moon awakes from a little sleep. It becomes a key held in the arm of a . . . a Guardian who is also a monster. The words of the Paiute bartender's vision quest came back to me.

That part had to refer to the waxing quarter moon rising behind the Rock Goblin.

It opens a path to twilight lands of peace and plenty, lands that a warrior may glimpse but never enter.

That part had to be Faery.

Only one warrior will rise above the ties that bind him to this earth to walk between.

And that meant me. And this happened only once in every ten generations.

Gulp. Tonight or never. In a few hours when the moon rose.

My hands trembled. I wiped sweaty palms on my jeans. This had to work. We only had one chance, one very small chance in a narrow margin of time.

The dancers did not perform on Monday or Tuesday night. By Wednesday when Lucia took over, no one would miss them.

Except Gregbaum.

Breven and Fortitude prowled the casino, gathering up any stray dancers. He refused to take Fortitude into the Valley Of Fire but seemed more than willing to help at this end of the operation.

Junior remained at The Crown Jewels, wringing his hands. I didn't want him broadcasting anxiety around me when stealth was the key to success. I suspected Lady Lucia kept an eye on him, though she didn't say where she'd be tonight.

Sister Gert supposedly had gone back to Pennsylvania. And if you believe that I have some oceanfront property in Arizona I'll sell you.

Gert and Juniper are giving Junior a serious talking to. She's really upset with him, Scrap said, flitting about, seeking shadows within shadows.

Fortitude has problems. Big problems. Don't trust him, Scrap continued curtly. *He listens to Junior more than to his Warrior. Junior is the one who dragged them down the current path of violence and total disregard for rules and the well-being of others. That's why Gert's giving him a hard time. Juniper is leaning toward Junior now, too.* He disappeared when I tried to get specifics from him.

Great. My allies were an angry faery changeling, a fellow rogue Warrior and his imp who had anger management problems, and a demon masquerading as a vampire crime boss.

Gollum and Mickey wandered around outside with a compass and GPS, setting tiny smudge pots at North, East, South, and West. Candles got tucked into crevices in between the pots. They'd both been unnaturally quiet all afternoon.

Donovan drove around and around in an oversized van. A tight fit for our crew and the dancers, but the most inconspicuous vehicle he could find on short notice that suited us.

I was just as glad he kept his sullen countenance away from me.

Me? I stayed hidden between the deserted back-stage and access to the dormitory. Scrap did my scouting for me.

"This is too easy," I whispered to Scrap. My internal clock told me the sun dipped below the horizon.

I can't find Gregbaum anywhere, babe, he growled, coming in for a landing on my shoulder.

"What about his guards?"

Missing in action as well.

"Do you think Donovan warned them about our operation?"

Scrap shrugged and took off again. *All twenty faeries present and accounted for in the dormitory.*

"Time to get this mission going.

My phone vibrated—no way I was taking a chance on a ring tone alerting the bad guys to my presence.

"The sun just hit the horizon. I'm lighting things up," Gollum hissed through the phone. "We've got to do this the exact opposite of when Lucia set the spell."

Sancroix came around the corner, looking tired. Fortitude looked like . . . well like Fortitude, gray-green skin darkened with age—more charcoal than green—wings held high, ready to flee in a heartbeat. He avoided looking at me or at Scrap.

Seconds later, Gollum and Mickey skidded to a stop in front of me.

"Is it working?" Gollum asked.

Nothing yet, Scrap replied.

"Try the dormitory, Scrap."

He mumbled and grumbled as he popped out and bounced right back in. *Still in place, babe.*

"What are we going to do?" I began absently turning the diamond ring on my right hand.

Mickey sniffed. "Something different . . ."

The magic smells different!

Fortitude nodded acknowledgment and spread his wings until they formed a curtain behind Sancroix. His skin grew darker, flushed with the barest hint of red. Sancroix winced as his imp's talons gripped his shoulder tighter.

Something was wrong between them. I could sense when Scrap did the same thing; he never hurt me.

Scrap flashed from gray to pink to red in an eye blink.

"Bad guys," I whispered to one and all.

"Where?" Sancroix turned in a circle, automatically extending his hand for Fortitude to land there and begin transforming.

I did the same for Scrap.

Scrap was still elongating when Fortitude's tail and ears curved into blades at opposite ends of a shaft.

I'd never seen an imp morph so quickly. He seemed a bit too eager to taste blood.

No time for questions. No time to think.

Fifteen black-and-red Faeries dropped from the flies above the stage, blued broadswords drawn and swinging.

Chapter 46

The Las Vegas Hard Rock Hotel & Casino uses only recycled metal, glass, and paper products.

"GOLLUM, MICKEY, GET the dancers out *now*!" I yelled.

Before Scrap had a chance to fully sharpen, I twirled the blade over my head, at the level of the black-and-red faeries' throats.

Flurries of movement all around me.

No rules. No confining fencing strip. No honor. We fought all out; to the death.

In the movies the bad guys politely wait to attack the hero one at a time. Real demons aren't so nice.

Fifteen armed bad guys against two Warriors of the Celestial Blade. "I've seen worse odds. Seen better ones too," I mused.

Scrap vibrated with agreement and a need to taste blood. The viler and blacker the better.

Sensing that my lack of height and reach made me the weaker prey, eight mutants descended on me, swords extended and slashing. Sancroix faced seven of the monsters.

I might be vertically challenged, but I'm fit and trained.

One opponent on my left caught the full curve of the blade across his middle. He stood staring and gasping as the wound gushed black blood. Before he could collapse, I'd taken out the guy on my opposite side with a backhand. He caught the tines of the outside curve in his throat.

Two down. Six to go. Sancroix had wounded but not taken out one of his attackers.

I didn't have time to gloat.

Three more black-and-red faeries landed between us.

Where were they hiding? Where did Gregbaum get so many goons to do his bidding?

I almost believed he recycled them back to life, like something in a science fiction novel.

We really needed some help.

Where the hell was Donovan when I needed him?

As if I'd conjured him with my thoughts, he burst onto the stage. In one swift movement he retrieved a sword from a fallen enemy and stabbed a black faery in the back.

Before he could recover his grip on the sword, he had five pressing him backward.

"To me," I called.

With barely a nod of acknowledgment, he sidestepped a blow and placed himself at my back.

"Just like old times, love," he said, almost gleefully.

I slashed at a goon that had sneaked under Donovan's guard in reply. His squirt of black blood covered my hands and made my grip slippery. A little heat and tingle, but my skin didn't burn like it would if these guys were truly demon-born and bred.

"Can we hurry this up? I'm double-parked," Donovan joked.

Slash, stab. Shift my grip, parry two blades, jump back from a third.

My shoulders ached. My thighs burned. The lingering groin injury flared back to life, feeling like a knife had ripped muscle. I kept changing my grip and the level of my blows to stave off fatigue. Fatigue that could get me killed.

The ring on my right hand twisted about my finger with every shift. Part of me registered fear that it slid too easily and I'd lose it before I really needed it at the Goblin Rock.

Presuming I survived that long.

And still they kept coming at us. Armed demons are ten times more deadly than unarmed. Worse, these guys had wings to lift them beyond my reach. No way we could even the odds.

"Tess, the magic net won't drop!" Gollum yelled from the corridor.

"Chant something. Light a candle." Damn, that blue-black blade almost cut me in two. I dodged and caught the tip on my upper arm. Blood dripped down to my hand, further threatening my hold on the shaft of my blade.

Scrap shuddered from within. He tired as much as I did.

"I've tried everything I know how."

"If we could just cut a door in the net rather than destroy it," Mickey said.

An imp can go anywhere, Scrap reminded me. His eyes blinked at me from the right-hand blade.

Imps open doors into any world. Could I break away from the fight long enough to slash through the magic?

Another faery came under my guard.

Donovan took him out with a swift stab to the solar plexus.

The ring twisted again on my finger.

I had a second imp trapped in the ring.

"Donovan, cover for me for two seconds." I kept twirling the Celestial Blade in my left hand, keeping at least one enemy at bay. All the while I ran my right hand up and down my leg, letting the rough fabric of my jeans turn the ring.

In my mind I pictured a door opening in front of the dormitory, and another to the outside. The image became so real I almost missed the black faery flying down onto my head, his leathery wings absolutely silent.

Just barely in time, I cut his hamstrings and he plopped into the middle of a phalanx of three of his buddies.

They went down like bowling pins.

I gulped air three times before I dove into the pig pile. Three of them died with a single blow. By the time I got to the fourth, Scrap began to dull and shorten.

My strength flagged.

We couldn't keep up this fight much longer.

"Hang in there." Donovan's voice came to me as if from a long distance.

I could barely lift my blade. He stepped in front of me and dispatched the last of the fallen foes. "The dancers are out. We've got to make sure they get away."

"I've got to go with them. They can't get home without me," I ground out. I lost my grip on the blade. It clattered to the stage and lay there inert for ten long loud heartbeats. I just stared at it, knowing I needed to do something, too tired to remember what.

The blade disappeared. Scrap crawled away to feed and rest.

My balance teetered.

Donovan grabbed me and braced me against his side.

I felt like I could stand there forever, letting him prop me up.

"I shouldn't admit this, but I feel an overwhelming need to watch over you and protect you," he whispered. His breath stirred my hair. "Put the ring on the other hand and we can make it official."

Something stirred within me. I couldn't decide if it was pleasure or terror.

"I owe it to Dill to take care of you, finish what he started."

Cold sweat broke out on my back.

A ruffling of black side curtains saved me from having to answer.

Without thinking, I grabbed the sword Donovan handled so lightly and leaped to the flurry of movement.

One last spurt of adrenaline carried me the ten steps I needed to go.

Gregbaum tangled in the yards of thin black cloth.

I held the broadsword to his throat. "Talk."

"I . . . um . . . uf . . . eek!" The last squeal in response to a nick from the sword tip. He bled red just like any normal human.

"How many more of your mutants await us at the Goblin Rock?" I pressed a little harder.

His throat apple bobbed as he swallowed. "A dozen," he squeaked.

"Donovan. Find us a car. Fast."

"Take mine," Lucia purred from directly behind me.

I like to think I had enough presence of mind to accept her presence and not let her sudden appearance startle me.

Actually, I was just too tired to jump.

"What do I need to do to restore the balance in Faery?" I spat, still holding the sword at Gregbaum's throat.

"N . . . nothing much."

"That doesn't tell me anything."

The drop of blood on his throat turned into a little rivulet.

Lucia licked her lips.

Gregbaum's eyes grew wide in fascinated horror. His pupils fully dilated.

Lucia came up beside me. She drooled a bit as her lips opened to reveal her fangs.

"C . . . close the portal behind the last faery. Kill all the mutants or throw them through the portal. Make sure all of them go. The leak will stop. They'll rebalance on their own," Gregbaum babbled.

"Go. Fight your battle," Lucia urged me. "There is food and drink in the car to restore you. I even managed a bit of mold for the imp." She half laughed, shouldering me aside so that she faced Gregbaum directly.

"It's not wise to accept food and drink . . ."

"The food is safe. It carries no obligation of hospitality. Just my little part in restoring the balance of portals. I, too, need to score points with the Powers That Be."

I backed away, keeping the sword close to my side. No telling if I'd need it out in the Valley of Fire.

"Where's Sancroix?" I asked, sagging more than a little.

The only evidence I could find that he'd ever been there was a pile of mutilated bodies. Not just dead enemies, but hacked-off limbs, severed heads, ragged slashes, and guts spilling all over the place adding their stench to the miasma of sulfur rising from the other corpses. And black blood everywhere. Great pools of it.

I gagged and had to clamp my teeth shut to keep my bile from adding to the stench.

Sancroix had gone far beyond defending himself or helping the mission to restore the balance. He'd succumbed to a berserker's bloodlust.

"Sancroix lit out as soon as the last black faery fell." Donovan cleaned his sword of black blood on the vest of one of the dead ones. "We've got to go if we're going to catch up with the bus."

"You aren't going to leave me alone with her!" Gregbaum screamed. "She'll ... she'll ... tur ..." He stopped in mid word mouth, moving but no sound coming out.

"Do not worry about the bodies. My crew will clean up," Lucia said. "Just remember to return the ring to me when you have finished." She opened her mouth wide and aimed her teeth at Gregbaum's throat.

He just stood there, frozen in horror, totally mesmerized by Lucia's exotic beauty and bloodthirst.

"You can't ..." I was equally horrified.

Donovan grabbed me and dragged me away. "That is a confrontation long overdue. None of our business," he ground out.

"But ... he's human!"

"None of our business how the lady takes her revenge for his deceit that jeopardized all the dimensions with imbalance and deadly consequences." With one arm around my middle, he pulled me backward toward the exit and the waiting black Hummer.

Chapter 47

In 2000 the Aladdin Hotel became the first hotel to be closed, imploded, and reopened without a name change.

"SHE TRULY IS A VAMPIRE," I whispered as Donovan maneuvered the powerful car in and out of congestion on the strip. "I thought she was Damiri, just pretending to be a vampire because humans might accept her better."

"She is. The demon in her needs blood just like a vampire. But vampires are much more socially acceptable than demons. There is power in the legends," he ground out, shaking his fist at a stretch limo that tried to cut him off from the freeway entrance.

"Has she pretended to live as a vampire so long that she believes her own lies?" I delved into the picnic basket—a real old-fashioned wicker one with folding handles and a top hinged in the middle that opened at either end—and produced rare roast beef sandwiches, cans of iced cola, and rich, dark chocolate bars. Sugar, caffeine, protein, and chocolate. All I needed.

In the very bottom was a jar of blue cheese that had gone moldy.

Or is that moldier?

I didn't care if it gave Scrap gas and an upset tummy as long as it helped him recover. I left it open in the basket. He could crawl in there to recover in private. "You've got an hour, buddy. Make the most of it."

Heaven, came his reply, weak and distant.

"As near as I can tell, she had no idea she might have demon blood in her until it took thirty years for her to age five. And she didn't know the value of the ring until many decades after she sold it." Donovan settled in for a long drive at fifteen miles above the speed limit. He drove competently with one hand, holding food with the other.

"An artifact of power of that magnitude must have left some kind of psychic trail," I mused. I thought of my lust for the ring.

Or was that the imp inside seeking an owner who might have the power to free him?

Got that in one, Scrap mumbled around a full mouth.

The headlights of an approaching car made the diamond on my right hand flash and sparkle.

"There are always rumors. Most of them false. When dormant, the ring doesn't betray its importance to any but the most sensitive. Lucia became sensitive enough to detect it after she investigated her demon ancestry. Her family always had an eccentric aunt or uncle who lived well beyond normal years and played with magic. They thought them witches and hid them." He downed half a cola in one gulp.

"If she didn't know, when did she start needing blood?"

"Once she'd tasted blood in her vampire act, she started craving it. The demon genes sort of leaped to life. That's one of the reasons Dill never allowed himself to indulge, even though he craved blood nutrition as much as he ached to transform." Donovan passed a line of cars only going five miles an hour over the limit in the left lane. His tires skidded on shoulder gravel, but he righted the car quickly and competently.

"Dill always did like his meat very rare." I dwelled briefly on a memory, then banished it as useless. I needed information about living demons. "When did Lucia leave Europe?"

"About forty years ago. The freewheeling hippie life-style in the States attracted her. She started speculating in real estate right off, in a small way. Built an empire in an amazingly short period of time. Most of her deals were cut at parties where she strewed just enough blood about to strike fear in the hearts of those with property to sell or develop. She can be up and about during the day when she has to. As long as she stays out of sunlight, she perpetuates the myth."

Hence the office with the painted windows and the covered patio below her bedroom. "You knew her then?"

"Yep."

"How well?"

"Not well enough for you to be jealous." He flashed me one of his anxiety-dampening smiles.

I did my best not to fall for it. Scrap said they were sleeping together now. I wasn't jealous. Not really.

"So, what exactly did Gregbaum do to Lucia to de-serve . . ." I tried to banish the sight of her fangs sinking into the pudgy rolls of flesh on his neck.

"He lied to her about the dancers. She knew they were real faeries. But Gregbaum told her they wanted to escape the imbalances in their home, not that he'd kidnapped them. He told her the magic net was to keep out Clean Up Teams from the Powers That Be. She had no idea in the beginning the spell she designed with Junior's help was to keep them trapped in the building and enslaved. He lied to her about the origins of his goons, too."

"Which is?"

"Mutations caused by the imbalance when Wind-Scribe killed the king of Faery and nearly set off a civil war in a dimension that had never known violence. Trickery, yes, but not the kind of rage and need to kill we found in those black-and-red monsters. Contrary to a lot of fiction and propaganda, vampires, demons, and witches do not seek violence for its own sake. But they have to get blood to survive somehow. Dill was the only Kajiri I've ever met who abstained. It nearly killed him at times."

He swallowed deeply, blinked his eyes rapidly, and reached for another cola to mask his emotions.

"Now that I think about it, Dill spiked a fever three times during the three months we were married. He ached all over and couldn't eat anything. I remember worrying about him, applying cold compresses, making chicken soup. I don't remember the timing to know if it happened on the night of the waxing quarter moon. But I'd have figured out a pattern eventually. He'd have had to tell me the truth."

"Reluctantly. He'd have put it off for a long time by arranging to be out collecting rock samples alone on those nights."

He swallowed and cleared his throat. "Junior kept leading more and more good faeries through the toxic waste dump their primary river became. They came out the other side, twisted, angry, more than willing to follow him as long as Gregbaum let them kill."

"Lucia has a point. Any time there is an imbalance, or a lot of dead bodies piling up, the threat of exposure increases. Witch hunts, demon hunts, vampire hunts, all become bigger threats," I mused. Europe in the seventeenth century. Salem witch trials. Jewish pogroms and the Holocaust.

Anyone "different" became fair game for execution.

In a way, that strengthened the need for Donovan's secluded resort that catered to sorcerers, demons, and vampires, where they could indulge their needs without fear of exposure.

I didn't like it, but I understood it, a little.

"I'm helping you tonight because Lady Lucia's long-term goals suit me better than Gregbaum's quick money grab," Donovan said reaching for another cola from the basket.

"Can we still be friends? We seem to fall into the same ... um ... social circles and require each other's help. And I'm not jealous of Lucia, or WindScribe, or any of your other women." Having been raised by a

Damiri—who are incredibly fertile—I don't think Donovan was capable of fidelity.

And I believe in monogamy once a commitment has been made.

Oh, God. Gollum and Julia! I think I just made my decision.

Anyway I looked at it, my relationship with Gollum was an unbalanced trio. Was I the third wheel? Or was Julia?

No way to naturally, or gracefully cut it down to two people.

One of us had to step away.

"We'll see. I take it Van der Hoyden-Smythe hasn't talked to you yet about that phone call."

I didn't like the feral satisfaction in the way he bared his teeth.

"Yes."

"Marry me, Tess. You and I are a better fit than you and him. I'll find a way to live with your imp, though I know you love him more than any man."

"I'll think about it." I twisted the ring again, wondering. Every time I tried to imagine myself committed to Donovan, I hit a blank wall that morphed into Gollum.

Shit!

"Is that our turnoff coming up?" Donovan wasn't the only one who knew how to change the subject without answering questions. I really didn't want to have to explain the sudden churning in my gut that had less to do with the three sandwiches and five cans of carbonated beverages than it did with the memory of all the color draining from Gollum's face when he recognized the caller ID on his phone.

We caught up with the van carrying the dancers as it careened around a sharp bend in the access road. Gollum had to be driving. Our headlights picked out few details.

The line of hoodoos appeared to be dancing families, frozen mid-step, hands stretching to join with another and failing. The one I'd put together to commemorate my first kiss with Gollum, was lost in the myriad of other ghostly forms.

Lost like our love.

As we crested the hill guarding the valley entrance the moon sent a shimmer of light along the eastern horizon. Not a lot of time left.

"Damnation!" Donovan spat as he pounded the steering wheel. "The gate's down."

"When has a little thing like a gate ever stopped you?" I dashed out of the car to raise the barrier, only to find it padlocked in place.

"A feeble attempt to cut down on vandalism, like we reported this morning," Gollum grumbled, coming up beside me. "This is a state park."

I wanted him to slip an arm about my waist, to reassure me that we'd find a way out of our dilemma.

He kept his hands to himself.

"It's at least a mile to Goblin Rock. Can we hike it before the moon lights the portal?" I asked surveying the landscape, what little of it I could see in the glow of the headlights.

"I think my friends are too far gone to walk that far," Mickey mused.

"Donovan, sword!" I commanded.

He emerged from the Hummer with the blue-black blade one of us had taken off the mutants. "Let me. I've got more strength." Before he'd finished speaking, he raised the sword and severed the hasp on the gate with one mighty blow. "Might have been easier to drive around, but that was more fun. And satisfying."

I held the gate open while they drove through, then closed it behind Donovan's vehicle. No sense alerting any passing rangers that we trespassed. They'd have to look close to note that the lock was gone.

Donovan pulled ahead of the van. He kept our speed reduced, compared to freeway excesses, but still faster than I would have driven the narrow road without streetlights.

We pulled into the gravel turnout. I checked on Scrap. He'd consumed the entire jar of moldy cheese.

Go away. I'm sleeping, he mumbled.

"You going to be up for a fight in a few minutes?"

Mft, phew, grl. Yeah, maybe. For you, babe.

At least the basket didn't smell like a toxic waste dump from his lactose intolerance. Yet. I'd hate to have to burn Lucia's gift.

"Moon coming up," Mickey said excitedly as he climbed out of the van.

Twenty faeries in varying shades of gray with mere hints of pastel in the folds of their wings and draperies tumbled out behind them. They twitched their noses eagerly, and as one turned to face the cave opening in the crook of the Goblin's "elbow."

"Home," they whispered breathlessly. "I smell home."

"No time to dawdle, folks," Gollum said. He began herding the dancers down the path, lighting the way with his flashlight. He had his backpack, stuffed with essentials.

"The Eagle Scout at work," Donovan sneered.

"That's why I love him," I said and followed along, taking the arms of two of the weaker faeries.

We made a great deal of noise coming down the path. No way to hide all those shuffling feet. The faeries might have been more silent if they could spread their wings and lift their feet more than half an inch. The desert chill on a clear night and near zero humidity didn't help them much.

Still we made good time on the hundred yards or so. We saw no signs of Gregbaum's guards.

"Is it too much to hope that when Lucia killed Gregbaum, his minions died, or reverted, or disappeared into the chat room and another dimension," I whispered to Donovan.

He paused while helping a male faery over a rough patch. The female he'd thrown over his shoulder.

I noticed Gollum had done the same thing.

"I don't think so. Once created, mutated, whatever, they take on lives of their own, separate from Gregbaum. They're here. I just can't tell where. Something about their Faery origins masks them from normal perceptions until they want to be seen."

"Scrap can you smell any bad guys."

Nope. He sounded a little more alert.

"You up to joining us yet."

Yeah, yeah, in a moment.

"Now, Scrap. You can doze on my shoulder as well as you can in that basket." I took ten long steps with faeries in tow before the imp roused himself long enough to pop onto my shoulder. He rested his head on my hair and wrapped his tail around my neck to keep himself in place.

"You aren't going to be much help if it comes to a fight, are you."

Mumble, mumble. Nothing coherent from him.

Great.

Good thing Donovan and I had brought swords along. He carried them across his back inside his shirt as a makeshift sheath.

"Moon coming into place," Gollum called the moment he reached the base of Goblin Rock.

"That's not the only thing in place." From my perspective ten yards back, with the moon just starting to glimmer behind the portal, I spotted the distinct shape of a bundle of dynamite jammed into the cave opening.

And three long wires trailing away behind the monolith. Some*thing* chuckled wickedly from the thorny shrubs in the near distance.

Chapter 48

The Apache was the first "high rise" hotel in Las Vegas with its own elevator. It towered three stories.

"*B*OMB!" I CALLED in my best schoolteacher voice. "Everyone freeze."

They obeyed.

"Gollum, can we cut the wires without setting that thing off?"

"You're asking the useless professor?" Donovan sneered.

"Not as useless as you may think. What do you know about explosives?"

"Um . . . a little bit of construction type demo."

"Not enough. Gollum, verdict?"

"Can't tell from here in this light." He edged closer, playing his light along the wires.

"Scrap, where are the bad guys?" I whispered.

Running for the hills like they're expecting the sky to rain down fire and brimstone, he replied on a yawn.

"We'll have to go after them."

Later, babe. Gotta get these faeries back home first. Close the portal, then black, red, and ugly are easy prey.

Tendrils of moonlight stretched through the opening portal in a dozen different directions, ethereal, wispy.

And turning to black smoke as they traveled closer and closer to the fleeing forms.

"They're drawing energy continuously from Faery. Cut off their power and they lose strength," I mused.

"It's only about ten feet up. I think I can get to it," Mickey said. He closed his eyes a moment in concentration. Royal blue energy shot out of the portal to enfold him. It shimmered around him in a glorious aura. The glow coalesced into a pair of magnificent wings that stretched from above his head to his heels.

Transparent wings, without a lot of substance.

"My God, he really is the crown prince of Faery!" Donovan breathed.

"You expected less?" I replied. "A true prince risks everything to save his people."

I almost heard Donovan's argument that he had risked his financial empire time and again to provide a safe haven for his people.

Only they weren't truly his people. He was a gargoyle turned traitor, condemned to live as a human.

The wings weren't enough to lift Mickey to the portal. They only kept his steps light so that fragile sandstone didn't crumble beneath his feet.

"It's just resting there. I can move it," Mickey said. He reached his right arm to encircle the bundle.

"Mickey, no!" Gollum ran to stand directly beneath him. "It's on a timer and going to blow. Get out of there."

"The moon is rising. The portal's going to close," Donovan added.

"I can do this." Mickey pushed off from the rock face, the dynamite cradled against his chest.

"Everybody down!" Gollum yelled. "Drop it, Mickey. Drop it now!"

Blinding light. Deafening noise. A whoosh of air knocked me on my ass.

Fire and rock rained down us.

I crouched, my head down, arms forcing two faeries into tight fetal balls.

Hot rock burned my hands, ate through the synthetic

fiber of my sweater. Not as much as I expected. I endured the brief pain.

"Mikhail," the dancers wailed as one.

I spread my wings over my Tess. Sparks bounce off them. Bigger embers scorch holes in my tender flesh. I endure. I have to protect my Warrior though the pain nearly drives me home to Mum.

Come to think on it, this pain is less than Mum's broom swatting my cute little bum.

If only I had a cigar to lessen the pain.

I've known worse. I will know worse still.

The fire threatens to engulf my soul.

I remember the Guardians and the black nothingness of their prison. This brief searing lessens.

I feel a wart or two breaking through on my spine. The pain is worth it to save Tess.

Are those elongated figures whipping through the smoke? They come to protect their valley. I am in no danger as long as I protect and serve.

Over the ringing in my ears, I heard a whump and a thud against the desert floor. "Mickey," I breathed and dashed to the fallen prince. Flying dust caught in my throat and burned my skin. I tasted grit and spat it out.

"Everybody up to the portal, now!" Gollum commanded. "You've got to get through before the moon moves and it closes again."

I sensed Donovan helping to herd the dancers toward their home. They kept trying to break free of his grip and return to their prince.

"Mickey?" I held a hand to his chest. He seemed intact, a little singed around the edges, but nothing severed or bleeding externally.

A faint whisper of air.

"He's breathing!" I told the assembly.

Vague forms scrambled up the rock face. As they neared the opening, they took on more color and definition. The gray of fatigue and separation washed away in a flood of benign light from home.

I tried to lift Mickey by the shoulders.

"Don't move him," Gollum said, coming up beside us. "He's bleeding internally from the fall. Probably concussed." As he spoke, the light from the portal began to close. "He must have thrown the bomb aside at the last second."

"Easy, Mickey, just keep breathing," I urged as I lay his head back down.

"Home? Did they make it home?" Prince Mikhail gasped for more air, painfully.

I almost didn't hear his words. Tears burned my eyes.

"Two more to go. They're going to make it, My Lord Mikhail," Gollum said with respect.

"I have served." Mickey closed his eyes. His breathing became fainter yet.

The light dimmed further.

"They're through, and the portal's closing," Donovan announced.

"You can't die. I won't let you die." I rubbed Mickey's face, willing him to open his eyes again.

"If he could get to Faery, he'd heal," Gollum mused.

"Too late," Donovan said.

An imp can go anywhere, anywhen, Scrap said.

"Scrap, can you take him home?"

Nope. But you can.

The ring near burned on my hand. I yanked it off and slipped it onto Mickey's thumb, making sure I twisted it.

"Mickey, I know you still live. You have to will yourself home. Think of home. Picture it in your mind."

A tiny glimmer of a smile lit his face. "Home."

"Yes. Think of home. Will yourself to go home." I twisted the ring again and again. "Just go home."

"I don't believe it," Donovan breathed. The portal's opening again. The moon has moved past, but it's opening again."

"Quick, help me carry Mickey up there." I kept twisting the ring, remembering bright flowers, a clear stream falling over a jumble of rocks, rainbow-colored beings flitting about in the sunshine. I'd seen it once before, the first time I entered the chat room in a fever dream years ago when the imp flu first possessed me.

Donovan slid his hands beneath Mickey's shoulders. Gollum took his ankles. I braced the faery prince beneath his back.

"On three," Donovan said.

We lifted in one smooth movement, keeping Mickey as level and still as possible. Desperately avoiding dropping him, we stumbled and slid the few yards to the base of Goblin Rock.

The monolith looked as if it sagged a bit. I didn't care. If we could just get Mickey up to the cave mouth . . .

Gollum pulled a coil of lightweight rope from his pack. Quickly, he fashioned a harness.

Donovan slid Mickey's legs through it and looped the length around his shoulders.

I placed Mickey's left hand over his right so that he could touch the ring.

By the time Donovan finished, Gollum had hauled himself up to the cave, the other end of the rope in his hands. He braced himself at the opening.

"Think of home," I reminded Mickey one more time, giving the ring a last twist.

"Oh, my," Gollum gasped, looking over his shoulder. "Even faded, it's beautiful. I think it's healing already."

"Home," Mickey whispered. His face twisted in pain.

"Tess, you've got to climb beside him, keep his body as level as possible," Donovan said. He scanned the height of the monolith. "The rock's too fragile to support my weight. You're the only one who can do this."

"I know. Okay, Scrap, it's you and me. You tell me where to grab and step so I can concentrate on Mickey."

Gotcha. The imp lifted free of my shoulder and flew back and forth. *Left hand here, right foot there,* he directed me.

Somehow we managed it. With one hand bracing Mickey so he didn't bang into the uneven rock, I held the picture of Faery in my mind. I let the others think through the climb for me.

Mickey gained enough strength and presence of mind to give the ring an occasional twist.

Gollum bless him, lifted a full-grown man smoothly.

Donovan boosted us from below, then directed the beam from the flashlight where I needed to be.

At last, sweating and breathless, I grasped the cave lip. With my shoulder under Mickey, Gollum hauled him the last few feet.

With the worst of the drag off me, I chanced a glance into the cave. About five feet high at the opening, it went back only a few feet.

But where a blank wall should define the end, the red rock dissolved and showed a distant view of light and color, like looking through the wrong end of a telescope. I couldn't move, couldn't think. I could only gaze with longing at the most beautiful of all the dimensions. I'd said the word "home" so often I almost believed that was where I needed to go.

Easy, dahling. Don't get lost. That is not home to you.

Gollum eased out of the cave to make room for Mickey's supine form. Together we pushed his feet, aiming his head toward the opening.

As we worked, the image at the end began to fade.

"Clap, Donovan," I called. My hands were too occupied with Mickey and keeping myself from falling.

"What?"

"Just do it. Like the end of 'Fairy Moon.' Clap as if Mickey's life depends upon it."

Strangely, he did. He brought his big hands together again and again. The willful slap of flesh against flesh resounded through the valley, picked up by the hills and bounced back to us. The sound doubled and doubled again, filling us with the resolve that this faery must live.

The lines of smoke and energy swirling around and around coalesced into vague outlines of beings with round heads and long triangular bodies that trailed off into wisps of energy. Red, black, gold, purple, and green, they gathered in a ritual circle around us. And they too clapped, continuing the magic through the dimensions. Helping us. Guiding us. Guarding us.

At the last second, two pairs of arms reached through from Faery and aided their prince home.

Just like the end of the dance.

Chapter 49

Ronald Reagan played Vegas in 1954 at the Last Frontier.

MY BABE LAUGHS AND CRIES as she and Gollum slide back to the safety of the ground. They hug joyously. Donovan joins them.

Each of the men vies with the other to kiss her. They both do.

I'd laugh, too, but my mind returns to the other side of the closed portal. Prince Mikhail has taken the ring with him. Now I'll never get a chance to free the black imp inside the diamond.

Is that such a bad thing? I feel for that imp. My fate could have been his. But would loosing him help maintain the balance among the dimensions?

I guess it's only fitting that the ring has returned to the faeries; they made it after all. They removed a violent imp from the universe for a reason. An imp too bloodthirsty to bond with a Warrior has no purpose in the grand scheme of things.

But still, I really, really needed to end the agony of that nameless imp. He calls to me across the dimensions through the cracks in the diamond.

Only my love for my dahling Tess saved me. I should rejoice with her.

A cigar and a big dose of beer and OJ will ease some of my pain.

Maybe Ginkgo will help remind me of the glory of life. I'll just pop over to the Citadel for a bit and give Tess and Gollum a little privacy to celebrate on their own. They need this time together, to remind themselves of the importance of their lives together.

They can't let a little thing like the insane Julia come between them.

That would be just wrong.

They're already starting with a deep kiss across the center console of the Hummer.

If Tess is going to get laid, so am I!

Donovan's going to ditch the van registered to Gregbaum out in the desert somewhere. My babe and her love will meet up with him at a nearby freeway junction.

They'll work it out on their own. No one needs me right now.

"Hey, Scrap," Tess calls. "Good work, buddy. Get some sleep. You deserve it."

Ah, Tess. She does think of me.

Life is good.

Exuberance carried Gollum and me all the way to the door of *our* hotel room. We touched, held hands, kissed often. A couple. Together. No doubts, no encumbrances.

While he fumbled with the key card, I held his mouth captive with my own, frustrated that I couldn't get his shirt off until he shed the heavy backpack.

At last, the door swung open and we tumbled inside, too eager for each other to think.

The pack hit the floor with a thud. My boots followed. I pushed him backward onto the bed, jumping on top of him, mouth open, hungry for more kisses, more everything of my Gollum.

Something chirped. An annoying sound interfering with my celebration of a job well done and beautiful lives saved.

The chirp continued.

"Um . . . Tess," Gollum mumbled around my mouth. "Tess, that's the alarm on my watch. I have a plane to catch." He sounded disappointed.

"Can't it wait?" I slid my tongue along his cheek, down his neck, amazed at the fairness of his midnight stubble.

"I'm sorry. I have to go back to New York. Tonight. Now." He groaned. His fingers clung to my back fiercely.

Then he pushed me aside and rolled off the bed.

Instantly chilled and sober, I knew I had to face the questions I'd hidden from since that phone call this afternoon that sent him into a terse funk.

"Talk to me, Gollum. I need to know what you want from me." I think I knew.

But I also had to examine my own role in this threesome.

Methodically he set about packing his few clothes and toiletries into a small duffel, zipping a vinyl bag around his suit.

"Gollum?"

He wouldn't look at me.

"Gollum, I understand why you have to go to her."

Damn, damn, damn. I did understand.

"You understand?"

I nodded, unable to speak, unable to think. I just had to hold myself tight enough to keep my damned heart from shattering into a million pieces.

"Thank you. You know I love you. I'd do most anything for you. Except . . . she depends upon me. She's more like a much younger sister than a wife. But . . ." He stood and gathered the last of his things.

"It's all about balance. I'm the one that threw you and Julia out of balance."

"Julia and I were out of balance long ago. But I'm her only hope of ever recovering."

"Gollum?"

"Yes, Tess?" At least he didn't call me "Sweetheart" or "Darling" or any other endearment. I couldn't stand it if he did.

"Gollum, I can't be with you. Not as a loving couple. That's wrong. Wrong for me, for you, and for her. Until you and Julia can find a peaceful way out of your marriage, I can't be your lover."

"I . . . I know. But I will be there for you when next you need an archivist. I'll not desert you."

"Just go. Please, go now before I . . . before I can't let you go."

"Good-bye."

I turned and stared out into the night that was never quite night in this city.

Agony! Pressure in my chest. My heart beats erratically. I'm dying.

I curl up into a fetal ball.

"What ails you?" my beloved Ginkgo asks. He enfolds me in his arms, closing our bodies together with his tail.

"Not me," I wail. "It's Tess. My Warrior . . ."

I can't stay here wrapped in love any longer. Tess needs me.

This kind of pain speaks of personal disaster. What could go wrong? She and Gollum are so right for each other.

I pop out of Ginkgo's arms and into the chat room without a thought. I barely register the Cthulhu demon on guard. I'm not there long enough for the ponderous water monster to notice me.

Then I am on Tess' shoulder, smoothing her hair, rubbing my cheek against hers.

I wish I could become solid in her dimension so that I can hold her as she needs to be held.

I can only share her tears and her pain.

Her agony is my agony. Her life my life. Not even death can separate us.

Chapter 50

Las Vegas no longer caters to a primarily adult crowd. It offers water parks, amusement parks, G-rated entertainment, and other activities aimed at the entire family.

SOMEHOW, POURING MY GRIEF and anguish into words for Scrap helped me gain some perspective. Yes, I loved Gollum. Yes, he had betrayed me by his silence and oblique promise of a future. But he hadn't totally abandoned me.

He'd be back. We'd have to renegotiate our relationship and find a way back to the friendship we'd shared before this weekend.

Do you remember when you claimed Gollum as your mate before the Windago and King Scazzy? Scrap reminded me of an incident last month. In order to protect Gollum from the Windago's vengeance—I had killed her mate so she would kill mine—I had to stake a claim on him.

"I claimed him as a friend."

You implied that he was your mate.

"If the Windago and the prison warden of the universe interpreted my statement that way . . ."

You claimed him before witnesses. He's yours by the laws of the cosmos.

"That doesn't mean we can be together. Not while Julia lives."

He's yours. He'll be back. Scrap blew a wisp of black cherry cheroot smoke up to the corner away from my face.

A small courtesy I hadn't expected from him.

"What I need to do right now is call Mom."

Yeah, you need to restore the balance of your relationship. Let her be your mom and take care of you. You've been taking care of her too much.

"Balance. It's all been about balances. Junior upset a balance by projecting his fears on the plane."

Before that. The faeries upset the balance by exchanging him for a human child.

"And he twisted the change into a hated exile."

You restored the balance on the plane with your songs.

"WindScribe upset the balance by killing the king of Faery."

Leaving the universe open to plundering by the likes of Gregbaum and Junior.

"But we put things in motion to heal that breach." The image of Lady Lucia sinking her fangs into Gregbaum's throat threatened to overwhelm me.

"How did Gregbaum kidnap the faeries? He was human. I know he had Junior's help, but they'd both have trouble getting into the chat room let alone into Faery. Otherwise Junior would have gone back a long time ago."

Scrap let that one sink into my mind.

"He had help. Not Lucia. She thought the faeries had come willingly to escape the imbalance in their home. Donovan?"

He's human now, too. But he will make sure any remaining mutant faeries are dealt with.

The place where the diamond ring had rested on my finger burned with emptiness. "An imp can go anywhere.

An imp can take his Warrior anywhere! Sancroix and Fortitude."

Scrap and I stared at each other in horror. The darkness of Fortitude's skin, almost black now, finally took on meaning. The imp had gone rogue and dragged Sancroix along with him.

Fortitude stopped listening to Sancroix and started working with Junior a long time ago. Sancroix may not have been involved.

"He had to have known even if he didn't participate. The bond between imp and human is too strong to hide something like that. He and Fortitude have become almost as evil as the imp imprisoned in the ring."

Junior started Fortitude on the path of darkness. Sancroix and Sister Gert believed him to be their son. They registered him as their orphaned nephew because of archaic prejudice against children born out of wedlock.

"Why'd they help me free the faeries?"

Because Fortitude likes killing things. Doesn't matter what side they're on, as long as he tastes blood. Just like the mutant faeries. Just like Junior. He gains pleasure vicariously when others kill.

They hadn't just killed the mutant faeries on the stage. They'd mutilated them with extreme violence even after they were all dead. Junior must have been watching from the wings.

Or maybe he diverted Gert away from the carnage, knowing she'd object.

A knock on my door. I dashed to open it, praying with every step, every rapid heartbeat that my Gollum had returned to me.

Lady Lucia stood before me in flowing red draperies from the Napoleonic era. The high-waisted gown, lace-trimmed scoop neck, and puffy sleeves suited her. She'd dressed her bleached locks in casual ringlets. More than a bit of her youthful beauty shone through her lustrous pale skin. The long strand of pearls, doubled and looped about her throat echoed the same luster.

"Invite me in," she demanded with almost no accent.

"Do I have to?"

"No. But you do not wish to discuss our business in public, and I may not enter without invitation." She tapped her foot impatiently.

More vampire mythology.

Don't do it, babe. She smells funny.

"For this one meeting I grant you permission to enter." Yeah, I'd read a bit of vampire fiction myself. I knew the rules.

She breezed past me and took up a position of command before the windows. The night lights of Vegas made a halo around her.

I didn't need my magical comb to recognize it for an illusion.

Scrap flitted about, trying to stay between us. I wanted to swat him away, but didn't dare betray his agitation to a potential enemy.

"The ring." Lucia held out her hand.

"No congratulations on a job well done? No questions about the disposition of the mutants? No polite 'Hello'?"

That's it, dahling, show no fear.

Lucia tapped her foot impatiently. "I know all of that. You promised me the ring. Now give it to me." Her eyes betrayed her. They shifted constantly, wary, only occasionally glancing at my neck.

If she could see Scrap, she didn't let her gaze linger on him.

Self-consciously, I shifted my shoulders so that the turtleneck of my sweater rose higher.

"I apologize, Lucia. I no longer possess the ring."

"What!" she screeched like a banshee. Her eyes turned funny. Not the vertically slitted yellow monstrosities portrayed on television. I can't describe it. They just looked strange.

Uh, oh. Pink flashed across Scrap's skin like a neon light on the fritz.

I shrugged. "I had to give up the ring to Prince Mikhail

as part of the rescue operation." I tried for casual and dropped into a chair. My knees continued to tremble even after I took the weight off them.

Maybe it was just that groin injury making them weak.

Yeah. Right.

Anyway, I knew better than to engage her gaze. I stared at my ringless fingers instead.

Damn. Now I'd never wear Gollum's ring. The only one I truly wanted.

"What happened to *my* ring?" she ground out.

"I had to put it on Mickey's hand to keep the portal open long enough to get him through. He got hurt. Badly."

"This is not acceptable."

"Sorry. That's the way it is. There is nothing you or I can do about it now."

"You owe me that ring." She grabbed my collar and lifted me to my feet.

I didn't see her move. I swear it. One heartbeat she was five paces away. The next she was on top of me, holding me upright by one hand. Baring her fangs.

This close I could see the seam of artificial dentures.

In my peripheral vision I saw Scrap turn vermilion. He dropped to my hand, half extended.

"Uh, I wouldn't do that if I were you, Lucia."

"By the rules of the Powers That Be, I claim you as forfeit." She opened her mouth, aiming for my neck.

"Want a Celestial Blade embedded in your spine? You may have a few drops of Damiri demon in you, but I can end your shadow existence before you can break the surface of my skin." To make my point (pun intended) I let Scrap's sharpening tail caress her ribs.

She dropped me abruptly.

"We are not finished, Warrior. You owe me."

"I acknowledge that I owe you an *honorable* service at some time in the future." I'd figure out how to break this rule later. Right now, I needed my life intact.

She dropped me abruptly.

My knees wobbled, but I remained upright. Scrap

shrunk back to his normal shape and size but remained bright red.

Lucia's nose wiggled. "I smell blood. Close. It smells like yours."

"I'm not bleeding." I checked to make sure.

"Not you. A relative." She aimed her rapid steps for the door.

"Mom!"

Call your mom, babe. I have a funny feeling. Scrap rubbed his very red belly.

I speed dialed her cell phone.

It went right to voice mail. She was either using it or had turned it off.

I called Penny's landline.

A sultry voice promised to call me back if I left a message.

"Where is she, Scrap? You've got to find her."

Parking lot. Now!

Elevator too slow. I pushed Lucia aside and fairly flew down the stairs, sliding on the banister when I could. Five flights. Ten landings. Too many.

"Time, Scrap."

Hurry!

"Go ahead. Do what you can."

My imp needed no other prodding. He popped out. Then came back to me as I launched myself out the fire door into the parking lot. He glowed bright vermilion and stretched longer than I'd ever seen him.

I hit the pavement, feet *en garde* and shaft of my blade twirling. Lamps on tall poles lit the entire area as bright as day.

Breven Sancroix faced me. Fortitude lounged on his shoulder, cleaning his talons with a long forked tongue. His skin had darkened perceptibly.

Then I saw my mother's body lying neatly on the ground, hands crossed on her chest. Her eyes stared sightlessly at the stars, her mouth half open in a surprised "Oh." Six long bloody gashes spread upward from her belly to her throat. Her favorite plum-colored slacks and lavender blouse were ruined.

"What have you done to her?" I screamed. I longed to run to Mom, to force her heart to beat and her lungs to breathe.

I knew in my head it was too late. I'd wasted too much time with that bitchy pseudo vampire.

I hadn't been here for my mom when she needed me most.

"I did the world a favor," Sancroix defended himself. He sounded almost casual, as if murder were an everyday incident for him.

Maybe it was. Fortitude didn't look particularly troubled.

"She was an innocent!" A red mist rose before my eyes as my temper soared. She couldn't be dead. She just couldn't.

I had to go to her. But I had to go through him to get to her.

"She carried a demon baby. No woman who lies with a demon is innocent," he sneered.

That stopped me cold. "Darren. Her husband died less than two days after they married!"

"Makes no difference. The Damiri are incredibly fertile. They breed and breed and breed again with as many women as they can. We took care of the problem."

"You idiot. How stupid can you be? She's too old . . ."

"Not for a Damiri."

He made to step past me.

I blocked him with the shaft of my Celestial Blade.

"You have broken your most solemn vow of the Brotherhood. To protect the innocent. You should have done your research before you took the law into your own hands. But you killed your archivist, too. Because he got in your way."

"I watched her for five days. She picked at her food.

Yet she glowed. She was pregnant. I had to dispose of the baby before it grew enough to take over her body and make her nearly invulnerable." His eyes became hard and cold.

"She glowed because she was happy, she'd finally found herself in her music. She picked at her food because she was trying to lose weight for her new career," I ground out, keeping my teeth clenched so that I didn't scream.

"That doesn't . . ."

"She had a complete hysterectomy right after I was born. She had no eggs to fertilize, no womb to nurture a fetus. You murdered an innocent woman. You murdered *my mother.*"

He lost some of his self-righteous calm. His imp looked up from his grooming. Fortitude nudged him. They communicated silently.

Can you catch what they're saying, Scrap?

A strong sense of negative emanated from my Celestial Blade.

"Don't listen to her, Dad. She's lying," Junior said quietly from the shadows. His voice carried a similar calming magic to Donovan's.

"Your mother married a demon. She had to die," Sancroix affirmed.

"That's right. She had to die," Junior echoed.

"Did she?" Sister Gert sounded hesitant, from right beside her son. Her *changeling* son, I reminded myself.

"No, she didn't need to die. Your imp, goaded on by your changeling son, needed to taste innocent blood. They elected my mom. You've lost control of your imp, Sancroix. Lost him to the man you raised to be your son."

"Impossible."

"Look at his skin. Look at how dark he is. The last time a rogue imp turned black, the faeries imprisoned him in a diamond, forcing him to stare at himself and examine his sins from inside the facets for all eternity." I shifted my stance, ready to lash out the moment I had the right opportunity. The fact that Scrap remained in Blade form with no demons present meant we faced incredible evil.

Sancroix had to die. I should turn him over to the law. But with an imp to whisk him away through the chat room, no prison could contain him.

Did I have the courage to kill another human being, no matter how evil? Would I be stepping along the same rogue path he'd taken if I did?

"What have you done, Breven?" Gert asked from behind me.

"Have you gone rogue, too, Mrs. Sancroix?" I sneered.

"An innocent. You have killed an innocent," she said. Anguish colored her voice. She moved forward, knelt beside my mother's body. "You have changed beyond recognition, Breven. I turned a blind eye to your bloodlust when it came to demons. I let you fight the mutants tonight without me because I knew you needed to spill blood. No more. You must kill no more."

Then, quite unexpectedly she bowed her head as in prayer. Juniper, her imp, did the same.

Gert's hand covered my own in the only act of tenderness I'd ever seen from her. "Take care, Sister. You are needed outside the Citadel. Don't let the monsters make you one of them. Go back home often to renew yourself and your commitment."

Fortitude saw us as no threat. Not even a hint of pink on his wing tips. Just that unrelenting deep green that bordered on black. I'd seen him completely transform in a heartbeat.

Overconfidence led to stupidity. These two had already committed that blunder once tonight.

I knew what I had to do.

"You need to go back to a Citadel, Sancroix," I said.

"Those useless, hidebound . . ."

Before he could finish his thought; before I had time to think, Gert rose up and clamped a choke hold on her husband. Juniper keened long and loud. She rose up and landed on Fortitude's back, talons out, all three rows of her teeth clamped upon his throat.

The two imps tumbled and rolled, snapped wings open and shut. Fortitude flipped himself on top of the battle.

I stepped forward, ready to break it up.

Go to your mother, Tess, Scrap commanded me. In an eye blink he'd morphed into a glowing white imp, far larger than I'd ever seen him.

"Stop it, Gert. They'll kill each other!" Sancroix screamed. He looked pale and sweating.

"Scrap?"

Imp business. Imp law. I must judge as a neutral party. Go to your mother.

A fake to the right, then Juniper sank her talons deep into Fortitude's spine.

At the same time his jaws clamped on her neck.

I heard bone crack.

"No!" Sancroix screamed, clutching his back in the exact same spot where Juniper hit Fortitude.

Gert gargled, releasing Sancroix to clutch at her throat with both hands.

The imps flashed into blade form even as death throes jerked them backward, toward the limp hands of their Warriors.

They all collapsed together onto their weapons. The tines of one penetrated Sancroix's heart, the blade of the other slit Gert's throat.

Scrap bowed his head, faded and shrank back to normal size. *So be it. I declare an end to this.*

I jerked out of my paralyzing horror and stumbled to my mother's side. Her hand already grew cold. A glaze covered her eyes.

She looked so peaceful, so relaxed.

All traces of the tense and waspish woman who'd raised me had vanished.

"Tess," she whispered.

I bent closer to catch those precious words.

"Tess, I love you. Tell Steph and Cecilia I love them. You are my baby. My last baby. I cherish you."

And she wilted, an almost smile frozen in place.

I wanted to believe the true woman, the *chanteuse*

who empathically projected love, compassion, and joy through her music shone through.

For a few hours each night she had balanced some evil in the world with her songs.

I couldn't speak. The horror of my dead mother lying on the pavement choked me.

As sirens erupted around me, Lucia bounded out of the fire door. She grabbed me beneath the shoulders and dragged me back inside the hotel.

"You can't be seen here. Let them believe this a love triangle gone wrong," she whispered. "But don't let them bury her with the pearls. You have to claim the pearls."

I nodded numbly. "Why?"

"No time to explain. They were mine once upon a time. Now they are yours. Guard them better than you did the ring."

"Junior?"

"I'll find him. He's finished in this town and he knows it. But I'll find him and bring him to the Powers That Be for justice. And you will help me. Later. Now you must flee."

Some morsel of self-preservation kicked in, and I followed her back up to my room.

Sister Gert's final words pounded into my brain. "I don't have the luxury of looking for a future, a normal life with Gollum, do I?" I said to no one in particular.

"If you stay with him, you will want a family. Your concerns will shift from fighting demons to protecting your children. Believe me. I know this." Lucia fixed me with her gaze.

Her sincerity penetrated my growing grief.

"I have to remain alone, focused and angry enough to complete the jobs the Universe hands me." That scared me more than a full pack of Midori, Windago, Sasquatch, and Damiri combined.

"Good-bye, Mom."

Epilogue

What happens in Vegas, stays in Vegas. Sometimes.

THE NIGHT BEFORE I took my mom home for her funeral and burial in the family plot on Cape Cod, I stood on the tiny stage of the lounge in The Crown Jewels Casino and Conference Center. I wore the midnight-blue dress spangled with pixie dust and my mother's pearls.

They caressed my neck with warmth and the memory of her love.

Donovan and Lady Lucia sat in the front row. Lucia had used her influence to end the investigation into Mom's death before it got started. She convinced high-powered lawyers and commissioners that the three bodies in the parking lot were a bizarre lovers' triangle gone sour with murder and suicide.

Everyone in Vegas and back home accepted that story as the truth.

I wanted to believe it.

Even more quietly, Lady Lucia bought out Junior's stock in The Crown Jewels. He disappeared. Even Scrap couldn't find him, and I know he looked long and hard.

Penny Worth and Mr. Stetson also sat in the front row. She wore a new wedding ring and had her heavily mortgaged house up for sale. She looked tired and resigned rather than a radiant bride.

Allie had come, too. That's what best friends do. They fly halfway across the country to hold your hand, help you make hard decisions, become a buffer between you and people who ask too many questions.

Gollum offered to come. I had to tell him no. Seeing him again this soon, while I was so fragile, would upset the tiny bit of balance I'd found within me.

"I'm dedicating this song to my mother," I said. No other words would come through the growing lump in my throat. I had to sing now or never.

"Take me in, yes, I'll be your victim,
I'll be the matchgirl, and you be the wind.
Take me in, yes, I'll be your victim,
I'll be Red Riding Hood, you be the wolf.
I'll be the girl who gets burned in the oven,
and you'll be the baker who serves me for pie.
I won't expect any boring old woodcutters
coming to save me at the end of the day—
In the end, yes I'll be your victim.
You'll be my frog and I won't be a princess.
In the end, no curtain, no laughter,
no pumpkin, no coachman, no happily ever after."

Gollum is standing behind a pillar where Tess can't see him. He clenches his fists and squeezes his eyes shut to keep the tears from leaking out.

He listens closely to Tess' music. In his heart he sings a different song, one that Mom sang often. A song from a different era.

A song people sang when they sent their lovers off to fight a war. "I'll be seeing you in all the old familiar places."

It ends, "I'll be looking at the moon, but I'll be seeing you."

P.R. Frost
The Tess Noncoiré
Adventures

"Frost's fantasy debut series introduces a charming protagonist, both strong and vulnerable, and her cheeky companion. An intriguing plot and a well-developed warrior sisterhood make this a good choice for fans of the urban fantasy of Tanya Huff, Jim Butcher, and Charles deLint."

—*Library Journal*

HOUNDING THE MOON
978-0-7564-0425-3
MOON IN THE MIRROR
978-0-7564-0486-4

and new in paperback:
FAERY MOON
978-0-7564-0606-6

To Order Call: 1-800-788-6262
www.dawbooks.com

DAW 70

Seanan McGuire

The October Daye Novels

"...will surely appeal to readers who enjoy my books, or those of Patrica Briggs." —*Charlaine Harris*

"Well researched, sharply told, highly atmospheric and as brutal as any pulp detective tale, this promising start to a new urban fantasy series is sure to appeal to fans of Jim Butcher or Kim Harrison."—*Publishers Weekly*

ROSEMARY AND RUE
978-0-7564-0571-7
A LOCAL HABITATION
978-0-7564-0596-0
AN ARTIFICIAL NIGHT
978-0-7564-0626-4

(Available September 2010)

To Order Call: 1-800-788-6262
www.dawbooks.com

Laura Resnick

Doppelgangster

"Resnick introduces a colorful cast of gangsters and
their associates as she spins a witty, fast-paced mystery around her convincingly self-absorbed chorus-
girl heroine. Sexy interludes raise the tension as she
juggles magical assailants, her perennially distracted
agent, her meddling mother, and wiseguys both
friendly and threatening in a well-crafted, rollicking
mystery."—*Publishers Weekly*

"Esther Diamond is the Stephanie Plum of urban fantasy! Unplug the phone and settle down for a fast and
funny read!"—Mary Jo Putney

"*Dopplegangster* is a joy from start to finish, with a
sexy hero, a smart heroine, a fascinating plot, and a
troop of supporting characters both lovable and otherwise. It's a wonderful blend of comedy and surprising
suspense. If you haven't met Esther Diamond yet,
then you're missing out on a lot of fun."
—Linda Howard

978-0-7564-0595-3

To Order Call: 1-800-788-6262
www.dawbooks.com

There is an old story...

...you might have heard it—about a young
mermaid, the daughter of a king, who saved the
life of a human prince and fell in love.

So innocent was her love, so pure her devotion,
that she would pay any price for the chance to
be with her prince. She gave up her voice, her
family, and the sea, and became human. But the
prince had fallen in love with another woman.

The tales say the little mermaid sacrificed her
own life so that her beloved prince could find
happiness with his bride.

The tales lie.

Danielle, Talia, and Snow from
The Stepsister Scheme return in

The Mermaid's Madness
by Jim C. Hines
978-0-7564-0583-0

"Do we look like we need to be rescued?"